VICTORIA FALLS

NATURAL WONDERS
BOOK 2

B.J. HILL

For Becky and Rebecca,
feminist, fearless, and faithful.
You sharpen the steel in my spine.
(also please tell Charly I love her)

A MESSAGE FROM B.J.

Hi friends!

Thank you so much for reading *Victoria Falls*, Book Two in my *Natural Wonders* series.

You don't <u>have to</u> read *Northern Lights* (Book One, about Alis and Dexter) first to enjoy Tori and Leo's story, but you'll definitely see some familiar faces and a few plot threads carrying over.

The series will eventually have six books total, each one its own complete love story with a happily-ever-after. However, since the timelines and characters weave together, the best way to get the full experience (and all the little easter eggs) is by reading them in order.

And don't worry... I'm already elbows deep in Book Three. That's kind of why this one took so long to write—because it lays SO MUCH of the foundation for books three, four, and five.

And with ADHD brain, that means I wasn't just writing this book... I was writing, like, four. At once. Like a crazy person.

Hope you love it! Say hi to Lois for me!

xx, B.J.

SENSITIVE SUBJECTS

It's important to be aware of the themes in this story before you start reading, that way you can decide what feels safe and right for you.

Victoria Falls includes the following sensitive subjects:
- Abandonment
- Alcoholism
- Divorce
- Infidelity
- Loss of a family member
- Physical abuse
- Religious trauma and manipulation
- Terminal illness (cancer)
- Verbal and emotional abuse
- And... math. Lots and lots of math.

Your mental and emotional health matters.

PROLOGUE
TORI

12 Years Ago, College

"YOU LOOK SO HOT!" my roommate, Lexi, says as she walks into our dorm room, her voice breaking through the soft hum of pop music playing from my phone. I'm blotting the excess fire engine red lipstick from my lips when I wink at her through the mirror.

"Thanks, sugarlips. Zip me up?" I fluff my long, brunette waves one last time as Lexi steps behind me, tugging the zipper of my little black dress until it hugs my body perfectly.

"Hot date tonight? It's about time you got out there. Lord knows where that twatwaffle Chase has been," she says, exasperated.

I should tell her I'm actually going to see Chase, but I don't want to hear the long list of protests that will follow. So instead, I turn, smile at her, and say, "Heading to a frat party. Don't know that I'm looking for anyone in particular, but figured I'd show up looking like a tall glass of water for whoever is thirsty and worthy."

Frat party. Baseball house party. Same thing.

The glow of my desk lamp casts a soft halo over the room as I grab my purse and do a quick once-over in the mirror. The dress clings to every curve, my lipstick pops just enough without being over the top, and my heels add the perfect amount of height to my petite frame.

I know I look incredible. I know when I walk into that party, eyes will be on me, and I know those eyes are connected to mouths that will immediately tell Chase I'm there. Because even when he's not mine, I'm still his. I hate it, but I also love it, because no matter who he's currently hooking up with, they know it won't last. He'll come back to me. He always comes back to me. And tonight, I'm done waiting.

He's had enough time to sow his wild oats, played the fuckboy baseball player for two months, and now it's time to come home. Not physically, as in Moraine, but back to me. I am his home.

I am his home. He will come back to me. We are endgame. We are fated. We are forever.

The cool night air brushes against my skin as I walk the few blocks to the baseball house. The faint sound of music and laughter grows louder with every step, and the distant glow of string lights comes into view. I keep these thoughts on repeat the entire walk to the party, not wavering once in my determination to get what I want.

I know to some I seem pathetic, but they don't know our history. I'm not some insecure girl clinging to her high school sweetheart with a vice grip. I know my worth, and I know his. The problem is that he doesn't know his own worth. He needs me to remind him. That's all.

Every time we break up, it's the same conversation: "You're too good for me. I don't deserve you. You'd be better off without me. I'm a fuck up. You should find someone better..." blah blah blah.

Skye says he does it for attention, and she's not wrong. I know he does it for attention, but is it any wonder he needs more affirmation than most people would? His parents didn't give two shits about him or his little brother when they were growing up—

always too high to care. I'm surprised Chase ever started playing baseball considering his dad's deep dive into drugs began with a painkillers addiction following a baseball injury.

They may have overdosed and left Chase and Trent as wards of the state, but the truth is both Dylan and Charity Martin abandoned those boys before they ever died.

I'm not his parents. I won't leave him. Even when he gives into his insecurities and leaves me, he'll come back. Granted, it's never taken him two months to come back to me—hence the reason I'm taking action.

I arrive at the baseball house, and as expected, the music is loud, the lights are dim, and the people are already sloshed. The smell of stale beer and cheap cologne wafts through the air as I approach the front door. I pause, closing my eyes and inhaling deeply before standing up straight and donning my game face.

"Tits up, Tori. You've got this," I whisper to myself, giving a final pep talk before pushing open the door and stepping inside.

The party is in full swing, bodies pressed together in tight clusters, the bass from the speakers vibrating through the floor. I scan the room, my eyes adjusting to the low lighting. Chase isn't here—yet. But I see the one person I know will get his attention: Aaron Taylor.

Target acquired.

Aaron is leaning against the bar, a red Solo cup in hand, his easy smirk practically oozing arrogance. I walk directly to him, ignoring the eyes that follow me, and slide my hand up his back before leaning in close. "Hey, Aaron."

He turns, his eyebrows lifting as his gaze sweeps over me. His smile widens, and I know I've got him hooked.

"Damn, Victoria. You look incredible." He places a hand on my waist, and I let him.

Bait cast. Now we wait.

"You noticed," I say, my voice dripping with honey as I place a hand on his chest.

Just as Aaron is about to respond, a growl cuts through the air behind me.

"Get your motherfucking hands off her, Taylor, before I break them."

Hooked. That worked faster than I thought. Thank God. I didn't want to actually kiss anyone else—just flip Chase's territorial switch so he'd get his head out of his ass.

I turn slowly, locking eyes with Chase Martin. *My* Chase Martin.

"That wouldn't be very kind, Chase. Breaking your teammate's hands and all. How ever will he pitch without hands?"

Chase ignores my words—he's too busy devouring my body with his eyes.

That's right, Chasey boy. I know what you like, and I dressed to impress.

"Fucking hell, Tor," he grumbles, his voice low and rough. "That dress."

Reel him in, slowly.

"You like?" I say, trailing my hand from my neck, down my front. My fingertips skim along the hem of my dress, drawing his eyes lower.

Chase's jaw clenches as his gaze lingers, dark and heated. His tongue darts out to wet his lips before he bites the knuckle of his right index finger—a move I know all too well. It's his tell. He's hooked.

Caught.

In one stride, he closes the distance between us, his arm snaking around my waist and pulling me flush against him. The heat of his body seeps through the fabric of my dress, sending a shiver up my spine. He leans down, his lips brushing against my ear as he whispers, "Tor, baby, I made a mistake."

My heart skips a beat. Eight weeks of heartbreak, doubt, and determination culminate in this moment. Finally. I knew he'd come back.

"I know," I murmur, my voice soft but sure as I slide my hand up his chest, letting my fingers trace the familiar line of his jaw.

My fingertips find their way to the back of his neck, tangling in the hair at the nape as I tilt my head to meet his eyes.

"How are you going to fix it?"

His lips quirk into a small smile, but I see the hesitation flicker in his eyes—the insecurity he tries so hard to hide.

"I'll do whatever it takes," he says, his voice rough with emotion. "I swear, Tor. Just… give me a chance to prove it to you."

Nevermind that last week he didn't want me. Nevermind that my roommate confessed he came onto her earlier in the year.

Nevermind the fact that I saw, with my own eyes, him leaning into another coed and fingering her hair when I left Accounting on Tuesday.

In short: I've made an art of ignoring all the red flags. When you're in love, those red flags look like a weird shade of green.

The familiar scent of his cologne—woodsy, with a hint of spice —fills my senses as I inhale deeply. His hand tightens on my waist, and I know I should press him for answers, demand accountability, but the pull of him is too strong.

"Have you been with anyone else?" I ask, already knowing the answer but needing to hear him say it.

His mouth twitches, the smallest flicker of guilt crossing his face. There it is.

"Chase. Answer me, and don't you dare lie to me."

His hand slides up to cup the side of my neck, his thumb brushing gently over my jaw. I hate how much I've missed his touch.

"I didn't sleep with anyone else, I promise," he says, his voice low and earnest.

He leans in to kiss me, but I press a hand against his chest, holding him back. If he kisses me, I'm done for, and he knows it.

No matter how many times he fucks up, he knows that if he

puts his hands on me and kisses my lips, I'll cave in an instant and forgive him anything.

Victoria Anne Foster, you do not give in, I tell myself, the words echoing like a mantra in my mind. Yes, you came to get your man. But you will stand your ground and demand answers. You love him, but you do not take shit from anyone.

"I want to know exactly what you've done, who you've done it with, and then I want you to promise me that you will not speak to any of those girls ever again. I mean it, Chase. I'm not doing this shit again. You are either with me or you're not. You either want me or you don't."

He looks at me, his expression softening as his thumb continues to trace lazy circles against my skin.

"Tor," he murmurs, leaning closer. "It's you, baby. Only you. I love you."

And then he's kissing me.

His lips are soft but firm, assertive in a way that leaves no doubt about his feelings. He kisses me like he's claiming me, promising me fidelity and forever. His tongue parts my lips, and I open for him, relishing in the feel of his hard body pressed against mine.

I melt into him, my chest pressing against his, my hands tangling in his hair.

I am home. He is home.

My God, I've missed him.

We've broken up and gotten back together four times since freshman year. I ask him the same question every time, and he never gives me a clear answer.

I have no idea how many other women Chase has hooked up with while we've been apart, and I probably never will.

Is that going to stop me from taking him back? No.

Because I love him. And we are inevitable. And these are just bumps along the road to our happily ever after.

Since the day we met in the tutoring lab in tenth grade, I've wanted him.

The math nerd and the baseball player.

I dreamed of us paralleling Nathan and Haley from *One Tree Hill*. The unlikely couple, falling in love, staying in love through all the bumps and pivots, ultimately living happily ever after. No matter the obstacle, nothing could separate us. No one could stop us. We'd defy the odds and have a love so fierce they'd write stories and songs about us.

"Let's go back to my place," he whispers against my lips, his voice rough with need.

"Say less."

ONE

TORI

THE HR BUILDING smells like floor polish and new beginnings.

I repeat my internal mantra as I cross the threshold: *Back straight. Head high. Be thankful. Be kind.*

Is working as a secretary for a pod of math professors my dream job? Not even close. But, it's a paycheck.

And after everything I left behind in Moraine—including ten years of a marriage that chipped away at my soul—I need this clean slate more than I care to admit.

I owe Dexter for pulling strings to get me in. I was on the cusp of partner at Smith Accounting, a title I practically bled for. Years of 4 a.m. mornings and 10 p.m. client calls.

I gave them everything.

And they gave me... nothing.

Well—worse than nothing. They let me think I had a chance. Maybe I did. But you can only break in the same spot so many times before the whole damn structure collapses.

My phone rings just as I reach for the door. I don't have to look to know who it is.

Chase. Again.

I silence it and shove it back into my purse.

Let my attorney handle him.

Well, the attorney I have yet to actually acquire. But I will. And when I do, the attorney will handle Chase.

Because I can't. Not now.

I miss him. God, I miss him.

But I miss *me* more. And I'm finally doing something about it.

Squaring my shoulders, I shake off the feelings bubbling up in my chest and walk through the door. The building is incredibly clean, more modern than I would have expected for a university. I locate the directory on the wall and see that Human Resources is, thankfully, on the first floor.

I really don't feel like stairs today.

The door is already open as I approach, and I knock quietly so I don't startle the woman typing at her desktop. She looks up and smiles brightly as I enter, greeting me warmly.

"Good morning! You must be Victoria Foster."

Yes, I gave them my maiden name. It's not that I'm worried about Chase finding and physically harming me, but I need the space and anonymity to think clearly and don't need him finding my place of work and disturbing the peace.

"Hi, yes. Good morning. Ms. Malcolm, is it?" She nods in the affirmative and gestures for me to take a seat.

"It was so wonderful to speak with you on the phone last week." My, she's bubbly.

"We appreciate your ability to start on such short notice, all things considered. Poor MaryAnne will be out for at least six months recovering from surgery. We were afraid we'd end up shuffling student workers around to fill the gap but this is much more preferable."

Six months. That's plenty of time to figure out what I actually want to do with my life. If I even want to stay in Grand River long term.

"I'm happy it all worked out. I just moved to the area and am excited for the opportunity."

If she senses the lie in my tone, she doesn't show it, instead pulling a folder with a stack of paperwork from the side of her desk and handing it to me.

"You can go ahead and fill these out here, and when you're finished I'll take you on a tour of the campus and then over to the mathematics department."

I smile, nodding along as she speaks. Am I smiling too much? I feel like I'm smiling too much.

"Do you need a pen?"

"No, thanks, I have my own," I say, taking the folder from her and opening it to see a handful of forms.

Some I've seen before: standard tax withholding forms and a straight forward employment application. Some that are specific to the university: employee code of conduct, an informational brochure, a campus map.

And behind it all, a sheet detailing the compensation package.

My God, secretaries make barely anything. How do these people afford to feed their families on this little income?

Trying not to react to the abysmal sum in front of me, I return my gaze to Ms. Malcolm, nod, and smile again—*my God, Tori, you probably look like a lunatic*—before getting to work completing the forms.

I stop when I reach the tax form boxes that ask if I am filing single, married filing jointly, or married filing separately.

I don't know.

Am I going back to Moraine? No.

Will the divorce be finalized before tax season is upon us? I'd hope so, but I can't be certain.

Ugh. All I want to do is keep a low profile and not clue anyone into my personal business, and here I am not five minutes into the day and I'm about to ask a stupid and revealing question, all because I can't figure out a tax form?

For fuck's sake.

I mark *single*.

If that's incorrect, I'll update it later. But for now, I'm claiming my independence, be it legally factual or not.

Once I've finished the forms, Ms. Malcolm takes me on a brief but informative tour of the campus. I won't need to wander much as my job is limited to one pod of professors, but it's nice to get the lay of the land nonetheless.

Finally, we make our way to the mathematics department and into the pod of professors I'll be working with for the foreseeable future. The pile of papers sitting on the secretary's desk—my desk, now—is a disaster of mismatched sheets and post-its, and I'm suddenly concerned about what I've gotten myself into. None of the six offices in this pod have the lights on, so I assume I'm here alone.

"Here you are, dear. Why don't you get settled and familiarize yourself with your workspace," she gestures toward the warzone that is my new desk and I plaster another awkward smile onto my face. "I'm sure one of the professors will be around soon if you have any questions."

I thank her and as she turns to leave I ask, "Do you happen to have any advice for how to best interact with these professors? I know personalities vary and I'd like to make a good first impression."

Ms. Malcolm chuckles and responds, "You just be yourself, dear. If they don't appreciate your first impression, that's their own problem."

Then she leaves.

That's their own problem.

Okay, so, I like her. I like her a lot.

I SPEND the next few hours organizing the warzone that is my new desk, sorting through papers and piecing together what Mary-Anne left behind. Most of it, thankfully, is just meeting requests from students—a scribbled, stapled, sticky-noted catastrophe that begins to feel like progress as I sort them into neat piles. A binder labeled **TASK MANUAL** catches my eye, and I crack it open.

Inside I find step-by-step instructions for logging in, navigating the email server, printing class rosters, and even a section with handwritten notes about each professor's quirks.

Damn, MaryAnne. You're a freaking unicorn.

The binder boosts my confidence, offering a whispered assurance that I won't drown today. I let myself breathe a little easier, flipping through her notes about things like Dr. Patel's obsession with calculators and aversion to scented pens and Dr. Johnson's need to be reminded to eat lunch. Every page is layered with a kind of quiet competence I both admire and envy.

By 10 a.m., the first professor finally arrives.

A short, elderly man with kind eyes and round glasses steps into the pod. He's got a shuffle in his walk and the kind of presence that immediately lowers your blood pressure.

"You must be our new administrative assistant," he says, smiling warmly. Thank you for not calling me a secretary. I'm not sure why that matters, but, it does.

"I am," I nod, standing up. "Hi, I'm Tori."

"Dr. Johnson," he replies, clasping my hand in both of his. "We're very thankful to have you here, Miss Tori."

Miss. I almost correct him, but don't. I'm not ready to explain anything yet. Not to a stranger. Not even to someone this gentle.

"I worked in accounting for the last ten years, so I'll probably have questions as I go."

He chuckles. "Questions are welcome. MaryAnne kept us all afloat, so we've been paddling in circles since she left. We'll figure it out together, yes?"

His kindness is disarming, and I find myself smiling—a real one, not a awkward one—as he disappears into his office. If they're all like him, this job might actually be bearable—maybe even enjoyable.

What does it say about my last workplace that a soft-spoken man remembering my name already feels like a balm?

I return to the meeting requests, checking them against posted office hours, highlighting conflicts and penciling in tentative time slots. The steady rhythm of the task settles my nerves.

Or, it does... until a voice slices through the air.

"Who are you?"

Okay, rude. I glance up.

Tall. Brooding. Displeased.

The man standing in front of me radiates judgment like heat off asphalt. I recognize him—he's Dexter's friend. Leo.

His eyes are dark brown and hard, the kind that search for weakness. Or maybe I'm just sensitive. Either way, he's staring at me like I'm the punchline to a joke he didn't laugh at.

I stand, smiling—awkward, not real—and offer my hand to shake.

"Hi. It's Leo, right?" I ask. I'm trying for polite.

Does it work?...

He glances down at my hand, not touching it, then returns his gaze to mine, obviously displeased.

...No. It does not work.

"Yeah. You're... Trina?" *Asshole.*

"Tori," I correct, my tone firmer. "I'm Alis's friend. We met at the apartment a couple weeks ago."

His eyes narrow slightly in recognition.

"Right." He scans my body, top to bottom. Still not impressed. *Still an asshole.*

"You're the one who ditched her husband."

The words slap harder than I expect, and I freeze.

It takes every ounce of composure not to let my expression crack.

I could explain. Could tell him how many times I begged Chase to care, to show up, to try. I could even tell him about the therapy sessions I booked alone, the nights I cried myself to sleep next to a man who didn't even notice.

But what's the point? He's already made up his mind about me.

Instead, I clear my throat.

"I'm filling in for MaryAnne while she recovers from surgery. She'll be out for around six months."

"Fucking hell," he groans, dragging a hand through his hair. "What kind of surgery takes six months to recover from? I thought she just fell or something."

I shrug, because honestly, I don't know.

"That's all I was told. But I'm here to help while she's out. If you need anything—"

"I'll handle my own shit, thanks," he cuts in, brushing past me.

He disappears into his office and kicks the door shut behind him.

The silence that follows is deafening.

I stare at the closed door for a beat too long, trying to decide whether I'm more embarrassed or furious.

Probably both.

My stomach clenches, but I square my shoulders and turn back to my desk.

Fine. Handle your own shit, then.

I didn't come here to be liked. I came here to rebuild, to prove to myself that I can start over.

Still, a knot sits heavy in my chest.

It's one thing to be judged by people who know me—family, friends, Chase's side of things.

But Leo? A stranger who knows nothing about me?

And yet, his words linger.

You're the one who ditched her husband.

I didn't ditch anyone. I survived him.

That's the difference. And I don't owe Leo—or anyone else— an explanation.

Still, I reach for MaryAnne's binder again and flip to the section labeled *Faculty Notes*.

There, scrawled in the margins under Leo's name:

· *Brilliant but volatile. Don't take it personally.*

And in slightly darker ink below it:

· *Keep chocolate in the drawer. Works better than logic.*

· *Random bouts of happy puppy behavior.*

I exhale a laugh through my nose.

So, he's in semi-permanent dementor recovery mode? Lovely.

And what the hell is happy puppy behavior?

TWO

TORI

IT'S 5:30 a.m. when I slip out of bed, tiptoe across our bedroom, and shut the bathroom door behind me as quietly as possible.

The faint glow of the moon filters through the blinds, casting pale stripes across the cold tiles. Everything feels still, like the world is holding its breath alongside me.

This is it. This has to be it.

I'm two days late for my period—always a good sign when trying to conceive.

Sure, it could be stress-related, but no. No.

This is it. I can feel it.

Ohmygod ohmygod ohmygod, I cannot wait to finally see that PREGNANT result on the digital test screen.

I picture the word lighting up in bold, happy letters, a beacon of hope that will finally change everything. My heart races at the thought.

I'll make Chase all of his favorite things for breakfast, careful not to overcook the bacon or undercook the eggs, and then sit across from him at the table with a single cinnamon roll on my plate. Nothing else.

He'll notice the differences in our plates—he will, won't he? Yes, of course he will.

This is going to be perfect.

He'll ask why I'm eating a cinnamon roll—more likely that he'll ask why I didn't give him a cinnamon roll.

Nope. No negativity.

He'll just be curious. Only curious.

Not condemning. Not rude. Just curious.

And I'll tell him, "Because I, Victoria Anne Martin, have a bun in my oven!"

We'll laugh and we'll cry and we'll hug and everything will be perfect and wonderful.

He'll be so happy, and he'll stop being so ornery and negative about everything. He'll see me and finally be excited about me again and we'll be a *real family*, not just a couple.

This. Is. Going. To. Be. The. Best. Morning. Ever!

I'm running in place, trying and failing to suppress my squeal of excitement.

Wait. Gotta pee on the stick first, dummy.

I grab a water cup off the bathroom counter, shimmy my way to the toilet room, pop a squat, and empty my hCG-loaded bladder into it.

Whaddaya know? I didn't even pee on my hand this time! Another good sign.

Walking back to the bathroom sink, I set the cup on the side and wash my hands before opening the test and placing it tab-side down in the liquid.

My hands tremble as I set it in place, like the weight of this moment is pressing down on me.

Three minutes. Shoot, I left my phone on the nightstand.

I sneak back into our bedroom, retrieve my phone from my

side of the bed, set the timer for three minutes, and sprint to the bathroom once more.

Chase is still sound asleep and snoring, so I'm no longer worried about waking him with any noises I make. If that man doesn't wake himself up with that freight train of a nose, there's no way he'll be disturbed by any sudden happy dances coming from the bathroom.

I'm pacing, biting my nails while I wait for three minutes.

Come on, come on.

I swear minutes are like hours. The timer ticks away, but every second feels like its own eternity.

As I pace, my mind wanders to various random places.

Why do people say things like, "We stared into each other's eyes for minutes before finally succumbing to our passion"?

I can't stare at anyone for more than five seconds before it gets weird. Do authors have no concept of time?

I wonder how many things I can think about in three minutes. Well, maybe two minutes and thirty seconds now.

What if the test is negative?

Nope. No, no, no not going there.

Positive thoughts. Only positive thoughts.

Positive. Positive. Math. Accounting.

I love accounting.

I'll also love being a mother.

Why do accountants always feel positive?

Because they know how to add up the good things in life! *Ba-dum-tss.*

Nailed it.

My kid is going to be so friggin' hilarious. With a mom like me they're bound to be.

A positive attitude creates a positive feedback loop—just like in calculus!

Ohmyeverlovingbananas why the hell is this taking so long?!

I should look.

Yeah. I should *totally* look.

These tests don't really take three minutes, right?

I mean, when Belle found out she was pregnant, the strip was instant.

Wham, bam, thank you ma'am; you're having a baby, let's party!

Ok. I'm doing it.

I'm walking toward the counter.

I'm looking at the test.

Shoot, it's flipped so the screen side is down.

I'm pulling the test from the cup.

I'm turning it over.

The test is...

Negative.

Wait... what?

It feels like someone has punched me in the chest. The air escapes my lungs, leaving me hollow, empty.

But, how?

I've done everything right. I exercise every day. I drink copious amounts of water and haven't touched caffeine in months. I take my vitamins, eat foods packed full of folic acid, take my temperature daily, and can literally pinpoint when I'm ovulating.

WHAT IS WRONG WITH ME?!

I set the test on the counter, bury my face in my hands, and cry. The sound of my sobs fills the small bathroom, echoing off the tiles as the reality of the moment crashes over me.

The weight of it all feels unbearable, suffocating.

I'm about to wash my face and crawl back into bed when the bathroom door opens and Chase walks in, dressed in only his boxer shorts and rubbing his hand over his buzzed hair.

The faint light from our bedroom window spills into the room, illuminating his disheveled figure. He doesn't notice my state of distress; he just walks past me to the toilet, slapping my ass along the way.

Should I say something?

Point out yet another failure so that he can look at me with disappointment and make some passive-aggressive comment?

I've just finished washing my face when he walks up to the counter to wash his hands. I stare at him in the giant vanity mirror, waiting for any hint of acknowledgment, when he sees the test on the counter between our sinks.

The moment he registers the negative test result, his face transforms from half-awake to accusation and contempt.

Our eyes lock in the mirror as he says, "Another one? Are you fucking serious?"

Dropping my gaze to the counter, I don't respond.

Chase scoffs, dries his hands, and heads to the closet, calling out over his shoulder, "You should go to the doctor and figure out what's wrong."

No sympathy. No shared grief.

No encouraging words of how we will get through this together or that it will happen when the timing is right.

Simply, accusation that this is my fault.

I need to figure out what's wrong with me.

I'm the problem. I'm the failure. I'm the letdown.

Not him. Never him.

I stand in the bathroom, staring at my reflection, tears still streaking down my face.

The woman looking back at me is unrecognizable—exhausted, defeated, broken.

All I ever wanted was to be enough.

Enough for him. Enough for this.

But I'll never be enough.

THREE

TORI

IT'S after six when I finally make it back to the apartment. My head throbs, my feet ache, and all I want in life is a whiskey sour and a bubble bath deep enough to drown in.

My key sticks a little in the lock, but eventually gives way, and the familiar smell of cinnamon and vanilla greets me as I push the door open with my hip and step inside.

The lights are off in the main room, late-afternoon shadows stretching across the hardwood like fingers. I toe off my pumps by the door, already halfway fantasizing about slipping into pajamas I haven't worn to impress anyone in years.

I head toward the closet to drop my shoes where they belong—only to find Skye's boots tossed haphazardly into the existing pile, her denim jacket draped over the pile like a flag of rebellion.

I sigh. Not in frustration—more in a fond, resigned sort of way.

Skye is a mess, and I love her.

Still, I shake out her jacket, smooth the arms, and hang it beside mine. Old habits die hard.

I do the same with my blazer, then pause, hand lingering on the hanger. The urge to organize the rest of the shoe rack itches in the back of my mind. Maybe rearrange the entry shelf, fold the scarves, color-code the umbrellas.

But I stop myself.

Skye doesn't need fixing. She never asked for that. And just because *I* prefer shoes lined up by season and heel height doesn't mean her chaotic pile is wrong.

We'd talked about it before I moved in—had a whole conversation where we set expectations and boundaries and made promises about communication and space and mutual respect.

She swore she'd changed after living with Alis and Sunny for half a year. Told me with complete sincerity that she was now "a whole-ass adult woman capable of washing a damn dish." Her exact words.

I didn't quite believe her. But I wanted to.

And maybe that was enough.

I glance around the living room. The throw blanket is slouched across the back of the couch, half on, half off, like it couldn't commit to one or the other. A half-empty coffee mug sits on the side table, steam long gone. But there are no clothes on the floor, no forgotten smoothie cups growing science experiments on the counter.

The house feels lived in. Imperfect, but intentional.

It's *nice*. Being in a space where I'm not constantly bracing for someone's disappointment. Where I don't feel like I have to clean the kitchen just to justify my existence. Where I don't have to quietly resent the invisible scorekeeping of a man who believed being married was the same thing as being owed.

I step into the kitchen, loosening my hair from its low chignon and groaning when the elastic pulls out a few strands. There's a note on the counter, written in Skye's 'serial killer' scrawl (get her to explain) on the back of a grocery receipt:

Ran to the store. Out of dish soap. Don't you dare cook anything without me. Be back asap. —S

I laugh, the tension in my chest loosening just a little. Of course she left a note. Of course it's bossy. And of course she wants me to wait to cook dinner *with* her like the domestic goddesses we are not.

She's a disaster. But she's *my* disaster.

And she cares. Not performatively. Not for credit. Not with some expectation of sex or praise or repayment. She just... shows up.

And damn, does that give me life.

I reach into the cabinet and pull down a tumbler. Two fingers of whiskey, a splash of sour mix, and a twist of orange, if I'm feeling fancy. I'm not tonight.

I drop in a half-melted ice cube and take a long, slow sip, letting the heat bloom across my tongue before trailing down to my chest.

I pad barefoot into the bathroom, switch on the light, and start the water in the tub. My body is screaming in places I forgot had nerve endings.

Who knew two months of unemployment and binge-watching true crime documentaries wouldn't keep me in pumps-for-hours shape?

As the tub fills, I catch my reflection in the mirror.

I look... different.

Not bad, exactly. Just *tired*. A little softer in the face, a little more hollow around the eyes. I look like someone starting over. Someone trying to believe that starting over is still allowed at thirty-two.

I stare at myself a beat too long, then shake it off and go to light the candle on the back of the toilet—Skye's "Pumpkin Ember" from her lifetime supply—and slide out of my clothes.

By the time I sink into the water, the day finally starts to unravel.

I think about Dr. Johnson. About his warmth and kindness. About how I didn't realize just how starved I was for that kind of basic decency until it was handed to me so freely.

I think about Leo and his glare and the way he said *you're the one who ditched her husband* like it was a fact and not his own assumption. Like it was something shameful instead of something necessary.

My stomach clenches again remembering it.

I don't know why his opinion bothers me so much. I don't owe him anything. And yet... it hits different when the judgment comes from someone who's barely spoken to you.

Who doesn't even know what they don't know.

Still. I'm not backpedaling. I'm not explaining. Let him think what he wants. He'll either come around or he won't. My years of trying to fix people have come and gone.

I soak until my fingers prune and the candle flickers low.

Then, from the other room, I hear the unmistakable clatter of grocery bags and the sound of Skye singing off-key.

"Guess who got Thaiiiiiiii foooooooood!" she warbles.

I smile. Really smile. Not the kind I forced at the university today.

The kind of smile that feels like home.

I TOWEL off and throw on an oversized sleep shirt—Skye's, actually. One of her old band tees she refuses to part with. The sleeves hang past my elbows, and the collar's been cut so wide it drapes off my shoulder.

I catch a glimpse of myself in the hallway mirror and laugh. I look like someone's girlfriend. And for once, maybe that's not a miserable thought.

Pfft. As if. This is my self-love era.

No, but seriously. I've had more orgasms in the last two months than I have had in the last ten years.

I should have known my housewarming gift from Skye would include an assortment of new toys for me to try out.

And try them out, I most definitely have.

Chase never wanted me to have anything for self-gratification, claiming that if I used a toy to get myself off that meant he wasn't enough for me.

He had all sorts of reasons for this twisted logic, the majority of those reasons some form of Scriptural manipulation, wrapped in fancy Jesus paper and tied with a bow of shame.

But no matter the reason, the core truth remained the same: my self satisfaction fed his insecurities.

It's truly infuriating how many ways I willingly made myself small for that man.

Never. Again.

When I get to the kitchen, Skye is barefoot, crouched over a paper bag and inspecting a suspiciously large takeout order.

"What did you do?" I ask, arching an eyebrow as I lean against the counter.

She looks up, grinning like a raccoon who just found a box of donuts.

"I panicked and ordered one of everything."

"Literally one of everything?"

"I had a coupon," she says, pitch so high I wouldn't believe her if she swore on her dead mother.

"You're lying."

Skye shrugs, not even attempting to keep up the charade. "I'm absolutely lying. But the point stands—we have drunken noodles, red curry, green curry, spring rolls, and what I *think* are crab rangoon, but I'm not entirely convinced."

"I thought you were just going for dish soap?"

"I did get dish soap. And then I got sidetracked by the call of coconut milk and MSG. Blame capitalism."

I laugh and grab napkins and chopsticks while she opens containers like a magician revealing tricks. Steam wafts through the air, the scent of lemongrass and chili hitting me in the face like a warm slap.

God, I didn't realize how hungry I was. I'm fairly certain I forgot to eat lunch today.

We sit cross-legged on the couch, food balanced in our laps, the coffee table a mess of plastic lids and sauce packets. The apartment smells like curry and soy sauce and something vaguely sweet that might be coming from the candle I forgot to blow out in the bathroom.

"So?" Skye asks, mouth full of noodles.

"How was day one?"

I take a bite of red curry, the heat catching me by surprise and making my eyes water just a little. "It was... fine. Dr. Johnson is a sweetheart. Very Mr. Rogers meets Einstein. There's a binder with all the instructions I could ever need. And the HR lady gave me a tour that somehow didn't feel like a punishment."

"See? Already thriving."

"Let's not go that far. I nearly cried filling out a W-4."

She winces. "Yeah, that'll do it. Nothing like federal tax paperwork to remind you that you're single and slightly unhinged."

"Exactly."

We fall into a comfortable rhythm of chewing and casual commentary, the kind of quiet companionship I didn't realize I'd been missing until I had it.

For a moment, it feels like I'm part of something again. Safe. Unwatched. Not weighed down by someone else's disappointment.

Then she glances over, a spark of mischief in her eye. "So... did you see Leo?"

I pause with a forkful of rice halfway to my mouth and roll my eyes. "Yes."

"And?"

"And... he hates me."

Her eyebrows shoot up.

"What? Not possible. Leo loves everybody."

"He called me *Trina*."

She nearly spits out her drink. "Shut up."

"Dead serious. I corrected him, and then he said, 'You're the one who ditched her husband,' like that is the sum of my life's work. Congratulations, here is your trophy. We will carve this onto your gravestone when you die."

Her mouth drops open in full horror. "*No.*"

"Oh yes. He's lucky I was standing behind my desk, otherwise I probably would have kneed him in the dick."

"Ugh, what an ass." She stabs a spring roll like it insulted her personally.

"Exactly. And honestly? I don't care if he likes me or not. I'm not interested in winning over every emotionally stunted man who can't separate someone else's choices from their own baggage. And besides, I'm only there for six months."

She nods in agreement, then leans back against the arm of the couch, tucking one leg under her. "Okay, so, you're gonna hate this, but based on his reaction, he might be fixated on you. Lord only knows what he'll do with that."

Yes, because that's exactly what I need.

I cut her a sharp look. "Doubt it. You should have seen the look he gave me. I got the full body scan, and homeboy was NOT impressed."

"First, it's literally impossible for a man to not be physically attracted to you. Like, HAVE YOU SEEN YOUR BOOBS? And second, I'm not saying he's for sure going to do anything," she says, hands up. "I'm just saying—when it comes to women, Leo's whole brand is indifference. If he didn't care at all, he would've barely looked at you. The fact that he stopped, glared, and offered a full body scan just from your mere presence? Top it off with shitty remarks and an intentional name fuck-up? That says you hit a nerve."

I narrow my eyes. "So, not a romantic fixation. Just judgmental fixation."

"Exactly," Skye nods.

"Congratulations, you're the human embodiment of his unresolved divorce trauma."

I laugh despite myself and shake my head, setting my plate down and curling my legs beneath me. "Wow. Goals."

She shifts her container of noodles to the side and softens. "Look, I should've warned you. He's not normally that much of a dick. I mean, he can be. But this thing with you? That's his shit, not yours."

I glance at her. "What thing?"

She sighs. "Leo's ex-wife left him a couple years ago. For her high school boyfriend, of all people. They'd been married since their early twenties, and then—bam—she reconnects with this dude online, bails on Leo, and is remarried within six months. Totally blindsided him."

"Oof," I mutter, instinctively reaching for my drink.

"Yeah. It wrecked him. So now, anytime he meets a woman who's left her husband—even if the situations are not remotely the same—he goes straight into fight-or-flinch mode. This one night, we went out clubbing together as each other's wingmen—you know, like 'Have you met Ted?' vibes—and I introduced him to this woman. I had no idea she'd just left her husband. She was gorgeous, smart, funny. Total catch. But the second the words 'I left his boring ass' left her lips, Leo tore into her so ruthlessly she started crying."

My eyes widen. "Seriously?"

"We were asked to leave," Skye says flatly, then shrugs. "Doesn't excuse the way he acted toward you. But it does explain why he saw your face and immediately decided you were the villain in his little trauma screenplay."

I blink. "So... I'm a trigger," I say, not quite a question.

"Um, not quite a trigger. More like a mirror. That's not the same thing."

I let that sit. Let it settle in my chest like something warm and a little sharp.

She leans forward again, pointing a chopstick at me. "But seriously—don't worry about what Leo thinks. The man is a literal Tinder whore. Like, swipes left on people who say 'dog mom' and right on anything with cleavage. He has the emotional maturity of a pubescent horn-dog."

"Charming."

"Oh, yeah. I may love him like a brother, but I've seen the receipts. He's a walking cautionary tale with a six-pack."

"And here I was worried he might try to be nice to me."

"Please. Let him hate you. That's way safer. Better he glares at you from a distance than tries to fuck you and ruin your life from the inside out."

I snort and toss a napkin at her.

"You always know how to make a girl feel special."

She catches it midair with a wink.

"It's a gift."

I pause, setting my drink down and tilting my head at her. "Okay, but, how did *you* end up in the friend zone with him? I mean, if he's constantly swiping and emotionally stunted and allergic to commitment, how did you bypass all that and end up as someone he actually trusts?"

Skye grins, then shrugs like it's the simplest thing in the world. "I told him I'd rather pull out my own IUD with salad tongs than sleep with him."

My eyes widen. "What?"

"Direct communication, babe. I'm telling you, it works

wonders." She bites into a crab rangoon like she didn't just drop a conversational bomb.

"No, seriously," I press. "That was it?"

"That and the fact that I never once gave him the impression he was God's gift to women. Leo is used to being charming. He knows how to flirt. I shut that shit down on day one and made it crystal clear I wasn't flattered."

I lean back, half-impressed.

"And he just... accepted it?"

"Eventually. Pretty sure I threatened to stab him in the balls a few times as well. Probably helps that I always keep that switch blade in my overalls. It made me more interesting to him, I think. Like, once he realized I wasn't an ego boost or a potential conquest, he let his guard down. He's better one-on-one than in a crowd. Still a disaster, but, like, a manageable disaster."

I nod slowly, absorbing that. "So the trick is emotional detachment and thinly veiled threats of bodily harm."

"Thinly veiled? Try direct."

She lifts her glass toward me. "To healthy boundaries."

We clink our glasses together with a soft laugh, and for the first time in weeks, I feel just a little more grounded.

FOUR

TORI

Past

Skye, 9:46 a.m.: Do we want nosebleed seats or should I try for something on the floor?

Tori, 9:46 a.m.: Floor, obviously. We've been waiting for this tour since we were twelve. Is Alis cool with floor seats?

Skye, 9:46 a.m.: True. And she doesn't care. You know her—she's whatever.

Tori, 9:46 a.m.: Does she even want to go?

Skye, 9:46 a.m.: I think if it was just the three of us she wouldn't care either way, but Belle wants to go so Alis is currently capable of giving a straight 'yes' to her participation.

Tori, 9:47 a.m.: 😏

Tori, 9:47 a.m.: K cool. I'm almost to my meeting so just let me know what I owe you.

> Skye, 9:47 a.m.: Can do. Is this the test results appointment?

> Tori, 9:47 a.m.: Naw. That's next week.

I just lied to my best friend. Again.

And the worst part? It didn't even make me flinch. Lying about my life has become so habitual I barely notice the sting anymore.

I turn off my phone screen and drop it into my handbag before reaching over to stroke the top of Chase's hand on the gear shifter. He tolerates it for two seconds before pulling his hand away and swapping his grip on the steering wheel.

The cold distance between us grows in the tiny space of the car, but I swallow it down like I always do.

"You ok?" I ask, knowing he's not, but also trying to reach out and connect with him.

My attempt at helping him not to feel so alone backfires, as usual, and he ignores me. His jaw tightens, the tendon flickering as he stares out at the road like it might give him the answers he's looking for.

"Who were you texting?" Chase asks, changing the subject so he doesn't have to acknowledge his own stress and worry.

"Skye. Tickets go on sale today for the tour, and we're hoping for floor seats. She's coming to Denver so hopefully we'll get that show, otherwise who knows where we'll have to fly to see her."

"That's stupid."

"What is?" I ask, my voice already laced with exhaustion because I know exactly where this is going.

"That you'd fly somewhere for a fucking concert. She's an old teeny bopper. Not worth the trip." His condescension is nothing new, but I know from experience that fighting back won't help.

Never mind that he was willing to drop two thousand dollars

on one bowl game ticket that required him to fly to California. I thought that was a waste of money, but it wasn't to him.

How someone can be so lacking in self-awareness is beyond me.

Not responding works its magic, and Chase goes back to driving in silence to our doctor appointment. The quiet feels oppressive, filling the car with a suffocating weight that makes it hard to breathe.

When I went in to figure out why my body refuses to get pregnant, the tests found a perfectly functioning uterus, free of endometriosis, PCOS, and all the other reasons why a woman's body would revolt against conception.

The doctor even made a comment about the perfect thickness of my uterine lining.

"Your womb is a Rolls Royce, Mrs. Martin."

As if a luxury uterus matters when the passenger can't drive.

I didn't tell Chase about the praise my womb received because I didn't want to see his eyeroll or hear his backhanded comments.

Don't take up too much space. Don't outshine. Don't rejoice in your clean bill of health. Keep the peace.

It was another eight months of negative pregnancy tests and biting my tongue against his continued passive-aggressive—and sometimes not-so-passive—behavior concerning our lack of conception before I finally built up enough courage to ask him to get testing of his own. He wasn't thrilled, but he also couldn't argue that I'd exhausted all my options for figuring out why my body wasn't doing its job, so, he reluctantly agreed.

I had to make the appointment. I had to remind him about it. I had to take the lead like I always do when it comes to any non-preferred task. But he went. He had the tests run. Came in a cup and also had bloodwork done.

And now we're on our way to discuss the results with the doctor.

I don't know why I didn't tell Skye the truth about where I'm headed—probably because I didn't want to get my hopes up that everything will be alright.

If I go into this prepared for the worst, then I can't be decimated when the floor falls out from under us.

I know that's an incredibly negative way to view things and is probably some sort of trauma response, but when your life is spent walking on eggshells you learn how to suppress the tiny morsel of hope locked in the deepest part of yourself and only let it out when you're certain it's safe to do so.

My current situation—riding in a car with Chase, a man incapable of processing his emotions, who will grow even more stressed, angry, and passive-aggressive at my attempts to provide a glass-half-full outlook—is not a safe time or place for my light.

Once we've arrived and parked—not close enough for Chase's liking, I might add—we exit the vehicle and make our way to the door.

The air is cool and heavy, like it's holding all the things left unsaid between us. I try reaching out for Chase's hand, needing some comfort for myself and hopefully offering some to him, but he deflects my attempt and slides his hand into his pocket instead. I understand he needs space, but he also needs a friend right now.

Please, complain again about how you always feel so alone?

I know how it feels to wonder what is wrong, why the one thing we want more than anything in this world is not happening. I know the weight and fear of having tests run to figure out why things are broken. I am well acquainted with the anxiety and darkness that so easily consumes the soul while waiting for a diagnosis.

I'm here for him. I want to be his partner and his support in this, but he continues to withdraw.

He arrives at the door a few steps ahead of me and opens it, opting to walk through it himself instead of holding it open for me. It's so easy to excuse these little jabs as unintentional or stress-related, rather than the indifference and selfishness I know make up his character.

I have enough nuggets of happiness to cling to that I don't succumb to the pain I feel at every instance of neglect, indifference, resentment—whatever.

Lately, though, I wonder how much longer those glimpses of light will sustain me.

God never promised marriage would be easy. If anything, the Bible teaches us that the Christian life is full of suffering. Suffering leads to holiness. Christ is close to the brokenhearted.

At what point do Jesus and I become conjoined twins?

Seriously, though.

Stop it, Tori. So many other people are in worse situations. Unfixable situations. You're not being abused. You're not being controlled or manipulated. Your husband is stressed out, and right now he's in a fragile state. Love keeps no record of wrongs. Love forgives. Love hopes. Love never fails. Chase is not responsible for your happiness.

But Chase *is* responsible for how he treats people. How he hurts people. How he hurts me mentally and emotionally. How he only knows I exist when he's pissed about something I've done or haven't done—or on Christmas, when he gives me an incredibly thoughtful gift that makes me feel seen for all of ten minutes.

Glimpses of happiness.

Nuggets of hope.

Specks of love.

I'm pulled from my inner monologue by the nurse calling us back.

"Mr. and Mrs. Martin, Dr. Ling will see you now." We both stand and Chase gestures for me to go before him.

Remembered your manners now, huh? Now that people are watching.

I shake out of that thought and offer the nurse a smile and a nod as I pass her in the open door and enter the hallway to the doctor's office.

The hallway is lined with generic art—landscapes that look like they were ripped straight from a discount catalog. The sterile smell of antiseptic lingers in the air, reminding me of all the other times I've been in this building, hoping, praying, leaving empty-handed. Chase walks a few steps behind me, his silence like a second shadow trailing me everywhere I go.

Dr. Ling is standing behind his desk when we enter his private office, his white coat freshly pressed, his kind eyes crinkling in an attempt to put us at ease. He extends a hand to each of us before offering us seats and bottled water.

I take the water gratefully, though my hands are trembling too much to twist the cap open. Chase declines, his arms crossed tightly over his chest as he slumps into the chair next to me.

The good doctor takes his seat, intertwining his fingers on top of a closed file sitting on the desk in front of him. His calm demeanor does little to settle my nerves. The file feels like a loaded gun sitting between us, its contents ready to shoot down whatever thin thread of hope I've managed to hold onto.

"How are we feeling today, folks?" he asks.

His voice is warm and steady, like he's trying to diffuse the tension with pleasantries. I appreciate the effort, but I can feel Chase bristling beside me. He's always hated small talk.

"We're alright, thank you for asking. A little nervous, but also hopeful," I reply, offering the best smile I can manage.

The words feel foreign in my mouth, like they belong to someone far more optimistic than I am. Still, I feel the need to fill the silence, to smooth over the cracks in this moment, even if Chase's growing impatience is palpable.

Dr. Ling nods, his reassuring smile never faltering. "Yes, certainly. Let's go over these results, and then we can talk through options moving forward."

Options? My heart leaps at the word.

We have options! This is wonderful! All hope is not lost! We will have a baby, a family.

Chase will be happy. *We* will be happy.

I sit up straighter, the hope infiltrating my spirit like a shot of adrenaline. A genuine smile spreads across my face as I glance at Chase, expecting to see the same glimmer of hope reflected in his eyes.

But he isn't looking at me. He continues staring at the doctor, his expression stony, his posture rigid. It's as if he's bracing for the worst.

"What do you mean by options?" Chase asks, his voice clipped and laced with annoyance. I flinch at the tone but try to push forward, clinging to the sliver of positivity in the doctor's words.

Dr. Ling opens the file and clears his throat, glancing between the two of us.

"There are a couple of areas where the results are lower than we typically like to see, but there's also some positive news that I want to highlight. Mr. Martin, the sperm analysis conducted on your provided sample shows that you have what we call severe oligospermia, which means your sperm count is below 5 million sperm per milliliter. For context, a normal sperm count is usually 15 million or more per milliliter.

"In addition to the low sperm count, we also found that your sperm motility is below the ideal range. Sperm motility refers to how well your sperm are able to move. Ideally, at least 40 percent of the sperm should be moving actively. In your case, the motility is lower, which means the sperm have difficulty swimming toward an egg, making it harder for fertilization to occur."

I reach over and slide my hand over Chase's, squeezing lightly to remind him that we are in this together. For once, he doesn't shake me off, though his hand remains limp beneath mine.

His eyes are locked on the doctor, his jaw tightening with each word.

"However," Dr. Ling continues, "I do want to point out that

your sperm morphology—the shape and structure of your sperm —is actually very healthy. More than 4 percent of your sperm have a normal shape, which is within the healthy range according to the criteria we use. This is encouraging because normal morphology is important for the sperm's ability to fertilize an egg.

"So, while the lower count and motility present some challenges, your healthy sperm morphology is a strong, positive factor. We can work with this, and there are various strategies we can explore to increase your chances of conception."

Dr. Ling pauses, giving us space to process the information. I glance at Chase, hoping for some sign of relief, but his expression remains unreadable.

His silence feels heavier than the words hanging in the air, so I step in, my voice softer than I'd like.

"So, we can still have a baby of our own?" I ask, the words trembling on the edge of my hope.

"It is possible, yes," Dr. Ling nods and offers a reassuring smile. "With a lower sperm count and motility, it might take a bit longer to conceive naturally, and we might need to consider some assisted reproductive techniques, such as intrauterine insemination or in vitro fertilization, if necessary. However, Mr. Martin, your healthy morphology means that the sperm that are moving have a good chance of being able to fertilize an egg. This gives us a solid foundation to build on as we discuss your options moving forward."

The rest of the meeting passes in a blur of medical terminology and acronyms I'd never remember without the brochures provided by Dr. Ling. I nod and smile at all the appropriate moments, clutching onto every sliver of hope like a lifeline. But Chase remains silent, his eyes fixed on some point in the distance as if willing himself to be anywhere but here.

By the time we're back in the car, the tension between us feels like a physical barrier, pressing down on my chest and making it hard to breathe.

I try for a moment of levity, desperate to break the silence.

"Oh! This one is called GIFT!" I say, flipping through the brochure. "That sounds promising. Let's see... Gamete Intrafallopian Transfer. No idea what gamete means. Eggs and sperm are placed directly into the fallopian tubes, allowing fertilization to occur naturally within the body. You think I'd be asleep for that? Or would I feel it? This is all so interesting!"

I ramble, filling the void with words, anything to distract from the weight of what we've just heard. But Chase doesn't respond. His hands grip the steering wheel so tightly his knuckles turn white.

I try again, my voice softer this time.

"Are you okay?"

A scoff. A head shake. Silence.

"Chase," I prod, unable to stop myself.

"I asked you a question."

Shit. Wrong choice, Tori.

Chase slams his palm into the steering wheel, the sharp sound slicing through the silence like a gunshot.

My heart leaps into my throat as he barks, "Can I have ten fucking minutes of silence, Tori?! Did you not hear what he said? I'm fucked up. My sperm doesn't work, and I'm fucking broken. Let me process this without your incessant chatter in the background. Just shut the fuck up and let me think for ten goddamn minutes!"

The car fills with a heavy, oppressive silence, the kind that wraps around you and squeezes, making it impossible to breathe.

My fingers tremble as I clutch the brochure in my lap, the words blurring together as tears pool in my eyes.

Did he not hear a single word Dr. Ling said? Were we even in the same room?

"You aren't broken, Chase," I say softly, carefully. My voice feels small, like it might shatter under the weight of his anger.

"And we can still have a baby."

I try to cling to the hope Dr. Ling gave us, to offer it to Chase like a lifeline, but he won't take it.

"Try not to think about all the negatives and focus on the positives," I continue, my voice shaking but determined.

"There's hope! It's going to be okay. We're going to be—"

"Jesus, fuck, Victoria! Stop fucking talking and let me think!" he yells, cutting me off mid-sentence. His words hit like a slap, leaving me reeling.

The brochure slips from my hands and falls to the floorboard, forgotten.

I was just trying to help. Trying to rescue him from drowning in his negative thoughts.

Offer a life raft. Let him know he's not alone.

But he only wants to be alone.

Except that he doesn't want to be alone.

I know that because when I leave him be and give him the space he seems to want, he'll come back later and berate me for neglecting him. For not caring. For being too consumed with work and friends to notice him.

Damned if I do; damned if I don't.

Trying to work my way through a maze with ever-changing walls and passageways. Never knowing which way is up. Always making the wrong decision.

But I keep walking. I keep studying. I keep learning the steps.

One day I'll get it right.

Won't I?

The rest of the drive home is silent. Not the kind of silence that offers peace or reflection.

No, this silence is heavy, suffocating, filled with all the words we aren't saying.

I stare out the window, watching the world blur past, wondering how we got here. How did the people who once promised each other forever turn into this—a constant battle of resentment and unmet expectations?

When we pull into the driveway, Chase shuts off the engine and immediately gets out of the car without a word.

I sit there for a moment, watching as he slams the front door behind him, leaving me alone in the car with nothing but the sound of my own ragged breathing. My chest tightens, and I bite my lip hard enough to draw blood, anything to keep the tears from spilling over.

I finally gather the strength to push open the door and step out, my legs feeling like lead as I make my way inside.

The house is eerily quiet, the only sound the faint hum of the refrigerator in the kitchen. Chase is nowhere to be seen, but I don't need to look for him. I already know he's in his office, hiding behind a screen, avoiding me like he always does when things get hard.

I make my way to the bedroom, my body moving on autopilot as I strip off my jacket and shoes.

My reflection in the mirror catches my eye, and I stop, staring at the woman looking back at me. Her face is pale, her eyes rimmed red from holding back tears.

She looks tired. Defeated. Broken.

The girl in the mirror looks nothing like the woman who used to dream about nurseries and matching Christmas pajamas. That girl smiled more. Spoke more. Laughed without thinking who might be listening.

"Pull it together, Tori," I whisper to myself. "You're stronger than this."

I close my eyes, taking a deep breath to steady myself. The weight in my chest doesn't lift, but I force myself to ignore it.

I grab my phone and sit on the edge of the bed, scrolling mindlessly through social media, anything to distract myself from the gnawing ache inside me.

I come across a post from Skye—a funny meme about the concert tickets—and I want to laugh, but I can't. Instead, I feel a pang of guilt for the lie I told her earlier. For pretending everything is fine when it's anything but.

I set the phone down and lay back on the bed, staring at the ceiling.

The silence in the house feels louder than any argument we've ever had. It presses down on me, suffocating and unrelenting, until I finally can't take it anymore.

I sit up, my hands shaking as I pick up my phone and text Skye.

> Tori, 12:26 p.m.: Hey. Got a minute?

I stare at the screen, waiting for the typing bubbles to appear. When they do, a small wave of relief washes over me.

> Skye 12:27 p.m.: Yeah bitch. What's up?

My fingers hover over the keyboard, the weight of everything I want to say pressing down on me.

I want to tell her everything—about the appointment, the results, Chase's reaction. But instead, I type:

> Tori, 12:27 p.m.: Nothing. Just wanted to say hi.

I hit send before I can change my mind, my chest tightening as I stare at the message. Skye's reply comes almost instantly.

> Skye, 12:27 p.m.: Hi. 😊 You ok?

No. I'm not. But I can't say that. Not now.
Not when I'm barely holding it together.

> Tori, 12:28 p.m.: Yeah. Just tired.

She responds with more memes about getting battle ready

before tickets go on sale tonight, but I can't bring myself to keep the conversation going.

I set the phone down and bury my face in my hands, the tears I've been holding back finally spilling over.

I cry for everything—my marriage, my husband, my dreams of a family, the person I used to be before all of this.

By the time the tears stop, I feel hollow, like I've poured out every last piece of myself. I wipe my face and stand, my legs trembling as I make my way to the bathroom.

I splash cold water on my face, staring at my reflection in the mirror.

"You can do this," I whisper to myself.

I don't know if I believe it, but I say it anyway.

FIVE

TORI

MY FIRST FEW weeks at Middle Peak are exactly as thrilling as one would expect organizing academic calendars and learning how to navigate a glitchy student portal to be—not one bit. I miss spreadsheets. I miss formulas. I miss the predictability of numbers that don't talk back or make passive-aggressive comments about departmental budget cuts.

Accounting had its downsides, but at least I wasn't fielding questions about professor office hours that don't seem to be posted anywhere or musical room assignments for professors who forget that I do not, in fact, know my way around this campus just yet. I hate feeling overwhelmed because when I'm overwhelmed, I act like a bitch. And in those moments when I'm feeling particularly bitchy, Leo decides that is the exact right moment he should talk to me.

I'm elbow-deep in a game of *match the syllabus PDF to the online course* when I hear his summons from his desk across the pod. He *could* pick up the phone on his desk and call. He could also get off his entitled ass and *walk* to ask me a question. But, no. He yells for me like his personal housemaid, at his beck and call.

"Victoria!" he shouts. "Got a second?" Of course, your

majesty. I have all the seconds for you. I am certainly not in the middle of sorting fifty bajillion classes worth of syllabi for four other professors.

I stand and walk into his office to find him sitting with his elbows propped on his desk, fingers steepled under his chin. The smirk on his face suggests he knows exactly how annoyed I am to be summoned like the help.

And the worst part? He looks *pleased* about it.

His office smells like coffee and sarcasm, like it's been marinating in his smug for years. Papers are spread across the desk in what I can only assume is his version of organized chaos. A Rubik's Cube sits near the edge—half-solved, just like him.

I force a polite smile. "What do you need, Professor Euler?"

He raises an eyebrow like he's debating whether or not to correct the formality. He doesn't. Just leans back like a man with all the time in the world.

"Copies. Calc exam. I need thirty." He slides a stack of papers across the desk and pats the top like it's the 1950s and we're in the Mad Men era. Sure, dude. Would you like to tack on a *'thank you, sweetheart'* to the end of that?

I step forward and take the papers, flipping through the pages as a reflex. I'm not even trying to be difficult—I just can't *not* double-check things. It's hardwired into me, like hitting the lock button on my key fob three times or shampooing my hair twice before using conditioner. A compulsion.

"Looks clean," I murmur, mostly to myself. But then—on page three—I stop. My brows draw together.

"Wait."

Leo tilts his head, eyes narrowing. "Problem?"

I tap the question. "Yeah. This integral's set up wrong."

He pushes back from his desk and comes around to stand beside me, arms crossed, shoulder nearly brushing mine. I don't step away, even though the heat rolling off him is annoying. Or maybe it's me. Either way, I hold my ground.

He peers over the page like I've just accused him of plagiarism. "No, it's not."

"It is," I say, not bothering to soften it. "Your u-substitution doesn't simplify the integral. You skipped a sign change, and the bounds don't align. If someone solves it as written, the final answer'll be off by a factor of two."

There's a beat of silence. Not just a pause—*a beat.* That subtle moment where something shifts in the air and both people know it.

He's still looking at me. Not the paper.

Then, flatly, "It's correct."

This smug asshole. I slap the exam against his chest, holding it there to let him know I'm not backing down. "I have two degrees in accounting. Took AP Calc my sophomore year of high school. I know how to spot a sign error. This one's textbook."

"It is *from* a textbook," he counters, that infuriating note of logic-meets-ego threading through every word.

I scoff. "Which doesn't make it right."

His jaw works. He opens his mouth like he's about to deliver a lecture, but nothing comes out. Instead, he snatches the exam from my hands—almost defensively—and flips to the equation in question. His eyes scan it fast, then slower.

I wait. Because I'm right. And I want him to *feel* that.

His fingers tighten at the top of the page. His posture stiffens. For a second, I think he might rip it in half.

Then, grudgingly, "I'll fix it."

"I'll wait," I say sweetly, stepping back.

His eyes lift to mine. And for the first time since I got here, something flickers behind that cocky exterior. Not irritation. Not condescension.

Respect. Or maybe... curiosity?

It lasts exactly one second before he smirks. "Didn't peg you for a math snob, Victoria."

"I'm not," I say. "I'm a math competent. Also, it's Tori. Stop calling me Victoria. You are not my father."

He chuckles under his breath. "Noted."

"I'm serious."

"I know. That's what makes it fun."

I roll my eyes and turn to walk out, but before I reach the door, I toss over my shoulder, "You can walk that corrected exam to my desk when you're done, Dr. Euler. I'm not a dog or a maid to be summoned."

"Noted again," he calls out.

But his voice sounds less amused this time. More like someone realizing they've underestimated their opponent.

I settle into my chair and pull my keyboard closer, pretending to be far busier than I am. Not that I'm not busy—but I make a point to look *very* absorbed. If he wants me to drop everything and jump every time he snaps his fingers, he'll have to try a little harder.

It's petty. I know that. But so is he.

A few minutes later, a revised packet lands silently on the edge of my desk. He doesn't say a word. Just drops it off like a sulky teenager handing in late homework and walks away. I don't even glance up, though I track him from the corner of my eye. His stupid shoulders are annoyingly broad for someone who eats vending machine Pop-Tarts for breakfast.

I wait until he's fully back in his office and walk to the copy room with the kind of pointed grace usually reserved for pageant contestants. I load the document, hit start, and listen to the comforting *whirrrrr-chunk* of paper feeding through the machine. Thirty clean copies. I check the page numbers twice. I may be spiteful, but I'm not careless.

I slide them into a file folder and walk them back toward his door. He sees me coming and doesn't move from his desk. Doesn't say a word. Just waits, fingers steepled again like some smug little academic mafioso.

Setting the folder down with more force than necessary, I affix a secretary of the year smile on my face and say, "Your precious exam, now error-free."

"Much appreciated," he says, his tone maddeningly even.

As I'm halfway out the door, Leo calls after me. "So, two degrees in accounting?"

I pause. Turn. "What, did that not come through loud and clear when I refused to copy your broken integral?"

He shrugs, unfazed. "Just confirming it wasn't a bluff."

"Not a bluff," I say, stepping just far enough back into view. "Earned both. With honors."

"Impressive. And yet here you are—babysitting professors and decoding department email chains."

I shrug. "When I left Moraine, Dexter mentioned this job was open. Figured if I was going to babysit anyone, math professors were at least numerically consistent."

He huffs a laugh. "Debatable."

Leo leans back in his chair, stretching out like we're settling in for a conversation neither of us really invited.

"So. Left Moraine, huh? What was so bad you had to run four hours south?"

I raise an eyebrow. "I think you've got the Cliff Notes version already."

"Maybe. But I haven't heard it from you."

"Not really your business."

He taps his pen once against his desk, then spins it between his fingers like he's weighing something heavier than office gossip. "Color me curious."

I cross my arms. "Look. We're not friends. We're barely coworkers. You can be friends with Dexter, Alis, and Skye, and still mind your own business."

Leo doesn't flinch. Just watches me, like he's waiting for me to realize something he already knows.

"I have enough shit going on in my life," I say, voice clipped. "I don't need you, or anyone for that matter, trying to figure me out like I'm a riddle to be solved between lectures."

He smirks. "You're assuming I'm trying."

"Oh, please. You're practically vibrating with it."

"That might be the caffeine."

"Sure. Let's blame the double espresso and not your fragile male curiosity."

He tips his head, amused. "So you do have a sense of humor."

"It's buried under layers of trauma and a spreadsheet fetish, but yes. Occasionally it comes out." *Did I just make a sex joke in front of a Tinder whore man child? Jesus, take the wheel.*

Leo grins and leans forward. "Good to know. I'll add that to the file."

"You have a file?"

Smirking, he taps his pen to his temple. "Mental one. For departmental productivity."

"Right. And how am I scoring?"

He pretends to think. "Somewhere between 'knows her shit' and 'has bite.' Jury's still out."

I give him a look. "Well, if you want a more comprehensive and accurate report, maybe update your attitude and stop yelling across the pod like I'm your grad student."

He smiles wider. "You'd make a terrible grad student."

"Damn right I would." I start to turn away, but something in his expression changes—subtly, just enough to stop me.

"So, that's it?" he asks, voice softer now. "You're just, what? Done with that whole life?"

I look at him. Really look. His tone isn't smug. It's not even mocking. It's earnest. Curious. A little too curious.

"Like I said," I say, arms folding before I can stop them, "I don't know you. You don't know me. We have mutual friends, but that doesn't mean we have to be pals."

His eyebrows rise, but I don't give him a chance to respond.

"I have enough shit going on in my life without worrying

about your opinion of me. You look at me and see some woman who up and abandoned her husband? Great. Think that. I could not give a single fuck less."

I step fully into his office now, tone flat, delivery razor-sharp.

"And I look at you and see a thirty-five-year-old divorcee hiding behind sarcasm, a chiseled jawline, and a rotating carousel of Tinder hookups. Super. Enjoy that. Remember to wrap it before you tap it."

"You think my jawline is chiseled?" he smirks, turning his head like he's modeling for a fucking cologne ad. "You like what you see?"

"Oh, sweetheart," I deadpan, "I've seen sharper angles on a soggy waffle fry."

He chuckles, low and amused. "Brutal."

"Accurate."

Leo leans forward, elbows resting on his desk, the smirk still playing at the corner of his mouth. "So, not a fan of sarcasm, chiseled jawlines, or Tinder hookups. Good to know."

"I didn't say I wasn't a fan," I say, turning on my heel. "But I don't have time for them. Also, go to therapy."

I'm once again halfway out the door when I hear him mutter behind me—just loud enough to be heard.

"Waffle fry."

I pause. Turn slowly. "What?"

He gestures vaguely toward his jaw. "You said you've seen sharper angles on a soggy waffle fry."

I cross my arms. "And?"

His grin curves, maddening and smug. "You looked long enough to notice."

I roll my eyes and walk off without giving him the satisfaction of a reply.

But I'm smiling when I sit back down.

BY MID-AFTERNOON, the department feels... abandoned.

The overhead lights hum faintly. The copy room door is open and I hear the machine kick on for no reason, then whir back into silence like it forgot it was tired. Most of the faculty packed up after lunch, slipping out with half-hearted waves and comments about beat-the-traffic Fridays and the sweet mercy of early dismissal.

But I stayed. Leo did, too.

He's in his office, door part way open. I catch glimpses of movement now and then—the scrape of a chair leg, the flick of his pen against a notepad, a soft muttered curse when the Wi-Fi blinks out again. Otherwise, silence.

It's peaceful. Slightly awkward, but peaceful.

I try to focus—on reorganizing a digital file tree that was clearly built by someone with a grudge against logic, on ignoring the pit in my stomach that's been simmering all week.

Then—

The door to the department office slams open so hard the file cabinet beside it jolts against the wall.

I flinch. Stand too fast. Adrenaline spikes.

"Tori."

I freeze. The voice is too familiar to mistake.

Lifting my head, I see him.

Chase.

He's standing in the middle of the room like he owns it—like he owns *me*. Tie loose, eyes wild, skin flushed from what I'm guessing was a four-hour, rage-fueled drive from Moraine.

"Oh for fuck's sake," I mutter. "You have *got* to be kidding me."

"You left," he says, stalking forward. "While I was in fucking Boston. I came home and you were just, gone. No call. No warning. Just an empty fucking house and a goddamn note."

"Not here, Chase," I say, grabbing my purse from beneath the desk and clicking my mouse to shut down the computer.

"I've been trying to get a hold of you for weeks!" he shouts, loud enough to echo through the pod.

I glance toward the hallway door—closed, thank God. No one else in the building will hear. But Leo will. *Fucking dammit.*

"Will you keep your voice down?" I hiss. "I will talk to you, but not like this. We need to have this conversation somewhere else."

"No, goddammit! You're talking to me right fucking now. If we walk out of here, how do I know you won't just drive off somewhere I can't follow you? Do you know how long it took me to find out where you work?"

How *did* he find out?

"Chase. Calm down. I know you're angry, and that's understandable, but this is my workplace. We cannot do this here. Please —just come with me and we can talk privately."

"You think I give a shit if you lose this job?" he snaps. "You need to get your ass back to Moraine. You have a job. A life. A *marriage* to get back to. Get your shit. We're leaving."

Excuse me?

Setting down my purse on the chair, I step around the desk, slowly. "You need to leave. You can't come in here and bark orders at me like—like I belong to you."

"Oh, cut the act. You're not some cold-hearted badass who can just pack up and erase *sixteen years*. You didn't even have the decency to say it to my face. You just took your things and disappeared."

Erase it? No. Walk away from it? Yes. "Because I knew if I said it to your face, you wouldn't hear me. You never do. I've tried to talk to you. So I made my decision. I wrote it down. And I left."

"I'm your husband!"

"And I'm not your property!"

His face twists. "This is what you want now? To be somebody's goddamn secretary? A used up, divorced, thirty-year-old failure of a wife? What are you supposed to do, Tori? Reinvent yourself? Act like we never happened? You think you're going to find yourself in some city?"

"Find myself?" I laugh—cold, bitter, a little unhinged. "I *know* who I am. I don't need to find myself. The only thing I needed was to stop *shrinking* so you could feel better about yourself for two fucking seconds."

I take a step closer. Stronger. Bolder. Angrier than I've been in his presence in years. My voice shakes, but it's not from fear. It's from release. From fury. From finally saying what should've been said years ago.

I'm not taking his shit any longer. And Leo's already heard every word spewed from this man's mouth, so at this point, I don't care what he hears. Let him hear *everything*.

"But you know what, Chase?" I hiss. "It didn't matter how small I was—you *still* hated yourself. And everyone around you. And I am the one who suffered for it. I'm the one who carried it. I'm the one who *nearly lost my fucking soul for it*."

My voice breaks, but I don't stop.

"So I left. Because I'm done doing everything I can to lift you up just so you can find new ways to *drown me* in your own goddamn misery!"

He stares at me, stunned. And for a split second, there's nothing—no fire, no sarcasm, no venom. Just silence.

Then he lunges forward and grabs my arm.

Hard.

But before he can say another word, the silence shatters.

"Let. Her. Go."

Leo's voice cracks like thunder.

He's already moving before Chase fully turns his head. Calm, precise, like he's done this before and doesn't need to rehearse the steps.

Chase drops my arm, but Leo's already between us.

"No," Leo says, low and firm, "we're not doing that."

Chase bristles. "She's my—"

"She's not your *anything*. And you're not welcome here."

Chase lifts a hand in mock surrender, but the tension in his jaw says he's one second away from doing something stupid.

Leo takes a small step forward. Not threatening. Just a shift in presence. His hands stay down. His voice stays even.

"Walk. Out. Now."

Chase looks at me again. One last scowl. "You *will* regret this."

"I already did," I say. "For years."

He doesn't answer.

He just turns and storms out, slamming the door behind him so hard it sounds like a gunshot.

The silence that follows is deafening.

I let out a slow, ragged breath. My whole body shaking now that it's over.

Leo turns toward me. "Are you okay?"

I look at the floor and nod before I can think better of it. Then, quietly, "I don't know."

When I return my gaze to him, Leo's eyes hold mine for a beat too long. I expect a joke. Some smart-ass comment. Anything to try and lift the weight of what just happened. But nothing comes. Just quiet.

He gives me a long look, then nods once. "You want me to call campus security? File a report?"

"No. He's not stupid enough to come back here." I pause. "Not now."

Leo studies me another moment. And in that moment, I realize something stupid and inconvenient—I'm glad it was him. Not anyone else. Him.

Because he didn't just defend me. He didn't posture or yell or make a scene. He de-escalated the situation with calm. With control. With that same maddening confidence he wears like cologne. Leo made me feel safe, where Chase has always felt out of control.

And suddenly, I hate that I noticed. I hate that it matters. I hate that a small part of me wonders what he thinks of me now—after seeing me at my absolute lowest.

"Still," he says gently, "if you change your mind—"

"I know."

A beat of silence passes between us.

Then, with quiet finality, I add, "Thank you."

He gives a short nod. No fanfare. No lecture. No condescension.

Just quiet steadiness.

Then he turns and walks back to his office—calm and steady—and leaves the door open.

He. Leaves. The. Door. Open. Why is that so important? Why does that make me feel more seen, understood, and cared for than I have by any other man in my entire life?

Lord only knows.

I sit down slowly, my arm still stinging where Chase grabbed me. My pulse should be erratic. My heart should beat loudly. Neither is true. My wrist may still hurt, but every other part of me feels calm. I don't know what to do with that.

SIX

TORI

Past

"INTO YOUR HANDS, O merciful Savior, we commend your servants, Alexander and Isabelle. Acknowledge, we humbly beseech you, the sheep of your own fold, lambs of your own flock, sinners of your own redeeming. Receive them into the arms of your mercy, into the blessed rest of everlasting peace, and into the glorious company of the saints in light. Amen."

The priest opens his eyes and raises his hands in invitation, addressing all of us gathered to mourn the loss of two of the best people I've ever known. The faint smell of incense mixes with the worn, earthy scent of the pews, and the weight of the sanctuary presses on me from all sides. I inhale deeply, fighting the urge to let my emotions spill over in the quiet room.

"And now, as our Savior Christ has taught us, we are bold to say:"

The congregation stands, the rustling of clothing and movement of feet breaking the silence. Together, we recite,

Our Father, who art in heaven,
hallowed be thy Name,

thy kingdom come,
thy will be done,
on earth as it is in heaven.
Give us this day our daily bread.
And forgive us our trespasses,
as we forgive those who trespass against us.
And lead us not into temptation,
but deliver us from evil.
For thine is the kingdom, and the power, and the glory,
for ever and ever. Amen.

I glance at Chase beside me, hoping for even the smallest connection, but he's shifting his weight from one foot to the other, his face contorted with irritation. As the congregation's voices rise around us, he pulls at his tie like it's a noose, muttering under his breath. I reach for his hand, a quiet plea for solidarity in our grief, but he pulls away to scratch his neck. My stomach knots. He's always been this way—restless, unable to sit with discomfort —but today, of all days, it feels like a slap.

During the priest's blessing, my mind drifts, unbidden, to Alex. I can't help but think about how he would've handled a moment like this. He was always the steady one—the kind of man who instinctively knew how to comfort Isabelle in her darkest moments. He never had to be asked or reminded; he simply showed up, fully present, fully attentive. The way he'd reach for her hand during difficult times, his thumb brushing over her knuckles, a quiet reassurance that she wasn't alone.

I glance at Chase again. He adjusts his watch now, tapping the face like he's timing how long this service will take. The ache in my chest deepens. How did we get here? How did I go from dreaming about a future with this man to barely being able to sit beside him without feeling the sharp edges of disappointment?

"And now," Reverend John continues, "The peace of God, which passes all understanding, keep your hearts and minds in the knowledge and love of God, and of His Son Jesus Christ our Lord;

and the blessing of God Almighty, the Father, the Son, and the Holy Spirit, be among you and remain with you always. Amen."

Amen.

"If you will please proceed to the burial grounds across the way, we will lay to rest our beloved brother and sister. Let us go forth in the name of Christ."

Thanks be to God.

"Thanks be to God this service is fucking over," Chase snipes, adjusting his tie before looking around the sanctuary at everyone waiting patiently for the pallbearers to carry both caskets down the aisle and out of the church.

I look at him, narrowing my eyes at the audacity of this man. "Really, Chase?" I whisper, trying to keep my voice down. "My best friend just lost her sister and brother-in-law—people who, I might add, we had dinner with weekly—and all you have to say is 'thank God that's over'?!"

Rolling his eyes, Chase chastises, "Calm your tits, Tor, it's fucking hot in here and that service was an hour longer than it should have been."

"Will you stop using that word in the sanctuary?!" I hiss. Another eye roll.

People have started filing out of their respective pews—not quickly enough for Chase, if his grumbling is any indication—and I decide I've had enough of him for one day. My heart is heavy, two of my favorite people are dead, my best friend just lost her other half, and I do not have the mental or emotional capacity to deal with my own husband's selfishness right now.

"I'm going to see if Alis needs any help with Sunny," I say, slinging my purse strap over my shoulder and turning to exit our row.

"Whatever. I'll just meet you at the gravesite." At least he didn't make some shitty comment about me giving my attention to someone besides him.

Without saying another word to him, I exit the pew and walk

to the front of the sanctuary, hugging Alis's parents before stepping up beside her to squeeze her shoulder.

"Hey, babe, need help?"

Skye is right behind me—where was she even sitting? I saved her a seat and didn't see her until right now.

"Hey," Alis sighs. The grief and exhaustion on her face are palpable. "Could you prepare her bottle? I need to check her diaper."

I nod and start rifling through the diaper bag for Sunny's bottle and formula while Alis gets to work changing Sunny. Skye makes some stupid comment that elicits a chuckle from Alis, and I've never been more thankful for a moment of levity.

While shaking Sunny's bottle, I glance out the open sanctuary doors and see Chase laughing with one of his friends in the parking lot. What the hell?!

He's not at the gravesite. He's propped against the back of his buddy's truck, shooting the shit and laughing while everyone else congregates across the street for the burial. I focus on his body language—his relaxed posture, the easy grin on his face, the way he casually leans against the truck like there's nothing at stake. A fresh wave of anger floods my veins. Does he even realize how much his indifference cuts? Does he care?

What is it called when you kill your spouse? Mariticide? Yeah, that's it. I mean, we're already here mourning the loss of two people. We could make it three. We could mourn two and feel relief for the third.

Whoa. Did my mind just go there? Seriously, Tori? I wouldn't actually do it, but what does it say about me that the thought of shoving a ballpoint into his jugular provides an internal chuckle and a moment of reprieve from the overwhelming weight of grief I've carried for the past five days.

Not five days. More like five years. The past five days have just compounded onto years of grief. Grief for the boy I love who wasn't loved well as a child. Grief for the emotional battering I take in the name of supporting him through his journey of healing. Grief for the millions of failed attempts at loving him enough for the both of us.

Love keeps no record of wrongs. Is grief considered a 'wrong'? There's supposedly no one way to work through grief, and professional psychologists talk about the journey through it as steps.

I don't want to hold his reactions to his own pain and grief against him. But when does the pain he inflicts on others finally warrant addressing? And is confronting those grievances showing that I've kept a record of wrongs against him? Is it loving to confront it?

I can put the things he's said and done out of my mind, but they are still there. I can forgive him and make excuses for him every time he hurts me, but no matter how much effort I put into forgiving and forgetting, my soul knows. When I look in the mirror I don't see the vibrant, strong, happy woman I was even just five years ago.

Where did she go? And is it his fault that she's gone? Or is it mine? When did I lose myself? I'm suddenly overcome with an added layer of grief and I didn't realize that was possible when I'm already so weighed down with feelings of loss and sorrow.

I can't grieve the loss of myself today. Or tomorrow. But there will come a time when I can no longer hide behind other feelings, acting as if everything is right in my world and I'm still here.

I don't know when that time will come, but when it does, how am I supposed to grieve something I can't even remember losing? How do I mourn the woman I might have been, the life I might have lived.

Might she have been happy? Might she have known love? Might she have been free? Free to laugh, to love, to live.

This is not the time for this train of thought. Focus, Tori. Today is not about you, your issues, or your husband. Today is about the Gilmores, their loss, and remembering my friends.

My mind drifts back to Alex again, to the way he showed up

for Belle without question. He was dependable. Kind. He would never have left Isabelle alone in the sanctuary while he laughed in a parking lot. Chase, on the other hand, has made a habit of walking away—not physically, but emotionally, leaving me to shoulder the weight of everything on my own.

I grip the bottle tighter, the plastic crinkling under the force of my hand. Maybe it's not fair to compare Chase to Alex. They're different men, with different struggles. But I can't help wondering if I've been making excuses for Chase for too long.

I don't know when I started feeling like a caretaker instead of a partner, but it's been years. Actually, I can't say that I've *ever* been his partner. I've always been his caretaker with the goal of becoming his partner, but that's never come to fruition. And now, every step of self preservation I take to distance myself from him— like walking out of that pew—feels like one step closer to the end of us. Maybe that's what I need.

"They're waiting. Let's go," I turn and say to Alis and Skye. I hope I don't sound like a dictator, but right now I'm keeping myself together by focusing my energy on holding my friends together instead. I won't be going home with Chase after this. I'm going to the Gilmores to make sure they are taken care of. Chase can get a ride from his dumbass friend in that ridiculous truck.

As I lead Alis and Skye out of the sanctuary, I realize something. Leaving Chase behind tonight isn't just about today's frustration or grief. It's the first time I'm choosing my own wellbeing over his. My first step toward choosing myself, even if it means leaving him behind.

SEVEN

LEO

WHAT THE ACTUAL fuck just happened?

I was at my desk, minding my own business, attempting to work while simultaneously daydreaming about Tori's smart ass mouth wrapped around my...

When I heard it—him. That voice. The anger and vitriol in his words. The sharp cadence of someone who's so used to being listened to that he doesn't even consider how ugly he sounds. The way he spoke to her like she owed him something—like he owned her. The words weren't just loud; they were sharp enough to scrape against drywall, echoing down the corridor like knives dragged across tile.

I knew who was standing at Tori's desk before I ever laid eyes on the prick.

She can handle herself, I told myself. She doesn't need a savior, I reminded the idiot rising from my office chair as he crept toward the slightly open door.

My rational brain said stay put. My body didn't listen. Every muscle was already coiled, bracing for a fight I told myself I wasn't walking into. My pulse ticked against my jaw. My hands flexed at my sides like they were already choosing bones to break.

I was fine—calm, even—watching the back-and-forth between them. Watching Tori handle the situation like a badass and not take shit from this asshole invading her workplace in the most inappropriate manner possible. Her tone was sharp, steady, unflinching. I felt a flicker of pride that didn't belong to me, like watching someone else's kid win a spelling bee. She was holding her ground. She shouldn't have to, but she was.

And then. He. Grabbed. Her. His hand closing on her arm like he had the right. Like she was property.

And I saw red.

Absofuckinglutely not.

Is she mine? No. But she's sure as fuck not his.

"Let. Her. Go." Three words, steady as stone. Low enough not to shout, sharp enough to slice. The kind of words that leave no room for misunderstanding.

He let go of her arm. Stepped back. Not because he respected me, but because he knew the sound of someone who wouldn't back down—or maybe because I forced myself in between the two of them. Forced a physical separation between his body and hers. Put her out of his reach.

He put his hands on her, and I want to break every fucking bone in that man's body. My fists actually itched for it. My pulse was a steady drumbeat against my palms, begging for an outlet. My teeth ached from the pressure in my jaw.

He had no idea I was in this office. Hadn't considered for even a second that anyone else would be here—or maybe he didn't care who heard his rant. Maybe he wanted someone to hear the vile words spewing from his toxic and entitled mouth. Thought if he said enough shit in front of her boss or some other superior she'd be fired and forced to return home with him.

Fat chance, asshole.

I was wrong. My god was I wrong. I have never been more fucking wrong about a person in my entire life—but I cannot think about that now.

Tori.

I stand there a second too long, my hands loose at my sides but the pulse in them buzzing like I've just gone ten rounds. The tension doesn't leave just because he did. It hums under my skin, an aftershock that makes every nerve feel like it's standing at attention.

I look at Tori. She's standing there, arms wrapped around her stomach. Her whole body drawn in tight, like she's holding herself together with sheer will. Her eyes are fixed on some middle distance, like if she doesn't move or breathe too loud, she won't crack. There's a flush across her cheekbones that wasn't there before, anger or embarrassment, maybe both. I notice the tiny tremor in her fingers, the way she tucks them under her arms to hide it.

I know I asked her something. Was she ok or did she want me to call security? Something. My voice didn't even sound like mine —it was too soft, too careful, like speaking too loud might shatter her.

And here's the worst part—she was still trying to act like none of it touched her. Still trying to hold the ground beneath her feet like she hadn't just been grabbed, like she hadn't just been verbally stripped bare by a man who thought cruelty was currency. She wanted to look untouchable. She wanted to look like she didn't need me, didn't need anyone.

And I let her.

That's what guts me. I let her walk out of that moment carrying it all by herself.

There's this split-second image seared into my head: the place his fingers had been blooming pink on her skin, the way she rolled her shoulder like she could shake him off the way you shake off rain. She didn't want comfort—she wanted distance from him, and maybe from me, too. I didn't reach for her. I didn't ask her to sit. I didn't even offer water. I carved space around her with my body and then retreated to my office like a coward and called it respect.

If that man put his hands on her in a public place, who knows what happened behind closed doors when she lived with him. If he said shit like that to her in this office within earshot of other people... I think I'm going to be sick. The thought of her silenced by him before, of her shrinking in private and pretending in public, makes bile rise in my throat.

"Thank you," she says. Quiet. Honest. Like what I did, what I said, matters. Like I helped instead of hurt her.

That sticks. Cuts deeper than it should. Because I've spent years believing I didn't have anything left worth giving someone else. And somehow she makes three words feel like I moved a mountain.

The ridiculous part is how specific that thank you sounded in my head afterward—like she was thanking me for not making a scene about *me*. For not puffing up, not grandstanding, not turning her terror into my ego trip. She thanked me for space. She thanked me for a boundary. I didn't know that could feel like a victory until she gave it to me.

I retreat to my office before I can make the mistake of saying something decent—or worse, cracking a joke because I don't know what the fuck else to do or say. My thoughts and emotions are everywhere. My office door stays open. I don't think about why.

GRADING quizzes is supposed to be automatic. Red pen, margin note, integer that makes or breaks somebody's GPA. But the first quiz has been staring at me for three minutes and I can't read a single line. My eyes skate over numbers and scribbles but none of it registers.

All I hear is her voice.

I already did. For years.

That isn't a line you throw to wound someone. That was truth. Heavy. Final. It carried the kind of weight you only get from scars that never fade.

And the worst part? It's familiar.

Stephanie. She regrets the years she was married to me, only our situation was vastly different.

The name itself is a bruise that never fully fades, no matter how much time passes.

I know what it is to regret years. I know what it is to look at a life you built, a life you thought would last, and realize it was made of sand. One tide and it's gone. I can still remember the exact way the kitchen smelled that morning she left—stale coffee grounds in the sink and rosemary from the plant wilting on the sill. I had just returned from a week away at a conference—no, the irony is not lost on me. The light overhead flickered every few seconds, throwing shadows across the counter like the house itself couldn't decide if it was still alive.

Her handwriting on the note was neat. Too neat. Like she'd practiced it a dozen times before leaving it behind.

I deserve happily ever after. This is not it.

That was it. No fight. No screaming. No ugly ending scene you could point to and say, This is when it broke. Just absence and a lack of accountability for any of her own unhappiness.

I remember walking through the house like a burglar, opening drawers and closets, searching for proof that this was all a joke—that she wasn't actually gone, that she'd changed her mind. Her toothbrush missing. The suitcase gone. Her favorite sweater no longer draped over the chair. Every piece of her absence screamed louder than words. And then, as if it hadn't been there from the moment I walked through the front door, the silence that came crashing down around me when I finally acknowledged the truth—my wife was gone. The silence was the loudest thing of all.

It crushed me. Not just because she left, but because of what it meant. It meant I wasn't enough. It meant years of trying—years of bending myself into something she might want—had still ended with her packing a bag and leaving. And not just leaving, but leaving me for someone else—a man who reminded her of high school.

That kind of betrayal doesn't just scar you. It rewires you.

Here's the mess I made out of that rewiring: I built a life around never letting anyone close enough to choose me *or* leave me. I pretend casual is freedom and numbness is maturity. I learn names at midnight and forgot them with the sunrise. I'm very, very good at clean exits. The trick is to convince yourself that leaving is power, so you do it first. Fear in fancy clothes.

I've carried it like armor and used it like a weapon. Until today, this afternoon, I had convinced myself women like her—women who smile politely while their hearts are already somewhere else—are everywhere. That charm is camouflage. That confidence is a mask. That anyone who looks too good at holding their ground is already planning their escape.

It has made me bitter. Distrustful. Has made me believe that the sharp-tongued, self-possessed women of the world aren't strong—they're dangerous. That they'll cut a man off at the knees just to stand taller.

And I've given it back, full throttle. I don my best smiles, keep myself in relatively great shape, swipe right on any woman who looks like a good time with a side of trouble. I'm here for a good time, not a long time. I'll fuck them and leave them—most of the time I don't remember their names.

It doesn't matter. They don't matter.

Nothing matters. Not when it comes to women.

And when I first met Tori, I slotted her into that box without hesitation. Beautiful. Smart. Guarded as hell. The kind of woman who could slice you open with a single word and then watch you bleed. In my head, she was just another Stephanie. Another selfish bitch in denial of her own flaws, unwilling to open her eyes and accept the fact that she is at least half at fault for the demise of her own marriage.

And I was wrong.

So. Fucking. Wrong.

Because what I saw today wasn't cruelty or calculation. It wasn't someone who enjoyed twisting the knife. It was survival. It was steel under pressure. It was a woman holding herself together while someone tried to dismantle her, piece by piece.

Stephanie walked away from me because she wanted something shinier, something that looked like a better story to tell her friends. But Tori... Tori walked away from Chase because she wanted to reclaim *herself*. And I can't stop replaying that difference in my head.

Maybe that's why her *thank you* gutted me. Because it wasn't flirtation. It wasn't manipulation. It wasn't the kind of sugar-coated line you toss out when you want someone to feel useful. It was raw, unfiltered honesty. She meant it.

And for the first time in years, I wanted to mean something back.

THE SOUND of the filing cabinet drawer closing outside my office snaps me out of my wandering thoughts and I'm suddenly staring at the same quiz. Same red pen in hand.

Perhaps I should have stayed with her after Chase stormed out. Talked to her. Tried to take her mind off of what happened. Instead, I walked back into my office, sat at my desk, and pretended to grade quizzes. Because that's what you do when you don't know how to be human in front of someone you don't want to scare off. Because you're terrified of saying the wrong thing. Because humor is easier than heart.

I tell myself I'm being respectful—giving her space. But really I'm circling. Like a goddamn shark. Every day I catch her out of the corner of my eye, the way she tucks a stray lock of that gorgeous brunette hair behind her ear, the way she keeps her shoulders tight. I hear the flicker of the fluorescent light above the copy room every time she walks by.

And I've noticed more than I should. Not just today, not just after Chase showed his face. I've caught myself cataloging things I had no business paying attention to—

the coffee ring on her desk from this morning, half-mooned and drying.

The paperclip she bent absentmindedly, left by the keyboard like a tiny silver question mark.

Her cardigan draped over her chair instead of the coat hook.

They aren't important. They aren't even remarkable. But they stuck anyway, like my brain wanted to memorize her without my permission. Even when I was still convinced she was another Stephanie waiting to happen, I noticed. I clocked the way she fidgets with her pen during phone calls. The way she lingers by the copier like she's buying herself a few extra breaths before heading back to her desk.

Why? Why did I notice? Why did I want to?

I don't care about women. Not really. I use them. Bodies, lips, legs—brief distractions that burn hot and burn out. I fuck them and leave them. Most nights I don't remember their names. That's the deal I made with myself after Stephanie: they don't matter, so I can't get gutted again.

But Tori... she doesn't fit in the box I built for women. She doesn't fit anywhere I try to shove her. Our banter earlier in the day—how the hell did that feel like foreplay when it was about a goddamn quiz? Why did I like sparring with her, testing her, pushing until she pushed back harder? Why do I want her mind just as much as her body?

I don't want this. I don't want *her*. I want easy. Disposable. Forgettable. Yet instead, I'm sitting here with a red pen in my hand, distracted by the echo of her voice, thinking about the curve of her mouth when she smirks at me and the way her eyes sharpen like she knows more than she says.

Why is this woman taking up so much space in my thoughts?

And now, now that I truly see her, I want to tell her to sit down, to let someone pour her coffee, to let someone make the world less sharp for a second. I want to fix it with a wrench and a curse word.

There's an ache, too. Not the old anger that burned when Stephanie left. This feels different. Softer. Riddled with something like... possibility, if that isn't too ridiculous. Seeing her try to keep it together makes me want to be better than the versions of myself that took things for granted. It pisses me off and fills me with something that's not pity. Maybe it's respect. Maybe it's something I'll have to name later when I've downed a few shots of whiskey and let the alcohol loosen the walls around my tortured heart.

And it scares me in a way I don't want to admit. Wanting things is how you get hurt. Naming them is how you get owned by them. So I don't name anything. I just sit here like an idiot with the sudden urge to be good.

I also know boundaries. I know not to barrel in and play hero in a way that makes her smaller. There's a fine line between being protective and being patronizing, and I don't want to cross it. So I'll do the only thing I can think of that's both cowardly and careful: I'll continue to leave the door open and keep my distance, make my presence obvious without smothering. If she wants me, she'll say it. If she doesn't, I'll be respectful. I'm not a saint. I'm not even sure I'm honorable. But I won't be the asshole who watches and does nothing.

The quiz still sits in front of me. The red pen idle. The paper is just a square of pulp and ink and some student's half-assed work. Not important. Not compared to this.

I push the stack aside and lean back in my chair, finally, the gravity of this place now centered on her.

Before I breathe out, I think—always stupidly melodramatic— about how people show up for others. Not with grand speeches, not with dramatic rescues. Sometimes with three stupid words that sound like a threat and sometimes with a quiet hand near a bag or a single text five minutes later that says: You okay?

I tell myself I'll step out there, be present, just in case. Someone needs to be on her side, even if it's just as a witness to the fact that the world didn't let him take her tone, her boundaries, or her dignity without consequence.

Except, she's not there. Her desk is empty. The cardigan's gone. The paperclip question mark sits alone. I look at the clock. It's 5:04 p.m. She must have shut that filing cabinet on her way out.

And now I'm left with the one question I don't want to answer: if she was just another woman, if she didn't matter, why the hell do I feel her absence like this?

EIGHT

TORI

UNION LODGE NO. 2 is Moraine's feeble attempt at a big-shot suit club, but it's trying too hard. The dimly lit space reeks of cheap cologne and ambition, with its pleather booths, polished brass fixtures, and a bar that pretends to be handcrafted mahogany but is too factory-cut for its own good. Everything about this place feels like a Pinterest board for fragile egos—leather that squeaks when it shouldn't, a fireplace that hasn't been lit since the Bush administration, and a row of framed vintage whiskey ads meant to suggest class but scream desperation.

Chase is in his element here, working the room like he owns it, greeting colleagues with loud handshakes and bro hugs. Nobody will call this place what it really is—a poser bar for small-town suits wishing they could step foot into the actual Union Lodge in Denver. Ha. As if.

I linger near Chase, trailing behind like a shadow, gripping the small clutch purse that doesn't quite match the black dress I put on just because he said he liked it. My heels click softly on the wooden floor, but the sound is swallowed by the dull roar of conversation and the clink of glasses. The air is thick with the tang of spilled beer and the faint musk of stale cigar smoke, making me feel even more out of place. Despite the effort I put into my hair and makeup, I feel like a prop, an accessory to Chase's overwhelming need for attention.

Sometimes I wonder why he wasn't named Chad. He really is *such* a Chad.

As we approach the bar, the lighting changes—a soft glow from Edison bulbs strung overhead casts long shadows, giving the illusion of sophistication. Chase introduces me to a few of his newer colleagues, their suits slightly ill-fitting and ties just a little too bold for the occasion. One of them, a younger guy named Matt, turns to me with a genuine smile, his blue tie a little crooked.

"So, Tori, what do you do?" he asks, his tone polite and warm, a stark contrast to the superficial energy around us.

I barely part my lips to respond before Chase waves a dismissive hand, cutting me off. "Oh, she just plays with numbers all day," he says, smirking like it's the funniest thing he's ever said. "She's an accountant. You know, spreadsheets and boring stuff like that. Nothing too exciting."

It's not the first time he's diminished me like this. Hell, it's not even the first time this week. I keep thinking I'm overreacting—that I'm being too sensitive—but that sinking feeling in my gut? It's becoming a permanent resident. The kind that moves in with a suitcase and changes the locks.

Heat creeps up my neck, and I feel my shoulders tense. The words hang in the air, mocking me. Chase's tone, his words, his very presence—all of it presses down on me like the oppressive weight of the too-warm room. Matt's smile falters, his gaze flicking to me with a mix of sympathy and awkwardness.

I manage a tight smile, brushing the moment off. "I'm an accountant at a small firm," I say, trying to salvage the conversation. "I handle a lot of different accounts, so it can actually be pretty interesting. Every day's a little different."

Matt nods politely. "That sounds great. I bet it keeps you busy."

"Yeah, it does," I reply, but my voice feels thin, barely audible over the clamor around us. I glance at Chase, who's already turned away, his focus locked on someone else. My stomach churns, and I swallow hard, fighting the lump rising in my throat.

"What about you? Are you an associate?"

"Junior associate," he says, his voice softening as if sensing my discomfort. "I just transferred to the Moraine office from Denver. I prefer a smaller town to the city."

"I get that," I reply, trying to ease the tension. "We went to UC Denver but moved back here as soon as we graduated. The city isn't for everyone."

The conversation dwindles as I turn to Chase, desperate for a distraction. "Babe," I call softly, placing a hand on his back. His body jerks, and foam spills over the top of his pilsner like a mini waterfall.

"What the fuck, Tor?" he snaps, spinning to face me with fire in his eyes. "Are you trying to spill this drink all over me?" The room suddenly feels smaller, the noise quieter, and I feel every eye in the vicinity shift toward us.

I force a laugh, though it feels like swallowing glass. "Sorry," I say lightly, trying to defuse his anger.

His scowl twists into a cocky grin, the one that makes me want to shrink into myself. "Always so eager to get your hands on me," he says, his voice loud enough to carry. "Spilling my beer so you can lick it off later? Aim lower next time."

My cheeks flush hotter than the bourbon Chase drinks on poker nights. Aim lower? Did he really just say that? Out loud? In front of his colleagues?

I'm about to respond, to do something—anything—when a voice cuts through the tension like a blade.

"Aim lower, Martin? Come on now. The only reason any

woman would aim lower on you is to knee you in the crotch for being a fucktwat."

I turn, startled, to find Skye standing there in all her fiery glory, her arms crossed and an eyebrow arched. I see it in her eyes—years of biting her tongue at family dinners, of pretending not to notice the way Chase talks over me, interrupts me, belittles me. She's warned me, gently and then not-so-gently, and I've always brushed her off. But tonight? She's had enough.

Chase glares at her, his ego visibly wounded. "The only place your knees belong is on the floor, Kennedy. Be a good girl and show Matty boy here how you got your nickname, Jizzebel."

The room seems to hold its breath. Even the faint jazz music playing in the background can't cut through the suffocating tension. My mortification is complete.

Taking my queue to leave, I turn back to the bar to retrieve my clutch. "Matt, it was wonderful to meet you. I apologize for my husband's lack of decorum and my friend's equally inappropriate response." I cast death glares at each of them before continuing, "Skye just got back into town so I'm going to head out with her."

Turning to fully face my husband, I say, "I'll see you at home." Chase waves me off, saying, "Yeah, whatever," before downing the rest of his beer in one go.

"Was that absolutely necessary?" I hiss, grabbing Skye's wrist and dragging her toward the door.

"Necessary? No. Paramount to my villain arc? Absofucking-lutely," she replies, her voice dripping with defiance. "I hate when he says shit like that about you, especially in front of other people."

The cool night air outside feels like a slap to my overheated face as we step onto the sidewalk. I can still feel the weight of the bar's atmosphere clinging to me, like a second skin I can't shed.

"You caused a scene."

"*I* caused a scene?" she scoffs, "Please, Tori. He caused a scene, embarrassed the hell out of himself and everyone around him. All I did was knock him down a peg. He deserves worse."

Skye crosses her arms, her expression a mix of frustration and concern as we walk down the sidewalk. The heels of my shoes click unevenly on the pavement, and I can't bring myself to look at her. She's waiting for me to say something—anything—but my mind is stuck replaying Chase's words over and over again, each one hitting like a gut punch.

"You know," Skye says finally, her voice sharp but not unkind, "you're allowed to be mad. You don't always have to make excuses for him."

I stop walking, my breath hitching. "I'm not making excuses. He's just... stressed. Work's been a lot for him lately, and—"

"Oh, for fuck's sake, Tori," she cuts me off, spinning to face me. Her eyes are fierce, burning with the kind of indignation I can never seem to muster for myself. "You're always so quick to defend him. Do you even hear yourself? You just let him humiliate you in front of his colleagues, and you're out here blaming it on stress?"

I flinch at her words, not because they're harsh, but because they're true. "It's not that simple, Skye."

"It's *exactly* that simple," she counters, stepping closer. Her voice softens, but the fire in her eyes doesn't. "You're married to a man who treats you like shit. Like you're just... a convenience? Not even that. He treats you like you're an inconvenience to him. A tagalong punching bag, there to take hits for his pleasure. It's humiliating, and it's not okay. And you just take it. Over and over and over again. You're so busy trying to keep the peace that you're letting him crush you in the process."

Her words hit like a hammer, cracking something deep inside me that I've been holding together with duct tape and denial.

"It's not like that," I mumble, even though I know it is.

Skye takes a step back, running a hand through her hair as she exhales sharply. "Tori, do you even hear yourself? You're miserable. You're always walking on eggshells around him, bending over backward to make him happy, and for what? So he can call you boring in front of strangers? So he can make you feel small every chance he gets? That's not you. The Tori I know is strong and fierce and takes up space, dammit!"

"I don't..." My voice falters, and I feel the tears welling up. I don't want to cry—not here, not now—but the weight of everything Skye is saying is too much to hold back.

"I know you love him," she continues, her tone softening. "But love isn't supposed to feel like this. It's not supposed to make you feel invisible or worthless. It's supposed to lift you up, not tear you down."

The tears spill over, hot and unrelenting, and I swipe at them angrily. "You don't understand," I say, my voice breaking. "It's not that easy to just... to just walk away. We've been together for so long, and he's been through so much. His parents—"

"Tori," Skye interrupts gently, placing her hands on my shoulders. Her gaze locks with mine, unwavering. "I'm not telling you to leave him. Not yet. I'm telling you to fight for yourself. Stop letting him treat you like you don't matter. Stop shrinking yourself to fit into his version of what you should be. You deserve so much more—so much better—than this."

The words hang in the air between us, heavy and undeniable. I want to argue, to defend Chase, to defend myself—but I can't. Because deep down, I know she's right.

"You don't have to make any decisions right now," Skye says, her voice softer now, almost tender. "But you need to start asking yourself some hard questions, Tori. What do you want? What do you deserve? And how long are you willing to wait for things to change?"

I swallow hard, the lump in my throat threatening to choke me. "I don't know," I whisper, the words barely audible.

She squeezes my shoulders gently before letting her hands drop. "Then start there. Figure out what you want. And when you're ready, I'll be here—whatever you need, whenever you need it."

The weight of her words settles over me as we continue walking, the silence between us thick but not uncomfortable. For the first time in a long time, I feel seen—really, truly seen. And while I'm not sure what comes next, I know one thing for certain: I can't keep living like this. Something has to change.

We arrive at her car, a beat-up Subaru she refuses to trade in because "it's got character," when suddenly it hits me—I wasn't expecting her tonight. I pause, frowning slightly as she unlocks the doors.

"Wait a minute. You're supposed to be visiting your brother. Why are you home early? And how the hell did you know we were at Union?"

Skye glances at me over the top of the car, a smirk tugging at her lips. "Bitch, please. I always know where you are. Location sharing, remember?"

"Stalker," I shoot back, but there's no heat in my voice. Just gratitude.

She laughs, the sound light and unapologetic as she slides into the driver's seat. "Call it what you want, but I knew you'd need backup tonight. That douche canoe doesn't know how to treat you, and I wasn't about to let him get away with being an even bigger asshole than usual."

I climb into the passenger seat, the familiarity of her car wrapping around me like a warm blanket. It smells like the coffee she always forgets to throw out of the cup holder.

"You still haven't answered my question. Why are you already back in town?"

Skye shrugs, pulling out of the parking lot and onto the main road. "Dad thing. Told him I'd help him with some stuff tomorrow morning, so I figured I'd come home a day early and see my favorite girl. Lucky me, I walked into Union just in time to see your boy showing his ass. Again."

I shake my head, a small smile tugging at my lips despite the lingering ache in my chest. "You've got impeccable timing, as always."

"Damn right I do." She glances at me briefly before turning her attention back to the road. "Seriously, Tori. You deserve better. And I'm not saying that as your best friend—I'm saying it as someone who's watched you bend over backward for a guy who doesn't even notice how much you do for him. You're not a goddamn doormat. Stop letting him treat you like one."

I don't respond, staring out the window at the streetlights blurring past. Her words echo in my mind, bouncing off the walls of my carefully constructed defenses. I know she's right, but admitting that feels like stepping off a ledge I'm not ready to leave.

"Like I said, you don't have to make decisions now or figure it all out tonight," Skye continues, her voice softer now. "But you've got to start thinking about what you want. Not what he wants, or what you think you're supposed to want. Just... you."

The weight of her words sinks deeper, settling into the corners of my mind like seeds waiting to take root. I don't know what I want yet. But for the first time, I'm starting to think it's okay to ask the question.

Skye reaches over, giving my knee a quick squeeze. "And when you're ready to raise some hell, you know where to find me."

I glance at her, a small, genuine smile breaking through the fog of my thoughts. "Wouldn't dream of raising hell without you."

I roll down the window. The scent of cold air chases out the last trace of Union Lodge—cheap cologne and something darker I can't name. I breathe deep. I don't know what comes next.

But I know I'm not walking back into that bar.

NINE

LEO

I DON'T USUALLY PUSH through George's front door at 9 a.m. on a Saturday.

Saturdays are ours, but they don't start this early. Most weeks I roll in closer to noon, let him have a slow morning, and we pick some replay to tear apart like the outcome isn't already decided. That's the rhythm. That's the ritual. But today I'm here three hours ahead of schedule, rapping my knuckles once on the doorframe out of habit before letting myself in.

The place smells the same—coffee, faint cedar from the woodpile stacked by the back porch. Everything looks the same too: paint peeling on the shutters, flag flapping lazily in the breeze, the ceramic bird feeder still hanging crooked from the porch beam. But George? George looks thinner than he did last week when he comes shuffling into the living room. His sweatshirt hangs looser, his cheeks a little more hollow. Cancer is carving at him piece by piece, and the fact that he still manages to smirk when I crack a jab about the Avalanche blowing another lead—that's everything.

I drop onto the sagging end of the couch, the cushion already molded to me from years of this routine. He lowers himself into his recliner with the care of someone who knows his body won't forgive him if he drops too fast. The TV's already cued up to a replay from earlier in the week—Avalanche collapsing in the third, again—and we treat it like it's happening in real time.

He rants about bad line changes. I tell him his goalie's washed. He tells me my Canes are pretenders who'll choke in the second round again. Stale pretzels in a chipped bowl, a flat beer for him and a cold one for me (it's five o'clock somewhere). That's the ritual. The safe place. The one constant left standing.

And for a while, it works. The tension from yesterday—the memory of Chase's hand clamped around Tori's arm, the sound of her voice undercut by his venom—starts to bleed out of me. For a couple hours, it's just hockey. Just us.

Until George breaks the ritual with eight words that send my beer down the wrong pipe.

"You going to tell me who she is?"

I cough hard enough I'm sure the beer's about to spray the carpet, bent forward with a fist against my chest. "The fuck, George. Who?"

"Acting like I'm stupid." He leans back, smug as hell. "Alright, I'll play."

I glare at him through watery eyes, but he just shifts in his recliner, straightening like a judge ready to deliver the verdict. Then he starts counting off on his fingers.

"For starters, you've been stuck in your head all morning, son. Don't give me that look—I know you. I know when Stephanie has done something to piss you off. You've got a whole face for that. Jaw clenched, shoulders stiff, like you're about to file for divorce all over again. And you tend to cancel our plans when she's the problem, because you don't want to bring it up around me out of respect for my relationship with my daughter."

I let out a slow breath. He's not wrong. I haven't answered her calls in months. Delete the voicemails without even listening. Out of sight, out of mind.

But the truth is, it's not that simple. It never has been.

Because Stephanie leaving didn't just rip a hole in my life—it left me with this strange version of joint custody. Not of kids—thank God we never had kids. But of her parents, George and Linda. The people who stayed when she walked.

And they did stay. They didn't make excuses for her, didn't pretend her choices were acceptable. They hugged me, fed me, pulled me into holidays and birthdays like nothing had changed—like the piece that broke off between their daughter and me didn't sever anything here.

I've thought about how weird that is more times than I can count. How most divorced people would give anything to not see their ex's family every week. But not me. George and Linda are mine. Family I chose. Family who chose me back. If there's any silver lining to the smoking crater of that marriage, it's them.

Maybe that's why it stings less that I've never been close with my own parents. It's not some deep abandonment wound or childhood trauma—it's just... distance. They were in their mid-forties when they had me, a surprise baby who landed in the middle of their already-established careers. While I was technically an only child, I was really more like the younger sibling to their teaching tenure. Their work was the eldest, the favorite, the one who got most of their attention. By the time I hit college, they were already packing up for their next stage of life—traveling, lecturing, chasing their own adventures.

We check in once a month or so. Obligatory updates, polite conversations. They're proud enough of me in a vague, distant way. But holidays? Those were never with them. Before the divorce, I spent them with Stephanie's family. After the divorce, now I spend them with Dex. It's easier that way. Cleaner. I assume that even with Alis and Sunny now living with him I'm still invited for Thanksgiving and Christmas, right? Sunny won't object—it just means more presents for her.

So yeah, maybe I cling to George and Linda harder than makes sense. Because while my own parents drifted, these two stayed.

Linda still calls me son. Still hugs me like I'm hers. Still insists I bring my appetite when I show up for dinner twice a week. And George—well, George is George. Grumpy as hell, stubborn as a mule, but steady in a way no one else has been. If he doesn't survive this fight with cancer, I'll shatter.

We don't talk about Stephanie. Ever. Our relationship is carved out separate, clean, untouched by her choices. What we talk about is hockey. Because it's safer than cancer, steadier than grief. That's our glue.

George knows when something's off with me. He's earned the right. But that doesn't mean I'm going to hand him the truth on a silver platter.

I've been quiet for too long, so I take a long pull of my beer, smirking around the rim. "Alright, Sherlock. What else you got?"

"Then there's the fact you showed up at nine instead of noon," George says, his eyes narrowing like he's got me cornered already. "You didn't go out drinking. Didn't bring a hangover with you. Which means you weren't out chasing a warm body last night. And that, my boy, is suspicious."

I bark out a laugh and shake my head, because, dammit, he's not wrong about that either. "And what about those two things makes you think there's a woman?"

"I'm not done, boy," George chastises, pointing at me like he's the authority here.

I motion for him to go on. "By all means."

Instead of lifting another finger, he points to my wrist. "The watch."

I glance down at it—silver band, scuffed face, second hand that ticks half a beat too slow. My grandfather's watch. I hadn't thought twice when I slid it on this week. It just... felt right.

"The watch?" I repeat, raising a brow.

"You only wear your grandfather's watch when you're happy," George says, smirking like he's already got me nailed to the wall. "And you haven't been happy in years."

I scoff. "You're joking, right? It's literally just a watch."

But the words don't carry the weight I want them to. Because I *did* stop wearing it somewhere between the last fight and the last time Stephanie slammed the door. And I *did* put it back on this week like it meant something I didn't want to name.

George leans forward, eyes sharp despite the frailty in his body. "You wore it on your wedding day. You wore it through the first few years. Then it disappeared. Except for Dexter and Alis's engagement party, a few other special occasions here and there. And now? Dinner on Tuesday. Dinner on Thursday. Today. That's not a coincidence, son. That's a man feeling lighter. Happier. And don't insult me by pretending it isn't."

His words hang heavy, heavier than the game on TV or the pretzel bowl between us.

I shift, stretching my legs out, trying to play it off. "I'll give you this—I am happier than I've been in a long time. But it's not because of a woman."

George tilts his head, unconvinced. "So what is it, then?"

I search for the words. "Maybe I'm just done with the bullshit. Done chasing cheap hookups. I'm too old to waste every Friday swiping through Tinder like it's a side hustle."

"And Saturday," he interjects."

"Asshole." I throw a pretzel at him and continue. "I'm tired of closing down bars just to wake up with strangers I don't care about. It's time that I slow down. Sleep more. Eat better. Do something responsible for once, like grade papers before deadlines instead of after. For the first time in a long time, I'm tired of being five steps behind in my own life."

George studies me, looks me over head to toe. "And how long ago did you come to these realizations and start making these changes?"

"I don't know. A few weeks ago?" I shrug.

"A few weeks." George snorts. "And this enlightenment— that's enough to put your grandfather's watch back on?"

I grin, despite myself. "Stranger things have happened."

He doesn't grin back. He just continues to study me, patient as stone. He knows there's more. This man sees through me like glass. And just like glass, I crack.

"There's... someone new in the office," I admit, finally.

George perks up, though he tries to hide it with a sip of his beer.

"She's the new secretary," I add quickly, holding up a hand. "And it's *not* like that." George rolls his eyes. Rolls his mother-fucking eyes.

"She just started last month. Moved here from out of town. Smart as hell. Caught an error in one of my quizzes before I even finished stapling it. Schooled me right there in my office. Didn't blink. Didn't stammer. Just laid it out like I was a freshman and she was the professor."

He sees how gone I am for this woman in my eyes before I can school my features, and his mouth curves into the kind of smug, knowing smile that makes me want to hurl the entire pretzel bowl at his head.

"I'm fucking serious," I warn, jabbing a finger at him, "it's not like that. She's just... competent. Direct. Which is... refreshing. And she's friends with Alis and Skye. So, no, it's most definitely *not* like that."

George's smile only widens, eyes glinting with mischief.

"Ah," he says, low and smug, like a man watching the puck slide clean into the net. "So she's the reason for the watch."

BY THE TIME I push back from the table and kiss Linda's cheek goodnight, I'm exhausted from the effort of pretending. George claps me on the shoulder as I leave, his grip lighter than it used to be, but steady enough to say what he doesn't out loud: *Take care of yourself.*

I nod, promise I will, and walk out into the night.

The drive home is silent. Radio off, phone facedown on the passenger seat. The roads are nearly empty, streetlights blurring through my windshield as I run back over every word from today. George's smug smile. His voice: *So she's the reason for the watch.*

I tighten my grip on the steering wheel. I don't want him to be right. I don't want her to be the reason for anything. And yet, no matter how many times I tell myself she's just a secretary, just a sharp tongue and a steady gaze, the truth presses in like a bruise I can't stop touching.

I roll through a yellow that probably should've been a red and catch my reflection in the rearview—the hard line of my mouth, the watch face ghosting in the corner of the glass. I flip the mirror down. Childish. Doesn't help. The image is still there in my head: her hand braced on the edge of the filing cabinet, the tiny tremor in her fingers she tried to hide. The way she said *thank you* like I'd taken a boulder off her spine with three words and a body in a doorway.

"Fuck," I say to the empty car, like swearing at upholstery might rewire me back to the version of myself that didn't care.

A light turns green. I don't move at first. The guy behind me taps his horn—polite, not pissed. I pull forward and breathe through my teeth. I need out. Out of this loop. Out of her voice in my head. Out of George's knowing, out of the way my chest feels strangely sore, like I've been running stairs.

I reach for the phone at the next stop sign and call Dexter.

He picks up on the second ring. "Hey, man."

"Hey." My voice scrapes. "You busy?"

Pause, the soft background wash of family noise. Clinking plates, a kid laughing. Sunny. "Kind of," he says. "Alis's parents are in town, we're doing a whole weekend thing. I can pull away for a beer later tonight if you need—"

"No." I say it too fast. "No, it's fine. I was just... driving."

"Driving where?" he asks, too gentle, like he can hear the weight in my throat.

"Home." I clear it. "From George and Linda's."

"How's he doing?"

I swallow. "Thin."

"Shit," he says softly. "I'm sorry."

"Yeah." I drag a palm down my jaw, stubble rasping against skin. "He's still himself, though. Still chirping the Avs. Still convinced my Canes are frauds."

Dex chuckles, then quiet again. "So, you good?"

I could say yes. I could say absolutely, I'm peachy, I'm a man without a single inconvenient thought in his skull. The lie rises easy. Too fucking easy.

"Yeah," I say. "All good. Go be charming with the in-laws."

"Leo."

"Yeah, man."

"You can call me later if you need to."

"I won't," I lie.

He exhales like he knows I'm lying. "Alright. Later, brother."

I end the call before I have to answer that back. Toss the phone face-up on the passenger seat and stare at the black screen until my face floats there, faint and unimpressed.

The quiet rushes in again. It's the kind of quiet that eats itself. I last four blocks, then unlock the phone and thumb the little red flame without thinking. Tinder blooms like a bad habit I keep in a glass case with a hammer beside it.

I swipe left on a brunette with sharp brows. Left on another with a smile that, if my imagination were crueler, could be Tori's cousin on a dark night. Left, left—too close, too many lips that look like hers. My thumb stutters over a profile that could have been Pull-and-Replace: same hair, same jawline. Left. Left. It becomes a small ritual of punishment.

Then a blonde pops up. Filter-soft, sunlit laugh in the thumbnail, bio that says *dogs, patios, over games under drama.* The part of me that's slightly functional snorts. The other part—the one that wants to combust out of my skull—doesn't care. I swipe right. Match in under a second. A green dot pulses like a detonator. Her name is Kelsey. She messages first:

> Hey there 😉 what are you up to?

My thumbs move on autopilot.

> Headed downtown. You around?

> I can be. Harper's on Main in thirty?

I check the clock because habits die hard. Doesn't matter. I type *See you there* and drop the phone back on the seat, laughing without humor. This is the choreography I know: girl, bar, banter, forgettable fuck, make up a weekend get together in the morning. Easy. Disposable. The religion I converted to after Stephanie.

I turn off the highway and into the familiar wide avenue of Main Street. Grand River at night is gutters of light and low music leaking out of brick storefronts—string lights swing over the crosswalks, planters push flowers into the cool air, and the Bookcliffs stand like watchmen on the horizon, dark and patient. People drift between doors, laughter spilling across the sidewalks; the smell of pizza from a place down the block mixes with hops and diesel and the faint woodsmoke from a late patio fire.

Harper's sits between a yoga studio that glows faintly and a gallery that likes to pretend its bronze sculptures aren't just abstract chaos. Its weathered wooden sign basks under two flood lamps. I wedge my truck into a slanted spot, kill the engine, and shove my hands into my jacket like that'll hide the watch. The face catches the streetlight. I want to take it off. I don't.

Inside Harper's the air is warm and loud—Edison bulbs, a mural of the Bookcliffs behind the bar, a row of taps that promises local IPAs, and a suspender-clad hipster bartender complete the vibe. The floorboards creak. The place smells like citrus, beer foam, and the kind of cologne guys wear when they want to be noticed for trying. Harper's is packed but not Denver-crowded; you can still move without elbowing someone's dignity.

I scan for the blonde. There are three. Of course. Two in black dresses, one in a jean jacket, all leaning against the bar like they're already half a story in someone else's night. I take a step forward to text Kelsey and then—because systems break for reasons you can't explain—I see electric blue.

Skye's hair flashes under the bulbs like a neon sign. She's tucked into a high-top, laughing with one hand slung over the back of her chair. Next to her, half in shadow, is Tori.

Everything in me freezes in that stupid animal way, like the brain's wiring is deciding between fight, flight, or the dumb, decorative third option: freeze. A guy behind me utters something about learning to walk in crowded places and sidesteps, but I don't move.

Tori's in a black top that dips at the collarbone, sleeves pushed to her elbows. Her nails are red in a way that makes small, terrible promises. She's mid-laugh—open, real—and when Skye says something offhand she throws back a look that's all mischief and teeth. The sight lands somewhere low in my gut and stays.

Relief hits first, oddly. Relief that she's laughing, not replaying Chase's hand on her arm like a bad loop. Relief that there's a friend at her side—Skye—someone liable to make a scene if some guy tried to be a shit. Relief that she's not alone carrying a shit moment she shouldn't have had to endure.

Then anger—at myself—for what I'm doing. For summoning a blonde as a decoy, a distraction. For the cliché I planned to act out like the rehearsed farce of fulfillment it's always been. For telling George the changes he sees in me aren't about a woman when every stupid action I take is a rebuttal in motion.

My phone vibrates in my pocket.

> I'm at the bar, black dress, red heels. Where
> are you?

I don't pull the phone out. I can't move in any direction that isn't toward the exit or toward them.

Skye spots me first, because of course she does. Her head rotates, blue hair a beacon, and her face lights up like she heard a joke she's about to tell. "Leo!" she calls over the buzz of a cover band playing something too earnest. The room pivots; Tori's head snaps toward me, eyes scanning, catching, sliding past one familiar face back to mine. She doesn't wave. She doesn't look away. She meets me as if she has time to make that call.

I lift a hand anyway—futile, boyish. She holds my gaze. She doesn't smile in an inviting way. She doesn't freeze me out either. It's a neutral that feels like a test.

Kelsey pings again.

> At the bar. Do you see me?

I see a blonde in red heels gesturing for a man with a hat. She does not see me. I could go. Walk over, play the role, let my head stop echoing Tori's voice like it's a drum. Or I could leave. Save myself the morning-after shame and the story I tell myself about not being that man. Or I could do something I haven't practiced in a long time: be a decent human.

Skye's grin widens to carnivore width as I edge toward them. She's always had that look—like she's found the game's best seat. "Fancy seeing you here," she says, sing-song and sharp. A trap with cushioned edges.

"Skye." I nod. "Tori."

"Leo." Tori's voice is steady, cool. My phone buzzes again.

> At the bar. I think I see you?

I flip the phone over in my hand, thumb the screen and for the first time in years mute a match.

Skye's mouth twitches at the motion. "Didn't know you were a Harper's guy," she says.

"I'm not," I say. "Came to meet someone." Then, because honesty keeps tripping me up, "Changed my mind."

Tori watches me with that unreadable expression—maybe relief, maybe judgment, maybe neither. I am not brave enough to ask for clarification. "You two good?" I say instead.

She studies me like she's weighing whether to trust the scale. Finally, she nods. "We're good." Then softer, a breath that almost folds into confession: "We're okay."

The promise of that little *okay* lodges in my chest and for one ridiculous second I believe it. Then Skye shoves Tori with her elbow. "We were about to order food. Sit. Or go meet your Tinder twat and pretend you didn't see us—I'll only tattle on you to Alis about it."

I should have kept moving. The blonde is still waving. I should have done the cheap thing. Instead, something in my ribs twists toward the honest option. "I'll get the next round," I say. "Food, too." I find myself looking at Tori when I add, "No strings."

Her face flickers—something unnameable—and she nods once. Skye beams and I know my wallet won't survive the night. "Burgers. Fries. Pretzel with the beer cheese for scientific comparison to George's bowl," she declares. I snort out a laugh. "His bowl is an artifact," I say. "It belongs in a museum."

I make the order at the bar, adding extra shots for good measure. I text one thing to Kelsey—*Can't make it*—and send without pausing for deflection. Three dots blink and die. I set the phone face down and for the first time since the filing cabinet slammed shut at 5:04, I breathe without reconstructing every syllable in my head.

The bartender asks for a name. "Leo." My name comes out

simple, certain. For once, it feels like enough. *I* feel like enough. I'm not lacking in anything tonight.

I lean on the counter, let the noise wash over me until it fades into background hum—the thrum of glasses, laughter, music seeping out of the back room. When I glance back, Skye is mid-story, blue hair slicing the air as her hands fly. Tori listens, one corner of her mouth curved in a smile that isn't armor, isn't survival—just living.

That smile wraps around my cold, dead heart like a blanket, and for once, I don't fight it. I don't overthink it. I let it warm me, because I can still hear what she told me in my office Friday morning: she doesn't have the time or space for me or my bullshit.

And maybe that's the safety net I didn't know I needed. Tori can't hurt me if she doesn't want me. Whatever this thing is—curiosity, infatuation, fascination—it won't matter, because she's not mine. She'll never be mine. By the time her divorce papers are signed, this will have burned itself out.

That's what I tell myself, anyway.

My thumb brushes the scuffed face of my grandfather's watch, finds the dent that's been there longer than I've been alive. George's voice echoes in my head: *So she's the reason for the watch.*

Maybe. Maybe not.

I pick up the shots and head back to the table. Skye's hair is a neon sign in the dim light, Tori's nails a streak of red against the wood. She's the woman who told me *thank you* like it cost her something, like it was an apology for letting me see her truth. Her shame.

But she'll see soon enough she has nothing to be ashamed of. Divorce, bruises, scars—none of it makes her small. And whether she thinks she has time for me or not, she's stuck with me now. I might be a fuckboy, but I'm a damn good fuckboy to have as a friend. Skye would vouch for that.

I set the four tiny glasses down with a flourish. "I believe you beautiful ladies are in need of more alcohol."

"Yas, bitch!" Skye slaps the table, hands out like a toddler begging for candy.

I slide two shots her way and push the others toward Tori. She lifts her brows. "None for you?"

"Not tonight, Tote. Someone has to drive your cute ass home."

The shot is halfway to her mouth when she freezes, eyes narrowing at the nickname. Confusion creases her brow—*what the fuck?* written plain as day.

Before she can say a word, I guide the shot glass the rest of the way, steady pressure on her hand until she tips it back, swallows, and slams it down again. I release her slowly, only when her gaze flicks away, back where it should be—on letting loose with her best friend.

Because I've seen how tightly wound Victoria Foster is these past few weeks. And Friday, I saw exactly why.

If I can't fuck the tension out of her, then at the very least I'll make damn sure she's safe while she unravels for a night out on the town.

TEN

TORI

THE SUN IS SETTING behind the Rocky Mountains, casting a warm, golden light over the valley. The crisp air carries the familiar scent of pine and earth, mixing with the soft hum of cicadas. Shadows stretch long and thin across the ground, the evening light painting the peaks in hues of amber and crimson. I'm sitting on the porch swing with Mom, the wooden slats creaking gently beneath us as we sway back and forth. The soft rustle of leaves in the breeze is almost hypnotic, a soothing melody against the backdrop of nature's orchestra. Normally, this view calms me, but today, the beauty of Moraine feels like a cruel contrast to the chaos inside me.

I came to my parents' house for dinner while Chase is on a work trip, partly because I wanted a distraction from the thoughts in my head and the growing discontentment I feel with my marriage, and partly because I need advice. Dad has always been a bit of an asshole and Mom doesn't seem affected by it. I don't know if that's because she is blind to how demeaning he is when he speaks to her or if she knows some secret I don't about how to maintain a happy marriage.

Is she happy, though?

I shake the thought. Of course, she's happy. I know her. She's my mother. I can trust her. I can talk to her. I don't have to keep bottling this up inside myself, constantly worried that I'm making a big deal out of nothing. This is something. This is a problem. This needs to be addressed.

The swing sways gently, the old chains groaning under our weight as the evening sky deepens to a rich lavender. Crickets join the cicadas, their rhythmic chirping creating a soft, pulsing background. "Mom," I start, taking another breath before continuing, "are you happy?"

That is not what I meant to ask, but I'll roll with it.

She looks at me, and for a millisecond I swear I see something hollow in her eyes, but it's gone and replaced with the serene smile I know and love before I can think too much into it. Her face is lit by the soft glow of the setting sun, which catches the faint lines around her eyes, hinting at years of quiet endurance.

"Of course, I am, honey. Why would you ask?"

Here goes nothing.

"Because I'm not." Again, not what I meant to say. Is it the truth? Yes. I had simply planned on offering that truth with more finesse.

Her brow furrows, concern evident in her eyes. Mom slides her hand over mine and squeezes gently, a physical sign of reassurance that this is a safe space. The warmth of her hand contrasts with the cool evening air, which seems to whisper around us, carrying with it the scent of distant rain and fresh grass. She's always been a safe space for me, for everyone. I can talk to her. She can help.

I'm thankful she doesn't press, just continues holding my hand while I gather my thoughts.

"I mean, I'm happy sometimes. But not... not in the most important aspects of my life." You know, for someone with such a high IQ and strong conversational skills, I'm doing a shit job of explaining myself right now.

"Such as..." she prompts. I shrug, suddenly nervous to say this out loud. I've never admitted these feelings to anyone, and while I know I can tell my mom anything, this suddenly feels different. Dark. Wrong, somehow.

The breeze picks up slightly, brushing against my skin like a whisper, as if the world itself is listening. The wind chimes hanging on the porch tinkle softly, a delicate, almost mournful sound.

"At home. I'm not happy at home. With Chase. With my marriage. I'm not happy when I come home from work, when he comes home from softball practice, when we have to ride in the same car to go somewhere. Basically, the only time I'm happy is when I'm not with him." There. I said it. I am not happy in my marriage. I do not want to be in my marriage. Nope. Can't say that. Don't go there. Let's focus on happiness, not leaving.

I continue, the words spilling from my mouth without a filter. *Get it out. Get it all out.*

"Mom, I don't know what to do. Chase... he's just so unhappy all the time. I study him, I know his favorite foods and his favorite movies and how he likes his pants folded and shirts hung and no matter what I do, it's never enough. I can't do anything right, and it's gotten to the point that I don't even want to be around him, let alone talk to him. I can't talk to him. It doesn't matter what I say —it's wrong or he dismisses it or he makes some backhanded comment to make me feel like shit. I read books about how to be a godly woman and a good wife and I do literally everything they say, and nothing changes. I'm tired, Mom. So, fucking, tired. Tired of trying to be exactly who I'm supposed to be and then being treated like I'm not enough. Tired of trying to connect with someone who clearly doesn't want me. I'm not happy, and goddammit I'm so tired of not being happy." Holy crap did I just say that? Out loud?

The golden glow of the sun is fading now, the horizon bruising into deep purples and blues. The valley below seems to exhale a soft mist, the cooling air wrapping itself around us. Mom turns to me, her eyes full of concern, but there's something else there, too —something that tells me she's about to give me the kind of advice I'm not sure I want to hear. She rubs her thumb over the back of my hand, and I brace myself.

"Tori, marriage is hard," she begins, her voice soft but firm. The sound of her words seems to blend with the creak of the porch swing and the distant hum of a car on the winding road below. No shit, Sherlock. I hold back my eyeroll, determined to hear her out. "It is a sacred covenant, a commitment you made before God. It's not about happiness, sweetheart. It's about holiness. Remember, the Bible tells us that marriage isn't meant to make us happy—it's meant to make us holy."

The twilight deepens, and the first stars begin to peek through the darkening sky. The air cools, brushing against my skin with a faint chill, and I fold my arms across my chest instinctively. I feel my stomach drop, but she continues, her voice steady. "I know you're struggling, and I know it's hard when it feels like you're the only one trying. But God calls us to be patient, to endure, and to submit to our husbands as unto the Lord. Have you thought about how you can serve Chase better? How you can love him more deeply, even when it's difficult?"

She pauses, searching my face, and I'm too stunned to respond.

"Sometimes, when we feel like our efforts aren't enough, it's because we're focusing too much on ourselves and not enough on God's will for our marriage. Maybe instead of focusing on your happiness, you should be asking how you can bring glory to God in your marriage. Pray for Chase, Tori. Pray for his heart to soften, for his burdens to be lifted. And pray for your own heart, that you might find joy in serving him, even when it's hard."

The words feel like stones being stacked on my chest, each one heavier than the last. I can feel the tears welling up, but I fight them back, not wanting her to see how much her words are cutting me. She squeezes my hand, mistaking my silence for agreement.

The shadows of the trees stretch further across the porch as the last light fades from the sky, and I feel enveloped by the growing darkness.

"Remember, dear, we can't control other people's actions, but we can control our own. Focus on being the best wife you can be, and trust God to do the rest. The Lord never gives us more than we can handle, and He will use this trial to strengthen your faith and refine you into the woman He wants you to be."

Does the Bible really say that? I'm fairly certain the whole "God never gives you more than you can handle" line is utter bullshit, twisted into some kind of inspirational platitude people use to justify suffering.

She leans in, her voice dropping to a conspiratorial whisper. The faint scent of her lavender lotion drifts toward me, a nostalgic but suffocating reminder of childhood comfort. "And sometimes, Tori, the enemy will use these feelings of discontent to try to pull you away from God's plan. Don't let him win. Fight for your marriage with prayer and humility. God honors those who remain faithful, even when it's hard."

The porch light flickers to life above us, casting a harsh, yellow glow that feels stark and unwelcome against the gentle fading colors of the sky. I nod mechanically, my mind spinning with everything she's just said. The weight on my shoulders feels heavier than ever, and I can't help but wonder if this is really what God wants for me—to be trapped in a marriage that drains the life out of me, with no hope of change.

A light breeze picks up, rustling the trees and sending a shiver through me. The night smells fresh, but it's cold and uninviting, a sharp contrast to the warmth I once found here.

And what about what I want? I'm tired of being trampled on all the time. Tired of reading and studying and serving and submitting. Tired of deferring and staying silent to keep the peace. Tired of being no one, when I know that I'm someone. Tired of being praised at work for a job well done, only to come home and feel the opposite. I can't share my victories with him. I can't share my heart with him. Fucking hell, I can barely share my body with him. Not that he cares what I want. As long as he comes, all is well in Chase land.

Until it happens again. The negative pregnancy tests. They always happen. Every. Single. Month. For the past seven years.

I don't know why I still take them. I know what they'll say. But Chase insists. He wants to see the evidence that once again he has failed to impregnate me.

I don't know why he does this emotional self-flagellation. It doesn't help anything. I've tried to help him focus on our marriage, on our relationship. To stop worrying so much about what we don't have and instead celebrate what we do. It doesn't matter.

He can't hear me—or he won't, rather.

The cicadas' hum swells around us, their unrelenting rhythm amplifying the silence between me and Mom. But I keep those thoughts to myself, forcing a weak smile as Mom gives my hand one last squeeze. This is not at all how I had hoped this conversation would play out. Instead of feeling safe and seen by the one person on this planet who loves me unconditionally, it's as if my feelings don't matter to her, to God, to anyone, really.

The mountains, now nothing more than blackened silhouettes etched against the star-speckled sky, seem to mock me with their stoic majesty—unyielding and indifferent, just like my marriage. They stand as silent witnesses to the dreams I once had of a happy life with the man I thought I loved, dreams now twisted into something hollow and cruel. The chill deepens, sinking into my skin, and the wooden slats beneath me grow harder, less forgiving, as though everything around me is conspiring to remind me of how far I've fallen.

Are you there, God? It's me, Victoria. Do you care, God? About anyone other than yourself and your fucking rules? Is this what your will is for my life? Suffering and oppression in a marriage to a man who is too selfish and broken to see anything beyond his own pain?

Fuck that. And fuck you. And fuck your rules. And fuck your holiness. And fuck my mother. And fuck Chase. And fuck infertility.

Fuck it all.

ELEVEN
TORI

I NEVER THOUGHT my life would look like this.

My hand hovers over the doorknob like touching it will detonate something. I'm dressed, handbag slung over my elbow, blouse buttoned, slacks on, feet in pumps. Pumps. I'm wearing fucking *pumps*.

Not sexy stiletto pumps, but the short, stocky ones. Like my mom would wear to church. They aren't even black. They are gray. Dark gray, but still. Gray.

Should I change? I should change.

Maybe that's why I can't open the door and leave. Because I need to change.

I don't have time to change my outfit. I'm going to be late, but my body refuses to take one more step and actually turn the knob and *open* the door.

Jesus, Mary, and Joseph what the ever loving *fuck* am I doing?

Divorce attorney. Jacob—what was his last name again? Something strong, something that sounds like it belongs on a campaign sign or stamped across a courthouse door. A name people take seriously. Finegan? That's not it. Because then I'd keep saying *Finegan Begin Again* in my head. Okay, so it's not Finegan.

Sterling. That's it. *Jacob Sterling, Esq.* I should feel better knowing that, but I don't.

Because the truth is, no matter what his name is, this life—life as a divorced woman at age thirty-two—is not the life I planned.

When I was twenty-two and wide-eyed, fresh from graduation, I thought marriage was the milestone that made you an adult. I thought forever was a thing you could will into existence with the right vows, the right person, the right dress. I thought I'd be one of those women who built a home around love, not fights and doctors and tension. Who celebrated anniversaries, not endings.

Skye is probably going to make me do that. Celebrate the divorce. She'll want to have a party. Like a bachelorette thing, but a *divorcette*? Part of me wants to ask her what the word is, but my smarter self doesn't want to accidentally inception an idea into her brain just in case it isn't already there.

Now I'm thirty-two and staring at a door like a child afraid of the dark, about to walk into a cold, leather-clad office to pay a man with a briefcase to help me unravel the life I fought so hard to build.

My chest feels hollow. My bones feel like rickety scaffolding, two seconds away from collapse.

And that's what really gets me—the collapse. Because at twenty-two, I walked down an aisle in a white dress, thinking I was walking toward solidity. Toward something permanent. People cried happy tears, toasted champagne, talked about our bright future like it was a fact. And here I am ten years later, staring at a different kind of threshold, going to talk to an attorney about how I can sign my name to an ending.

It's not an ending. It's a beginning.

If I say it to myself enough times, I may actually start to believe it.

"I. Am. Ready." My voice cracks on the last word, like it already knows I'm lying.

The click of a door down the hall startles me. Skye's voice

follows, steady and casual, like this is any other Tuesday. "Hold up. I'll grab my bag."

I frown and turn just as she steps out of her room, jean skirt, boots, leather jacket, keys twirling in her fingers like she's heading to brunch. Her eyeliner is perfect, blue hair pulled back in two french braids that end in messy buns on each side of her head. She looks effortlessly beautiful, fun, and totally badass. If only I looked half as intimidating.

"What are you doing?" I ask.

She raises a brow, like I'm the one being strange. "What do you mean? I'm coming with you."

"Skye—"

She shakes her head before I can say another word. "There is no way in hell you're walking into a divorce attorney's office alone, Tori. Not happening."

I blink at her. "I didn't ask you to—"

"Pfft," she cuts me off. "You think I'm gonna let my best friend sit in some buttoned leather chair across from a stiff white man in a suit, talking about legal separation and marital assets, without backup? Not a fucking chance."

Her tone is flippant, but her eyes are not. They're sharp, steady, and full of the kind of loyalty that doesn't ask permission. My God, I love her. I also hate that right now I'm dressed like I could be her mother. Whatever.

Something inside me cracks. Not enough to spill, but enough that I feel the fissure spread. I press my lips together, trying to swallow the lump in my throat.

Because part of me is relieved. The bigger part is ashamed.

I should be able to do this on my own. I should be the kind of woman who walks into a law office with her head high, her voice clear, her resolve unshakable. Instead, I'm standing in the doorway of my borrowed apartment with sweaty palms and a heartbeat that feels too loud in my ears. I feel twelve years old. Like a child playing dress-up in divorce papers instead of tiaras.

"Skye..." My voice thins, tears welling in my eyes. "What if I can't do this?"

She closes the distance in two strides, hands on my shoulders, grounding me. "You can. You already are. The hard part was leaving him. This is paperwork."

I laugh, short and humorless. "Paperwork that will decide the rest of my life."

She tilts her head, bangs falling over one eye. "Exactly. *Your* life. Not his. Not the one he controlled. Yours. And I'm gonna be there every step of the way."

Her certainty is a hammer to the shaky scaffolding inside me. For a moment, I almost believe her.

Almost.

But as Skye reaches around me to open the door and we step out into the crisp Colorado morning, the air biting my cheeks, I can't shake the gnawing voice in my head. The one that whispers how broken this looks. How this wasn't supposed to be me. How my parents might act supportive to my face but will whisper behind their polite smiles. How the girl I used to be—the one who dreamed of love and babies and happily ever after—wouldn't even recognize this version of herself.

I haven't spoken to anyone in Moraine since I left. Not a text, not a call, not a single word. Just my mother's cautious updates, lacking any real details about the goings on of neighbors and her friends at church. But I don't need details from my mom to know the truth. Moraine is a small mountain town, the kind that thrives on tourists in the summer and gossip all year long. Everyone knows everyone. Everyone knows every*thing*. And when they don't? They invent the details until the story fits whatever narrative makes the best entertainment around the coffee shop tables and church steps.

So I can only imagine what they're saying now. How my name rolls through town faster than a middle school game of telephone. How people lower their voices after church on Sundays, standing in little clusters outside the stone steps, whispering like they're praying. *She left him. Ten years and no kids—no wonder. She was always too ambitious, too focused on her career. She couldn't make it work. Bless her heart.*

And Chase—God, Chase knows how to play that audience.

I can see him now, polished to perfection, sliding into the same pew every Sunday with his tie knotted just so. Head bowed, voice heavy, letting himself be caught in the spotlight of pity. *Pray for me. She left. I don't know why. I did everything I could. She didn't even say goodbye. Took off like a thief in the night while I was out of town.*

He'll paint himself as the abandoned husband, a noble victim. And the congregation, his friends and coworkers, everyone will eat it up, will nod and murmur and pat his shoulder, will fold him into prayers and well wishes with the kind of sympathy that makes me the villain without ever saying the word or considering that every word out of his mouth is bullshit.

The shame flares sharp, hot. But right on its heels comes something harder. A low, coiled defiance.

Let them whisper. Let him make a show of being abandoned. Let him cry crocodile tears into offering plates and soak up the sympathy. He can perform sainthood until the end of time, but he can't rewrite what happened inside our walls. They didn't live my life. They didn't survive his refusal to heal from his own goddamn trauma.

Skye taps the steering wheel to a song on the radio I can't name. She glances over, a half-smile pulling at one corner of her mouth. "You okay?" she asks, like she's asking about the weather and not the slow collapse of my former life.

"No," I say honestly. "But I will be."

My throat tightens. I stare out the window, watching power lines blur into sky. "I just keep imagining all the bullshit being said about me back home. What they're probably whispering in Moraine. How Chase is probably showing up to church every

Sunday looking like a martyr, making me the villain in his fucking sob story."

Skye snorts. One hand on the wheel, she takes my hand with the other and squeezes. "Let them talk. We never liked those motherfuckers anyway."

"Very true," I laugh.

"And besides," she continues. "If I hear of one person calling you the villain in his sad little sob story, I'll drive up there myself, punch those snooty bitches in the vag, and light the church pews on fire. Metaphorically." She pauses, then adds, "Or not."

Another laugh hiccups out of me. It's small and crooked, but it's real, and laughing definitely helps to ease the tension and stress I've felt all morning. "You can't punch every person who has an opinion."

"Watch me." She slants me a look, then softens. "Let them whisper whatever bullshit they want, T. They don't know shit. They don't get a vote."

Let them whisper. The words flare warm in my chest, quick as a match. Maybe that's the only answer there is. Let them whisper. Let them talk themselves hoarse while I sign the papers that release me to build a life they won't recognize. Let them call it failure, while I call it truly, *finally* living.

We turn off the main drag into the heart of downtown, the part with the string lights crisscrossing overhead and the little boutiques stacked shoulder to shoulder with cafés and bookstores. The kind of street that looks pretty on a postcard. Skye practically lives down here—her coffee shop is just up ahead, the front windows already buzzing with mid-morning traffic.

A block down from it, the vibe shifts—less cozy charm, more clean and clinical. Glass windows, cold symmetry, metal letters gleaming across the façade: **Sterling Law Group**. The kind of signage that says *we win* before you even step inside.

My pulse hammers. I smooth my blouse, which is suddenly the wrong fabric, the wrong weight, the wrong life. The pumps pinch. I deserve better shoes than this. *Did these shoes just become a metaphor? Probably. But I'm the math geek, not the English nerd.*

"Okay," Skye says, as much to herself as to me. She pulls into a lot where the lines are freshly painted and the landscaping has zero personality but is definitely judging us. "We go in. We do the consult. If he's a good fit, we move forward. If he's not, we walk out and get someone different. Either way, when this is over, we get obscene mimosas."

"Giant margarita glass mimosas," I correct her.

"Giant margarita glass mimosas," she echoes.

We sit there for a beat, both of us staring at the building like it might blink. My mouth is dry. "It looks... expensive."

"Good," Skye says. "Expensive is the energy we want."

I nod because it's that or laugh until I cry. My hand finds the door handle, slips, finds it again. The seatbelt catches when I try to get out too fast, tugging me back like a toddler on a leash. I take that as a sign to slow down, breathe, and unbuckle like a normal adult human—not a person who requires child locks.

Outside, the air has teeth. Cold bites the naked slice of my ankle between my pant hem and pump. Somewhere a truck rattles by, and a woman in a pencil skirt clips across the lot like a woman on a mission. I wonder if she, too, ever stood in front of a door and thought she might explode from the inside out. And if she has, did anyone notice?

We walk side by side-ish, Skye's boots thudding confident and sure, my pumps clacking behind like they're trying to keep up. I wish my heels sounded as confident as the other woman from a few seconds ago, but they don't. Her's were more of a *click click click*, and mine are definitely more *clunk*.

Ah, yes. The difference between a woman to be desired and a woman to be pitied. I wonder if her shoes were also gray? Doubtful.

The glass doors loom. I can see us in them—Skye's braids, my careful blouse, the way we lean slightly toward each other. A small, stubborn unit.

We stop at the threshold. *Deja fucking vu.* I stare at the handle like it's the same one from our apartment, like I've been walking a slow circle and landed right back where I started.

Here's the truth I don't say out loud: I am both the woman who can do this and the girl who wants to run. I am both the version of me that stayed too long and the one who finally left. I am a thousand messy contradictions mashed into a person who can barely stand upright in these stupid, clunky, pinchy gray pumps.

Skye nudges my arm with her elbow. "Want me to open it?"

I shake my head. "No. I've got it."

I swallow, find the handle, wrap my fingers around the metal. It's cool and solid and real under my palm. My reflection stares back—eyes a little too bright, mouth too tight, hair behaving for once. *At least something is working for me today.* I look like a woman on a mission. Not a desperate woman looking to escape her marriage, but a woman taking control of her life and her future. I do not feel like her. Maybe that's okay. Fake it til you make it? Done.

Let them whisper. Let the building shine and the letters gleam and the pumps pinch. Let my hands shake. Let my heart race.

I'm getting divorced, bitches.

TWELVE
TORI

I'M NOT sure when I drifted off, but the slam of the front door jerks me awake like a gunshot. My heart launches into my throat as I bolt upright on the couch, the blanket tangled around my legs. The room is dark, except for the glow of the TV screen still playing some rerun I wasn't watching.

"God fucking dammit."

Chase. I hear him in the foyer, tripping over his own feet as he stumbles to take off his shoes. I hear his body slam against the entry table, keys dropping to the floor instead of hanging on the hook next to the coat closet.

He's drunk. Of course he's drunk. Still mumbling to himself, Chase turns the corner into the living room and stops short when he sees me sitting there. For a moment, I'm not sure if he realizes it's me. His body halts, but his words continue as if he's been conversing with the person in front of him the entire time.

He reeks of stale alcohol and cigarette smoke. Something sour —vomit, maybe?—clings to his clothes. I can't remember the last time he was so drunk that he threw up, but I also can't remember the last time he smoked. His drinking has grown worse over the years, and I've tried to talk to him about it, to no avail.

I used to try everything—pouring the bottles out, hiding them, begging him to stop. At some point, you stop playing tug-of-war when the other person drops the rope.

Tonight, though? Something is wrong. Something is terribly, terribly wrong.

"What the fuck are you looking at?" he asks, breaking his monologue of "Of fucking course this would happen" sentiments.

I rise slowly, unsure of whether I should speak or wait. My heart is already pounding in my chest, my hands clutching the blanket like a shield.

"I asked you a question, goddammit!"

Speak it is, then. "What happened?" I ask gently, trying not to further agitate the situation. "Are you okay?"

He scoffs, then laughs—a bitter, broken sound that holds no real humor.

"Just. Fucking. Peachy," he spits, taking a mocking stance, hands on his hips and venom in his tone. "Everything in my life is fucking perfect."

I literally don't know how to respond to this. So I wait.

Tossing his arms in the air, Chase shouts, "I'm going to be a fucking uncle!"

Oh. *Oh.*

My throat goes dry. "Trent and Fallon?"

He nods, jerky and exaggerated. "Yep. Trent and Fallon. Golden boy and his golden girl. Knocked up and glowing. Of course they are."

Wrapping my arms around my middle, I lower myself back onto the couch slowly. I'm happy for Trent and Fallon—truly, I am—but if there is one person in this world who sets off Chase's insecurities and feelings of inadequacy more than anyone else, it's his little brother.

"Chase, I'm sorry. That must've been hard to hear," I say

softly, trying to sound steady, even though my body is already bracing for impact.

"Hard to hear?" His voice climbs, sharper now. "Hard to hear? Jesus fucking Christ, Tori. Do you even fucking get it?"

He starts pacing, hands clenching and unclenching like he doesn't know what to do with them.

"It doesn't fucking matter what I do. That punk-ass kid will always be a step ahead of me. He bought a house before I did. He made partner before I did. And now he's having a goddamn baby before me. Before *us*."

His words are laced with fury, but the way he says "us" feels like an accusation. A punch without the wind-up.

"We grew up in the same house. Had the same fucked-up parents. Same genetics. Same foster houses. Same lack of fucking opportunities. And still—*still*—he's always one step ahead."

He paces faster now, fists clenched at his sides like he's holding back something too big to name.

"He's always got the upper hand. Better looking. Better job. Better fucking cars. Hot as fuck wife. She actually *likes* him."

My chest tightens, bracing for what's coming. The oxygen in the room feels thinner with every word he spits.

"And what do I get?" He spins on me, venom in his voice. "A wife who fucking *pities* me. A *mediocre* life. And a cock that can't even do the *one* thing it's created to do."

The words hit me like a slap. My hands instinctively press against my stomach as though to protect it from him, from this moment, from everything he just said.

I force a breath through my lips and stand, taking a step toward him. I want to withdraw from him, but I know it's in these moments that I need to draw near. He needs me more than ever right now. He just doesn't know how to ask for it.

"Chase, please don't talk like that. We're doing everything we can. We're going to figure this out, okay?"

"For fuck's sake, just shut up." His voice curdles. "You always have something to say. Always trying to spin it. You think your optimism makes you helpful? It makes you a *fucking joke!*"

I take a small step back. He follows.

"You think I don't see it in your eyes? The *disappointment?* The *pity?* You think you could do better than me? You think I can't do better than you?! I fucking know I can!"

I don't even know who he's attacking anymore. All I know is that I don't want to be here. I don't want to hear any of this.

His finger jabs through the air, inches from my face. I take another step back, heart racing.

"Chase, you're scaring me," I whisper. "Please, just—"

"I'm scaring you?" he snaps. "*I'm the one who's scared, Tori!* Everything about me is broken. Nothing is ever enough! I'm not enough for *you.* I'm not enough for *anyone.* I'm always gonna be the fucked-up version of the man I'm supposed to be! And then I come home to you—*you*—the one person who's supposed to have my back, and all I get is pity and your fucking optimism and your empty womb!"

I flinch, my whole body trembling now. "That's not fair," I whisper, tears slipping down my cheeks. I inch back further and my heel hits the baseboard. "I don't pity you. I love you."

An eerie calm settles over him, so quiet it almost makes me sicker than the shouting. He moves with intention, placing one hand on either side of my head against the wall, caging me in. His breath hits my cheek—hot, rancid, sharp with the bite of whiskey and something rotten. I don't dare breathe.

Lowering his face to mine, Chase locks eyes with me. There's nothing in them now. No warmth. No recognition. Just a man hollowed out and hunting for someone to blame.

When he speaks, his voice is low—quiet enough to be mistaken for tenderness by anyone not standing in my place—but every syllable is laced with cruelty.

"Love?" he murmurs, so close it curls in my ear. "Was it love when you latched onto the broken foster kid because you wanted to fix him? A little project for you to heal and patch up with your sunshine and spreadsheets?"

My stomach churns, bile burning the back of my throat.

"Was it love when you decided your perfect life would look better with a tragedy in the prom pictures? When you told yourself I just needed stability? That you were the answer to all my fucked-up questions?"

I blink rapidly, trying to hold back tears I know will only provoke him more.

He leans in closer—too close—his voice dipping into something almost soft, almost intimate, but soaked in venom.

"Was it love when you manipulated me into marrying you? When you smiled and promised me I'd be happy, that you'd be enough? Because you thought a good woman and a white picket fence would fix all the cracks in my fucking soul?"

I shake my head, barely, just barely, afraid even that motion will send him spiraling.

He doesn't flinch. Just stares at me like I'm the reason he hates his own reflection.

"All I feel is dead inside," he breathes, "all the goddamn time. And you? You're the one who pulled me under."

He pauses just long enough to lower his voice into something more dangerous. More accusatory.

"You're nothing but a burden. A fucking anchor. You hold me down, and you smile while doing it."

The pause is worse than the yelling. The calm before a punch that hasn't landed.

"You think your little encouragements make me feel better? They make me small. Useless. FUCKING. TRAPPED."

He slams his fist into the wall beside my head, hard enough that he punches clean through the drywall.

The force sends a puff of dust into my face. I scream, hands covering my head, waiting for the next hit.

But it never comes.

I stay there, shaking, the sob trapped in my throat. Maybe if I stay still enough, silent enough, I'll disappear. Maybe if I don't move, he'll remember who I am and not who he thinks I've become.

He steps back, panting, chest heaving, and without another word, storms toward the bedroom. The door slams behind him so hard the frame rattles.

And I slide down the wall, legs folding beneath me as the tears come.

Big, heavy, silent sobs that feel like they're tearing something loose inside me.

I don't know how long I sit there. Long enough for the rage in the walls to settle. Long enough for the ache in my chest to dull into something more manageable.

Something like numbness.

The room is quiet again, except for the flicker of the TV and the sound of the heater clicking on. I focus on that noise—the heater—like it might ground me. I count the clicks. One, two, three. It hums. It breathes. It's something solid.

I think about texting Skye. My phone is only a few feet away, abandoned on the coffee table. All I'd have to do is reach. But what would I say? He punched a wall tonight? I'm scared, but I still love him? Please come get me, even though I'm not sure I'll go?

Instead, I crawl the few feet to the couch, resting my back against the side so I see the evidence of what just happened. And I stay there, tracing the outline of the hole in the drywall with my eyes. It's jagged. Raw. Exposed.

Just like me.

THIRTEEN

TORI

MY EYES ARE WATERING, and my vision is blurred. Of course my contact lens would decide to act up today of all days. I'm already late for the monthly departmental meeting, and now I'm stuck in the bathroom, blinking furiously, trying to get the damn thing to settle back in place.

Doesn't matter if I'm on time if I can't see to take minutes, though. They can wait.

Finally, after a solid two minutes of furious blinking and swearing under my breath, I manage to pry the lens off my eye. It perches on the tip of my finger, wobbling there like a soap bubble about to burst. Victory feels short-lived because the sound of a toilet flushing breaks the silence.

I freeze.

Heart slamming against my ribcage, I glance at the closed stall door behind me in the mirror. My brain short-circuits. I am literally the only woman on this floor today. Who the hell is in my bathroom?!

And then—Leo.

Leo?!

He steps out of the stall, looking maddeningly casual for someone who's just shattered my sense of personal safety.

"Jesus, Leo!" I gasp, jerking my head back from my fragile little lens like he might make me drop it just by existing. "What the hell are you doing in here?"

For a split second, panic spikes. Did I wander into the wrong bathroom? Am I the idiot here? But no—the wicker basket of panty liners, the jasmine diffuser sticks, the row of sinks exactly where they're supposed to be—this is definitely the women's bathroom.

Leo, meanwhile, leans against the stall frame like he has every right to be here. Smirk firmly in place.

"Your soap smells better," he says, rolling up his sleeves to wash his hands, as if that's a perfectly logical explanation for male faculty trespassing into the land of jasmine and tampons.

Something shifted after that afternoon two weeks ago when Chase showed up in the office. At first, I thought it was pity—that Leo had heard the venom in Chase's voice, seen the way his hand clamped down on my arm, and started seeing me less as someone to begrudge and more as someone to pity.

But then came that night at Howard's. And there wasn't a trace of pity in his eyes. Not one. He didn't hover. Didn't handle me like glass. He ordered half the damn menu, kept the whiskey flowing, laughed so hard at Skye's dumb jokes he nearly fell out of his chair. I can't remember the last time I'd had that much fun outside the safety of our apartment.

And for once, I didn't have to be on guard. Nobody could hurt me. No man was going to take advantage of me or Skye. We laughed, we drank, we danced. Hell, I even danced with Leo—*Leo* —for a few songs. And I'll admit it: the man has some serious moves. Suddenly, Skye's nickname for his Tinder conquests—the Tinder twats—made a lot more sense. I could see why they lined up to climb him like a tree.

She wasn't wrong about him. When he wants to be, Leo is pretty great.

That is...when he's not trespassing in my bathroom.

"Our soap... smells better?" I repeat, incredulous.

"Yep." He smirks, rinsing his hands. "Plus, it's quieter in here. No one bothers you."

"You are literally killing that vibe by being here. Right now." I blink furiously at the lens on my fingertip, trying not to think about how ridiculous this situation is. I'm half-blind, late, and dealing with a man who has apparently claimed dual citizenship in both bathrooms.

"Do you do this often?"

"Often? Naw." He steps closer, and suddenly, he's too close. Close enough that I catch the clean mint of his toothpaste under the warm spice of his cologne. Close enough that I remember the way his scruff brushed my temple on the dance floor.

And then, voice low, he murmurs: "Only when I feel particularly confident I'll run into you."

A shiver zips down my spine. I hate that it does.

No. Nope. I do not find him hot. He's a fuckboy, Tori. A. Fuck. Boy. Every word, every movement, every bit of proximity is deliberate—designed to provoke. And right this second, it's working.

I snap back, clinging to the one thing still under my control—the contact lens. "You're unbelievable," I mutter, focusing on the delicate disc balanced on my finger, as if willing it to slip back into my eye will save me from whatever game he thinks he's playing.

"Maybe." His smirk lingers in my periphery. "But you have to admit—it's a good strategy."

"A strategy for what? You work in the office next to mine. You see me every damn day. There is no reason for you to sneak into the women's bathroom to 'run into me.'"

He grins, cocky as hell. "For cementing myself as your GBF, of course." And then he winks.

He motherfucking *winks*.

The sound that bursts out of me is part snort, part feral laughter, and completely unhinged. It's so violent that my poor contact lens launches itself off my finger, sailing into oblivion. RIP, little guy.

"Please, sir, enlighten me," I manage between hysterics. "What *exactly* do you think that stands for?"

Leo looks at me like I've just asked what two plus two equals. "Guy best friend, obviously."

I lose it. Doubled over, tears leaking from the corners of my eyes, arms clutched around my stomach.

"Guy." *inhale.* "Best." *inhale.* "Friend." *inhale.*

"Jesus Christ, you're actually an idiot," I wheeze, swiping at my face before the non-waterproof mascara betrays me. "This might be the single greatest moment of my life."

He frowns, brow furrowed in confusion where his smirk used to be. "That's what it means."

"No, honey." I'm still half-laughing, half-choking. "GBF stands for *gay* best friend. And you might be a fuckboy, but you sure as shit aren't gay."

"Aw, Tote," he croons, leaning in again, crowding me with heat and scruff and confidence. "Are you jealous? Think calling me a manslut will hide the fact you want this dick?"

He did not.

I stop laughing. Instantly.

I turn, nose nearly brushing his, glaring daggers. "I called you a fuck*boy*. I have never, not once, called you a man."

Then I shove him. Hard. He stumbles against the stall frame, startled.

"And I wouldn't touch your dick if my life depended on it, Professor."

My emergency glasses come out of my bag. Neon lime green—yes, these were Skye's idea. The worst possible choice with this outfit. Okay, *every* outfit. I jam them onto my face, shoulders squared, dignity maybe, possibly, intact.

We're late for a meeting. I'm still half blind. My glasses clash like a toddler picked them out.

Wait. How am I still half blind if my glasses are on my face? Shit, I forgot to take out my other contact.

BY THE TIME I make it into the conference room, my pulse has barely slowed. I slip into the last open chair at the long table, grateful the lime green frames don't clash *too* catastrophically with the polished wood surface. Six professors look up from their folders and mugs of coffee as if I've just interrupted a sacred ritual. Because of course, my having to remove the other contact lens meant Leo arrived before I did.

I am the late one. Or, the lat*est* one. Super.

Dr. Johnson gives me his customary nod—for such a gentle old man he sure knows when to step into his department head shoes. His nod is stern, efficient, already turning back to his notes. Dr. Patel offers a polite smile. Dr. Liu adjusts his glasses and clears his throat, always ready to redirect the conversation to whatever data set he's been obsessing over lately.

And then there's Dr. Wallace.

Mid-thirties. Thick-rimmed glasses. Crisp tie knotted too tightly under his sweatervest, like he wants to be taken *very* seriously. His gaze flicks toward me and lingers—too long. Not lecherous, exactly, but weighted, like he's trying to calculate me along with his equations.

I swear I had set my laptop in front of a seat on the other side of the table before heading to the bathroom to fix my contacts earlier, yet here it is, in front of the empty seat next to him. Did he move it so I would sit next to him?

Surely, not. That'd be weird.

Then again, *he* is weird. Not creepy, per se, but definitely socially awkward.

I drop my bag quietly beside the chair before taking my seat and opening my laptop to take notes. Dr. Wallace leans forward, folding his hands on the table. "Good morning, Victoria," he says smoothly, as though I need reminding of my own name. "Rough commute?"

"No," I answer simply, offering him a thin smile. Was that his attempt at a joke?

Leo's chair creaks beside mine as he leans back, arms crossed. I don't have to look at him to know his jaw is set.

Dr. Wallace chuckles like I've missed his joke—so, yes, there was an attempt—then launches into a five-minute "question" about the midterm schedule that is really just him showing off how thoroughly he's thought through every possible contingency. By the time he's finished circling the point, all he's really said is: I'd like my exam proctored on the 17th.

I type it in without comment.

Leo shifts again, louder this time, like the chair is just as annoyed as he is. *We get the point, dude. You don't want to be here any more than we do.*

When Dr. Wallace glances over at me again—whispering something about "make sure you block out extra time, I'd hate for you to feel overwhelmed"—Leo exhales through his nose in a way that's one step short of a growl.

I bite the inside of my cheek to keep from smiling. Why is he acting like such a caveman?

The meeting rolls on. Syllabus adjustments. Departmental budget complaints. Everyone drones their way through the agenda. Dr. Patel mentions a student caught cheating; Dr. Liu proposes stricter proctoring protocols; Dr. Johnson agrees with a decisive thump of his hand against the table. His palm catches the side of Dr. Patel's beloved calculator and I swear it's about to fly off the table, but before it catapults across the room, Dr. Patel steadies it and carefully sets it on the other side of his laptop, away from Dr. Johnson's demonstrative affirmations.

I record everything neatly, typing deadlines, dates, and whatever else into my document. My fingers move on autopilot, but my mind keeps tugging on loose threads.

And through it all, I feel it—Leo watching me when he thinks I won't notice, gaze steady enough to make my skin hum. Dr. Wallace's lingering looks, pretending to skim my notes when I know he's glanced at my boobs at least four times since I sat down.

Maybe I should take back my thoughts about him not being creepy. Because staring at my boobs is not cool.

I keep telling myself to focus—this meeting, these minutes, this list of directives—but my head won't stay put. It drifts into questions I don't want but can't shake.

I never thought I'd work anywhere other than that accounting firm in Moraine. Never thought I'd be single, starting over. New city. New people. And yet here I am, smack in the middle of a university departmental meeting—hell, not even an accountant anymore—wedged between two mid-thirties, single men. Both conventionally attractive. Both at least physically attracted to me.

And instead of soaking it in, instead of maybe even enjoying it, I spiral. What do they see in me that Chase couldn't? What was so absent in me that my husband couldn't be bothered to notice—let alone appreciate—when I dressed up for him, when I made his favorite dinner, when I packed his bag before a business trip? What variable did I miscalculate? What part of me never balanced out?

The irony twists in my chest—because if anything, sitting here between Leo's quiet watchfulness and Wallace's too-obvious stares only proves what I've had to repeat to myself over and over since I left: I was not the problem. I'm not perfect. Every marriage is made of two imperfect people. But there was one person in ours who refused to treat the infection buried deep in their psyche, and that person was not me.

Finally, Dr. Johnson closes his folder with a sharp snap. "That's everything for this month."

Chairs scrape back. Papers shuffle. Conversation splinters into casual chatter. Dr. Patel asks Dr. Liu about his latest research grant. Dr. Johnson mutters something about the dean. Dr. Wallace lingers, deliberately slower than the rest.

He leans toward me, lowering his voice just enough to feel intimate. "You handled that very efficiently, Victoria. I've been impressed with your organizational skills."

Before I can thank him—or sidestep the weirdly loaded compliment—Leo cuts in.

"She's good at what she does," he says flatly. "That's why she's here."

The edge in his voice makes the air heavier. Wallace blinks, adjusts his glasses, and mutters something about heading back to his office. He leaves, and the tension leaves with him.

But not Leo.

He's still leaning back in his chair, watching me with that unreadable expression. I shut my laptop with more force than necessary. "What?" I snap, finally meeting his gaze.

He smirks—slow, infuriating. "Nothing. Just, your GBF duties are safe with me. I'm here to protect you from Dr. Sweater-vest's poorly delivered mansplaining come-ons. Who knew Deondre Wallace had a passive-aggressive degradation kink?"

I groan, pushing to my feet. "At least he doesn't say stupid shit like 'you want this dick.' Or sneak into the women's bathroom. If I need saving from anyone in this office, it's you."

Slapping his palm against his chest, Leo mock-groans. "You wound me, bestie."

I roll my eyes, done with this conversation. "GBF. You'll never live that one down."

"Wouldn't dream of it, Tote."

That makes me pause. I sling my handbag up my arm, hug my

laptop to my chest. "Okay, seriously. What's with that nickname? Tote? It sounds like a purse. Or laundry detergent."

His grin widens, lazy and smug. "Relax. You know, like Dorothy. Toto—the scrappy little dog. Small, feisty, loud bark, doesn't back down from anybody. Remind you of anyone?"

My jaw drops. "You did *not* just compare me to a dog."

"Survived a tornado, saved her girl a dozen times," he says, shameless. "Honestly? Solid résumé."

I glare, fighting the twitch of a smile. "You're lucky I didn't shove you harder in that bathroom."

Leo stands, sliding his hands into his pockets and, thankfully, does not step closer to me. "If you had shoved me any harder we could have ended up *in* the stall… *together*. That would've been way more fun than this meeting."

He's shuffling backwards, already heading for the door, grin carved deep enough to make me want to smack it off. "What can I say? It'd be fun to play tangent to your curves."

Then he turns and exits the meeting room, leaving me standing there. Speechless.

My pulse hasn't quite settled since the bathroom… incident? And I can't decide which unsettles me more: Wallace's too-probing looks, or the way Leo keeps finding his way under my skin. And did he just make calculus *dirty*? Of course he did.

If I'm honest, I haven't had this much fun with a man in… well, ever.

Either way, it's only 10 a.m., and it's going to be a long freaking Tuesday.

FOURTEEN
TORI

THE DRIVE TO MY PARENTS' house is quiet. Too quiet. The kind of quiet that lets your thoughts run wild and loud and sharp. The kind that leaves room for second-guessing. For imagining different outcomes. For wondering if this decision—this monumental shift in the trajectory of my life—could somehow still be walked back. But I know it can't. Not this time. I've made my decision. I'm choosing myself. And no, that is not selfish.

I've tried everything. Tried to be patient. Tried to be understanding. Tried to hold all the pieces together with duct tape and grace and optimism and self-help books and Bible verses and counseling and pure, fucking will. But you can't patch something that keeps breaking the same way. And love shouldn't demand I keep bleeding to prove it. I'm done here. Done pretending that I am strong enough for the both of us. Done holding together someone who refuses to put forth any effort to repair himself. Just. Fucking. Done.

My hands grip the steering wheel tighter as I pull into the

driveway. The porch light is on even though it's barely dusk. She always turns it on when she knows I'm coming. The gesture tugs at something in me. A memory of being small and loved and safe. Before I knew how complicated love could be. Before that night— almost two years ago now—when I came to her broken, raw, and honest about how unhappy I was in my marriage, hoping to find safety and rest in her and instead finding myself met with manipulated Bible verses and hollow platitudes.

When I step inside, I find her in the kitchen, humming to herself and stirring something on the stove. The scent of garlic and rosemary fills the house. It's comforting. Familiar. A piece of home I've always carried with me. It's strange, that word, home. It's so complex. I feel comfort, love, safety, betrayal, loneliness, anger, sadness, regret, hope, thankfulness, weariness, all at once.

"Hey, sweetheart," she says, turning to smile at me. Her eyes scan my face, and the smile falters. "Everything okay?"

No, Mom. Things haven't been okay for a long, long time.

I nod, thinking I can have a few minutes of happy small talk, before giving up and shaking my head. I don't know how to put on a show anymore. I'm too tired to fake anything.

She sets the spoon down and wipes her hands on a towel. "Come sit. Tell me what's going on."

The last time I did that, you told me to submit better. That's not fucking happening this time.

I sit. I breathe. And then I say it.

"I'm leaving Chase."

Silence stretches between us like a rubber band pulled taut. Her eyes widen slightly, then soften, then cloud.

"Tori," she says, her voice already carrying the edge of disapproval. "Honey, I know things have been hard—"

I cut her off. "Mom. Stop."

My protest means nothing. She continues, "I know you're hurting. But you can't just throw away a marriage because of a rough patch. You made vows."

"I know," I say. "I meant them. And I kept them. I've stayed. I've supported. I've tried. But Mom, it's not a rough patch. It's a pattern."

She sighs and sits down across from me. "What about counseling? Or talking to Pastor James? Sometimes getting things out in the open with someone neutral can really help."

"We've gone to counseling," I say. "Both together and separately. Nothing changes. This is so much deeper than counseling. I'm not trying to say this is all on Chase, but this truly is something I cannot fix for him."

She frowns. "Well, maybe this time would be different. Maybe if you gave it one more shot—"

"Mom." I cut in again—gently, but firm. "I love you. I know you want to believe that all marriages can be saved if people just try hard enough or pray hard enough or trust God enough. But that's not always true. I can't keep setting myself on fire to keep someone else warm. Chase doesn't value himself, and until he does, he'll never be able to value anyone else—not truly, and definitely not me. I've tried to love him enough for both of us. That's not how love works. And I'm done."

Her lips press into a line. Her eyes shimmer, but she doesn't cry. She never cries easily. "I just worry you're giving up on something sacred."

"I'm not giving up," I whisper. "I'm letting go. There's a difference. Giving up is quitting. Letting go is accepting that holding on is killing me. And don't I deserve better than that?"

She closes her eyes. A breath. A pause. "Tori—"

"HE CALLED ME AN ANCHOR. A BURDEN. A WORTHLESS PIECE OF SHIT. THEN PUNCHED A HOLE IN THE WALL TWO INCHES FROM MY FACE. I. AM. DONE. THE END. NOT ANOTHER WORD OF PROTEST."

You need something to open your eyes to the reality of my situation? There.

Her face pales, eyes widen. She swallows, and nods.

"Oh."

Yeah. Oh.

"Does he know? That you're leaving, I mean," she asks.

"Not yet. But he'll figure it out when he gets back from Boston and I'm gone."

Her voice is small, quiet. She doesn't sound disappointed, just shaken. "Do you have somewhere to go?"

"Yes. I have a plan. I've been saving. I'm not making this decision recklessly. I just need you to respect it. And not tell anyone. Please. Not even Dad."

She nods slowly. "Okay. I won't. I'm assuming Skye is helping you?"

I laugh, for the first time in days. "Yeah," I say, smiling. "She may be chaos, but she's my chaos."

Nodding once more, she says, "So you're going to Grand River, then?"

"I am," I confirm. "I think it will be good for me to have a change of scenery. Skye needs a roommate now that Alis and Sunny are moving in with Dex, and I'm sure I can find a job in the city somewhere. I have enough saved to hold me over for a few months while I look for something."

Mom crosses her arms on the table, leaning into the conversation and entering inquisition mode. Now that she's accepted my fate, she may as well gather all the details. "Does Alis know?" she asks.

I shake my head. "No. She's had so much going on, and with things finally coming together for her I didn't want to burden her with any of it. Skye is the only person who knows anything about it."

"She's wild, but she's loyal."

I smile, thinking about my purple-haired firecracker of a friend. "Yeah," I say, smiling.

"And you'll be safe?"

"Always."

Mom is quiet again for a moment, then clears her throat. "How long have you known?"

I blink. "That I needed to leave?"

She nods.

I exhale slowly, picking at a thread on the edge of my sleeve. "I know this sounds cliche, but I think on some level I've always known we weren't compatible. In pieces. In moments. But the night he punched the wall... that was the breaking point. I knew in my bones it was over."

"And before that?"

"Before that, it was the backhanded comments. The distance. The way I felt lonelier with him in the room than I ever did by myself."

She sighs, the sound full of something heavier than judgment. "I wish I had been more help to you before now."

"You did the best you could with what you knew," I say gently. "I see that now. And I forgive you for not seeing it then."

Tears threatening to spill over, Mom reaches over and wraps me in a hug. "I love you, you know that, don't you?"

"I do, and I love you, too."

"And I'm proud of you."

Now that, I did not expect.

I pull back, looking her in the eyes to gauge the sincerity behind her words. "Really? You're not disappointed in me for leaving?"

Mom laughs, wiping the tears now falling from her eyes. "Victoria, I've never once been disappointed in you in your entire life. You've put up with more crap than any one woman should ever have to go through with that man, and you've handled it with grace. To be honest, I'm almost jealous."

Say what?

I arch my brow, clearly asking for her to go on.

She shakes her head, still chuckling. "I love your father, I really do. But if I had half the courage you do, I would have stood up for myself years ago."

"You still can, Mom," I assure her.

"Maybe," she shrugs. "You just keep doing what you're doing, and maybe you can teach this old dog new tricks."

This conversation is completely bass-ackwards from the one we shared on the porch swing two years ago, and for the first time all day, I feel like I can breathe.

Suddenly, leaving my marriage doesn't feel like failure. It feels like freedom.

A freedom I thought I might never get to taste. A freedom that I now realize I had to carve out with my own two hands. I feel the weight lifting, not all at once, but enough to believe that something better is possible.

When I finally stand to leave, Mom walks me to the door. We linger there, awkward in the way only two women raised to suppress our own wants and will can be. And then she wraps me in one more hug, tighter this time. Tighter than she used to.

"Call me when you get home,"" she says.

"I will."

"And if you need anything, anything at all, you come here. Understand?"

"I know. Thank you."

Driving away, I glance back at the porch. She's still there. Watching. Arms folded over her chest like she's holding herself together. But she's there.

And maybe now, she's holding space for me too.

On the drive home, my mind wanders back to something I said during our conversation—something I hadn't realized fully until the words left my mouth this evening: that I feel lonelier *with* Chase than I do by myself.

I don't know how long it's going to take me to get over that realization, but I can already envision thousands of dollars of therapy bills in my future. And to think, I *chose* him. I chose to stay. I chose to love him. Nobody forced me into a relationship with him. Nobody guilted me into loving him. The hollow, empty feeling at the core of my being is the result of my own, conscious choices.

I've been so focused on building up my nerve, believing in what I deserve, that I haven't stopped to think about the fact that I put myself in this situation to begin with. Throughout the years, all my complex feelings about staying have focused on Chase and his need for me. Until tonight, the only complex part of my new perspective was coming to the realization that it is not selfish to prioritize my needs.

Now, however… now I'm faced with the realization that I'm not only angry at him; I'm angry at myself. How might my life have been different if I hadn't held on so tightly to him?

"Was it love when you latched onto the broken foster kid because you wanted to fix him? A little project for you to heal and patch up with your sunshine and spreadsheets?"

I don't know. I don't think so. Was it?

"Was it love when you decided your perfect life would look better with a tragedy in the prom pictures? When you told yourself I just needed stability? That you were the answer to all my fucked-up questions?"

I didn't think my life was perfect. Did I? I didn't think I was the answer to all his problems and questions. Did I? Is that why I kept choosing him? Because I thought I was the answer? Like I could fix him? Do I have a savior complex? Am I the problem here? *AM I THE PROBLEM?*

Take a deep breath, Tori. Deep, deep breath.

This is why I need to leave. I can't do this anymore. I need space. I need a new life. I need a new… everything.

I don't know what the next few weeks will look like. I don't know how Chase will react. I don't know what grief still lies ahead.

But I know who I am. I think. And I know I deserve better than what I've lived the last decade of my life. I'm pretty sure. Yes. I do. I deserve better. Even when I don't feel like it, I know it, intellectually. So I'll keep saying it until I believe it at my core.

And for the first time in years, that feels like enough.

FIFTEEN

TORI

THE APARTMENT IS DOING that thing quiet does—pressing in from every corner like soundproof foam. The heat kicks on and off in little breaths, the Betty Boop clock above the TV ticks one second at a time like it's proud of itself, and my brain—mashed potatoes. I'm in my comfiest leggings and an oversized hoodie with a hole in the left cuff, hair in a messy bun that's more a metaphor for my current state of mind than an actual hairstyle. On the coffee table: a legal pad from Jacob Sterling's office; my neat, anxious handwriting; a capped pen I've been uncapping and recapping for the last two hours. Fairly certain the tiny circle imprinted on the tip of my thumb is permanent.

I can still hear Mr. Sterling's voice. Measured. Even. Exactly how you'd want a man to sound if he were holding a sharp knife and cutting your life in half—careful enough not to sever a finger, steady enough not to slip. I left work at lunchtime today so I could meet with him this afternoon. I had planned to attend this one solo, but once again, my trusty, blue-haired—nay, now purple-haired—sidekick met me at the stairs to the building just as I was about to enter.

"I'm not here to destroy your husband," he said, sitting back in that too-perfect leather chair, palms flat on the desk as if to say *no tricks here*.

"Thank you, Mr. Sterling."

"Please," he said, "Call me Jake."

I nodded. That definitely made everything feel less formal, less stuffy and uncomfortable.

"Destroying someone else is not the point of this process, and it's not how I practice. I'm here to ensure you're taken care of and this is fair. We will be firm where we need to be and humane where we can be. You shared real years. I won't pretend they didn't happen."

Humane. Firm. Fair. Words that feel like a level surface after months of walking on marbles. During our first meeting I got the impression that Skye was not the biggest fan of Jake, but she is not in the habit of making decisions for me and refused to offer any opinions or guidance after we left. She simply asked questions about what I wanted, and had me answer whether or not Jacob Sterling fit the bill. He did. She asked if I wanted to meet with anyone else or if I felt comfortable with him. I felt comfortable. That was that. Jake was my guy.

He went line by line, patient, precise: house in Moraine (primary marital asset; equity to be split), the joint checking and savings (trace the deposits, freeze the account from any surprise withdrawals), Chase's 401(k) and pension track (QDRO—Qualified Domestic Relations Order—filed if needed; "Don't worry about the acronym; that's on me," he'd said with a small smile), my tiny retirement from the accounting firm (barely a blip, but it's still a piece on the board), the cars (titles, current value), the shared credit card (close it; we'll divide responsibility based on dates of use). He even asked about furniture, and I told him about the coffee table we bought from that antique shop the summer we first moved back to Moraine—the one with the drawer that sticks and the carved elk antlers on the legs. Not because I want the coffee table. But because I ramble when I'm nervous and he wanted to know if I had any sort of attachment to things that might surprise me later.

I didn't. Not to objects. Not anymore.

"Spousal maintenance," he continued, "is not a punishment. It's a tool. You've been the lower earner the last few years. The court looks at need and ability to pay, length of the marriage, standard of living, both parties' earning capacities. We'll run the numbers. We don't posture; we present."

He said *we* every time. Not you. Not I. *We.*

I thought the word would make me feel small—like the person with the law degree was creating the illusion of partnership to get me to sign things. It didn't. It made me feel... held? Not in a romantic way. In a *someone competent has the wheel* way. My mother likes to say *Jesus, take the wheel* when she's overwhelmed.

Well, *Jake, take the wheel.* Because I sure as hell don't know what I'm doing. I'm glad he does.

At one point, I'd blurted, "I don't want to ruin him." It came out too fast, too raw, right in the middle of something he was saying, and Jake nodded like I'd just solved for x on a chalkboard and he'd been waiting for me to catch up to myself.

"Good," he said. "We're aligned. We don't litigate vengeance. We litigate clarity. And if we can do this without court? We do. If not, I know that road, too." His mouth twitched. "But I don't leave people limping. Your husband won't leave with nothing. He'll leave with what's fair. So will you."

I exhale. My shoulders drop. I hadn't realized they'd been lodged up by my ears since noon.

This—this is why I hired him. Because while he can be heavy-handed if someone forces him there, he also respects the reality of a shared life. He isn't going to turn our last decade together into a bloodbath just to spike a win percentage. I never wanted that. I want clean. I want done. I want to sleep again without waking up with my molars clenched.

I flip the legal pad to the next page. My own notes look like a stranger's handwriting—not because the actual writing looks any different, but because the words don't feel like my own. The act of getting divorced is still so foreign and unfamiliar. *Gather tax returns (last 3 years). Bank statements (12 months). Retirement plan statements. Car titles. House deed. Itemize furniture only if it'll matter to me emotionally later—(it won't). Passwords—already changed, but double check.* A doodle of a tiny box labeled "marital property" with a stick figure version of me climbing out.

I should feel better.

I do. A little.

The clock still ticks. The heat still clicks on, then off. On again.

Skye's not home—closing the coffee shop, probably doing a latte art competition with herself and talking to regulars about their dogs. The whole apartment feels like a waiting room. Waiting for, what? Who even knows.

And then, because it always happens, the ache sneaks in. The missing.

Yes, I still miss him. Every. Single. Day.

Does it make sense? No. And also, yes.

It isn't the missing of who Chase is now. I'm not that delusional. It's the missing of the man I married—the boy with the cocky grin who I tutored in tenth grade, who kissed me behind the gym like I was his nerdy little secret, who told me he loved me and meant it. The man in college who wanted to marry me and build a life with me.

Where did he go? Was he ever truly there, or am I remembering glimpses of reality but not the whole picture?

That's what terrifies me—constantly wondering if my own memories are lies. If I distorted reality because I saw potential instead of an actual person standing in front of me each day. Was our love a lie? Our marriage a farce? Was it real? The connection? The intimacy? Or was it all fabricated, forced. Held together by the sheer will of a fifteen-year-old girl who saw a beautiful, broken boy who needed someone, *anyone*, to love him, and she thought that person could be her.

Come here, broken boy. I'll love you. I'll make it all better.

I mourn for her naivety. The hope she had for the future—for *their* future, together.

I wonder if he's okay. What if he's not okay?

I pick up my phone. Set it down. Pick it up again. It's pathetic. *I'm* pathetic.

Chase's name stares back at me from the screen. The photo is from years ago—Denver weekend, rooftop bar, sun in his eyes, squinting smile. I should change it. I should delete it. I should do anything besides what I'm about to do, which is tap his name like my thumb has a mind of its own.

Would he even answer?

Of course he'll answer. He wants me to come home.

Would he be happy if I called?

Do I care if he's happy? I don't want him to be unhappy. I also don't know that I care about making him happy. He can be happy, but I don't have to be the one who made it happen. It's not like I was ever any good at contributing to his happiness before.

The call screen hovers. I freeze, then swipe it away like it's hot. End. End. End. I back out, opening a new text instead, because typed words feel safer than his voice. That voice I know too well.

> I met with an attorney today.

My thumb hovers over send. I delete it.

> How are you?

Delete.

> I love you.

Nope.

I hate you.

No, but, also yes. But, also no.

I miss you.

My chest clenches. I delete that so hard my thumb hurts.

The sickest part? I do miss him. And I hate that I miss him. I hate that grief and relief coexist in my ribcage like roommates who refuse to move out.

Hi, hello, my name is Victoria Foster and I am a walking contradiction. Yes, mhmm, it is incredibly frustrating. What's that you asked? How close am I to Britney 2007? About as close as I am to throat punching you for asking that question in the first place.

My thumb finds the microphone icon by habit. I almost press it. I want to ask if he's eating actual meals. If he found the gray sweater I left in the dryer. If he's sleeping. If he thinks about me when he pours his coffee or if I've already been edited out of the morning routine.

I put the phone face down on the far side of the coffee table like distance will save me. I know it won't. I could walk across the room and throw the damn thing into the kitchen sink and it would still hum in my bones like a mosquito in the dark.

There's only one thing I can control right now, and it's not my heart. It's my body chemistry. And if I can't calm my mind, I can at least calm my body. Decision made, I stand from the couch and head to my room.

Skye's welcome box lives under my bed, tucked behind a tote of old sweaters I swear I'll sort next weekend. She packed it like a fairy godmother with a sense of humor: bath bombs, chocolate, eye masks, a bottle of Trader Joe's prosecco, and, like, five different vibrators wrapped in tissue paper like they might be fragile. She'd set it on my bed the day I moved in and said, "We do practical here. And orgasms are practical. Time to get your rocks off with your socks off, bitch! Or, on. Whatever you're into. No judgment."

I'd laughed until I almost cried.

Now, I pull the box out and sit on the floor beside my bed, cross-legged, the U-shaped vibrator in my palm like a ridiculous, necessary secret. I'm pretty sure Skye said this one was meant to be used with a partner, but in my late-night exploratory sessions I've determined this one is my favorite. I'm probably using it wrong, but it gets me off faster and more effectively than the others and doesn't leave me sore between my legs the next day, so that's a win in my book. (*The weird thruster one with the suction piece for your clitoris is super aggressive and scary and makes me walk funny the next day. Zero stars. Do not recommend. But again, I'm probably doing something wrong.*)

I tell myself what I'm about to do isn't about anyone in particular. This is not about Chase. It's not about Leo—*Wait. Why would I even think about Leo right now?* It's not about proving I'm alive and my body still works and someone could want me. Of course someone could want me.

This is purely mechanical. It's Advil for a headache. It's stretching before a run. It's—*for fuck's sake Tori,* just stop thinking and get in bed and give yourself an orgasm already!

I crawl under the covers and roll onto my stomach, left knee drawn up. The sheets are cool; my skin is suddenly too hot. I close my eyes and will my mind to empty.

Do not think. Do not picture. Do not invite a single face into the room.

The vibrator hums to life in my hand, a sound like a purr. The tiny remote is in my left hand, ready to adjust the vibration at will, and I use the other to slide the toy lower, down my stomach, between my legs, until I reach my clit. I'm not yet fully turned on and ready to slide anything inside, so I rub the larger end of the toy against my bundle of nerves, slowly, hoping for something, anything to awaken my core and coat this vibrator with enough natural lubrication to nestle inside where it belongs.

I'm working too hard to keep my mind blank. Literally working against myself, against my body, by overworking my thoughts.

So I let go. Let my mind wander into uncharted territory. My breath catches. My mouth opens. My spine arches just a little and—

Harper's.

The whiskey. The music. And Leo. Swaggering through the door like the human embodiment of a good time. I hadn't wanted to want to look at him. And yet—there he was. Big, loud, and magnetic in the way that always ends in mistakes.

Let's dance, he'd said. Not a command; not quite a request. He took my hand and pulled me onto the dance floor, his arms around my body like they belonged there, mine up around his neck, hands toying with the hair at the base of his neck.

I'm soaked. I push the toy down to my entrance and it slides in, effortlessly, settling into place exactly where it belongs. The large end of the U nestles against my G-spot, the smaller end against my clit.

My palm presses down and the vibrator finds a rhythm. So does the memory. Leo's hand at my hip, warm and unambiguous. The way his thumb slid across the bare skin between the hem of my shirt and top of my jeans. The exact rasp of his scruff when he leaned in to talk into my ear, lips brushing skin by accident but not really accidental. How he smelled—clean and expensive in a way that shouldn't work in a bar that smells like beer and salt and whatever hipsters were smoking that week. His chest against my back for one song, then my front for another, our bodies slotting together like something that had been sitting on a shelf and was always meant to interlock.

I was drunk, but not wasted. He was sober, but never crossed the line. It was friendly, it was hot. It was sexual, it was safe. I knew he wouldn't make a move, and that emboldened me to move. My ass against his crotch, back arched, arm stretched up and around his neck. The music slowed and he didn't spin me to face him. Just wrapped both arms around my front, dropped his chin to my shoulder and held me, swayed with me, while I rested my head back against his shoulder.

What if he hadn't been such a gentleman? What if he'd invited me home?

I try not to imagine it. My body refuses to obey. My thumb clicks the remote once, twice, as the scene escalates in time with the pleasure between my legs.

His mouth—God, his mouth—is suddenly between my legs in my mind, that scruff turning into friction, into heat, into a kiss where no one has kissed me like that in... I don't even know how long. His hands are too big to be gentle and that is exactly the point. One grips my thigh, pushes it open; the other locks around the other thigh so I can't move, like he knows I'll try. Not because I want him to stop, but because I want to climb out of myself and see if this is real. His tongue finds a pattern, deliberate, devastating. He pays attention. He listens with his body. He doesn't stop when I gasp; he changes tempo, angle, pressure until my brain forgets my own name. My fingers slide into his hair in the fantasy; in reality one twists into the sheets, pulling, yanking, searching for purchase while my hips press deeper into the mattress, my palm working the vibrator against my clit and my G-spot in tandem.

He'd said the other day at that meeting, mouth turned up in a smirk, sexy and tempting as sin, *It'd be fun to play tangent to your curves.* I'd rolled my eyes. Brushed him off. Now, the words shiver through me and land low. *Tangent to your curves.* It's obscene in my head. It's perfect.

Like my vagina is a horny little mathematician.

The orgasm hits like lightning in a canyon. Sudden. Loud. An initial jolt, closely followed by shuddering echoes that ripple throughout my body. My thighs clamp around my hand and wrist;

my belly pulls tight; my breath goes ragged, stuttered, caught. I hear a sound, a drawn out curse, and it's mine. I ride it. I let it take me. My eyes squeeze shut so hard I see stars and behind the stars is a jawline I shouldn't be mapping with my mouth.

How I ever compared that jawline to a soggy waffle fry, I'll never know.

Then, it's over.

The silence afterward is not the good kind. It's a vacuum. I pull the vibrator from between my legs and depress the button, turning it off as quickly as possible like I can shut up my own choices. The object drops to the mattress with a soft thud; my hand falls to my stomach. For a breath or two, I float. For a breath or two, I think maybe this is what forgetting feels like.

Fat chance.

Shame creeps in slowly, like tide water under a door you thought was sealed. It soaks my skin, my hairline, the base of my throat. Just ten minutes ago I had Chase's name glowing on my phone screen and my thumb hovering over a call I didn't make. Ten minutes ago I was a woman who missed her husband. Now I am a woman who just came to the image of another man between her legs. A man who is not mine. A man who should not matter. A man who—if we're tracing lines and calling things what they are— is a complication I never asked for and cannot seem to stop thinking about.

I am STILL. MARRIED.

I turn onto my side and tuck my knees against my chest. My throat stings. I try to swallow the tears back the way I've been swallowing every other thing I don't have time to deal with. They don't listen.

I cry quietly—first because I don't want Skye to hear me if she comes in, then because embarrassment is my default, factory setting. Then because the embarrassment turns into grief I didn't schedule and the grief turns into a weighted blanket I can't get out from under. I cry because I miss the life I was supposed to have, and because I don't miss it enough to go back. I cry because imagining someone else's hands on me made me feel wanted for the first time in… I don't even know how long. I cry because I still wear a ring-shaped dent on my finger like my skin refuses to fill the space. I cry because I'm still married. Because I left. Because I stayed too long. I cry because I still want to be married. Because I don't want to be married. Because I'm confused and alone and my skin feels too tight and too different and nothing feels normal. Because I made myself small. Because even in my quest to stop doing that, sometimes I still am.

Eventually, the tears slow. The room reappears—lamp casting a soft cone of light onto the wall. I left the open legal pad on the coffee table like a promise I made to future me, my phone sitting face down nearby. I can feel its gravity from here, the way an object holds a planet in orbit. But I can't see it, so it doesn't have any real power over me.

I should get up, clean up my mess in the living room and plug in my phone so it's not dead before morning, but I won't. Tomorrow is Saturday. I have nowhere to be. No one to see. Let it die.

I don't move. I don't go get it. I don't text Chase *sorry* or *are you okay* or *I miss you* or *I shouldn't but* or any of the thousand dumb things that would unravel me. I don't text Leo *you're an idiot* or *stop being hot near me* or *please keep being hot near me I hate you*—because if I start, I won't stop, and the only thing worse than shame is the hangover after you toss it a shot and call it a plan.

I drag the blanket up to my chin and stare at the ceiling. Jake's words drift back, one by one, like buoys you can grab if you're tired of treading water.

> *We present, not posture.*
> *We don't litigate vengeance.*
> *I won't leave either of you limping.*
> *You'll be taken care of.*

I didn't know how much I needed someone to say that until he did. Not just *you'll win*, not just *you'll be free*, but *you will be taken care of.* It lands in a place inside me that isn't greedy; it's just, empty. For years I tried to fill it with effort and patience and prayers that never made it past the ceiling fan. Tonight it fills with a simple, practical promise: this will not ruin you. It will simply, and finally, end.

I breathe in through my nose, out through my mouth. Count to four. Again. Again.

My eyelids go heavy. Shame is still there, a low weight at the base of my ribs, but exhaustion sets a hand on its head and tells it to hush. I turn my face into the pillow, thinking of glass doors and metal letters, of broken high school boys and giant mimosas with Skye. I think of a dance floor and scruff and a mouth that said *tangent to your curves* like calculus was foreplay. I think of a church pew and a man who will always be adored by people who will never know the darkness that lives in his soul.

Somewhere between all of these thoughts, I slip under.

Sleep doesn't save me. Not really. But it holds me still long enough to forget wanting to call, long enough to not reach for the phone, long enough to give morning a chance to be kinder than tonight.

SIXTEEN

TORI

Past

SKYE PULLS into the driveway just as I do.

She's halfway out of her car when she spots me and grins. "Damn, Foster. You've got impeccable timing, as always."

For the first time in ten years, I don't quip back with, "It's Martin, you whore."

I spot her purple space buns over the roof of my SUV and smile, soaking in the half-light of dusk, cicadas buzzing somewhere in the trees. Skye knows exactly why I called her home for the weekend, and I'm grateful she doesn't kick off our girls' night with a heavy *are you okay* or a pity hug. Instead, she rounds the front of my Telluride in cut-off shorts, combat boots, and a yellow crop top that reads *Daddy Issues*. She bumps her shoulder into mine, grins, and says, "Hey, bitch," before heading for the door.

The second we step inside, I breathe in the familiar scent of wood polish and whatever aftershave Skye's dad has used since we were kids. It's cooler in here than I expect, and still so eerily unchanged it makes my throat tighten. The floor creaks the same way it always has, and I can't tell if the shiver that runs through me is from memory or the quiet panic of knowing I'm actually going to do this—I'm about to sit down with my best friend and talk through the logistics of leaving my husband.

I drop my bag next to the couch and stand there for a second, letting my shoulders fall. This house shouldn't feel like sanctuary. It's not mine. But after years of bracing myself at every threshold, walking into a place where no one's waiting to corner me with silence or sharpened words feels like crawling out of a cage.

Skye kicks off her boots and flops into her usual spot on the couch. "Shoes off?"

"Obviously."

"Pants or no pants?"

I raise an eyebrow. "It's nine p.m. and I'm emotionally unraveling."

She nods solemnly. "No pants it is."

I peel off my jeans and curl up on the other end, snuggling under a plush blanket I found haphazardly draped over the edge. The quiet between us is soft, familiar. We've done girls' nights countless times before, but never like this.

She waits. Then, finally, I speak.

"I'm leaving him."

The words don't punch the air like they used to. They settle. Still a little sharp. Still capable of bruising. But now, instead of sending shockwaves through my system, they feel like truth—like something I'm allowed to say without flinching.

Skye doesn't react right away. Just tilts her head a little. "Yep. You said that already. Now, say the rest."

I look around the room. My eyes land on the dented coffee table from that one party we swore we'd never talk about, the scratch on the TV stand, the dusty old family photo that was taken before Skye's mother passed away all those years ago. Everything here has a history, and somehow that makes it easier to say the next part.

"He's going to Boston in four weeks. A work trip. Five nights."

Skye straightens a little. "Nice. Ok. So that's your window."

I nod. "That's my window. I'll leave the morning after he flies out."

She doesn't interrupt. Doesn't fill the space with commentary or reassurance. Just listens.

"I've been saving since the Christmas fight," I continue. "Opened a credit union account he doesn't know about. Birthday money, some of our tax refund, random cash from the grocery budget—I funneled it all there."

Her eyes narrow, impressed. "You sneaky little badass. Who knew your accounting skills could be used for evil—or in this case, salvation?"

I don't respond to that last comment. At first, I felt guilty about building myself a secret fund in case I ever mustered up the ovaries to leave. Then, as the months went on and the glimmers of hope and happiness we were able to find in previous years were nowhere to be found, I tossed all semblance of guilt out the metaphorical window and prepared myself for the day I'd finally reach my limit.

"I've got enough for six months without a paycheck. Maybe longer if I get creative. I cook more than I eat out. My clothes are all in great condition so I won't need to go shopping. I'm not someone who lives in excess."

"You won't need six months," she says confidently. "But even if you did—you'd still be okay."

My throat tightens. I look down at the blanket twisted in my lap.

"I'm planning to move in once Alis and Sunny are settled with Dexter," I say. "If that's still—"

Skye cuts me off with a look. "That room's already yours. You're just coming home to it."

Hot tears press behind my eyes, but I blink them away.

"It's weird," I admit. "Everything's lining up. Like God or the universe or whatever was just waiting for me to finally stop stalling."

Skye studies me for a second. "Are you ready?"

I shrug, but the motion feels too big and too small all at once. "Yes? No? I don't know. But I know I can't stay. It doesn't matter if I'm ready or not. I made my decision. I told my mother. I'm not changing my mind."

She doesn't push. Just nods and waits for me to sort through the back-and-forth in my head.

"I need your help," I say after a beat. "On the day. When I leave. I don't want to do it alone."

"You won't," she says, shaking her head. "I'll take off work, drive to Moraine the night before and crash here, head to your place in the morning and help load what fits. We'll ghost out like pros."

"I'm not taking much," I tell her. "Only what fits in our cars. He can have the rest."

"Anything you'll miss?"

I shake my head. "Not enough to fight for. I just need my clothes, my books, a few personal items. Everything sentimental is at my parents' house, not mine."

She grabs her phone. "Alright, checklist time."

This side of Skye always amazes me. As off-the-wall and fly-by-the-seat-of-her-pants as this woman might seem, Skye never fails to have a plan and make things happen. That's what she does when shit hits the fan and everything feels like it might float off the edge of the world.

"Okay," she murmurs, typing on her phone as she speaks. "Passport, social, birth certificate?"

I nod. "Fireproof folder. Already packed."

"Laptop?"

"With me. Always."

"Jewelry?"

"Figured I'd leave my wedding rings on top of the goodbye

letter on the kitchen counter? Other than that, I'll have my few precious items in my purse. Everything else can stay behind."

"Forwarding your mail to my place?"

"If you don't mind."

"Duh. You'll be living there. Need a burner?"

I blink. "A what?"

"In case he shuts your phone off or won't stop calling. I'll grab you a prepaid one just in case."

My stomach flips. "I'm still on my parents' phone plan so he can't shut it off. But you think it'll come to that? Like, he won't stop calling me?"

Her tone softens. "I think we're not leaving anything to chance."

She keeps going—passwords, account logins, prescriptions, documents. I nod and answer, but somewhere in the middle of it all, I drift.

I'm imagining my SUV packed to the roof with boxes of the life I'm shedding. I'm imagining Chase coming home to an empty house. Finding my letter on the counter. Throwing my rings across the room in a fit of rage. Slamming cabinets and doors searching for alcohol that won't be in the house. Will he shatter the framed photos of us? Throw a lamp into the wall? Will he sit at our dining room table with his head in his hands and mourn my absence? Will he even care?

A tear slips onto the hand propping up my face at the edge of the couch, right as Skye nudges my foot.

"Hey. You're not weak for being sad," she says, voice low. "Even when it's the right thing. Especially then."

I nod once, swiping away the tears that pile into my eyes before they can fall.

No one talks about this part. Social media is full of memes about the joy found in choosing yourself, breaking free, owning your future. And sure, those things are probably true. But every women's empowerment blurb I've seen leaves out one detail: Freedom? It's heavy as hell once you finally pick it up. And it hurts. My God in heaven it hurts.

We sit there in silence for a while. The kind that isn't awkward or rushed, but quiet and open. Space to breathe. Space to fall apart a little more if I need to.

And I do. I really do.

"It's not just about me," I say finally, my voice quieter now. "I mean, yes—I'm leaving because I deserve more. Because I can't keep being his emotional punching bag every time he spirals. But, it's more than that."

Skye knows all of this. She's listened to me talk in circles for hours. Thankfully, even though she's heard it a thousand times, she just listens.

"I love him," I admit. "God, I've loved him so long I don't even know who I am without that ache. He's not some villain I'm escaping from. He's... just a broken boy who never learned how to stop bleeding on the people who try to love him."

Skye exhales slowly. "Correction. He's also a fucking asshole."

I huff out a laugh, even as my chest tightens.

"I'm serious," she goes on. "You can feel sorry for the scared kid inside him—but don't forget the man he became. The one who tore you down and twisted your words and made you question your own worth. That wasn't just trauma. That was choice. *His* choice. And he doesn't get a free pass because he's sad and haunted."

She leans forward, eyes sharp. "You're allowed to love him and still call him what he is. Call his behavior what it is—abuse. Verbal, mental, and fucking emotional abuse. You're allowed to say you're escaping, because you are. Just because he hasn't been chasing you with fists doesn't mean he hasn't been ripping you to shreds for years."

I press the heel of my hand to my chest, willing the crack in my voice not to split wide open.

"I've been trying to protect both of us," I say. "Trying to carry both his pain and mine. But it's like all I did was enable him. Like he never healed because he just used me as a shield to hide behind, and I let him."

My fingers twist the edge of the blanket.

"I used to think if I just held on a little longer, he'd wake up. Like he'd see me standing there in front of him. He'd one day believe he was worth fighting for and he'd stop trying to destroy everyone and everything in his path. But that's not how it works. You can't outlove someone's self-hatred."

I swallow. "I want him to get help. Real help. But he won't. Not as long as I'm there to cushion the fall."

Skye squeezes my thigh. "He's needed to hit rock bottom for years. Maybe this time, he'll finally feel it."

I nod, slowly.

"I still hope he heals," I whisper, no longer fighting the tears falling down my face. "He deserves to heal."

Skye interrupts. "Tori—"

"No, Skye. Don't." I stop her. "I'm serious. Yes, he's an asshole. And yes, he has chosen, time and time again, to hurt me and belittle me and take out every bit of pain inside himself on me and his brother and whoever else is around him. But that doesn't change the fact that he is a goddamn human being. He is a person worthy of love and a full life. He is broken, in need of help and healing, and just because I am walking away from him and this marriage does not mean I believe for even one second that he deserves anything less than that."

She nods, not daring to interrupt again.

My voice wavers, faltering under the weight of my hope for Chase's future and my fear that reality and hope are two very, very different things. "I hope he gets to live a full life. I do. I just know now—I'm not the one who can give it to him."

Skye reaches over and laces her fingers through mine.

"You've bled enough for him," she says. "Now it's your turn to heal."

Skye doesn't say anything else. She doesn't have to. Her hand is still wrapped around mine, thumb brushing lazy arcs over my knuckles like she's grounding me to the moment—to the reality that I'm allowed to choose something else. Something better. Even if it terrifies me.

"I don't even know what it's going to feel like," I whisper. "Waking up without him. Living each day without the constant need to protect myself from whatever shit flies out of his mouth at any given moment."

"You'll love it. And, you'll also probably hate it," she says, not unkindly. "At first."

I smile a little. "Thanks for the pep talk."

"I'm serious. You're going to feel like your skin doesn't fit. Like you've stepped out of the life you were cast in and now you're standing there naked on stage. But that feeling fades. The emptiness starts to feel like... space."

"Space for what?"

"Whatever the hell you want," she says. "Your own thoughts. Peace. The kind of quiet that doesn't come with consequences."

God, I want that.

I lean my head back against the couch and close my eyes.

"I think I'll miss his voice," I say quietly. "Even when he was cruel, there was something about the way he said my name. Like I was his tether to the world."

Skye doesn't answer right away. When she does, her voice is soft. "Maybe you were. But you shouldn't have to be someone's anchor if they're just going to drag you under."

That one hits somewhere deep.

I open my eyes, blinking against the sudden sting.

"He's never been okay," I say. "Not really. Not since the beginning. I used to think he just needed more time. More love. Like I could patch the holes if I just stretched myself thin enough. But I was never the solution. Just a distraction."

"Yeah," Skye says. "A convenient one. Because if he focused on your flaws—real or imagined—he didn't have to look at his own."

The weight of it settles heavy in my chest.

"I was fifteen when we met," I say. "Can you believe that? Fifteen. And I made it my mission to save him."

"I was there. I remember. And you weren't equipped for that. No one is. Not even now."

"I didn't want to give up on him."

"I know." Skye nods. "You're not giving up. You're choosing yourself. And I hate that it took this long for you to believe you could."

We sit in the quiet for a while. Just breathing.

"I done word vomiting. Is there ice cream in the freezer?" I say after a minute.

Skye's already on her feet. "IS. THERE. ICE. CREAM. IN. THE. FREEZER. What the hell kind of house do you think this is?"

I laugh. "I don't know. You arrived at the same time I did."

"Yeah. From the Gilmores' house. I had dinner over there tonight and already stocked the fridge earlier today. And even if I hadn't—there's always ice cream in this house. My dad treats pints of Ben & Jerry's like stock options."

She disappears into the kitchen and returns a minute later with two pints and a pair of mismatched spoons. "Half Baked or Cherry Garcia?"

I reach for the first one without thinking. "If you know the answer, why do you ask?"

"Because I'm committed to the illusion of choice."

We eat in silence for a few minutes, curled up on opposite ends of the couch like we're twenty again and staying up late to dissect dreams we didn't know would unravel the way they did.

"Do you think he'll hate me?" I ask eventually.

"Chase?"

I nod.

"He'll pretend he does," she says. "Because that's easier than admitting he lost the one person who never gave up on him."

I stab my spoon into the pint. "He's going to go ballistic."

"Maybe he needs to."

I glance at her.

"I mean it," she says. "Let him rage. Let him fall apart. He's never had to face himself. Not really. Maybe this is what it takes. You stepping away."

I swallow hard. "I just... I want him to find peace. Even if it's without me."

Skye leans forward, rests her elbows on her knees.

"You can't build your healing around his potential," she says. "You've already tried that. You gave everything you had, and then some. And maybe, someday, he'll do the work. Maybe he'll even thank you. But that part's not yours to carry anymore."

It's both freeing and devastating. I let it settle in my bones.

We finish our ice cream, the room thick with unspoken things.

Skye sets her empty pint on the coffee table, then stretches her arms overhead with a soft, contented groan. "Alright. Let's go. Bedtime."

I lift a brow, still wrapped in my blanket. "You're not gonna make me sleep on the couch like some stray you found on the porch?"

She snorts. "Please. Like I'd pass up the chance to relive our glory days of sharing a bed and fighting over boy band soulmates until two in the morning."

I smile—small, but genuine. It slips out before I can stop it, catching me off guard with how right it feels.

"Come on," she says, standing and holding out a hand like I need help remembering the way.

I don't. I know this house as well as she does.

Still, I take it.

We walk down the hallway side by side, steps softened by the rug worn threadbare in the center. Skye's bedroom door is already open. She doesn't even bother with the light.

The lavender walls are still covered in old posters—concerts we never actually went to, cheesy motivational quotes we taped up for finals week and never took down. Some of them are curling at the corners now, browned slightly at the edges. A corkboard still hangs near the dresser, filled with pushpins and fading snapshots. Right in the center is our senior year photo booth strip, still perfectly intact—Skye mid-laugh, me sticking my tongue out like a girl who hadn't yet learned how much damage could hide behind a smile, Alis pushing up her glasses that never seemed to stay put.

Three unstoppable best friends. And I haven't even told one of mine that my life is literally falling apart. Part of me feels guilty about that, but with everything she's had going on and the happiness that has finally come her way I didn't want to spoil it with my own sob story. Alis will find out soon enough. I'll explain everything when I get to Grand River in a few weeks.

I sit at the edge of the bed while Skye digs through the dresser, tossing me a pair of pajama shorts so old the logo is barely legible.

"Camp Long Pine," I read aloud, squinting at the faded print. "Pretty sure these predate my first real kiss."

"Vintage," she says, completely unbothered. "You're welcome."

We change without commentary, the silence between us soft, easy. Skye climbs into bed, pulling the blanket up to her chin and patting the space beside her like I haven't claimed it a dozen times before.

I slide under the covers, the mattress dipping in the exact spot I remember. I stare at the ceiling for a while, the fan whirling above us.

There's something safe in this room. Something steady. Like all the versions of us that once existed here still linger.

I can't sleep, and when I finally speak my voice comes out

quieter than I mean it to. "You remember how you swore you were going to follow in Belle's footsteps?"

Skye hums, turning slightly toward me. "Study abroad, fall in love with some dreamy foreigner, elope by twenty-one? Oh yeah. That was the grand plan."

"You never talk about Italy," I say. "Five months is a long time. You really didn't meet anyone?"

She huffs, but her voice stays light. "Not anyone worth mentioning."

"Come on," I tease, nudging her leg with mine beneath the covers. "Nobody special?"

"I've already told you," she says with a lazy shrug. "I found my true love in Italy, and that was espresso. The boys were a dime a dozen." She smirks, wiggling her eyebrows suggestively, "And I definitely sampled at least a dozen."

I laugh—not at all surprised—but I don't push for more. If there is something she's not saying, I'll let her keep it tucked away. We all have corners we don't invite people into. Some truths only come out when you're ready to let them go.

The room settles into stillness again, the kind that feels like a held breath. And then it creeps in—that dull ache in my chest. The one I keep shoving back down, pretending I'm brave enough to handle all of this without breaking.

"I don't know how to be single," I whisper, staring at the ceiling like it might hold the answer.

Skye shifts beside me, her voice calm. "You don't have to know yet. Right now, just be free."

"I'm scared."

"I know."

"I'm scared I won't know how to exist without him."

"You will."

My voice breaks a little. "But what if I miss him so much I forget why I left?"

The bed shifts slightly as she turns toward me. "Then I'll remind you."

Of course she will. Her reassurance is simple. Solid. No hesitation.

Skye doesn't say anything else. She doesn't need to.

And finally—*finally*—I fall asleep.

Not without fear of the future, but with the calming reassurance that no matter what happens, at least I'll have my friends at my side to help me through it.

SEVENTEEN

LEO

SATURDAY CARRIES the kind of chill that sneaks into your lungs and makes every breath feel sharper than it should. Not winter yet, not really, but the air has shifted. The last of the cottonwoods along George and Linda's street are more branch than leaf, the few stragglers clinging dry and curled, rattling like brittle paper when the breeze stirs them. The sky is a hard, cloudless blue, sunlight bright but cold, throwing everything into sharp relief.

I should've known something was wrong earlier this week. Linda canceled dinner Tuesday, then again on Thursday, said George wasn't feeling well. Both times I offered to stop by anyway, just to sit with him, watch a game, keep him company. Both times she told me, "Not a good time, honey. He needs rest."

Saturdays, though... Saturdays never need planning. Saturdays are automatic. Me walking in with a six-pack, George in his recliner, hockey already queued up, him swearing that offsides wasn't offsides because back in '86 the refs called it with "common damn sense." That's the rhythm we keep.

I don't bring the six-pack today.

I stand on their porch half a beat too long, cold biting the tips of my ears, empty-handed and pretending that's why my chest feels tight. I knock anyway—one knuckle rap out of habit, but I don't wait. I push the door open like I always do and call, "It's me."

Linda is already in the living room. She turns, that soft smile she keeps for me stitched to a face that hasn't slept. Her lipstick is on; her eyes are tired underneath it. "Hi, sweetheart. Come in."

The heat is up too high. The house feels sealed—like the air hasn't changed out in a while. The recliner is angled at the TV the exact way George likes it. The afghan is folded. The remote is on the side table, lined up with his reading glasses. Everything is where it should be—except him.

My stomach bottoms out.

Linda folds her hands in front of her and steps around the recliner, into the entryway where I'm still standing. "He's in bed," she says. "It's been... a week."

I nod because my throat is occupied trying to keep it together. "Can I—?"

"Of course." She reaches for my forearm and squeezes, the way she has since I was twenty-two and scared of my first real Thanksgiving with her family. "He's awake. He'll be glad you're here."

The hallway creaks under my shoes. The frames along the wall catch the light—weddings, graduations, a photo of me and George at a hockey game with foam fingers and a stupid-thick pretzel. Stephanie and Aaron on their wedding day. My jaw tightens, then lets go. Not today. Today isn't for that.

I nudge the bedroom door open.

George is propped on pillows, smaller than last week, the angles of his face sharper. An IV line curls from his arm to a bag that catches the afternoon light, another line loops to a nasal cannula resting along his upper lip, the tubing glinting against weathered skin. The oxygen mask is clipped to the bedrail, waiting for when he wants it. The Avalanche are on the TV mounted opposite—the Wednesday rerun—crowd noise low, commentators more hum than words.

He sees me and lifts a hand with all the bravado he can

muster. "It's just fluids, son. Don't be such a bitch about it." His voice is gravelly but amused. "I'm not dead yet. You can cry when the morphine comes, but that won't be for at least a month."

My laugh shows up late and sounds wrong. "Dammit, George, you stole my opening line."

I take a step into the room and toward the old, floral-patterned sitting chair on his side of the bed, but before I make it three feet into the space George slaps the mattress beside him.

"Don't you dare sit all the way over there. Linda won't mind. Come on. This thing even has a remote; it's basically a recliner with a headboard. And if your ass goes numb, hit the massage button. It'll rattle you like a paint can."

Shaking my head—because this man, I swear to God—I walk around to the other side of the bed and toe off my shoes. I climb on, awkward as hell, settling on top of the covers beside him, careful not to sit on tubing or wires, and the individual twin-sized mattresses are firm, but comfortable.

Being in this bed, next to George, I'm instantly twelve again—climbing into my parents' bed after a nightmare—except there's no waking up to fix this. This is reality. This man, the man who has been more of a dad to me than my actual, living, breathing father, is dying. And I'm just supposed to be okay with that? Pretend like it's a part of life, like I'm not falling apart inside and terrified of what life will look like without him in it?

He's watching the television, eyes fixed on the game. The puck drops and the announcer's voice fills the room, but I can't stop cataloguing details about him—how thin his wrists look against the sheets, the slack in his cheeks, the way the IV tubing tugs when he shifts. I'm studying him, hoarding the sight of him like I'll never get another chance.

Without taking his eyes off the screen, George snorts. "Christ, son, you're staring. Take a picture—it'll last longer. But just so you know, my left side's the good one."

I laugh, shaking my head as I turn my attention to the game. "Not staring. Just making sure you aren't tangled up somewhere."

"You think I'm flopping around in this damn bed like a fish?" he huffs. "I can barely breathe well enough to walk myself to the shitter, let alone roll my old ass over to tangle my tubes. Stop being so fussy. That's what Linda and the nurses are for."

"Noted."

We settle into the game. I jab at him when one of his defensemen drifts offsides. "Your boys can't line up to save their lives. It's like watching a drunk conga line."

George grunts, eyes sharp on the screen. "Better than your goalie, who's holier than Swiss cheese. Man couldn't block a beach ball if it was tied to his forehead."

I smirk. "We still won on Wednesday."

"Barely," he fires back, coughing a laugh. "Ref handed it to you on that penalty call. I've seen toddlers take hits harder than that."

The banter is easy, familiar. We've had this same back-and-forth a hundred times in recliners, in bars, in the cheap seats. But now it feels like I'm clutching at it, hoarding it the way I hoard every detail of him—because who knows how many more times I'll get to hear his trash talk?

Silence sneaks in during a commercial break. George's breathing rasps, steady but thinner than I like. My mind drifts to the nights we sat shoulder-to-shoulder in real arenas, beers sweating in our hands, his voice booming over the roar of the crowd. He's been here for every win and every loss of mine, even the ones that had nothing to do with hockey. And now...

George is dying. And while I won't be alone, not really, there's no denying that of all the people in this world I love, George takes up the most space in my heart.

"Now, listen." George turns his head, breath hitching with the effort, and for a second the light catches the freckles on his temple. "We're gonna have a talk, and you're not going to like it much, but you are going to listen."

My shoulders stiffen, but I try not to let my reaction show. Instead of looking at him like I'm terrified of whatever is about to come out of his mouth, I school my features and nod, letting him know that I'm ready, and willing, to listen.

He holds my gaze, steady as bedrock. "I'm dying, son. Don't look away from it. Don't pretty it up. A month, maybe less. Which means I don't have time for you to keep bullshitting yourself. You've been running ever since Stephanie. You let what she did to you—how she lied, how she left you for Aaron—set the rules for your life. And you've been living by those rules ever since. That's not living. That's hiding."

The words cut straight. They always do when he says her name. Stephanie. The choice she made to walk out. The image of her hand in another man's—George's own son-in-law, for Christ's sake.

"I know, George," I manage, voice tight. "And I'm trying. You know that I am."

"I said you're going to listen. Not talk," he snaps, but it's not cruel—it's conviction. "Now hush."

I huff a laugh and motion for him to continue.

"You said you've turned the page." He studies me like he's weighing every muscle in my face. "But saying it doesn't mean shit if you don't live it. It's one thing to tell yourself you're moving on. It's another thing to actually open the door when something good comes knocking. You hear me?"

He pauses, breathing hard, then pushes through. "I love my daughter. I love Aaron. But don't mistake that for approval of what she did to you. She gutted you, Leo. And it was wrong. But you are not going to spend the rest of your life letting her decision rot you from the inside out. Not while I still have breath to tell you otherwise. You are my son, too. And I'll be damned if I watch you throw away the years you've got left just because you're too scared to let someone in again."

The words lance me open. I can't meet his eyes. I stare down at my hands, picking at a callous on the side of my thumb for something to do, something to focus all this nervous energy into while he speaks.

He doesn't let up. "You've been alone too long. And if that woman—the one you keep pretending is *just a friend*—is who you want, then don't hide behind bullshit excuses. Don't tell me 'it's not the right time.' Life doesn't wait until the right time. If she's worth it, you go after her. Will she hurt you? Maybe. But that doesn't mean she's not worth loving."

I exhale, long and heavy, and finally look back at George. "Her name is Tori."

"Tori," he repeats. "I like that."

"Me too," I laugh. Then, more seriously, "She's... she's going through hell right now. And I don't know if I'm drawn to her because I feel obligated to be her friend through all of the shit she's dealing with, or if I'm drawn to her because it's more than that."

George's face sombers; it doesn't take but a second for him to understand my meaning. "She's going through a divorce."

I nod. "She's right in the thick of it, and he's a fucking asshole."

"You've met him?" George seems stunned by this revelation— as was I the day that prick barged into our office.

"Not on purpose, but, yeah. That's a whole other story that I don't want to get into." He nods and I'm thankful that he doesn't press for more.

"Even if I could sort out whatever the hell I'm feeling about her, she doesn't need me trying to push anything on her. Not anytime soon."

"So be her friend," George says simply.

I scoff. "What the hell do you think I've been trying to do for the last few months? Exactly that. Turns out, I'm pretty good at it —I think—until I'm not."

His brow lifts. "And why's that?"

I rub the back of my neck, half embarrassed and half hoping

George has the magical words of wisdom to help me keep my foot out of my mouth—permanently. "Probably because as soon as she relaxes around me I say something stupid and come onto her like a douchebag."

George lets out a bark of laughter, coughs, then pats my leg. "Well, son, when every bit of female interaction you've had in the last three years has been with Linda, students, or hookups, it makes sense you wouldn't have a clue how to be *just friends* with a woman."

"I'm friends with Skye," I protest.

His laughter continues, stronger than before. "Oh, Lord." *Cough.* "Now that," *cough.* "That right there, is the funniest damn thing you've said in a long time."

I furrow my brow, perplexed. George shakes his head, his laughter finally calming down to a chuckle, a knowing smirk in his eyes. "Leo, that girl is just as foul-mouthed and horny as you are. The two of you are twins separated at birth. She absolutely does *NOT* count."

Ah. Good point. I shrug. "Okay. That's fair."

"Does this Tori still come around," George asks, "even after you say something stupid?"

I think about it. "Yeah. She does."

He nods, satisfied. "Then you're doing fine, son. You're doing just fine."

I grin, but it fades quickly as the quiet settles again. The game drones on, crowd noise muffled by the four walls, but I'm not really watching. My gaze keeps drifting back to him. To this man who never once had to claim me but did anyway. Who showed up to my graduate school commencement ceremony when my own parents couldn't be bothered to return from their Mediterranean cruise. Who bought me my first real suit when I landed my first teaching job, and celebrated the fact that it was at my alma mater and not some fancy ivy league. Who, when Stephanie left, let me rage and break down in the same breath without making me feel pathetic for it.

And it's now that I realize I've measured everything in my life against him. What would George think? Would he be proud? Would he tell me I'm being an idiot? Most of the time, both.

He notices, again, of course. He always does. "Don't get that wet-eyed look, son," he rasps, eyes still on the screen. "I told you, I'm not gone yet. And if you cry, I'll have to hold your hand, and then Linda will come in and start crying, and before you know it, we'll need a canoe to get out of here. If I can't even laugh without coughing, what the hell makes you think I have the energy to row a goddamn boat?"

I snort. "Yeah, well, you're the one who started getting all deep and philosophical."

"That's because I don't have time to waste on bullshit," he says flatly, though there's no heat. "Not anymore."

We fall back into the game. The Avs score and George perks up enough to raise a fist. "That's how it's done," he crows, voice cracking but proud. "None of that weak-sauce slap shot crap."

"Fluke goal," I mutter, hiding my grin. "Bounced off his skate. Even I could've scored that one."

"Boy, I've seen you skate. Your stick handling looks like you're churning butter," he fires back. "Fucking dairy maid," he says under his breath. "Don't talk to me about flukes."

It's dumb, juvenile, perfect. Exactly us.

The third period winds down and Linda peeks in, a tray in her hands—two mugs of tea, a bowl of broth, crackers on the side. Her eyes soften when she sees me on the bed, shoes kicked off, settled in like I belong there. Which, I guess, I do.

"Thought you boys might be hungry," she says.

George waves her off. "I'm fine. Leo'll eat it."

She sets the tray on the bedside table anyway and gives me that look that communicates *don't you dare let him talk his way out of food*. I nod, and she disappears again.

George exhales slowly, watching the last few minutes tick down. "You know," he says, "people think dying is the hard part. It's not. The hard part's knowing what you'll miss. The games. The dinners. Watching you screw something up and fix it anyway." His lips twitch. "That woman, Tori... once all this bullshit settles down, if she makes you want to try, don't you waste that. Not one damn day. You hear me?"

I swallow hard. "I hear you."

"Good. Because if you keep waiting for the right time, son, you'll wake up and realize the right time never came. And then it's too late." His hand squeezes mine, papery but steady. "You don't have to marry her tomorrow or even next year. Hell, you don't even have to kiss her yet. But don't you dare keep her out just because Stephanie did a number on you. That'd be letting my daughter's fuck up keep winning, and her mistakes don't get that privilege."

I'm trying so damn hard not to get choked up. He's right; I know it.

We sit with the weight of every truth spoken today. The horn sounds on the TV, players skating off, and George mutters about bad officiating one last time. I laugh, grateful for the normalcy of it, the ordinariness of our banter layered on top of everything heavy.

When I finally drag my shoes back on and stand, George pats the mattress like he's stamping me into it. "Same time next week. Don't come empty-handed. I expect beer, even if I can't drink it."

My throat tightens. "You got it."

"Good man." His eyes close, but there's a smile tucked at the edge of his mouth.

I step out into the hall, and Linda's waiting. She doesn't say a word—just reaches for my arm, squeezes once. I squeeze back, and lean down to kiss her cheek. Then I walk out into the chill, lungs burning, heart heavier than it was when I came in.

And still, somehow, lighter.

EIGHTEEN

TORI

Past

"TOR, have you seen my blue tie?" Chase calls from our walk-in closet.

I'm trying to keep my cool. Trying to act like nothing out of the ordinary is happening today. Or tomorrow. Or every day for the rest of our lives.

Everything is fine. Totally fine. He's going on a business trip. Status quo. I'm helping him pack—currently ironing his shirts in our bedroom. Not getting distracted and leavingtheironon-theshirtfortoolong—dammit.

"It's rolled in your tie box—left side, middle," I call back, yanking the iron away from the white button-down just before it can leave a mark.

Keep your shit together, Tori.

"Found it!" he says. Amazing what happens when you look for something where it belongs.

I finish the six shirts, buttoning each to his specifications—all the way to the top, because God forbid a floppy collar—and slide them into the garment bag with his suit trousers and jackets. Three suits. Six shirts. Two extra pairs of trousers. Seven undershirts, seven pairs of socks, seven boxer briefs, two pairs of shoes. No toiletry bag—the hotel concierge will handle that before he arrives.

Chase walks out of our closet with four rolled neckties and hands them to me. "Make sure these are steamed before putting them in the garment bag." Not a request—a demand. Then he leaves the bedroom, and I hear the television click on.

Am I going to steam these? Not today. I turn the iron down to the silk setting, unroll the ties, and run it slowly over each one. They're flat, as requested. Not burned. He'll never know the difference.

Once they're folded over the pants hangers in the garment bag, he's packed and ready for Boston. Five days.

Five days on the other side of the country, rubbing shoulders with whatever finance bros make him feel both important and inferior. And he has no idea that while he's kissing their asses, I'll be packing my shit and leaving.

This is fine. Everything's fine.

I poke my head out of our bedroom. "Do you have something pulled out in the closet to wear on the airplane?"

He's holding a beer—of course he is.

"Yes." He doesn't even look at me.

"Do you need a tie for it?"

"Why do you think I handed you four fucking ties, Tori? I obviously need one for tomorrow," he snaps, eyes still glued to the television.

I don't argue. I don't ask which color. I'm too tired to hear him snap again. It's late. I want to crawl into bed.

I retrieve the blue tie he was looking for earlier from the bag, walk it into our closet, and drape it over the pants hanging on the nearly empty rack he uses for tomorrow's clothes.

I'm at my dresser in our closet, about to grab a set of unattractive matching flannel pajamas, when I see it—a satin, lace-trimmed nighty I bought for our anniversary a few years ago. Deep purple, beautiful against my skin. I only wore it once, and it stirs a memory I don't ever want to lose.

Chase and I had been in a good place then. We'd gone to counseling for a while, and things were going well. We weren't fighting as much; his words were mostly kind. On our anniversary, he actually brought home flowers. I walked out of our room wearing only that nighty, my hair falling in loose waves down my back.

That night was more than sex. We connected. We made love. There was passion, connection, love, mutual respect. He touched me with reverence, kissed me with tenderness. Told me how much he loved me, and I said it back—wholeheartedly. We fell asleep in each other's arms, content. Happy, even. For a while.

Suddenly, I wonder.

God, this is stupid. What am I doing? I've already made up my mind. Made my choice. I'm leaving.

But what if—

No. No, I can't.

...Can I?

Fuck it.

I drop the flannel set back into the drawer and reach for the satin instead, the fabric slipping cool and traitorous through my fingers. Today's clothes go into the hamper. The nightgown gets folded in half on the vanity like it might change its mind if I let go.

I close the bathroom door quietly and turn the lock—not that Chase is likely to peel himself away from the television—and twist the bathtub faucet on. A quick shave to smooth my legs. Lotion. A spritz of perfume. The small, almost pathetic rituals of someone still trying. Maybe I'll comb through my hair, brush my teeth, pretend I'm not clawing at the frayed edge of something already gone.

He's watching football. They have a name for this play, right? A Hail Mary. That's what this is—one last, reckless throw into the end zone. My final gamble to see if there's even a flicker left to save us before I pack my bags and walk out the door forever.

Once I'm done shaving, I smooth lotion over my legs until they shine, spritz perfume at my wrists and the hollow of my throat, run a comb through my hair until it falls just right. The woman in the mirror looks soft, inviting. Ready to be loved.

The woman in the mirror is really fucking confused about why she just put all this effort into someone who definitely does not want her.

Why am I doing this, again? Hope. I have to know. One last time. Hail Mary.

When I step out of the bathroom, Chase is already in bed, phone in hand. The blue glow illuminates his face. He doesn't look up. His shirt and shorts are crumpled in a heap on the floor—because of course they are.

I pause in the doorway, satin brushing my thighs. Wait for him to notice. He doesn't.

I cross the room and slip into my side of the bed, close enough that the scent of my perfume should reach him. "Hey," I murmur, fingertips grazing his arm like an invitation.

He doesn't even flinch. Just keeps scrolling, the blue light from his phone washing over his face, making him look miles away.

"Chase?" My voice is quieter this time, because I already know.

He finally looks. No smile. No warmth. Just a bland acknowledgment that I'm here, breathing in the same room.

I lean in anyway, pressing my mouth to his shoulder, my hand sliding along his side, trying to coax something familiar from him. A spark. A memory. Anything. He exhales—impatient, not affected—and sets his phone on the nightstand before lying back, waiting for me to take the lead.

I straddle him, hoping muscle memory will wake him up, pull him toward me. My lips trail up his jaw, my hand skimming his chest, but he gives me nothing—not a kiss, not a touch. Just stillness.

I grind down, searching for connection, but before I can ask if something's wrong, his hand is in my hair, pushing me under the covers. No words. No tenderness. Just a silent order: put my dick in your mouth.

It stings. But I go. Because maybe if I do this—if I give him what he wants—he'll see me again, even if only for a second.

I take him into my mouth, slow at first, teasing the tip with my tongue, then swallowing him deep before pulling back with a hard suck. The rhythm is muscle memory for me. I work him until he's fully hard, until I can pretend for just a second that this is foreplay, not a transaction.

I climb back up, guide him to my entrance, and sink down, satin pooling at my waist. I want him to grip my hips, to drag me closer, to touch me like I matter. But he just props his arms behind his head, his hips lifting every so often to meet mine halfway, like this is a chore he's willing to finish but not invest in.

I lean down to kiss him—God, I want to kiss him—and he turns his head, giving me his jaw like I'm an inconvenience.

I keep moving. Not because I want to. Because I have to. Because if I stop now, I'll have my answer before I'm ready to hear it.

No, Tori. There is no hope to be found here. This was a waste of time and effort. All you've done is stabbed yourself in the heart once again.

My hands press to his chest. My hips shift, aligning with his, begging silently for him to join me. To meet me halfway, in more ways than one. His eyes stay closed, his mouth slack, his focus entirely inward.

I feel it when he's close—the tightening of his stomach, the change in his breathing. I'm nowhere near, but I adjust my angle, searching for friction, willing my body to catch up to his. Maybe we can still finish together.

Of course, we don't.

He grunts, releases, and stills. For one suspended second, I think he's going to reach for me—wrap his arms around me, offer a smile, a kiss, anything. Instead, he taps the side of my thigh, a perfunctory signal to get off him. *Time to get off the horse, lassie. Ride's over.*

I move away, a new understanding of *hollow and alone* settling over my entire being. He leans over the side of the bed, grabs his crumpled T-shirt from the floor, wipes himself, and tosses it at me without looking.

I hold the shirt in my hands for a long moment before using it, the damp fabric clinging to my skin like proof of something ugly I can't unsee. Proof I asked for this—invited it—because I needed to know, once and for all, if there was anything left worth saving.

When I finally use it, the fabric drags against my skin, erasing more than just the evidence of what we've done. It wipes away the last version of me that believed in him.

I lie back and pull the comforter to my neck. He's already turned away, bare back to me, breathing evening out like nothing happened.

Years ago, I used to watch him like this and feel safe, warm, claimed. Now, the space between us feels like an ocean, and I'm treading water while he sleeps on shore.

The satin nightgown twists at my waist, cool against my over-heated skin. Tears slip into my hairline, pooling before sinking into the pillow. I let them fall. They feel like they've been waiting for this moment.

The ache in my chest is heavy, unrelenting. And he has absolutely no idea what's coming.

I knew better. God, I knew better. I needed one last chance—one last fragile thread of hope. That maybe he'd see me. That maybe he'd wake up and remember who he is when he's not drowning in alcohol and his own misery.

I think about that one anniversary night—the way his hands were steady but tender, how he'd brushed my hair back just to look at me, how we'd fallen asleep tangled together. I convinced myself we could find that again if I just tried hard enough.

But tonight proved what I didn't want to face. I handed Chase

Martin the last intact piece of our marriage, and he crushed it without even looking.

The room smells faintly of him—soap, sweat, stale beer—my perfume clinging in the air like an afterthought. My mind drifts to all the nights I went to bed alone while he stayed up drinking and watching TV, the times I reached for his hand and felt him pull away, the moments I realized halfway through speaking that he wasn't listening.

As soon as memories of his harsh words, drunken temper, and fist in the wall flood in, I shut them out. I lived through enough of those moments for one lifetime. I have no need to replay them in my mind.

It wasn't always like this, but the good moments became crumbs scattered between months of fighting, drinking, distance. And I was the one crawling to collect them, pretending it was enough.

Tomorrow he leaves for Boston. And tomorrow, I'll pack my life into my SUV and drive away from this marriage, this town, and this version of myself. I'll leave behind the woman who begged for scraps and called them meals, who tiptoed through her own home.

I picture loading the last box into the back, the slam of the hatch final. I'll climb into the driver's seat, check the mirror, half-expecting to see him in the doorway. But he won't be there. He won't even know I'm gone until the key turns in the lock and the silence greets him instead of me.

For years, I feared life without him. Now, I fear the life I'd have if I stayed.

When I hit that button to start the ignition, it won't just be the end of us.

It will be the beginning of me—untethered, unhindered, and free.

NINETEEN
TORI

"WHEN YOU MOVED OUT, that didn't give you permission to disappear, bitch." Skye shoves Alis with her foot from across the couch, nearly tipping a very full glass of Cab Sauv into Alis's lap.

She yelps and jerks the glass overhead like she's blocking a volleyball spike. "I'm sorry! I'm so bad at peopleing."

"The worst," Skye says. She is in pajama shorts with tiny lightning bolts on them and a cropped sweatshirt that reads COFFEE & CHAOS. Her purple hair is twisted into two messy space buns and, somehow, she has eyeliner wings sharp enough to slice cheese. Add in the retinol under-eye patches, and she's truly a sight to behold.

I pat Alis's knee. "Our sweet little hermit. We still love you."

Alis relaxes back into the cushions, the tiniest smile tugging at her mouth. "I love you, too. I just... forget that 'let's hang out' doesn't mean 'sit in my house with a book, a dog, and a man who brings me tea.'"

Skye points at her with a cracker. "You hear that? She forgot us. Otis outranks us. Dexter outranks us. *Tea* outranks us."

"You forgot Sunny. Sunny has always outranked you," Alis says.

I gasp, hand over my heart. "She's spicy now. Look at her, a real person who says things."

Skye leans forward to refill her glass. The coffee table is a thrifted trunk covered in coasters that we never use, a plate of grapes and sweating brie, a tragic pile of broken crackers we keep pretending are rustic. "Tell me about Canada, Madame Married-But-Not-Yet-Legally. Was Montreal all cobblestones and croissants and sex in French?"

Alis makes a face. "Oh my God. We were visiting his family."

"Ignore her. Canadian Thanksgiving," I prompt. "Dexter's parents. How did Sunny do with the French?"

"It was lovely," Alis says, and her voice softens around the word in a way I recognize—like she's smoothing a favorite page. "Dex's parents switch between French and English so naturally. I didn't realize they speak English so much. I was worried Sunny would feel lost, but she thought it was a game. His mom taught her how to say 'pass the potatoes' and then Sunny wouldn't stop asking for potatoes, like, in perpetuity."

Skye snorts. "A worthy cause."

"And the city was absolutely stunning," Alis adds. "He took us to this tiny place with bagels baked in a wood-fired oven, and there was this old man who told Sunny stories about his cat in like three languages. Sunny ate two bagels by herself and tried to feed the pigeons. Dex had to rescue a poppy-seed-eating pigeon from her loving clutches. Like she was determined to take this bird home with us so it could be best friends with Otis."

I rest my chin on my fist, smiling. "Oh, Sunny. Ever the optimist."

"So much like her favorite aunt," Skye chimes in.

"And equally as feral," Alis nods in affirmation.

"I bet you loved seeing Dex in rescue mode," I say, nudging Alis's knee with my own.

"I mean, obviously," Alis says, quietly, and the blush returns.

Skye's eyes light with fresh mischief. "Speaking of Sexy Dexy...

the French. We require details. Preferably salacious. At minimum, educational."

Alis hides behind her wine glass. "Absolutely not."

"Come on," I coax. "We're living vicariously."

She peeks at us over the rim. "He... he doesn't switch to French mid-sentence to be sexy. It's not performative. It just—happens. He'll murmur something without thinking and I'll feel it in my spine. Which is mortifying."

"Give me one," Skye pleads. "One phrase."

Alis hesitates and then, as if bargaining with herself, says, "He calls me *mon cœur* sometimes." She shrugs, eyes flicking down. "My heart."

Skye presses a hand to her chest and groans. "Ugh. It's official. I'm obsessed."

"And—" Alis clears her throat, mustering up the courage to continue. "When we're alone he'll... he'll say things that are... less... sweet."

"Such as?" Skye is practically vibrating.

"Skye," Alis warns.

I grin. "I bet Dex's dirty talk could fund our serotonin for the quarter."

"Or charge the batteries in our vibrators for a fucking year," Skye quips.

Alis covers her eyes with one hand, attempting to hold out on us before giving in with a whisper so soft we have to lean in to hear what she says. "*Il n'y a que toi.* There's only you." She swallows. "And sometimes—" Her blush is so deep, I'd almost swear she's sunburnt. "*Je vais te faire oublier ton nom.*"

"I have no idea what you just said, but that was hot as *fuuuuu-uuck*," Skye sings the last word like a soprano, and I take a sip of my wine, impressed that she got the words out at all.

Alis remains quiet, smiling to herself. She traces the rim of her wineglass with her pointer finger nonchalantly, as if she's forgotten we are even in the room.

Lifting a brow, I ask, "You are going to tell us what that means, right?"

Alis smirks, her expression no longer shy, but knowing. This woman is about to flip our everloving lids. "I will make you forget your name."

"STOP IT!" Skye yells, kicking her feet back and forth, at the same time I squeeze my thighs together, eyes wide.

"Holy shit," I exhale. "I think I just came."

No longer hiding behind her shyness, Alis tosses her head back and laughs. "You asked!"

That little minx. She enjoys getting a rise out of us.

I soak in this moment. The three of us, together. A moment of complete and utter happiness. Soul sisters; best friends.

I love these two women more than my own life.

"I did ask," Skye concedes, and then, magnanimous as ever, changes the subject. "Okay. Wedding. Give me a morsel. Venue? Dress? Cake I will pretend to be allergic to while eating three slices?"

Alis's smile flickers. "We, um... we haven't gotten far. I've been so busy, you guys."

I nudge her knee. "Busy is valid."

"I know," she says, but she's looking at her hands now, rolling her stemless glass in small circles. "Also, I didn't want... I didn't want to be insensitive. To you." She lifts her eyes to mine, careful. "It felt weird to walk in here and babble on about wedding stuff when you're... doing the divorce thing."

The room shifts, the air going quieter around the edges. The candle on the side table—something Skye labeled "Put your books here" because of course she did—pools amber light over the spines. Skye's gaze jumps to me and back to Alis, like she's waiting for the right quip to re-inflate us.

"It's okay," I say, and I mean it the way you mean something and also have to push it through a narrow place inside yourself to mean it fully. "Your joy doesn't hurt me. Not even a little. It helps."

Alis's throat works. She nods, sits with me, eyes steady, then inhales and tips us on a different axis.

"Can I ask you something?" she says. "And you can tell me to shut up if I'm out of line."

"Always," I say.

"I don't pry. I never have. I try to respect your boundaries, because I want people to respect mine. But—we've been best friends since kindergarten. Why didn't you tell me?" The words aren't sharp. They are soft and bewildered, like she found a bruise and is trying to remember how it formed.

The questions come in rapid fire. "What happened? Why did you leave him? You showed up at the apartment and said you were moving in while I was moving out and I had absolutely no idea what was happening. Why didn't I know anything?"

The sip of wine I took while she was speaking hushes in my mouth. I look at Skye on instinct—half for backup, half for a map —and she only lifts a shoulder. Absolutely not at all helpful.

"I keep your secrets," Skye says, simple and unadorned. "I kept hers, too, when I needed to. I'm a vault, babe."

It hits two ways at once: relief, hot and immediate, that Skye didn't dump me into anyone's lap to be fixed; and a thin, embarrassed sting at how I have to explain practically everything to someone I love—my best friend, no less.

"Okay," I say, and my voice is steady until it isn't. "Okay."

I don't offer up a play-by-play, but I also don't do her the disservice of skimming over the truth of what happened. I tell her the most important parts—the infertility, the comments, the fights. Walking on eggshells, never being enough. The breaking point that was Belle and Alex's funeral, the night Skye finally said something at that bar. The night he came home drunk and punched a hole in the wall right next to my face. How I made the decision right then that I was leaving, and how Skye drove to Moraine to help me make a final plan to leave while he was out of town. How I asked her not to tell anyone—partly because I was ashamed, but mostly because everything seemed to happen either when Alis's life was falling apart or finally coming together, and I never wanted to add to or take away from those things.

When I finish, Alis has both palms over her mouth like she's trying to press the air back in. Tears streak down her cheeks. She shakes her head, once, twice, and then lowers her hands and her gaze to her lap. She's quiet, contemplative, and then...

"I knew he was selfish," she says, breathless with it.

"Alis—"

"No," she stops me. "Let me say what I need to say."

I nod, and she continues. "I knew how he was in college. I didn't want you to marry him, Tori. You know that—I told you I was worried. But after the wedding, I thought... people change? Or they don't and you learn to... I don't know."

She gives a helpless little laugh that isn't a laugh. "I knew you were trying for a baby, but then you started grad school and I thought—I don't know what I thought. And then Belle..." Her mouth trembles. "Everything changed when she and Alex died. All I could see was Sunny and my grief. And even when Skye moved back to Moraine, and then you and Chase moved home and we were all together again... I don't know. Was I selfish?"

"No, honey," I reassure her. "You've never been selfish a day in your life."

"I feel selfish because I didn't see it," she says, wiping fresh tears from her eyes. "We were all there. Literally, right there, in the same town, living our lives together, every single day. And I didn't see it."

She's getting worked up, and I don't want that. But I also know Alis. I know that she's not typically a verbal processor, so the fact that she's saying any of this out loud, in front of us, is huge. I'm not about to interrupt her.

"Skye saw it. Said something. Hell, she helped you get out. But

I..." Alis's sobs rip through her, self-control be damned, and I pull her into my arms, Skye following close behind.

The three of us stay there, tangled together, a crying mess of pain, sorrow, and friendship, for what seems like hours but is probably only a minute or two. The couch sighs under our combined weight. The lit candle tunnels lower. Betty Boop ticks on the wall, a subtle reminder that as much as we might want to go back and do things differently, time always, only, moves forward.

Once Alis calms, I loosen my hold on her and swipe my thumbs under her eyes, cupping her face while I place a soft kiss on her nose.

"You gonna be okay, honeybun?" I ask, squishing her cheeks together.

Alis furrows her brow, her glasses now foggy from my exhale and the humidity built up from her tears and from being sandwiched between Skye and me in that bear hug. She looks like an adorable, angry chipmunk, and I can't help but chuckle.

"How do you always end up taking care of me instead of the other way around?" she grumbles.

"Because she's the mom, duh," Skye quips from her end of the couch, already tearing into the sleeve of Oreos we said we weren't going to open.

I release Alis and nestle back into my corner of the couch, running my fingers through my loose hair to detach the strands that stuck to my face while crying it out in our huddle. The apartment smells like wine and warm sugar and that stupid bookstore candle Skye keeps lighting when she wants me to unclench.

"Not to be the insensitive one," Skye says, "but have we heavied enough for one night?"

I laugh, "Yeah, babe. That's enough heavy for now."

"OHTHANKFUCK," she huffs. "Because I need so much more of that Sexy Dexy dirty talk in my life it's not even funny."

The groan that comes from Alis is unmistakable. *"Ben là, tabarnak!"*

Skye nearly spits wine. "Give me more of whatever that was. Like, right now."

"That was me telling you to please, for the love of God, stop," Alis says, cheeks pink again. She reaches for a grape and misses, plucking a rogue olive instead and making a face. "Also—this olive is lying about being a grape."

Skye's grin goes sly. "Okay, fine. New game. I'll give you outrageous English lines, you translate into French, and T will judge if it's hot or not."

"No," Alis protests, already laughing. "I refuse."

"Too late." Skye clears her throat like she's about to recite Shakespeare. "'Your mouth is my favorite sin.'"

Alis drops her head back and groans. "*Ta bouche est mon péché préféré.*" She covers her face. "Happy?"

Skye points both index fingers at me like pistols. "You hear that? I'm bilingual by association."

"Absolutely not how that works," I say, but I'm grinning. "Ten out of ten hot, though."

Skye scrolls through nothing on her phone because she just likes the drama of it. "'I'm going to kiss you so slow you forget your address.'"

"Your address?" I ask. "That's what you're going with?"

Alis half-laughs, half-wheezes. "*Je vais t'embrasser si lentement que tu oublieras ton adresse.*"

"Rude," I say, pressing my knees together again. "Arson-level rude. That absolutely should *not* be as hot as it just sounded."

"Last one," Skye announces, feigning sobriety. "'I want you like coffee wants mornings.'"

Alis squints. "*Je te veux comme le café veut ses matins.*" She looks horrified by herself. "That didn't even make sense."

"Neither do we," Skye says, smug. "So it's perfect."

Alis's phone pings on the table. She glances down, then tilts the screen toward us. It's a photo: Otis asleep, half on Dexter's foot, half on a book, under a throw blanket Sunny clearly swiped from our couch last time she was here. Dex's caption: *Mes monstres préférés*. "My favorite monsters."

"Seriously though," Skye says, smiling at Alis. "I love him. Like, for you. I love him for you."

Alis's smile is so big, and her eyes lit up with pure, undiluted happiness. "Last night he made shepherd's pie and saved me the corner so it gets crispy. He's the best."

"Okay," I say, clapping once softly to get both their attention. "This is girls' night, and we have action items. One: wedding spreadsheet. I'll build a prototype tomorrow at work—budget, vendors, tasks, color-coded tabs that will make you wet."

Skye perks up in the way only she does at the word *spreadsheet*.

Alis asks, "Can there be a tab for vows? Not like... to write them, just to collect ideas. Quotes. Lines from books."

Skye fans herself. "If you don't put a line from a smutty Regency novel in your vows I will riot."

"Action item number two," I continue, ignoring her. "We pick a standing girls' night once a month. Literally put it in the calendar. Like, right now."

Skye snatches her phone and starts a new event called **SHE-WOMAN MAN HATERS CLUB**—because of course she'd call it that. "First Thursday?"

Alis nods. "First Thursday."

"Three," Skye says, wagging a finger at me, "Tori lets her friends help. No Lone Rangerette mentality. You put your attorney meetings on the shared calendar so we both know about them."

I open my mouth to argue and then close it. "Fine. Yes. Okay."

Skye looks unbearably pleased. "Growth."

Alis chimes in, "I don't need all the details, but just so I'm caught up: that ball is rolling and the things are happening?" I nod in affirmation.

"Her attorney's office is, like, right next to my shop, so it's hella convenient for me to attend all the meetings," Skye says. "Even the ones she 'forgets' to tell me about, since my phone pings whenever one of you shows up in my vicinity."

"Mmmm, yes." My voice is not at all laced with sarcasm, nor are my shoulders lifted up to my ears. "I love the stalker setting on our phones so, so much. It's my favorite."

"Shut up," Skye chastises, standing and snagging the empty wine bottle off the table.

We migrate to the kitchen for tea because we've hit that age where two bottles of wine means death tomorrow. The kettle clicks on; the tile cold under my heels. Skye hums to whatever indie-pop music plays on repeat in her head while Alis stacks plates, rinses olive juice from her fingers, and lines everything on the drying rack like tiny dominos.

"Tell me one fun thing about wedding plans," I say over the kettle, nudging her shoulder with mine. "Anything. Color palette? Cake flavor? Will Otis wear a bow tie?"

Alis soft-smiles. "Sunny wants constellations somewhere. She keeps drawing them on scrap paper and telling me which one is 'Sunny's Star.'" She shrugs. "I like the idea of something in the night sky watching us."

"Babe," I say, throat thick for half a second in a good way, "that's perfect."

Skye bounces on her toes. "We can do starry escort cards. Or a constellation seating chart. Or tiny cookies shaped like moons that say dirty things in French, just to see who knows the language and who doesn't."

"Absolutely not," Alis says, scandalized. "You forget that my in-laws will be there."

"Thus the basis of its appeal!" Skye quips back in her best impression of Kat Stratford.

Alis starts pulling tea bags from canisters—mint for her, chamomile for me—but stops when she realizes the Earl Grey is empty.

Before she can ask what Skye wants in its place, we turn to see she's already popped a new cork and is filling her mug with wine.

"You don't want tea?" Alis asks.

"No, thanks. I'm recently monogmugamous."

"Monogmu... what?" I, too, have no idea what she just said.

"Monogmugamous. I'm faithful to coffee. He'd know if I stepped out."

Then she lifts her mug of wine to her lips, takes a sip, and walks out of the kitchen. As if what just happened was perfectly normal and not the most absurd thing she's ever done.

Which says a lot, considering she's Skye Kennedy and you never know what the hell is going to come out of that woman's mouth.

Tea brewed and bodies settled under blankets on the couch, we spend the next half hour talking about Sunny's school project on plate tectonics and how she drew a fault line under her teacher's patience. We talk about Dexter's new lecture series, the way he gets lost in his research and babbles on about Madeleine de Scudéry as if she's an old friend instead of a seventeenth-century author barely anyone knows about—(I literally have no idea who she is). We talk about Otis's new trick: "shake" with either paw depending on which hand you offer, which is unreasonably impressive for a dog with the attention span of a toddler who got ahold of Mountain Dew.

Somewhere around the bottom of the mugs, our laughter thins to the soft contentment that only shows up when you've said all the words. Alis sets her cup down and tucks her feet under a blanket like she's putting herself away, settling in for the quiet part of the evening.

"Thank you for telling me," she says to me, quiet but steady. "Even the hard parts."

"Thank you for asking," I say back. "Even when you were scared to ask."

Skye reaches all the way around Alis to my hoodie, pulling

both of us in for another group hug. "I love you bitches so damn much," she says.

"I love you, too," Alis mumbles. "But can you please let go? Because my face is smashed into your boobs."

"Shhh," Skye coos. "Rest in my bosom, sweet Alis."

"Um, no thank you." Skye continues to hold us in her death grip—her arm wrapped around my neck in more of a chokehold than a hug, Alis smashed between my chest and hers.

Finally, Skye loosens her grip enough that I'm able to duck out from underneath her arm and Alis resurfaces, making a show of inhaling as if she couldn't breathe before.

"And remember. Vault," Skye declares, tapping her chest. "The good kind. The glittery kind."

"Those exist?" I ask.

"Only the most secure. Super rare," she says.

We put on our favorite rom-com and quote over all the dialogue, as is our sacred custom. When the credits roll, Alis stands and collects her things slowly, like she's not quite ready to break the spell. At the door, she hugs us both in a three-person tangle, and for once none of our elbows stab anyone in the boob.

"I'm here," she says, one last squeeze.

"I know," I answer. "Me too."

After she's gone, Skye leans her forehead against the door and lets out a soft, tired exhale. "I love her."

"Same."

She turns, eyes flicking over my face like she's checking for cracks. "You okay?"

I think about tonight. About having to explain the shitstorm that was my marriage to my best friend, and how the three of us held each other in the aftermath. I think about how, even in the midst of so much pain and heartbreak, with these two women I am always safe, always completely at home. "I'm okay," I say, and it's true.

Skye bumps my hip with hers. "Next month, we make Alis say 'integrate me' in French."

"Good God, woman," I huff. "You really are feral."

She grins, smug and soft. "Love you, too, mon cœur."

"Don't start," I warn, but I'm laughing as we kill the lamp and let the string lights do the rest—our little apartment warm and bright, the night outside knocking softly and deciding to leave us be.

TWENTY

TORI

THE COPY ROOM hums like a lazy beehive—not that I can hear it—printer warm and breathing, the big industrial copier chewing through a packet for Dr. Patel one thunked ream at a time. It smells like hot paper and toner and that faint plasticky scent of fresh lamination, even though I have yet to find the magic laminator. I've commandeered the only clear stretch of counter—left to right: quizzes, stapler, paper clips, sticky notes with my reminders in tidy loops—while my audiobook chatters straight into my skull.

Maybe "chatters" isn't the right word. More like, *caresses* my senses.

It's supposed to be background noise, something to keep my brain from gnawing on itself while I alphabetize the chaos in front of me. Except... it's not background. It is very much foreground. The narrator's voice drops and I swear the room temperature climbs five degrees.

"...his hand slides along her hip—firm, claiming—and she tilts toward him like a tide pulled by—"

Okay, um, wow. I click the speed to 1.3x like that'll make it suddenly SFW. It does not. I should switch to a podcast about amortization schedules or something, but my hands are full of three-hole-punched seduction. I set a neat stack, reach for the next—

A warm palm lands on my hip.

Every nerve in my body misfires. The book in my ears says hip and my hip gets touched and my hindbrain, that traitorous bitch, responds before the human part can vote. I inhale and—God help me—lean back, ass first. My hips press into firm muscle. A breath catches behind me—his or mine, I don't know, but I felt it—and heat spikes at the nape of my neck.

Oh. *Oh no.*

Reality slams in a beat later. I jerk forward so fast a stack of quizzes avalanches, whirling around, heart in my throat, earbuds still droning on, noise canceling still in full effect. Leo is inches away, palm lifted in a useless *oh-hey-don't-freak* gesture, eyes wide like a kid who set off a firecracker in a library.

The slap leaves my hand before I decide to use it.

Crack. Except, still, I don't hear anything save the foreplay ramping up from two to five chilis super hella fast in my ears.

Leo's head snaps to the side. A faint red bloom rises on his cheek, slow as a Polaroid. For a split second we are both statues— me with my chest heaving, him with his jaw clenched and his eyes carefully *not* on mine.

I yank an earbud out. Silence floods in except for the copier's steady *chunk-chunk*, the clack of a paper tray reseating itself. The audiobook, disrespectful little hussy, keeps going in one ear about how she opens for him like—

This has to stop. Like right the fuck now.

Pulling out the other earbud, I slam it down on the countertop next to its partner.

"I—" My voice comes out shredded. "You cannot—*do not*— touch me like that." I'm trying to breathe through it. The adren- aline spike. The shame and heat climbing up my throat. The way my body moved all on its own like I'd been wired to a switch.

Leo lifts both hands now, palms out, fingers spread. No swagger, no grin—he's looking at me like I'm a spooked animal, seconds away from fight or flight.

He's probably not wrong.

"You're right," he says, and it's quiet and immediate, the apology tucked right into the first syllable. "I'm sorry. I thought —" He swallows, recalibrates. "I didn't think. I saw your earbuds and... I shouldn't have touched you. That's on me."

The thing about anger is that it comes with friends. Embarrassment. Mortification. A slideshow of moments I will replay in my brain at three a.m. night after night for the rest of... forever? Yes, forever.

"Why would you think—" I stop, inhale, try again. "Why would you touch me? At work?!"

"I was trying not to startle you with my voice," he says, wincing like he hears how stupid that sounds as it exits his mouth. "Which, when said out loud, is dumber than the dumbest option available." A beat. "I'm sorry."

The handprint on his cheek is perfectly shaped where it rises above his stubble, finger lines extending toward his cheekbone. Suddenly, I don't know what to do with my hands. I put them on my hips, then cross them, then aim them at the stapler like that's a weapon I could use.

"I—" I suck in a breath that shakes. "I leaned back." Why am I admitting that out loud? No idea.

Leo blinks. The corner of his mouth twitches like he's not sure if he's allowed to acknowledge that sentence. But of course, he does. "You did."

"Don't," I warn, finger up, because if he smirks even an inch I will shove him into the recycling bin and call it a day.

"I won't," he says quickly. "I'm not. Tote—Victoria—Tori— I'm serious. I'm sorry." He points vaguely toward the pod offices beyond the copy room door. "I'm going to give you some space. And get some ice. For your hand or my face or maybe your pride... or mine—whatever needs it most. Probably all of those things."

He pivots, then hesitates. "Can I— Are you okay? You look... frazzled?"

Am I? My pulse is a drumline. My face is on fire. There's a dry spot on my tongue that no amount of swallowing fixes. And beneath the humiliation is the whisper of something I don't want to admit: the way my body said yes before my brain remembered where we are, who we are, how complicated all of this is.

For fuck's sake—I didn't even know who had walked up behind me! My body wants to say it knew, instinctively, that Leo was the man touching me. But can I honestly say that? Nope.

The sexy book said he put his hand upon her hip, then the mystery man put his hand upon my hip, and then my body was like, "Mmmm, yes. When I dip, you dip, we dip." *Absolutely mortifying.*

"I'm fine," I lie, because I don't have a term for this particular flavor of meltdown. "Just... go."

He goes. The door sighs shut, and I exhale. I press my palms to the countertop and drop my forehead to the cool metal, breathing until the strobe-light thud under my skin slows enough to be mistaken for a heartbeat. On the floor, a sad disaster of disorganized paper fans across my shoes.

Looking up, I growl, "Pull it together," at the stapler. Sure, it is not at fault, but it is listening.

The door opens again. Leo returns with a ziplock filled with ice, wrapped in a brown paper towel and donning a blue sticky note that reads SORRY in block letters big enough to be read from space. Cute.

He takes three careful steps in, once again approaching that frightened animal. He sets the ice on the counter, then retreats to a safe distance near the paper-cutter, hands back in his pockets like he's disarmed himself.

"I brought reparations," he says, tone tentative. "For your—" He gestures at his own face, then my entire existence. "Everything?"

A painful laugh barks out of me. I pick up the ice and, for reasons unknown to science, press it to my cheeks one at a time. It's cold, and it helps. I set it down, then smooth my blouse like it misbehaved. Nope. Not the blouse. Just your horny hips and ass, Tori.

"Thank you," I say. "And I'm... I'm sorry I slapped you."

"Totally earned." He tips his head toward the mess of papers on the floor. "Want me to fix your paper massacre while you choose something... else... to listen to?"

I squint. "You didn't hear—"

"Just a murmur," he lies so quickly I almost admire the technique. "Sounded... super... plot-driven."

A sound escapes me that could be a laugh if I wasn't so embarrassed. "That was... not plot."

He holds up both hands again, playful surrender reappearing by degrees. "You're killing my lie, Tote."

We move around each other ever so carefully, simultaneously playing a game of "clean up" and "the friend is lava." He crouches to gather the escaped quizzes; I restack and re-straighten until my edges line up in a way my life does not. The copier snarfs the last set of prints and spits out a neat pile with a triumphant whirr, like *See? I told you I could do it!*

When I speak, it's once again to the stapler. "You can't touch me from behind."

"I won't touch you at all unless you tell me to," Leo says, no hesitation. "And if I ever forget that, feel free to brand my other cheek."

That shouldn't make me feel better. But it does, a little.

He slides the rescued stack my way. "And I know this isn't about me, but I want you to know I didn't mean—" He searches for the right words, brows knit. "I wasn't trying to—whatever it felt like. I should've gotten your attention with a 'hey' and some jazz hands like a normal person."

"Jazz hands would have been worse," I say, and the quip falls out before I can help it. "You in the doorway like a deranged mime? Please, no."

His smile makes a careful cameo, small and lopsided. "So you're saying I should not keep a white glove in my pocket for emergencies?"

I roll my eyes at him, dismissing his ridiculousness with a shake of my head.

We work. The quiet is different now—not awkward, per se, but full of things neither of us knows how to set down yet. I shove a fresh stick of staples into the stapler and watch the neat silver spine click into place. If only brains and feelings worked like office supplies. If only desire had a tray you could slide back in.

I'll pull you out when it's appropriate and file you away when it's not your time to play, thankyouverymuch.

If only.

"Hey," Leo says after a minute, gentler. "Can I ask a clarifying question that will not get me slapped?"

I side-eye him. "Proceed with caution."

"If I accidentally make you laugh again in the next five minutes, is that allowed? Or do I need to submit a request to HR for a sense-of-humor permit?"

I snort. This man. "You are HR's worst nightmare."

"Incorrect," he says. "I am HR's favorite problem. Big difference."

I hate how my mouth curves. I hate it and also I don't. "You can joke," I say, and then add the boundary I should've led with. "But not about this—the book and hip thing, I mean."

He nods, sober again. "No books or hips. Understood."

A knock raps the door frame. Dr. Johnson appears, eyebrows already communicating displeasure. "Is the copier free or are we all neglecting desk duties and hiding from students in here today?"

Leo slides sideways like a magician, revealing the machine. "All yours, Doc. We were just—" He chokes on any answer that could get either of us fired. "Stapling."

"Mm," Dr. Johnson says, which is tenured for 'I do not want to know.' He shoulders in with a stack of midterms and the room gets smaller—as if that's possible.

Leo brushes past me—careful, so careful, no touching—to the doorway. He pauses just outside Johnson's line of vision, tips his head, and winks.

He's mid-turn, about to exit the room, when the traitorous bitch in my brain, still apparently wearing a headset from the audiobook, decides to fling me under a bus.

"Leo," I say, voice low enough not to draw Dr. Johnson's attention.

He turns back, hopeful in a way that slices me and makes me warm all at once. "Yeah?"

"It wasn't—" My tongue trips. God, Tori. "I didn't slap you because I hated it."

Something like hunger flickers in his eyes, then he boxes it up so fast I doubt what I just saw. "Noted," he says softly. "But also, not the point. I won't touch you again unless you ask. That's the new rule."

New rule. I nod, trying the words on the inside of my mouth. "Okay."

He gives me one last look—a look that feels so much like longing, but might just be me projecting—and then he's gone. Dr. Johnson mutters about the copy machine's built-in stapler being jammed and I take unholy joy in fixing it in two seconds flat while he blinks like I performed witchcraft.

When he leaves, I sag against the counter and pick up my earbuds, twirling them around in my palm before placing them back into my ears. I click my audiobook back on for noise, then immediately swipe out of that app because *absolutely not*. Instead, I swap over to a cheerful podcast about a woman who rescues raccoons. The host's voice is bright and happy. She says 'babies' way too many times.

I stack the last quiz and straighten the edges again, even though they don't need straightening. My palm still tingles from the slap; my hip still remembers the heat of his hand. Shame and want take turns elbowing each other in my chest.

I think about the way Leo didn't make excuses. About how he stood there, hands open, and let me set the terms. About how he said my full name—Victoria—like I am a person he respects, not a hurdle he has to charm his way over.

I put the last stack in Dr. Patel's box and label it with a sticky note in my neat handwriting. Then I pick up the ziplock once again and press it to my cheek because it gives my body something to do while my brain recalculates.

I don't know what we are. Friends? More? I don't know that I'm allowed to want more. I only know that today, in a too-warm copy room smelling like hot paper and toner, a man—Leo Euler— touched my hip and my body reached back before my history could stop it—and then that same man apologized with his whole being and listened when I told him how to treat me.

New rule. I can work with rules. I like rules. Especially when people follow them. Even more so when people follow through on what they say they are going to do.

And I truly believe he's going to follow through on what he said. He won't touch me again unless I ask him to.

Outside, the pod is quiet. Thanksgiving break begins next week and students have already begun the trek home to visit family and friends, leaving us to our own devices. Fewer meetings, fewer interruptions, more time to complete daily tasks and prep work before finals at the beginning of December.

I savor the quiet days, especially since people in our office typi- cally means someone has a problem that needs to be solved. I have enough problems in my own life at the moment, thank you.

Like the separation agreement and affidavit being served to Chase by my attorney's office today. I do not foresee him responding to that anywhere near as calmly as Leo responded to my slapping him across the face.

So, yes. Chase is definitely considered a problem in my life.

And Leo... I'm still not entirely sure what he is, but a problem, he is not.

BACK AT MY DESK, I line up my pens like little soldiers and open a new email I don't need to open just to stare at the subject line until my pulse stops trying to stage dive out of my neck.

My fingers type before I overthink them into silence.

Subject: Copy room
Body:
For the record, I don't hate you.
New rule stands.
– T

I hover over send. This is nothing. This is air. This is also me handing him a match and telling him not to light anything on fire.

I hit send.

The reply lands thirty seconds later like he's been sitting there waiting with a defibrillator.

Subject: Re: Copy room
Body:
Received.
Rule: No touching unless asked.
Sub-rule (per HR's favorite problem):
No jazz hands.
Addendum: May request permission to make you laugh in non-hip-related contexts.
Optional Addendum: Can we agree that two negatives make a positive?
– L

A smile sneaks onto my mouth, uninvited, then pretends it's always lived there. I type back.

Subject: Re: Re: Copy room
Body:
Addendum approved.
Violation results in stapler-related consequences.
And no, don't test the double-negative theory—you'd end up squared and I'd still be negative.
– T

Before I can close the tab, his typing dot pops up again—like he's texting inside of email, which is illegal but also, apparently, on brand.

Subject: Re: Re: Re: Copy room
Body:
Noted. I respect the stapler.
Also... you okay? (You don't have to answer.)
P.S. For the record, you had me at acute angle of that slap.
– L

The corner of my lip betrays me, curving up. Acute angle. God help me.

Subject: Re: Re: Re: Re: Copy room
Body:
Working on it.
And don't get clever. That slap was 180° of justified.
– T

His last reply comes slower, like he's thinking too hard about it.

Subject: Re: Re: Re: Re: Re: Copy room
Body:
Fair. But if 180° is a straight line… maybe someday we find the curve again.

– L

I close the laptop before I melt into my chair. He's impossible. And infuriating. And exactly the kind of math-pun Don Juan who could make me blush just by mentioning geometry.

Once again I am reminded that my vagina is, no doubt, a ridiculously horny mathematician. How did the fuckboy become my personal brand of kryptonite?

I fish my phone out to text Skye and Alis because if anyone can metabolize secondhand embarrassment for sport, it's Skye, and Alis, because… well because I'm trying really hard not to leave her out of things.

Tori, 1:08 p.m.: Accidentally listened to porn in the copy room and then hip contact happened and I slapped Leo across the face.

Skye, 1:08 p.m.: LMFAOOOOO STOP IT! Also wdym by 'hip contact'??

Tori, 1:09 p.m.: Hip contact like, he touched my hip and I maybe kinda pressed my ass into his groin before I turned around and slapped him?

Skye, 1:09 p.m.: …

Skye, 1:09 p.m.: You did WHAT?

Skye, 1:09 p.m.: Do I need to bring emergency pastries? Like a croissant that whispers "you are insane and also so fkng hot"

> Tori, 1:09 p.m.: It was weird and the book was playing in my ear and … GAH. We established a new rule: No touching unless asked. He apologized. Like FOR REAL apologized.

Skye, 1:10 p.m.: See???? Unhinged yet respectful. Proud of him. Proud of you. Proud of your hip and your ass for trying to get. you. some.

Alis, 1:10 p.m.: I am so confused RN.

> Tori, 1:10 p.m.: I'm moving out.

Skye, 1:10 p.m.: Damn babe. That's super fast for just getting some hip action. Does Leo know ur a stage5 clinger?

Alis, 1:11 p.m.: Still confused.

Skye, 1:11 p.m.: also i'm naming a latte after this. The Copy Room. notes of toner, seduction and regret.

> Tori, 1:11 p.m.: absolutely not

Alis, 1:11 p.m.: ARE WE TALKING ABOUT LEO, LEO?! LIKE MY FIANCES BEST FRIEND, LEO?

Skye, 1:11 p.m.: too late it's printing on the menu LOVE YOU BYEEEEE

Alis, 1:12 p.m.: ONE OF YOU WHORES BETTER ANSWER ME.

I set the phone down, laughing because damn, it feels good to have not just one, but both of my best friends in the know about my life. Alis may feel confused right now, but she'll catch up.

The pod door is open, and footsteps drift down the hall. Dr. Wallace's voice filters in, low and precise, as if he's rehearsing lines before stepping on stage. He appears in the main doorway, holding a stack of papers balanced on the edge of a clipboard.

"Victoria," he says, tone overly formal. His gaze does a quick, literal up-and-down like he's scanning for injury to the upper half of my body that is not hidden behind the desk, then latches on to my face. "If you're planning to go to the supply closet later, I could... accompany you. Carry a box, in case it's heavy. I don't want you to... strain anything."

The words aren't oily, just factual, as if he's making a case for himself in bullet points. Still, they land with a thud, and my shoulders try not to climb into my ears. If I had to compare Dr. Wallace to a book character, he'd be Mr. Collins from *Pride and Prejudice*. Means well, but damn. The man is so awkward it hurts.

"I'm fine, but thank you," I say, polite and brisk, a smile neat enough to staple.

Behind him, Leo's office door opens. His timing is suspiciously perfect. He leans casually against the frame, holding up a slim folder like it's Exhibit A.

"Hey, Wallace," he calls across the pod, breezy. "Didn't you want those lecture notes from 2019? Found the whole set." He wiggles the folder. "In my office."

Wallace blinks, recalibrating. The offer of notes is apparently more compelling than my supply-closet muscles. "Ah. Yes. Thank you." He adjusts his glasses and makes a beeline for Leo's office instead.

The moment the door clicks shut behind them, I rub at my temple. Half gratitude, half exasperation.

Five minutes later, the pod is quiet again, my inbox halfway wrangled, when Leo's door clicks open once more. He strolls out, folderless this time, and without breaking stride, deposits a sheet of paper squarely on my desk like he's delivering campus mail. No eye contact, no pause—just a half-smile tucked into his cheek before he vanishes back into his office.

I glance down. A half sheet of printer paper, trimmed with scissors. Across the top, in his neat block caps:

INCIDENT REPORT: COPY ROOM
Date: [Today]
Reporting parties: T. Foster (hand of justice), L. Euler
(face, left cheek, now better than right)
Cause: Miscommunication + Audiobook Spiciness (Cate-
gory 5)
Injuries:
- Redness (cheek, L.); treated with ice + humility
- Ego bruise (V., mild); treated with apology, organiza-
tional assistance, smoulder
Corrective Action:
- New Rule implemented (No touch unless asked; see
Sec. 1(a))
- Jazz hands banned (Sec. 2)
- Consent stapled to office policy (Sec. 3)
Signatures:
L. E. _____________
V. F. ____________

I shouldn't grin at a fake, hand-written incident report delivered like contraband in a spy movie. But I do. I slide it under my
planner like a ridiculous secret I'm choosing to keep.

The afternoon continues on, slowly but peacefully. I answer
emails, fill out a room request for finals week. I order a box of the
good paper clips because no one else will. At some point, the sun
angles low enough to throw a pale bar of light across the carpet
from the window across the hall and the building fully settles into
that pre-break quiet I adore.

My phone buzzes again. A new text from an unknown
number with a link preview. My stomach drops before my brain

catches up—Chase? No. It's Jacob Sterling's office. The process server has confirmed delivery.

> Unknown, 3:47 p.m.: Separation agreement and affidavit: served.

I stare at the confirmation, watching my name and his name sit there beside the word *served* like it's just a verb and not the ground shifting under my feet. A small tremor moves through me that isn't panic, but not quite steadiness. It feels most like the after-sway when you've stepped off a boat.

I type back: *Received. Thank you.* Then turn my phone to 'do not disturb', lock it, and set it face down, because I'm not going to let my peace get hijacked by whatever reaction might be brewing in Moraine.

Across the pod, Leo's laugh carries—soft and short, the kind people let out when they're trying not to. I picture his cheek earlier today, still faintly pink, and the way he stood with his hands open, no excuses. The way he wrote "consent stapled to office policy" like a dork and a gentleman at the same time.

Today was supposed to be unbearable—the day Chase got served, the day my life tilted harder into paperwork and split assets and lawyers and divorce and all the ugly aftermath. And yet, somehow, between his terrible flirting and stupid math puns, Leo Euler managed to take my mind off the stress without even knowing he was doing it.

TWENTY-ONE
LEO

THANKSGIVING BREAK. The most wonderful time of the semester.

Students vanish and the campus goes quiet in a way that feels almost holy—no lines at the café, no one jamming the printer with a 200-page dissertation draft, no herd of freshmen clogging the stairwells. The break is too short for an intensive, too long for the university to grant faculty the entire week off, which means most professors take PTO or invent conferences in exotic locations so they can disappear until the following Monday. The campus looks like a ghost town.

But not for one Leopold Christopher Euler III.

Oh, you thought Leo was short for Leonardo? Leonard? Leocifer? That last one isn't technically a name, but one of my nannies disliked me enough to call me that when I was six. My mother thought it was charming. I did not.

As I was saying—Thanksgiving break is my favorite break of the year. Two whole days of undisturbed office work, where I can actually accomplish things instead of being ambushed by hallway questions or committee meetings. Then Wednesday with George and Linda. Thursday with Dexter—this year we'll add Alis, Sunny, Skye, Tori, and the whole Gilmore contingent for dinner. And Friday through Sunday? That's reserved for leftovers, alcohol, too many sports channels, and sleep. In years past, Dexter and George were the constants of that long weekend. This year, my weekend plans feel less certain.

Still, I'm determined to enjoy the silence while it lasts. I stroll into the office at 8:36 a.m., twirling my keys around a finger and whistling *Fly Me to the Moon.* Thirty-six minutes late, but when you're the only human in the building, who's keeping score?

Except... I'm not the only human in the building.

The pod lights are already on. Odd. I keep walking toward my office, mentally scrolling through my three-page to-do list, when I see them: Tori's handbag, her phone, a purple knit sweater draped over the back of her chair, and her laptop open and glowing faintly on her desk.

Strange. She said just last week that she and Skye were driving to spend the first part of the break with their parents before heading back Wednesday night for Thanksgiving dinner. So why are her things here?

I glance around the pod. Empty. No sign of her.

I shrug and retreat to my office. But twenty minutes later, with no sound from the open space, curiosity edges into worry. If her phone wasn't sitting on her desk, I'd text her. Instead, it resides between her bag and laptop like a witness to something I don't yet understand.

I push back from my desk and head into the hall. The women's bathroom is the logical guess. Maybe she's not feeling well. I knock, call her name. Nothing. Empty stalls, humming light, no Tori.

Next, outside. Her car is parked right in front, gleaming in the thin November sun. No Tori inside it. The benches out front are empty, too. The weather is mild, late autumn sunshine catching on the last stubborn leaves, but she's nowhere in sight.

I head back inside, check the other offices. All locked. All dark. The pod is still empty except for her things, sitting exactly where I saw them before.

There's only one place left. The copy room.

I knock softly and push the door open.

I expected to find Tori, earbuds in, humming over a stack of papers with the steady whir of machinery filling the room. What I find is the opposite: Tori on the floor, knees pulled tight to her chest, face buried in her arms.

"Hey," I say, stepping inside. "Tote?"

She huffs, raises her head just enough to glare. She looks... wrecked. Not crying-today wrecked, but the slow-burn kind of wrecked. Exhausted. Mad. The kind of mad that simmers behind your eyes when you've had no sleep and too much to think about. Two seconds away from murder.

"You okay?"

"I'm fine. Just go away." She drops her head back into her arms.

"You don't look fine."

"Fuck off, Leo."

"See, that's interesting. Those words communicate the exact *opposite* of fine."

Her head snaps up again, eyes blazing. "Why are you even here? It's Thanksgiving break, everyone's gone. I came here today so I wouldn't have to be around anyone. But of course, you're here. Because you're always here. Showing up to witness every fucking moment of misery and embarrassment life decides to toss my way. Like I can't catch a fucking break."

That... stings. I thought we were friends now. Flirty friends? Maybe, one day, more than friends? Her tone, though, makes me sound like a nuisance. An issue.

No, that can't be right. She's upset.

"You can talk to me, you know," I say carefully. "Or scream at me. Curse me out. Tell me why you hate the world. I told you, GBF. Full service. At your service."

Her brows rise, a thin slash of disbelief. "Full service, huh?"

"Anything your heart desires, milady." I throw in a wink, just to be insufferable.

"Can you drive to Moraine, knock some sense into my soon-to-be ex-husband, and get him to sign the separation agreement and affidavit agreeing to entry of divorce so I can finally move on with my goddamn life?" Her voice cracks with fury. "Because that —*that*—would be great."

I blink. That is... not what I was expecting.

"He's refusing?"

"Oh, he's more than refusing. He called me screaming, losing his shit, said he couldn't believe I hired an attorney without talking to him first. Which, sure, whatever. Expected."

Hm. Expected outcomes do not result in copy room hideouts.

"But, he's not why you're hiding in the copy room, is he?"

She's quiet for a second, her face re-buried in her arms, head shaking 'no.'

Then, she returns her emotionally spent and broken gaze to mine. "My father."

I still. She's never said much about her parents, except the throwaway mention of her plan to visit them this week.

"What about your father?"

She blows out a humorless laugh. "Not three minutes after I got off the phone with Chase, he called. Out of the blue. Haven't heard from him in months. And he didn't ask if I was okay. Didn't care. He called to tell me it's time to stop my 'little tantrum,' repent—yes, *repent*—and return home to the 'safety of my marriage.'"

"Safety?"

"Yep," she says, popping the 'p.' "Because apparently a man who punches holes in walls is *safe*." She scrubs a hand over her face, fury sparking hotter. "And when I tried to explain, he cut me off. Kept talking over me like nothing I could possibly say mattered. Told me Chase had already confessed his heartbreak and his failures, that he's in counseling now, that I'm the one destroying a covenant. Dad's solution? Go home. Cook dinner. Pray more. Pretend my life is fine."

Well, this explains why she decided not to visit her parents this week.

"That's..." I shake my head. "That's messed up."

"Believe me, I know. He spits out Bible verses, cherry-picks them to justify being cold and distant, and calls it leadership. Like he knows better or best or whatever because he's a man with a swinging dick between his legs, so us women better listen! We better obey! He's been doing it to my mom for forty years." Her laugh is sharp, her voice rising with each word. "And now he thinks I should *thank him* for teaching me the same lesson."

She slaps the floor on either side of her—no longer speaking, now she's shouting. "No! No, I will not listen and I will not obey and... JUST. NO!"

She's unraveling in front of me: tears forming, hands flailing. Her knees uncurl from her chest and she drops them into a crossed-pretzel position on the floor, gesturing wildly as she continues the rant, cataloguing every grotesque detail of the conversation with her father. Anger pours off her like steam, filling the room, saturating the air.

I let her go until I realize she's spiraling into the kind of rage that leaves you worse than when you started.

She pauses to take a breath, and that's my cue— "Do you want to get out of here?" I cut in.

She freezes, mid-rant, hands suspended in the air. "What?"

"Do you. Want to. Get out. Of here."

"Like... the copy room?"

"Well, yes. But also the building. The campus. Go do something exponentially more fun than folding yourself into misery on the floor.”

“We can’t just leave.”

I make a big show of glancing around. “You’re right. We’d get in so much trouble leaving the office when literally no one else is on campus. Absolutely criminal.”

Her eyes narrow, the faintest flicker of a smirk slipping through her anger.

“So, you coming or not?” I hold out my hand.

She stares at it for a beat, then sighs, slaps her palm into mine, and lets me pull her up. “Fine.”

“Good. Because you need a serious dose of Vitamin D.”

Her mouth drops open and she slaps my shoulder, hard. “Ugh. Pervert.” (At least she didn’t slap my face this time.)

“I meant sunshine.” I deadpan. “But honestly, you could use a solid dicking.”

The glare she aims my way is lethal.

“What? It’s medical advice. Builds bone density.”

She glares, but her lip betrays her, twitching like it might smirk. “Kick rocks, Leo.”

Now that’s an idea. I clap once. “Perfect. Let’s go hiking.”

The look of terror on her at the word ‘hiking’ is priceless.

“Relax,” I tell her, turning and strolling out of the copy room. “I’m not marching you up Everest. Just a short trail, trees, air, sunshine. It’s more of a walk. It’ll be fun. I promise.”

Tori follows, begrudgingly, muttering something about preferring a lobotomy while she packs up her laptop and gathers the rest of her belongings. But when I step out of my office, jacket on and truck keys in hand, she follows without argument.

Small victories.

BY THE TIME we swing into her apartment complex and I watch her step out of her car, I can see the fight has gone out of her shoulders. She still looks tired, but not curled-up-on-the-floor tired. She disappears inside while I wait in the parking lot, tapping my steering wheel in rhythm to nothing. When she comes back, she's traded her slacks for jeans and swapped her flats for sturdy shoes. The purple knit sweater stays, sleeves shoved to her elbows.

"You sure that's warm enough?" I ask when she climbs into the passenger seat of my truck.

"It's practically tropical compared to Moraine," she says, tugging at the hem. "Besides, this isn't a hike, it's a walk. Your words."

"True," I concede. "But it's a scenic walk. With incline."

"Then I'll just roll downhill when I get tired." She shuts the door, seatbelt snapping into place. "Problem solved."

Her sarcasm is adorable, and much preferred to the agony and rage that tinged her words just an hour ago. Less fury, more teasing. I'll take it.

We make one last stop on the way out of town—this one at my place. She goes quiet when I pull into the driveway of a small cottage-style house—the kind with a peaked roof, a modest front porch, and enough shrubs out front to look like I might actually care about landscaping.

"This is... your house?" she asks, climbing out slowly, like we are most certainly in the wrong place.

"Last I checked," I say, jogging up the front steps to unlock the front door.

"I guess I've always pictured you in an apartment," she shrugs. "Something more bachelor-pad-like, with bare walls, a futon, and maybe a sad fern you keep forgetting to water."

I snort. "That was my life for a while, yeah. Stephanie and I always lived in apartments. She could never settle on a house—every one we looked at had some flaw that made it unworthy. The kitchen wasn't big enough. The neighborhood wasn't polished enough. The paint color wasn't trendy enough. Nothing ever cleared her bar for perfection, so we just... stayed in limbo. Apartment after apartment, always temporary, never rooted."

"Sounds exhausting."

"Oh yes," I nod. "It was. After the divorce, I couldn't stand that feeling anymore. Everything else in my life was falling apart—my marriage, my routine, my sense of what the hell I was even doing. I needed something solid. Something I could point to and say, This is mine."

I open the door and step inside, motioning for her to follow. I spread my arms as if to say, ta-da!

"So I bought this place. It's not big, it's not flashy, but it's a house. Comfortable, manageable, and completely mine. No memories of anyone else. No leases or landlords. No shared walls with weird ass people I don't know. Just me deciding how it looks, how it feels, how it stands."

I gesture around the cozy living room: books stacked on built-in shelves, a real couch with real throw pillows, a guitar leaning against the corner. It's not flashy, but it's lived-in. Warm.

"Whatcha think?" I ask, studying her expression as she takes in my space. My home.

Tori nods, eyes softening. She gets it. Of course she does.

But does she like it? And why does that suddenly matter so much to me?

"I love it," she says, a warm, wide smile on her face.

She means it. She really does love it.

That's good. That's really, really good.

Then she huffs, a humorless sound. Her smile transforms from warm to wistful, happy to hollow. "I'm in the opposite situation. Trying to figure out how to force Chase to sell the house we bought together so I can afford to start fresh. Right now I feel—" She hesitates, then throws caution to the wind and opts for full vulnerability. "Homeless. Like I'm crashing on my best friend's couch. Even though I know that's not really what this is. Skye would fight me to the death if I ever called her generosity 'crashing.' I pay rent. I live there as a fully contributing roommate."

Her laugh is weak, but her eyes say the rest.

"I feel like I'm going backwards." She's wringing her hands together, no longer taking in the home around her but instead thinking of the home she's lost.

Shit.

"Tori," I say, taking a step closer. "May I touch you?"

She nods, still staring down at her hands. I lift a finger to her chin, tipping her face up so her gaze meets mine.

"Hi." I smile at her, hoping it'll help the light return to those beautiful hazel eyes.

"Hi," she whispers. This woman is so goddamn beautiful, so strong and brave and smart and funny. And also in so much pain. All I want to do is hold her together. To take it all away. But I know that's not how this works. I know that's not what she wants or needs.

She needs a friend. Someone who understands what she's going through and doesn't try to fix it for her. Someone who stands with her and reminds her that she's got this, everything is going to be okay, and that even when everything is falling apart both around and within her, it's okay.

It's okay because everything happens for a reason, and that reason is because she is meant to rise like a motherfucking phoenix.

She doesn't see it yet, but it's already happening.

I lean in and place a soft kiss on her forehead, then step away and walk to the kitchen to grab two bottles of water and some snacks from the pantry. I swipe an empty backpack from the coat closet by the front door and toss our sustenance inside, thankful I do not have to change since I'm already dressed in light hike-appropriate clothing since I didn't dress for anyone else to be in the office today.

"Alright, Tote. Here's the deal." I sling the backpack over my shoulder, locking eyes with my hiking companion before we exit the premises. "Today, you are not homeless. You're not a divorcee. You are hot, but you are not a hot mess. You're not anything except a woman in a purple sweater who's going to take a walk in the woods with a man. Deal?"

Her mouth quirks sideways, almost a smile. "Deal."

"Did that sound as weirdly creepy as I think it did?"

"I'm totally texting Skye so she knows where to find my body."

TWENTY-TWO

TORI

THE TRAIL SMELLS like sun-warmed pine and clean mountain air, which is frankly rude because my lungs keep letting go of stress I was planning to hold onto out of spite. Needles jostle under our boots. A jay laughs somewhere above us like it knows a secret—again, rude.

"You undersold this," I say, swatting a branch. "I was expecting more... walk... with trees."

Leo grins like a man who lives to be right. "You're welcome. It's one of my favorite spots. Scenic, quiet, excellent geology for punning."

"Please," I beg. "Don't."

"But my puns have so much sedimental value!"

"Oh my God." I shove his arm, laughing anyway.

"Come on, Tote," he teases. "You love my rock-solid sense of humor."

"I will throw myself off this incline."

"And I will calculate your trajectory, velocity, and force of impact," he fires back. "Physics, baby."

"You're insufferable."

"And yet..." he lifts an eyebrow, "here you are. With me. In the wilderness. Alone."

"Dude. You really do sound like a serial killer."

"Nah. Serial killers don't pack snacks." He pats the backpack. "Rookie mistake."

We fall into a rhythm: crunch, crunch, breath, flirtatious insult. Sunshine sifts through the branches in skinny gold bars, and the valley flashes between the trees every time the switchback turns. My sweater sleeves are shoved to my elbows by the second turn; by the third, the knot behind my breastbone starts to loosen. I'd planned to stew all day, to marinate in my righteous rage—Chase, my father, the whole flaming pile—but apparently the forest didn't get the memo.

Relax, it says. *Breathe*, the breeze beckons.

"Observe," Leo says in his best nature-documentary voice, pointing at a tree. "The majestic ponderosa pine, otherwise known as a giant air freshener."

"Okay, Attenborough."

His grin is easy. So is the silence that follows. Every few minutes he points out something—lichen on a rock, a woodpecker tattooing a trunk, the *green besideus* (seriously, he is such a dork), clouds stacking like meringue over the far ridge. It's... nice. Uncomplicated in a way my life is not.

ABOUT AN HOUR later we reach a flatter stretch.

Leo glances over. "How's the heart rate, Foster?"

"Elevated," I deadpan. "Due to your proximity."

He winks. "Acute observation."

"Stop."

"Can't. Rising slope. We're approaching a peak in this function."

I groan. "You're banned from math."

"Impossible. That's like telling a fish to stop calculating wave functions."

I snort so hard a bird complains and darts deeper into the trees.

By the time the trail opens onto a shoulder of rock with a clean view, my hairline is damp and my bad mood has retreated to a manageable simmer. The sky is that too-blue Colorado does better than anywhere else, and the pines below us look like someone combed the mountain with a green brush.

"Snack break," Leo announces, dropping the backpack by a sun-warmed boulder.

I climb onto the rock so I don't sit in dirt and immediately stretch out my hands, reaching for snacks like a hungry child. Leo hands me water and a granola bar like I'm his favorite cranky hiker. He doesn't crowd. Just leans against the boulder, forearms braced behind him, head tipped back like he's letting the sun find the parts of him that were too busy hiding beneath the trees.

For once, he's quiet.

"Thanks," I say, twisting my water bottle open.

Leo opens one eye, waiting for me to continue.

"For, you know." I make a vague gesture that means the whole day.

He nods like, yeah, he knows. A breeze moves through and lifts the hair at my nape. The quiet changes—stays easy, but deepens. Now he's lifted his head, looking out over the trees, jaw working like he's chewing something he isn't sure how to swallow.

"You don't have to say anything," I offer, because silence doesn't scare me the way it used to.

He huffs a laugh, small. "I kind of want to." He doesn't look at me when he starts. "I've never really told anyone the whole... thing."

Thing?

"Not like this. Dexter knows the headlines. George—" His voice tightens and then steadies. "George knows most of it. But."

Oh. Stephanie. I wait. The wind does a low hush through the pines, like the mountain decided to listen, too.

"We were young when we got married," he says. "Stupid young. Literally hadn't even graduated college, young. We didn't communicate. Or, I tried in the way I knew how and she... didn't. Not with words, anyway. Stephanie wanted what she saw in movies. Fireworks, grand gestures, the feeling of the first two months—forever. We were both still in school, then I was in grad school, then I did my PhD. Which is not exactly a fireworks factory. I thought she understood what it would take."

He shakes his head. "She knew I wanted to be a professor, but I never actually asked if she understood what that meant. And then, every time I buried myself in research or grading, she'd—" He searches for the word. "Withhold. Eye rolls. Sighs. Snide comments. Ask her parents for things instead of talking to me like we were adults building a life together."

His mouth twists. "We both worked. She was never a mooch. She's a hard worker. So smart. So fucking talented. I swear, that woman could run circles around me when it came to business sense, investing, tech—she's just one of those natural-born geniuses, you know?"

He looks over at me and I nod. I know the type.

"I think that's a lot of what drew me to her. I mean, she's beautiful, yeah. But it was everything else, too. And I knew if I didn't marry her, she'd wake up one morning and some other guy with better looks and better brains and deeper pockets would swoop in and take her away from me. So, after we'd been together for only six months, I asked George and Linda for their blessing. I proposed, she said yes, and we eloped."

I let out a small laugh at the absurdity of it all. The whirlwind romance is very on brand for him. "You asked for their blessing, but then eloped?"

"Yep," he nods, that adorable smile stretching wide across his face.

"And how did they feel about that?"

Leo leans in closer and says, conspiratorially, "They already knew."

I gasp, and he laughs at my shock.

"I knew Stephanie would be swept up in the moment and want to do something crazy, so when I asked for their blessing I went ahead and asked if they would be okay with us eloping and having a reception for family and friends afterward. They actually praised me for knowing their daughter so well, and appreciated my forethought."

"Wow. That's just... wow."

"Yep," he nods. "So we eloped, I moved out of the frat house and into her apartment the next day, and a few weeks later we had a reception."

As soon as he says the word "apartment," Leo's laughter subsides, his smile weakens. "We always lived in apartments because no house was perfect enough. The backsplash was wrong. The neighborhood was wrong. The paint, the porch, the... whatever. Nothing cleared the bar in her head, so we lived in limbo. I told you that part."

"You did," I say softly.

"She would get so angry when her parents supported me. If they congratulated me on passing comps, she heard it as a criticism of her—she wasn't doing enough, reaching high enough, whatever. If anyone praised something I did, she'd find a way to make the day about everything she wasn't getting."

He's not cruel when he says it; he's tired. Honest. "She's the middle kid. Always felt overlooked. Her parents are good people—*great* people. They love her. I loved her."

He swallows. "Was I great at loving her? I don't know. I thought I was... okay at it. But I never quite met her standard. And I didn't realize until it was too late that her standard was 'make me your sole focus, all the time.'"

Leo's staring out over the valley, arms crossed over his chest. I slide my palm along his shoulder and offer a gentle squeeze. "You know that's an impossible standard to live up to, right?"

He nods. Of course he knows.

That nod lands in my chest and sits there, humming. My marriage wasn't quite the same shape, but the ache of being measured against a rulebook you can't see? Playing a game you'll never win? Yeah. That ache is familiar.

I slide my hand across his shoulder, over his neck and to the other side, lightly dragging my nails back and forth. He doesn't shrug me off or ask me to stop, doesn't show any signs of discomfort or tensing, so I don't stop.

"She got tired of being unsatisfied. Aaron Lassen, her high school boyfriend, popped up on her social media as a suggested friend. They reconnected, started sending secret messages back and forth. And then a few months later she left a note. And she was just... gone."

He draws in a breath like it still hurts to use his ribs. I pause my caresses, a sudden stab of guilt at the familiarity of how I left Chase.

No notice. Just a note, and I was gone. *The circumstances were different.*

"Please don't stop doing that," Leo whispers. So I resume.

"George called about a week later. Asked me to come over. I walked in, and Stephanie was at the dining room table, crying. George looked at me, then at her, and said"—he slips into an impression of an older man that's so good it makes my throat sting —"*You're gonna look your husband in the face and tell him exactly the kind of shit you've been doing behind his back. And so help me God, Stephanie Marie, if you lie, I will never speak to you again.*"

I close my eyes for half a second. I can see it, even though I've never met either of these people in person. George at that table, steady as a mountain. Stephanie, small, in a chair she's sat in since she was a teenager.

"And she told me," Leo says. "All of it. About how unhappy she'd been. About reconnecting with him. About when it changed from talking to meeting up for coffee to fucking behind my back."

He pauses, fist to his brow, eyes closed. "Then she looked me dead in the eye and said, 'I love Aaron. And I want a divorce.'" He laughs once, humorless. "That was the only direct sentence she gave me in who knows how many years."

I don't realize I've moved until the inside of my thigh brushes the heat of his torso and my hand is no longer simply grazing his shoulders. I've spun him toward me, both arms now wound around his neck, pulling him into my body before I can think better of it.

He stands there, frozen, like he's trying to process why I've suddenly turned into a koala. But when I whisper, "I'm so, so sorry," he understands what kind of sorry it is—the deep kind, not the cheap kind—and he steps into my embrace, arms wrapping tightly around me.

We stay that way, wordless, for a long minute. His hand moves slow and steady up and down my back; I press my face into the warm curve of his neck. Hugging my girlfriends is one thing, but being held like this—by him—feels entirely different.

He's warm. And safe.

He makes me laugh. He understands my pain in a way nobody else does right now. Leo sees me because he's lived this—walked through the fire, the chaos, the pain, and survived it. And without me even asking, he's helping me survive it, too. Not because he wants anything. Just because that's who he is.

"Truly, I'm sorry," I whisper again into his neck. The kind of sorry that means I'll sit in the ruins with you, even if I can't rebuild them. "And I'm so proud of you."

He nods. "Thank you." He doesn't let go, but he does ease back enough to look me in the eye. He's standing between my knees now, his hands sliding from my back, down my thighs, until they rest on my knees. My palms settle against his chest like they've been waiting there.

"That's the greatest hits," he says with a shrug. "Divorce paperwork. A house. A series of terrible choices on my part that added up to... a lot of noise. Hookups, mostly." His smile is crooked, not quite reaching his eyes. "You've met the ghost of that man."

"I've met you," I say. Simple. True.

His smile softens. It's real.

This. This moment is real.

I can feel his heartbeat under my palm. A whisper of cotton under my fingers. I trace up, slowly—his sternum, collarbone, the angle of his jaw. His not-quite-beard is rough along his jawline, and my thumb catches on the scruff in a way that makes my stomach drop like a ride just started.

His eyes flick to my mouth, then back to my eyes, and he doesn't move an inch. Not until I do.

I lean in, carefully, gently, pressing my lips to his. It's just a peck. A question. But I linger, not pulling back. Not just yet. He exhales against my lips and the sound goes straight through me.

I break the kiss for a breath, close enough to feel him smile. "Is this okay?" I whisper, because, rules.

His hands slide up and tighten on my hips, just enough to answer the question twice. "This is more than fucking okay."

He pulls me in and the kiss goes from sweet to something that feels like stepping into warm water: deeper, all-encompassing, inevitable. He tastes like spearmint and granola and something that is just—him. I slide closer and he presses his body into me, fitting himself between my knees like his body has known this geometry longer than his brain. My fingers curl at the back of his neck. His thumb settles at my waist, not possessive—anchored. I'm very aware of the incline, of the way my sweater has gone too warm, of the small, embarrassing noise I make when he tilts his head and changes the angle.

This kiss doesn't turn frantic. It doesn't need to. It's a steady climb, an easy yes. There's the slow press of our bodies, the rhythm of two people figuring out exactly how they like to fit, a barely-there grind that pulls a swear out of him against my mouth and a shiver out of me that has nothing to do with the wind.

When I finally ease back, my breath is wrecked in the best way, and his forehead finds mine like we're both surprised the physics of standing still still apply. His eyes are dark and soft at the same time, and for a heartbeat I forget why anything ever felt complicated.

He brushes his nose against mine and I have to fight not to lean in and claim his lips once more.

"I get that your life is complicated right now," he says, low. "I'm not expecting you to want more. Or less. Or to even understand why you wanted to kiss me." His mouth curves, something tender and wrecking. "But, Jesus, Tori, I'm damn glad you did. If for no other reason than because you're so fucking beautiful and you deserve to be kissed."

My laugh comes out shaky, like my insides are still readjusting to gravity. "That was... a lot of words to say you liked it."

"I did," he says, solemn as a vow. "Extensively."

"Extensively is not a feeling," I say, pushing him back a step.

"It is in calculus." He grins. "We just integrated for a while."

I palm my forehead. "Oh my God."

"Don't worry," he adds, mock-serious. "We stayed within bounds."

I drop my head back and groan at the sky. "You promised no math."

"I promised no jazz hands," he says. "Math is a free variable."

"You're lucky I'm too blissed out to push you off this mountain."

He glances down the slope, then back up at me. "Based on current slope and friction coefficients, I'd survive. But I'd be so, so hurt."

I reach out and snag the front of his shirt, pulling him back in between my legs—and he shuts up exactly the way I want him to. We kiss again—one more slow drift that feels steady, uncomplicated, and warm.

When we pull apart, he doesn't apologize and neither do I. We just breathe the same air for a second, smiling like stupid teenagers.

"Ready?" he asks, grabbing the backpack off the ground and tossing it back over one shoulder.

"For the walk or for the part where I pretend none of that just happened and you pretend you're not smug about it?"

"False dichotomy," he says, smug.

I nudge his shoulder. "Help me down, nerd."

"New rule," he murmurs, palms firm and careful at my hips as he eases me off the rock, setting me steady on my feet. "No touching... unless asked."

"Smart man," I say, even as my fingers hold his a second longer than strictly necessary.

We repack the crinkled wrappers and empty bottles—"Leave no trace," he says—then start the descent. The trail feels different now. Same trees, same sky, but like we stepped through a door. We don't talk about it. We don't have to. He points out a squirrel with delusions of grandeur; I tell him his socks don't match. We trip into the kind of ease you don't get often, and when we reach the truck, I'm flushed for a whole new set of reasons.

He opens the passenger door and waits, hand on the frame like chivalry accidentally grew some scruff and a totally nerdy, yet adorable, sense of humor.

"Thanks for the walk," I say, climbing in.

"Anytime," he says, and means it.

As he rounds the hood, I catch my reflection in the side mirror —hair wild, cheeks pink, a smile that didn't have to ask permission to be here.

Complicated? Totally. Over? Not even close.

But when it comes to my sexual chemistry with Leo Euler, there's no denying that the math checks out:

something about me + something about him + fresh air + a purple sweater + a sun-warmed boulder + his sexy as hell smile = a variable I'm not afraid to solve for.

... and I just punnuendo'd myself. Awesome.

TWENTY-THREE
LEO

I BARELY GET my coat hung before Sunny comes barreling past me in socks, hair flying like she's got a wind machine blowing right at her. Otis thunders after her, tail wagging hard enough to rattle the picture frames, tongue flopping out of his mouth in pure joy. That Aussie always wins, but Sunny never accepts defeat without a rematch. She shrieks with laughter and darts around the corner, Otis hot on her trail.

God, I love it here. Dexter's house smells like roasted turkey and cinnamon, and the noise—I don't believe I could hear myself think if I tried. From what I gather, there are too many hands in the one kitchen, the men are most likely in the den watching football, and my favorite almost-eleven-year-old will sprint back around that corner in three... two...

"Gotcha!" I grab Sunny and launch her over my shoulder right as she makes the turn. Feet kicking and arms flailing, she screams, "Uncle Leo! He'll win! You're letting him win!" as we both watch Otis sail past us, down the hall, and leap into the giant bean bag strategically posted inside the open bonus room door.

I refuse to let down my captive, carrying her through the living room and into the kitchen where I know I'll find a gaggle of women talking over each other and cooking all my favorite foods.

"Absolutely not!" Skye.

"You're insane," Tori fires back.

Alis's laugh cuts through both of them. "You're both wrong."

"Daddy's home," I announce, just to see if anyone's paying attention.

The women don't hear a word I've said, but they instantly stop their bickering when Sunny lands a solid punch to my back, a knee to my stomach, and yells, "You're not my dad! Dexter is my dad, you dummy!"

I drop the little shit. Because, obviously.

"What did you just say?" Alis whispers, eyes watering and face so lit up with happiness I could puke.

Please. Nobody rush to help or even notice the man doubled over and out of breath from being assaulted by the four-foot-ten-inch tyrant.

Dex enters the kitchen and claps a hand on my shoulder, not reading the room whatsoever. "Why is everyone so quiet?" he asks, looking from me, to Alis, then Sunny, and back to Alis.

"And why are you crying, love?" He can see that her tears are not from sadness, so he doesn't rush to comfort her. Instead, he wraps an arm around Sunny's shoulders and ruffles her hair, leaning down to whisper, "You know she's staring at you, right?"

Sunny looks up at him and nods. "Yeah. I know. I said the dad thing."

"Ah," Dexter acknowledges, not at all surprised by this revelation—the complete opposite of Alis. "I thought we were going to talk about that as a family before you started saying it in front of people?"

Huffing out a breath, Sunny rolls her eyes before gesturing toward me. "That was the plan, until this loser walked in the kitchen and said, 'Daddy's home' like some gross old mall Santa and, I don't know. It just slipped out."

"Slipped out," Dexter laughs.

"Someone had to put him in his place," she shrugs. "Especially after he made me lose my race. Again."

Before I can fire back, Alis's parents appear from the direction of the den like reinforcements. Julia spreads her arms, all warmth, perfume, and holiday cheer.

"Leo, darling, you made it!"

Finally. The recognition I deserve.

"Mama Gilmore," I throw my arms wide and step into her embrace. "At last! Someone in this house appreciates me."

"Don't encourage him," Tori groans.

"Too late," Skye adds.

Jim chuckles and pushes his way through the mess of bodies crowding the kitchen, heading straight for the turkey and muttering something about quality control.

And just like that, the chaos resumes. The kitchen fills with clatter and chatter, Skye and Tori bicker over who's in charge of the potatoes, Alis wields her dishtowel like a weapon, Sunny and Otis zoom past every few minutes—I still don't understand how that girl hasn't broken an arm, or her neck, running through this house—and Dexter makes the heroic save of the stuffing tray before it burns.

I slide into the rhythm of it, grabbing a pack of dinner rolls from the counter and tearing the plastic with my thumb. The kitchen's packed shoulder-to-shoulder, so I start arranging the rolls into a basket, making them look more presentable than "straight from the bag."

I claim counter space beside Tori, who's furiously whisking like the fate of Thanksgiving depends on her wrist strength.

"Need a spotter?" I ask, nudging a roll into place like it's fine art.

She side-eyes me, whisk still flying. "You'll just start punning about peaks and slopes again."

"True." I dip closer, lowering my voice so only she can hear.

"But honestly? I'd rather watch you whisk than listen to Skye butcher another O-Town lyric."

Her lips twitch, betraying the laugh she's trying to bury. "Careful, Euler. You're dangerously close to charming."

I hold up the basket like I've performed a miracle. "Please. These rolls look homemade. I deserve a medal."

She glances over, unimpressed. "You opened a bag."

"And elevated the presentation." I grin. "That's called flair, Foster."

"As Sunny would say, 'delulu is your solulu.'" She bumps my hip with hers, still whisking. "But sure. Keep telling yourself you contributed."

The contact is brief. Just a bump. Just a tease. But the heat lingers like she left a match pressed to my side.

I let the silence stretch, lean in just enough for my shoulder to brush hers as I glance into the bowl. "You always whisk this hard, or is today special?"

She snorts, catching the innuendo immediately. "It's mashed potatoes, Leo."

"I'm just saying..." My grin is shameless. "If there were an Olympic category for wrist stamina—"

"Stop." Her cheeks flush, but she's smiling now, teeth biting into her bottom lip like she can hold back the laugh.

I set the basket down, fingers tapping against the handle of the whisk instead, deliberately grazing hers. "Tell me to go and I will."

She doesn't tell me to go. Instead, her hand stills for half a beat, then she keeps whisking, slower this time. Her shoulder brushes mine again, maybe by accident, maybe not.

"Fine," she mutters. "You can stay. Quietly."

"Quietly is not my strong suit." I pitch my voice lower, leaning close enough that her brunette waves graze my jaw. "But I'll make an exception for you."

Her breath catches, just enough for me to notice. She doesn't move away.

"Don't read into this," she says, eyes fixed on the bowl.

"Oh, I'm reading into everything."

Her laugh comes out shaky, and when she finally risks a glance at me, it's loaded—she knows exactly what we're doing—and exactly how much trouble we're both in.

"Scootch, hootch." Skye wedges in between us, obliterating the moment.

"You forgot the cheese!" she whines, her tone drenched in accusation.

Tori grabs the bowl of potatoes and spins away from Skye, keeping it just out of reach. "Don't you fuck with my potatoes, woman!"

I knew they were arguing about the potatoes earlier, but I didn't realize the argument had become so heated.

"You know," Dexter says, stepping up beside me while we watch two grown-ass women engrossed in a game of keep-away, "they could have just made two different types of mashed potatoes."

I nod in agreement. "Sound logic. But, women."

The crack of the dishtowel sounds a millisecond before my left asscheek lights on fire. "The fuck?!" I spin just in time to see Alis locked and loaded to deliver another lashing to my backside.

"Women? Are you kidding me right now?" She pops the towel once more but misses, and before she can try again I push Dexter in front of me like a shield. He's too busy laughing to offer any real assistance or come to my defense, so I leave him to handle his fiancée, twisting and ducking my way through women and bowls and Julia pulling a pie out of the oven before I finally make it into the front hall.

Am I in the clear? Of course not. Because right as I think I've avoided all possible collisions I hear a high-pitched squeal, a bark, and then I'm airborne—tumbling sideways through the open bonus room door in a tangle of fur and claws and screaming eleven-year-old.

And thank fuck for this giant bean bag.

DINNER IS DONE, the last of the pie plates scraped clean, the kitchen a battlefield of dirty dishes and half-empty wine glasses. Inside, the noise keeps rolling—football commentary, women laughing over coffee, Sunny and Otis still tearing through the halls like caffeinated maniacs.

Isn't the tryptophan supposed to knock that kid out at some point?

Out here on the back porch, it's quiet.

Cold air bites at my cheeks, sharp with pine and woodsmoke from a neighbor's chimney. Dexter sets two heavy tumblers and a bottle of whiskey on the porch rail, then fishes two cigars from his shirt pocket and offers me the matchbook.

"You want the first light?" he asks.

I shake my head. "Nah. You're the host."

He grins, tucks a cigar between his lips, and strikes the match. The flame flares, then dims as he pulls. I light mine and wait until the end glows. The first draw is familiar—smoke and burn, a ritual. The whiskey chases it down, smooth enough to make me sigh.

For a while we stand shoulder to shoulder, saying nothing, watching our breath curl into the dark.

"How's George?" Dexter finally asks, voice careful but steady.

I keep my eyes on the tree line. "He's... hanging in there. Some days are worse than others. But he's still George. Still making everyone laugh, still giving the nurses hell."

Dexter's mouth lifts. "Sounds about right."

"Linda's doing her best," I add. "She's strong. Stronger than me most days."

Dexter nods, takes another drag. "I can only imagine."

We sip in silence again. The night is heavy but not suffocating.

I let the whiskey burn its way down, loosening knots of grief, little by little.

Dexter breaks it next. "I hate to ask, but... I know you still care about her. How's Stephanie handling everything?"

I exhale smoke and watch it vanish into the dark. "I haven't spoken to her. Not really. But I know she's at her parents' every day that I'm not. So, yeah. She's there, doing what she can."

He nods once, slow. A man of few words, like that was all he needed to know. He doesn't push further.

From inside, laughter spills through the glass—Tori's laugh, sharp and bright, rising above the rest. I turn, catch sight of her through the window. She really is so goddamn beautiful. Her head tipped to the side, hands covering her face, laughing hysterically while Skye gestures wildly about who knows what. I love seeing her happy.

The sound cuts through my heaviness like a blade, unraveling more knots in my chest, warming me more than the whiskey. I don't want to, but I do—I picture what it might be like to let her in. Really let her in.

"So. What's that all about?" Dexter tilts his glass, eyes narrowing as he studies me.

I blink. "What—"

"I saw you in the kitchen. Then you sat next to her at dinner. And don't think I didn't notice the two of you sneaking looks at each other the whole damn meal."

I huff a laugh, low, more exhale than sound. "That obvious, huh?"

"Obvious enough," he says, grinning. "Alis didn't catch it—or at least, I don't think so—but I did. And I'm asking."

I don't answer right away. My thumb taps the glass, restless. I think of her shoulder brushing mine in the kitchen, the way her hair grazed my jaw when she leaned close, how the world shrank down to the two of us on that trail.

"It's... complicated," I say finally, voice rough. "But I can't seem to stop looking at her."

Dexter takes another pull from his cigar, exhales slowly. His other hand rests easy on the tumbler on the rail. When he turns back, his face is full of concern.

"Does she know? About Stephanie?"

I nod. "Yeah. She knows."

"All of it?"

I take another sip of whiskey before answering. "Strangely, yes. I'd say she knows more than you."

"Damn." He laughs, shaking his head. "And here I thought I was your shoulder to cry on."

"Fuck off," I mutter, landing a playful punch to his shoulder.

He chuckles, but when it fades, his expression sharpens. "But do you know?"

That pulls me up short. "What do you mean?"

"I mean, sure, you've told her everything. But has she done the same with you? Has she let you in the same way?"

It's a fair question, but I still feel myself bristling. Of course he's not prying—this is Dex, he'd never come at me sideways—but still. My instinct is to guard her. To protect what's hers to share.

"I don't fucking know, man," I snap before I can reel it in. "It's not like we're dating. She's still married, for Christ's sake."

"Whoa, brother." Dexter holds up both hands, the picture of surrender. "I wasn't trying to pry or make assumptions. I was asking because I care about you. If you decide to pursue something with her, I want to make sure you're not the only one cutting yourself wide open."

I drag my hands through my hair, tug hard, then drop them. "I know. And you're right." My voice is quieter now, the fight gone. I press the heel of my hand to my brow, take a breath. "My head's everywhere. George, work, Stephanie's random shit—and then Tori bulldozes in like the most perfect temptation I've ever seen, right there in front of me, every damn day."

I let out a laugh, half amusement, half exasperation. "In one day—hell, one hour—I'll feel grief, annoyance, happiness, contentment, and more turned on than I've been in years. And those last three? Entirely because of her." I gesture toward the dining room window, where she's still laughing with Alis and Skye.

"Do you know how much of a mind fuck that is? When all I've felt for more than three years now is empty?"

Dexter doesn't answer right away. He just nods, slow, steady. He knows. He's seen it—watched me burn down into someone angry and bitter and broken. Watched me try to claw my way back.

"And how's that working out for you?"

"What?"

"Feelings," he says, hiding a smirk behind the lip of his glass.

TWENTY-FOUR

TORI

FINALS WEEK IS HELL. It's the week before Christmas break, students are feral, professors are cranky, and the copy machine is on its third nervous breakdown of the morning. The room smells like scorched toner and hot plastic, the kind of air that roughs up your throat. Someone left a half full coffee mug cooling into bitterness beside the paper cutter. I am one jammed paper tray away from committing a felony.

And to top it off? I've spent every day this week proctoring exams, babysitting grown ass adults with graphing calculators, and running errands for Dr. Johnson like I'm his personal assistant instead of the faculty secretary for this entire pod.

So yeah. I'm over this week. It's Thursday, but it should be Friday.

I'm once again in the copy room, feeding a thirty-page exam into the machine, when I feel him enter.

Leo Euler doesn't knock. He doesn't clear his throat. He doesn't even pretend to give me warning. He just shuts the door, locks it (why though?), and suddenly the room feels about three sizes smaller. The lock clicks like a period at the end of a sentence I didn't agree to. My shoulders clock his proximity before my brain does—skin prickling, heat sliding between my shoulder blades (and thighs, no lies), pulse ticking in the soft spot under my jaw.

His palms land on either side of me, bracketing me against the copier, heat rolling off him like I somehow forgot what it feels like to be near him.

"Good morning, Tote," he growls into my ear, voice low and smug and entirely too aware of itself.

I close my eyes. Inhale. His cologne is spice, pine, and something darker, and it's not fair. I can't remember the last time a scent has pulled me under like this—dragged me straight back to that trail, to that kiss, to the Thanksgiving kitchen where he leaned too close and we shared stolen glances like foreplay. Sun on my eyelids. His mouth opening against mine. The stupid, perfect sound he made when I pulled him closer. It's all there, tucked behind my ribs like contraband.

I exhale, praying my voice doesn't crack. "Dr. Euler. Can I help you with something?"

He chuckles, soft and lethal. And, because the universe hates me, my nipples pebble against my satin blouse like I'm starring in an HR complaint. Thin lace bra = zero protection. Fantastic. Truly an inspired day to wear fabric with the structural integrity of a dandelion.

Nope. Absolutely not. I swat his hand and circle to the other side of the machine to gather Dr. Johnson's copies.

"If there's nothing you need, I don't know why you're in here. Don't you have exams to prep? Papers to grade? Other people to irritate?"

He shrugs. Completely unconcerned. "Probably. But this seemed more fun."

Cocky bastard. Sweet bastard. Fuck-hot bastard. *DAMMIT, TORI.*

I reach for the stapler, too fast, the copies in my hand knocking it straight to the floor. Perfect. Excellent. Ten out of ten execution.

Leo crouches, scoops it up, but instead of handing it back like a civilized adult, he presses it against his chest.

I reach for it, but he doesn't move. Suddenly I'm not grabbing a stapler, I'm grabbing his hand, holding a stapler, against his chest. His heart is right there under my fingers, steady and solid, and then he steps closer.

The filing cabinet presses into my back. No escape. Not that I want one.

I can barely breathe. Is he going to kiss me? Do I want him to kiss me? That's a stupid question.

He doesn't kiss me. Instead, that infuriating, adorable, oh-so-kissable half smile crests his face, and then stupid, stupid words fall from his lips.

"You always this clumsy with your variables," he says, voice like silk, "or am I just the X you can't solve for?"

Sweet Jesus. I cannot with him. "I don't do equations with unreliable inputs."

"Then let's simplify." His grin sharpens. "No distractions. Just you, me, and some hands-on calculus."

"When are you going to realize that this isn't calculus."

"It is now." His nose traces my jaw, deliberate, slow. When he reaches my ear, he whispers, "Because Tote... I'm about to find every curve on your graph."

And I—snort. I actually, fucking, snort. The sound is undignified and exactly what I need—like popping a balloon in a too-warm room.

"You're ridiculous."

"Don't worry." He tips his head, lips close enough to graze. "I'll start slow. Run a derivative. See where the slope's steepest."

"Oh my God." My laugh bubbles up, half mortification, half arousal. "You're so bad at this." But also, like, why is this so fucking hot?

"Maybe. But I'm converging. And unless you want this function to go undefined—you might want to stop looking at me like that."

"Like what?" I whisper.

"Like you want a little chaos."

"Fat chance."

But he doesn't back off. His chest brushes mine. His eyes burn into me. Every nerve ending in my body screams Yes. God, yes.

"You know what I think?" he murmurs.

"What?" My voice barely makes it out.

"I think what you really want is some nonlinear dynamics."

NOPE. STOP THAT. STOP THAT RIGHT NOW.

Not today, horny mathemetician!

I duck, shove past him, and yank the door open before I can make the worst decision of my life. Thank God for push locks that pop open when you turn the handle.

The office air blasts my face, and for two seconds, it almost works to calm my racing pulse.

I don't turn back. I don't need to. I know exactly what he looks like right now—smirk cocked, smug as hell, knowing full well I'm not immune to him. He's probably watching me walk away, adjusting the start of an erection in his slacks—good God, woman, don't think about that.

"Get back to work, Professor!" I call, chin high, even as my pulse tries to punch out of my throat.

My legs are jelly and my spine is steel; apparently both things can be true. I march because marching feels like backbone, and backbone is the only thing I'm willing to show him right now.

I grab my phone off my desk as I pass, clutching it like a lifeline, and march straight toward Dr. Johnson's class with the stack of exams balanced like an offering. He never asked me to proctor—I'm fairly certain he's scheduled one of his grad students for this one—but I suddenly find myself in need of a morning activity. I need the walk. I need the air. I need the space.

Because the truth is, Leo is not the problem. I am.

And I want him. Like, right now.

I TELL myself I'm professional and composed and that the fact I flushed halfway to my ears is just the price of being a functioning adult. I tell myself this as I walk straight out of the pod, phone in one hand and thirty exams in the other.

The hallway hums with fluorescent light and sneaker squeaks. A student laughs too loudly for 9 a.m. and a passing professor shushes him. It's finals week, after all, and every one of the classrooms in this building is filled with testing students. The building exhales heat in uneven bursts, old radiators clanking like they're in a fight with winter.

I pass Dr. Wallace's open classroom door—he's teaching Intro to Differential Equations this semester, which is quieter than everything else on campus, probably because half the students are asleep. When I nod, he nods back in that literal, slightly panicked way he always does, like he's not sure how humans work. Poor, awkward turtle of a man. I keep walking.

Dr. Johnson's room is a tiny shoebox of polyester and lecture chairs with fold-down desks. His grad student looks hung over and desperately in need of sleep, and is halfway out the door before I even finish saying, "I've got this."

The students file in—hoodies up, earbuds tucked away, faces set like they're heading into battle… most of them unarmed. I stand at the front, drop the stack of exams on the desk, and start passing them out myself because otherwise they'll end up crumpled and coffee-stained before the first page is even read. Once everyone has a packet, I lay down the rules in my dry, non-negotiable voice, then settle at the little wooden desk in the corner like an executioner waiting for heads to roll.

I plant the proctor stare—the one that says 'I can spot a hidden phone from orbit and I will end you with a whisper.' It works. Mostly. Maybe. Probably not.

It's a strange kind of silence, the hush that settles once twenty-something undergrads have an exam in front of them. Not reverent silence, not focused silence—more like the quiet hum of collective dread. Papers rustle, pencils scratch, someone clicks a mechanical one like it's a fidget spinner. *Good lord that clicking is annoying.*

The kid in the front row chews on the end of his hoodie string. *Gross.* Another keeps tapping her sneaker against the tile like Morse code. I wonder if she's communicating anything. Like she's an undercover spy, sent to Middle Peak University by some black ops organization to communicate secret messages to Russia through Dr. Johnson's Linear Algebra II finals.

I huff a laugh at the absurdity of my thoughts, trying my best not to draw attention to myself. I cross my legs and pretend to check my phone, but really, I'm people-watching. Exams bring out the weirdest survival instincts. One girl has three sharpened pencils lined up like weapons. A guy in the back pulled out a bag of baby carrots, crunching away with his mouth open—*again, gross*—not a care in the world for the noise he's making. I half expect someone to start stress-knitting.

But no matter how interesting a distraction these students prove to be—despite the very reason I came in here in the first place—my brain drifts straight back to Leo.

Leo, with his smug growl in the copy room.

Leo, with his mouth so close to my ear I nearly lost my balance.

Leo, with his cocky, ridiculous, infuriating math puns that shouldn't make me laugh but do, and his body heat pressed against mine until I couldn't tell if I wanted to strangle him or climb him like a freaking tree.

I snap my attention back to the exam room. *Jesus, Tori. Focus.* You're here because you needed space. You volunteered to proctor this exam so you wouldn't be trapped in the office with him. So you wouldn't risk finding another excuse to knock staplers with that numbers wrangler in the copy room.

Knock staplers? Numbers wrangler? What the hell is wrong with me? My brain is writing cowboy fanfic while my body's supposed to be a hall monitor. Fire me. Someone fire me.

One student raises his hand. "Can we use graphing calculators?"

I point to the exam packet. "Rule three. It's right there, in bold."

He glances down, sheepish, then nods. They always ask questions they could answer themselves if they just looked. Maybe it's nerves. Maybe it's the belief that exceptions are always negotiable. Either way, it's irritating.

I settle back into my chair, cross my arms, and stare at the clock. Only ten minutes down. Nearly two hours to go.

Super. Love this for me.

My mind drifts again, this time to the trail, the boulder, to Leo's mouth curving into a smile and saying *This is more than fucking okay* right before he kissed me back. I can still feel the pressure of his hands on my hips, the way his voice went soft when he told me he wasn't expecting more but was damn glad I kissed him.

A pencil snaps in the front row, and I jolt. The kid mutters a curse and digs around in his bag for a backup. I fish a spare from the desk I've occupied, stand, and walk it over. His hand shakes when he takes it.

I remember being nineteen and convinced one broken pencil could ruin my whole life.

"You're fine," I add, softer than I mean to be. He is. Maybe I am, too. He takes it with wide eyes, like I just handed him the holy grail.

"You'll survive," I mutter, returning to my seat.

He might, but the truth is, I'm not sure I will.

Not if Leo keeps this up. Not if I keep letting him under my skin. He doesn't apologize. He doesn't back down. He doesn't do the dance of pretending nothing happened, the way I keep trying to. And dammit, part of me respects that. Wants that.

Which is exactly why I'm sitting here in this classroom instead of back in the pod where I belong. Because if I'd stayed, I know myself well enough to know—I would have found my way back into that copy room, and I would have kissed him... again.

And this time, I don't think I would've stopped.

WHEN THE LAST exam thuds onto the front desk and the room empties in a stampede of relief, I stack the packets with the care of a jeweler.

Order is a spell I know how to cast. Yet today it barely holds.

Exams complete and submitted to the lockbox at the center of the building, at about eleven I duck into the women's bathroom to relieve myself and freshen up. I wash my hands and then stare at myself in the mirror, taking a moment to give myself a mental pep talk before heading back to my desk.

The mirror shows a woman with flushed cheeks and a blouse that did not seem too low cut when I put it on this morning, but now I'm questioning my wardrobe choices. Twisting the faucet cold, I press wet fingers to the nape of my neck until the heat steps back.

I just pray that by the time I return Leo hasn't left for lunch.

I mean *has*. That Leo *has* left for lunch.

Ok, ma'am. Pep talk time.

This has to stop. Like right. the fuck. now.

I have no business wanting him. Legally, I'm still married. Is that relationship completely over? Yes. But still.

Legally. Married. Marriaged. Filing taxes *juntos*.

Wait, we don't have to do that. We can totally file separately.

We're filing separately.

FOCUS. PEP TALK.

Chase may refuse to acknowledge it's over—those papers were served to him, what... three weeks ago? Almost four? Other than him calling to scream at me, I haven't heard a peep. Before that, I hadn't heard from him since the day he came barging into the office and Leo shut him down. And before that, the last time I spoke to him was the night before he left for Boston.

Which, when I think about it, is insane.

I've been in Grand River, what, five months? Almost six? He refuses to answer my attorney like an adult. Refuses to do anything except throw fits and ghost me in between.

This could have been done by now. It *should* have been done. But the reality is that Chase is not a variable I can solve for. He is a wildly unsolvable differential equation I have been trying to linearize my whole adult life.

Escaping Chase is not the reason I want this... whatever this is with Leo. God, no.

But Chase is a heavy, exhausting weight that I've carried far too long. And right now, the person who makes me not only feel completely free of that weight, but also beautiful, seen, and just... *desired*... exactly as I am, is Leo Euler.

This pep talk is not going in the direction I thought it would be going.

But we'll keep going. Because even though this is not going to plan, it is very much ridiculous and terrifying and feels like the most honest thing I've admitted to myself since... well, since I realized my marriage had been a series of compromises in which I was the only one compromising.

I was tired of compromising by giving more of myself than Chase was willing to give.

And, dammit, now I'm tired of compromising by giving *less* of myself because Chase is holding me back.

He doesn't get to make the fucking rules. He doesn't get to dictate my happiness. *I do.* I have been living my life according to someone else's thermostat for years—too hot, too cold, and never my hand on the dial.

And since I am the one who dictates my happiness, I have decided that my first order of business as Mistress Dictator(ess?) of Thine Life is to walk out of this bathroom, into Leo's office, shut the door, and tell him that yes, Professor of Corny Math Puns and A Beautiful, Not-Quite-A-Beard Jawline, I do, in fact, *want. that. dick.*

The thought is a flare in a midnight field, and everything in me rushes toward the light. I dry my hands, square my shoulders, and head for the door.

EXITING THE BATHROOM, I expect to return to my office and find Leo behind his desk, or, worse case scenario, out to lunch.

What I don't expect is to be intercepted halfway down the hall by a frantic, stressed out looking Alis. The snap in her voice she usually saves for Dex is gone; what's left is frayed edge and white knuckles.

"Tori," she says, pulling me aside. "Have you seen Leo?"

"Earlier, why?" The look on her face is terrifying. "Is everything okay?"

"Dexter has been trying to get ahold of him for about an hour, and he's not answering his phone."

Weird. But also, not the end of the world?

"I've been proctoring a test, so I haven't seen him since this morning. Have you checked the office?"

"I did. He's not there." She's wringing her hands together, looking around every which way. Something is obviously very, very wrong.

"Alis." Saying her name turns her attention back to me. "What happened?"

"It's George," she says. George. Leo's George? Obviously,

otherwise Alis wouldn't be looking for him. Still, I repeat the name.

"George?"

"Stephanie's dad. They're close."

I nod. I think I knew this. We're going to pretend that I most definitely knew this.

"Ok, what happened?"

The look Alis gives me communicates that I have said something stupid. Awesome.

"He... died." My eyes go wide. "From cancer." My mouth drops open. "Today."

The hallway tilts a fraction, that vertigo when an elevator stops one inch off level. Somewhere, a copier starts, and the mundanity of it makes my eyes sting.

"I'm so sorry. I had no idea."

"Leo didn't tell you? Skye didn't tell you?"

I shake my head, because no, he hasn't told me anything about his life. Not his life *now*, anyway.

And... wait. "Skye?"

"Yeah. She's close with them, too. Both George and Linda."

I swear it's like I don't even know the people in my own life. Where the hell have I been the past year?

Oh, right. In Moraine. With Chase. *Not here.*

And after I moved here? I've been coddled. Everyone focused on all my trauma and drama. Nobody sharing *their lives* with me because they're too focused on the shit storm happening *in mine*.

The realization lands like a stone in my gut. For a second I can't find words, so I reach for action instead. "Okay," I say, voice steadier than I feel. "Where would he go? House? Hospital? With Stephanie? Do you know if Linda—"

Alis shakes her head, biting her lip. "Dex thinks he might be at the house or—honestly—just... driving. He does that when he doesn't want to break down in front of anyone."

I nod. That, I understand. "Text me if you hear from Dex. I'll check his office, the lot, and then I'll call him. If he doesn't answer, I'll go to his place."

"Thank you," she whispers, eyes glassy.

I squeeze her forearm once—brief, decisive—and head for the pod, already pulling up Leo's contact. The screen reflects my own worried face back at me as his line starts to ring.

One ring. Two. Voicemail.

"Leo," I say, and my voice is softer than my spine feels. "It's me. I—call me, okay? I'm here."

I end the call and stand in the corridor, phone warm in my palm, the hallway suddenly too long, the air too thick. A week ago, I would've told myself to mind my business. Today, I don't hesitate. I turn toward the stairs, toward the parking lot, toward wherever he is, because grief is a language I understand and because— whether or not I'm ready to say it out loud—he's become one of my people.

Maybe even my *person*.

And my people don't do this part alone.

TWENTY-FIVE

LEO

THE LINE MOVES, slow and unending, a tide of black clothes and murmured condolences. I barely hear the words anymore. My place is beside Linda, steadying her when she wavers, and I don't let go of her hand. She clings to me, fingers shaking, and I keep my grip firm because it's all I can do. Stephanie is on my right, Aaron hovering close to her, Adam and Ethan with their families nearby. We're all here, lined up like some formal arrangement of grief, but nothing about this feels orderly. It feels hollow. Off balance. Wrong.

Because he isn't here. And no matter how many people stream past, saying how sorry they are, that's the only thing I can hear in my head.

My mind keeps circling back to that Thursday morning. The last time.

Tori had just walked out of the office with Dr. Johnson's exams when my phone lit up with Linda's name. I knew before I even answered. Her voice was steady, but her words cut straight through me. *He doesn't have much time left, Leo. You need to come now.*

I didn't think. Didn't grab a coat. Didn't say goodbye. I just left. Keys and wallet in my pocket, my whole body ran on instinct —*get to him. Get there before it's too late.* I don't even remember half the drive, only the ache in my chest and the way my hands shook on the wheel.

But I made it.

When I walked into that bedroom, I could feel how close the end was. His breathing was shallow, his eyes half-lidded, but he was still George. Still himself, in the ways that mattered. Linda held one hand, Stephanie the other. Aaron standing close, his face pale and useless—*because you didn't really know this man.* I sat at the foot of the bed because I couldn't stand still, because I needed to be close, needed to be touching him, needed him to know I was here.

I told him everything I could fit into those last hours. That I loved him. That he had been the best father I'd ever had. That he'd given me more than I could ever repay—his trust, his laughter, his stubborn belief in me when no one else thought I was worth a damn. I told him I'd carry him with me, always. That he would never be gone from me. I even told him that if I ever did settle down and have a kid that I'd name the first one after him—even if it's a girl.

With my luck I'll probably end up getting a dog named George. Or a monkey. Probably a yellow hat to go with it.

I don't know how much he heard. But I swear he did. I swear he knew. His mouth twitched—just the faintest smile. His fingers curled, weak but sure, around Linda's hand. And that was enough.

When the end came, it was soft. No drama. No pain. Just one final breath, and then silence.

Linda and Stephanie stepped out to make calls. Aaron disappeared down the hall, useless as ever. And I stayed. Sat in that floral chair next to their bed, staring at the man who had been my compass, my anchor, my proof that not every man in this world valued their careers over the people they loved. I stayed until they came to take him away, because I couldn't leave him alone, not even then.

I was grateful for that time. Grateful to sit with him in the stillness, just the two of us. But now—now I don't know what to do with the hole in my soul he left behind.

Because George wasn't *like* a father to me. He *was* my father. The one who loved me, not because he *had* to, but because he *wanted* to. The man who chose me even after the divorce was final and the State of Colorado said, "No, George, he's not your son anymore." He said, "You're mine, son." And losing him—it feels like someone carved out the part of me that could breathe, that could stand steady when everything else went to hell.

So here I am, a week later, standing in a funeral home line, listening to people tell me how much he loved me *like* a son. They don't know. They'll never understand. He was the best man I've ever known. The only one I've ever truly wanted to make proud. And now he's gone.

Linda's hand trembles again in mine. I squeeze tighter. For her. For me. For him. It's the only way I know how to keep from falling apart right here in front of everyone.

I STEP out of the line once the crowd thins, handing off Linda to Adam—I won't leave her alone, I just need a minute. My body feels like stone. Too many hands on my shoulder. Too many murmured *he was a good man, he'll be missed*—like anyone in this room could possibly put words to who George was, to what we lost. I need air. Space. A room that isn't suffocating me in the smell of lilies and the press of other people's grief against my own.

There's a hallway off to the side, narrow and dim, that leads to a few small family rooms. I slip into one and shut the door behind me, the latch clicking too loud in the quiet.

The room is staged for comfort—soft lamps, high-backed

chairs, a table with a box of tissues placed like a centerpiece. There's a coffee urn in the corner. I pour a cup out of habit, but my hands shake so badly the liquid sloshes over the rim, and I set it down, untouched. I sink into one of the armchairs and lean forward, elbows on my knees, staring at the carpet until the patterns blur.

For the first time all day, I let myself feel it. All of it.

The weight of his absence hits me like a full body blow, the kind that steals all the breath out of your chest. I see him everywhere—George in his recliner, George standing over the grill, George tossing me a beer with that look that said he already knew my answer before he asked the question. I hear his laugh in my head, that deep rolling sound that made any room brighter, lighter. I can still feel the press of his frail hand in mine those last few weeks before he passed, the way his mouth twitched into the faintest smile as I told him I loved him on his last day. That I'd always carry him with me.

And then he was gone. Just... gone.

I couldn't cry in front of all those people, but now, the tears come. Unbidden. Relentless. A sob rips from my chest and I bend forward further, pressing the heels of my hands into my eyes until the darkness behind my lids swirls.

He's been gone for seven days, and for every one of those days I've stood here pretending like I know how to be upright without him. Pretending like I know how to breathe when every inhale cuts. Pretending like I can carry Linda's grief and my own without breaking in half.

But I can't. I can't do it.

I thought I knew pain. I thought I knew heartbreak and loss and what it felt like for my entire world to fall out from beneath my feet. But that... that was nothing. Not compared to this.

Because even when everything else in my life was ripped to shreds, George was with me, holding me together, every step of the way.

And now? When the most important person in my life is gone? When the man who glued my soul back together, piece by piece—even after his own daughter was the one to destroy it—is gone?

The door opens softly behind me, and I drag my hands down my face, wiping away what tears I can before looking up. Stephanie.

Her eyes are swollen—I assume mine look much the same— her mascara smudged, and she looks younger than I've seen her in years. She looks almost like the girl I met in college, only now, instead of an added layer of confidence and sex appeal, she's stripped down and fragile.

Stephanie hesitates, hovering just inside the doorway like she's not sure if I'll tell her to leave.

"Can we talk?" she asks, her voice trembling.

I nod because what else can I do? This is her father. My father, too, in every way that mattered. If she needs me, I won't turn her away.

I stand as she crosses the room in slow, uncertain steps. And then, without another word, she leans into me. Her body folds against mine like she's been holding herself rigid for too long. I wrap my arms around her, steadying her as more sobs break loose.

"I feel like he died disappointed in me," she chokes out against my chest. "Like he never forgave me for what I did to you. Like—" She sucks in a jagged breath. "Like every decision I've made in the last four years was the wrong one."

Her words slice through me. She's grieving, and grief is cruel. It lies. It claws at every scar you thought had healed. But I can't stand hearing her tear herself apart like this.

"Steph," I murmur, tightening my arms around her, my palm against the back of her head, stroking her hair. "That's not true. Those thoughts in your head? Those are lies. All lies. He loved you. He was proud of you. And there was nothing for him to forgive. You know that. It's not like you hurt *him*."

She pulls back a little, tears streaking her face, eyes desperate for something to hold on to. "But I did," she whispers. "I hurt him when I hurt you. Because he loved you, just like he loved me."

"I know he did."

"And you," she continues, eyes bouncing back and forth between mine. "Did you ever forgive me?"

I swallow hard. "Yes," I nod. "I did. Maybe not all at once. But I forgave you. Somewhere along the line, I let it go. And your dad knew that."

Her lips tremble, and her expression shifts, and she buries her face into my chest again.

I forgot how small she is. The top of her head barely reaches my shoulder. It almost feels like I'm hugging a child.

I think her tears are subsiding, but then she asks the last question I expect: "What if I do it again?" she whispers.

My brow furrows. "What do you mean?"

"What if I mess up again?" She pulls her face from my chest again, tilting her gaze back up to mine. "What if I hurt Aaron the same way I hurt you?"

Her words knock the wind out of me. For a second, I just stare at her. "Why would you even ask that? Have you—" I hesitate, the thought tasting bitter. "Have you cheated on him?"

She shakes her head, gaze dropping to the floor. "No," she whispers.

Then she looks up again, and her eyes flick to my mouth, lingering there. "But when dad got sick, I started thinking about... well, everything. About the past, and how I ruined everything. And what if..."

It's not just grief in her face now—it's something else. Something dangerous. Something that used to belong to us.

And for one suspended heartbeat, I feel it too. The echo of what we were, tangled with the raw ache of losing George. The air between us is heavy with everything unsaid, everything that should stay buried but refuses to die.

Before the moment can tip into something neither of us can take back, the door swings open.

Skye's voice cuts through, sharp and merciless. "I hate to break up such a tender moment, but the service is about to begin—and your husband is looking for you, Stephanie." She spits the word *husband* like it tastes sour.

Stephanie startles, stepping back fast—almost too fast. She wipes at her face with trembling hands, forcing a weak smile for Skye.

She doesn't look back at me.

Stephanie slips past Skye and into the hallway without another word.

I drag my hand over my mouth, pulse hammering. "That wasn't what it looked like—"

"I don't care what the fuck it looked like," Skye snaps, fire in her eyes. "What you do with your ex-wife is none of my damn business."

"Skye—"

"None. of. my. business," she repeats, biting off the words. Then she steps aside, revealing Tori behind her.

Her eyes lock on mine, and Skye adds, "But it might be hers."

Shit.

Has she been there since Skye opened the door? Did she see...

And just like that, everything I've been holding—grief, guilt, temptation—presses down harder than ever, threatening to crack me wide open in the middle of this goddamn funeral home.

TWENTY-SIX

LEO

BY THE TIME I leave the funeral home, the sky's already dark. It's only a little after seven, but the parking lot lamps glow against patches of ice and the cold sinks straight into my bones. The whole day feels heavy and endless, but the thought of going home makes my stomach twist. If I walk through my front door, I'll drink myself stupid. I know it. I'll crack open a bottle, call it "just one," and by midnight I'll be staring at an empty glass like it owes me answers.

I can't do that tonight.

But I also can't stomach being around anyone else. I've been surrounded by people since morning—hands grabbing mine, voices whispering condolences like they mean anything, eyes watching me to see if I'll break. I've done enough breaking for one day.

So instead of heading toward my house, I find myself pulling into the Middle Peak lot. Three days before Christmas, the campus is dead quiet. Most students cleared out last week, professors scattered soon after. It's eerie, all those dark windows and empty sidewalks, like the place has gone hollow.

My spot is open, like it's been waiting for me.

Of course it's open, you dumb fuck. Nobody else is even here right now.

I cut the engine and sit for a second, listening to it tick in the cold. My hands don't move from the wheel. The truth is, I don't even know why I came here. But maybe I do.

My office is the only place I can think of where I'll be left alone. No bottle waiting, no well-meaning neighbor showing up with a casserole, no memories pressed into every corner of the house. Just a desk, four walls, and silence.

I take my keys, shove them deep in my coat pocket, and head inside. The halls are dim, the kind of half-light you get when maintenance sets the timers wrong, buzzing fluorescents overhead. My footsteps echo too loud, like I don't belong here. But the quiet—the quiet is what I need.

When I unlock the pod and step in, everything is in its place. Familiar. Safe. Neutral. I don't even bother with the lights, there's no point, and lean back against the door until my knees remember how to hold me up.

It's pathetic, probably, retreating here of all places. But tonight, it feels like the only option that won't destroy me.

Because George is gone. Skye's furious. Stephanie nearly kissed me. And Tori—

Christ, Tori.

I have no idea what is running through her mind right now. What she saw in that room. Assumptions she made. She should be furious—hell, Skye is livid. But when she said goodbye tonight, she didn't seem angry at all. It didn't make sense. She adjusted my tie. Like it mattered. Like *I* mattered. And then she pulled me down just enough to brush her lips against the corner of my mouth.

"I'll see you later."

That's all she said before walking out.

My legs are stable enough to support me now... I think... so I push off the pod door and head toward my office. Only, when I step inside and look around, it isn't enough.

Isn't safe enough. Warm enough. Secure enough to hold me together when all I feel like doing is falling apart.

And suddenly, I completely understand why Tori curled herself into a ball in the back corner of our copy room, even when she was the only person here.

Because the copy room—it is safe, and warm, and small enough to help someone feel secure when everything else is chaos. When everything else hurts. When everything else is broken beyond repair.

When I step into the small copy room, the contrast to my office is immediate. I breathe in paper and toner, listen to the faint hum of the machine. It's white noise—not loud enough to jar, but steady enough to ease the weight of unbearable silence.

I'm not even halfway across the tiny room when someone else enters behind me, shutting the door and locking it.

"What the—" I turn around and see... "Tori?"

Calm. Steady. Eyes like flint. She walks toward me with slow, deliberate steps, like she's hunting something she's already wounded.

"Tor—"

Then she shoves me. Just enough to press my back to the filing cabinet. And drops to her knees in front of me.

"Wha—what are you doing?"

She doesn't answer. Just reaches for my belt.

I catch one of her wrists. "Tori—wait."

Her eyes flash.

And then she *pinches* me. Right behind the knee.

Hard.

My leg buckles.

"What the fu—"

"Shut up, fuckboy," she says evenly, "and let me swallow your sorrows. Try and stop me again and I'll do that to your balls."

Jesus Christ.

My cock twitches before I can stop it, and holy shit... this is really happening.

Victoria Foster, the woman I am entirely too enamored with and who saw me not two hours ago in a nearly compromising position with my very married ex-wife, is on her knees, in front of me, about to swallow down my cock like a goddamn hoover.

I'm sorry, but, have I died? Because there is no fucking way this is actually happening.

She doesn't smile. Doesn't flirt. Just unbuckles my belt, pulls down my slacks, and palms me with single-minded focus. Her fingers curl around my base—rough, impatient—and then her mouth follows.

She licks the underside first.

Long, slow, deliberate.

And then—

She freezes.

Tongue pausing right as she reaches the head. Brows drawing in. Her eyes flick up, just a beat of surprise before they narrow into something darker. Curious.

And then, she scoffs.

"You would."

"Would what?" My voice is low, strangled.

"Be so desperate for someone to touch your dick that you'd let someone fondle you and stick a needle through it."

For fuck's sake. The last thing I expected tonight was Tori's mouth on my cock, so no, I didn't think to clue her in to a frenum piercing.

I groan and grab a fistful of her hair. She started this; now she better fucking finish it.

"Are you scared of a little metal, Tote? I thought you were swallowing my sorrows."

Her eyes flick up, sharp and steady.

"Now, be a good girl and put my pretty pierced dick back in your smart ass mouth, *Victoria*."

And, she does.

She fucking *does.*

No hesitation, no comment, no smug grin.

Just lips parting, mouth hot, tongue sliding over me and taking me deep into the back of her throat like she means to suck every ounce of sadness, pain, and regret out of my body and replace it with the best. fucking. head. of. my. life.

Just when I think this is all too good to be true—that Tori's actually submitting to me, swallowing my cock without a fight—I flinch.

This salty bitch pinches my fucking taint.

And *holy shit.*

I bite down on my knuckle to keep from screaming, the pain sharp and blinding—right behind my balls, precise and punishing —and I can't fucking help it.

I have never been more turned on in my life.

This should *not* feel good.

Why does this feel *so fucking good?!*

I glance down and look at her.

She's got her other hand under her skirt, between her legs, but she's fumbling. Frustrated. Uncoordinated.

She finally pulls it out, bracing that left hand against my thighs —heaven forbid she relinquish the death grip on my goddamn taint.

That's fine, Tote. Two can play this game.

She's whimpering now. Struggling. Shifting on her knees.

Still sucking my cock like her life depends on it, relaxing her throat, swallowing around my head, using her tongue and her teeth to play with my piercing each time she draws her mouth back to the tip—*my God*—but she will *not* let go of that pinch.

This woman is driving me insane.

"Fuck—Tori—"

I *snap.*

Gripping her hair with both hands, I thrust into her mouth the way I've wanted to for weeks—brutal, ragged, raw.

She moans like she's starving, takes everything I give her, the burn between her thighs practically vibrating in the air around us.

And when I come, it's violent. Fast.

Her nails dig in. My vision whites out.

And I lose every last shred of composure I have.

She finally pulls off me, her lips swollen, spit slick on her chin, eyes glassy and wild and so goddamn *beautiful* I almost forget how to breathe.

But I can't let her have the last word.

Not after *that.*

She's still on her knees, thighs clenched together in obvious arousal. I brush a strand of hair off her sweat slicked forehead—gentle, almost reverent—and murmur, "Did that turn you on, Tote?"

Her eyes go wide, electric. Is that... hope of reciprocity?

"Tell me," I say, tracing my finger from her hair down her jawline. I use my pointer finger to tip her chin slightly more upward. I want to see her fire. "Are you desperate enough for me to touch your wet pussy that you'd let me stick a needle through it? Because I don't think you deserve to get off after talking shit like that."

I watch the flicker in her expression—shock, then offense, then something *feral.*

She stands.

No words. Just calm precision as she rises, straightens her skirt, and then *spits.*

Right in my face.

A thick stream of my own release splats against my cheekbone, some splashing into my eye.

"Swallow your own sorrows, then."

And she walks out, slamming the door closed behind her.

Back straight. Head high. Tori leaves me standing in that copy room like the fucking asshole I am.

And the worst part?

I deserve it.

I DON'T MOVE. Not right away. My pants are still open, halfway down my thighs, my shirt rumpled, my face sticky with my own release and... yep. It's no longer just on my face, but has traveled down my jaw, to my neck, and if I don't find some sort of napkin or paper towel or—

Fuck it. I use my shirt sleeve like a toddler eating spaghetti to clean up my neck, then my cheek and around my eye. There's probably cum smashed into my facial hair, but I'll have to wash that out in the shower.

I'm honestly shocked that she 1) hadn't swallowed, because who wants to sit with jizz in their mouth for that long, and 2) actually had the audacity to then spit it in my face.

Who even does that?

Victoria Foster. That's who.

And, fuck, she was right. Because what she did? That wasn't cruelty. It wasn't malice. It was the kind of thing only someone who actually gave a damn about me would do.

She followed me here. After the funeral. After seeing me in that room with Stephanie. After every reason in the world to walk away from me and never look back—she still came. She didn't want me to be alone. She wanted to take care of me in the only way she thought I'd accept.

Our banter—that shit was fire. And I, like the absolute prick I am, couldn't just let it be what it was. I had to push. Had to say something stupid. Had to remind her that no matter how close I let her get, I'll find a way to ruin it.

But she accomplished exactly what she came here to do. She

swallowed my grief right out of me, even if only for a few minutes. And Christ, if I'd shut my mouth—if I'd just let her give without trying to twist it, without turning it into some ugly game—maybe tonight would've been different.

Maybe she would've gone home with me. Maybe I could've held her, just held her, all night. No words, no explanations, no past, no future. Just the heat of her body against mine, her breath steadying me, her presence keeping me from drowning. Even if we hadn't had sex, even if nothing more happened, I could've slept beside her. I could've woken up tomorrow morning not empty, not alone.

Instead, I'm here. Alone in a copy room with my dick out and remnants of my release smashed into my scruff.

I didn't think I could feel any worse today, but alas... here I stand.

I zip up. Straighten my clothes. Run a hand through my hair like that'll fix anything. It won't. The damage is done.

And now, the whole reason I came here—to avoid the bottle, to avoid making a mistake with someone who means nothing—feels like it just went up in smoke. I can't stay here. Not after this.

Instead, I think through the options, already knowing the answer.

I've already fucked things up with Tori enough for one night. I won't make it worse by finding some random body to sink into, pretending that will numb me. It won't. It never does.

George would hate seeing me like this. The thought of me hiding away, covered in shame, debating whether to drink myself blind. He'd tell me to stop wallowing, to go home, to try again tomorrow. He'd tell me I was worth more than this. And I want to believe him. I do. But right now? I don't feel like that man. I feel like the fuckup he never wanted me to be.

I won't call Dexter because I don't want to ask him to leave Alis and Sunny to come to my place. Or maybe because right now I don't feel like I deserve any more sympathy. I won't go to Skye, won't ask her to sit with me, because she already made it clear she's furious. I can't go to Linda's because her boys and their families are there, and *fucking Stephanie*.

I still just want to be away from people. The only exception to that rule was Tori.

So I'll go home. I'll shut off my phone. And without the comfort of her warm, sweet body curled next to mine, I'll get lost in a warm, smoky bottle of Scotch instead.

Because it doesn't matter what asshole bullshit I say to Johnnie Walker—he's heard it all before.

TWENTY-SEVEN

TORI

CHRISTMAS IN GRAND RIVER doesn't feel like Christmas.

The streets are quiet, shops closed, half-hearted strings of lights clinging to telephone poles. It's the opposite of the Christmases I grew up with, when silence was a sin and noise meant you were doing it right.

Back then, the house was full every year—people from church, neighbors with nowhere else to go, my parents insisting Christmas wasn't Christmas unless it was bursting at the seams with bodies and voices and casseroles lined up on the counter. Mom would crank carols from the old CD player until the speakers crackled, Dad would launch into Luke 2 like the living embodiment of a Christmas Eve pageant, and as the only kid in the house, I was the built-in entertainment.

"Play us something on the piano, Tori."

"Tell us your favorite Bible verse."

"Show us what Santa brought you."

There was never any hiding. No excuse strong enough to keep me from the center of it all. Every eye on me. Every voice pushing me into the spotlight whether I wanted it or not.

And then came Chase.

For someone who claimed to hate Christmas, he had a way of thriving in it. All that attention I used to drown under? He soaked it up like he'd been starving for it—and maybe he had. The boy who spent so many years in foster care, who never really had a family Christmas after his parents died, suddenly became the shining star of mine.

He slipped into those loud nights like he'd been rehearsing his whole life. He laughed at the right moments, teased my uncles about football, let my mom fuss over his plate until it was stacked high. He and my dad got along famously, which still feels strange to remember.

My dad never gave his approval easily, but with Chase, it wasn't just approval—it was admiration. They'd sit shoulder to shoulder at the table, trading stories like they'd known each other for decades, my dad laughing so hard his face turned red while Chase played the role of charming prodigal son.

And the strangest part was how much I liked it. For the first time in my life, people weren't doting on me or asking me to play carols on the piano. The spotlight shifted, and I was grateful. Chase fit into my family's holiday chaos so easily, it almost made me forget he'd sworn up and down that he hated the holiday.

Maybe that was the irony of him—he hated Christmas until someone handed him the microphone, and then he loved it.

Looking back, I see it for what it was. He wasn't faking it, not really. He was hungry. Starved for attention, for belonging, for a seat at a table where people actually cared what you had to say. He took up the space because no one had ever given it to him before.

And I let him, relieved to fade into the background for once.

But now, sitting in this little apartment in Grand River, with the streets outside silent and my own living room still, I realize this is the first Christmas I've ever spent without noise. Without the performance. Without my parents, without Chase, without anyone.

It feels... right.

No casserole dishes. No CD player skipping on *O Holy Night*. No awkward piano solos.

Just the hum of the fridge, Betty Boop ticking away on the wall, and the faint whistle of wind against the windows.

Dexter, Alis, and Skye packed up yesterday morning, heading to Moraine to spend the holiday with their families.

Skye argued, of course. She hated leaving me, hated the thought of me being here alone. It took everything I had to push her out the door, to look her in the eye and say, *I'll be fine.*

Because I will be. I want this—*need* this.

There's no pressure to perform happiness for my parents. No arguments with Chase about where we're going and what time. No pretending everything is picture-perfect when my whole body is unraveling under the surface.

I want the quiet.

I spend most of the day cleaning the apartment. Wiping down counters, vacuuming under furniture that hasn't seen daylight in months, finally tackling the sweaters stuffed in that plastic bin under my bed. I pull them out one by one, shaking out any folding lines embedded from months gone by, and hang each sweater in the closet. A neat row of color-coordinated warmth right next to my jeans.

Organization sparks so much joy in my heart.

One box waits in the corner of the closet, half forgotten. The one I shoved full of random clothes from my old closet when I left Moraine. I never sorted it—just dragged it here like baggage I wasn't ready to unpack.

Today, I open it.

On top is a tangle of shirts I barely remember owning, a pair of jeans that don't fit anymore, a cardigan with a hole in the sleeve.

And then I see it.

The dress.

Black, short, snug in all the right ways. At least, it was when I was twenty. Now it probably fits more like a sausage casing—*these hips don't lie.*

I hold it up, and the memories crash over me before I can stop them.

That night. The party. Lexi zipping me up, telling me I looked hot. Armed with red lipstick, my game face, and a plan.

I walked into that baseball house knowing exactly what I was doing, knowing Chase would hear I was there and he'd come running back the second I cast the bait.

And he did. I played that boy better than the piano at a Christmas party—and I'd been taking lessons since age four.

I wore this dress the night I pulled him back for the last time. The night I decided I was done waiting for him to choose me and went out to force his hand.

I baited the hook with Aaron Taylor, and Chase bit like I knew he would. He always came back, because I was his home, his constant.

And also because Chase Martin can't stand for someone else to play with his toys.

That's what I'd always been—his. He knew it, I knew it. But that last time we broke up he took his sweet time coming back to me, so I changed the rules. He wasn't allowed to leave anymore without consequences. If he walked away, I'd stop waiting.

So he stopped fucking around and then never had to find out.

I smooth the fabric over my lap, remembering how confident I felt slipping it on.

How determined. How... desperate?

Because looking back, I see that it wasn't just Chase who kept coming back to our relationship as his foundation, his constant.

I did the same thing.

Every time we broke up, I felt unsteady.

What if he doesn't want me anymore? What if he doesn't need me?

Being Chase Martin's girlfriend gave me a purpose—something more than just being the girl who was good at math or the sweet deacon's daughter at church.

I didn't play a sport, I wasn't popular. I wasn't the crazy and wild one in my friend group or the one with the super cool older sister.

I was always just... Tori.

And there's nothing wrong with that. Nobody had ever made me feel like there's anything wrong with that.

But I think somewhere, deep down, at the core of every person, is a desire to be something... more.

Not just ordinary, but extraordinary.

Like we're born with this ingrained sense of not being enough, and we spend so much of our lives thinking we need to do or be something different, something more, to fix it. To exceed the unrealistic expectations we put on ourselves—or, in many cases, that others have put on us without ever asking if we wanted them.

I can't say that my parents ever put those kinds of expectations on me. Mom has always been proud of me, in her own way, though her pride often came wrapped in platitudes and soft, church-approved smiles.

And my father... I guess I never considered his expectations unrealistic because, until now, I'd always met or exceeded them. Good grades, good behavior, a clean reputation polished enough to reflect well on him at every church gathering. I never tested the limits of his patience or his disappointment.

I was surprised, honestly, that he didn't have an opinion or a comment when I never became pregnant during all those years with Chase. That probably had more to do with him being too self-involved to care about when or if Chase and I ever reproduced. He only would have cared if it disrupted his image—if it had forced him to step down from his role at church or explain away something that didn't fit his picture of a tidy, respectable life.

Mom never asked either. She's not one to pry. But whenever I'd talk to her about it—about the silence in our house, about the ache in me she also felt but never acknowledged—she'd give me a hug and whisper the same thing every time:

All in God's time, Tori. All in God's time.

Not helpful. Not actually comforting.

Reflecting back on my upbringing, on the way my parents never really took the time to go deeper than surface-level, faith-based answers and manipulated Bible verses, I can see why I was so drawn to Chase Martin.

In my fifteen-year-old brain, if my perfect, God-loving parents never had to fix me or themselves, then we must have been the perfect example of a stable, loving family.

That's exactly what Chase needed, right?

A boy who had no parents, who had been passed around in foster care, who carried scars he never admitted out loud but showed in every reckless decision he made—he needed someone steady.

Someone pure. Someone who could play savior.

And if I was solely focused on what Chase needed, then I never had to look too closely at myself. I never had to acknowledge how hollow and weak an entire life of perfection and Christian platitudes had left me.

The truth is, Chase didn't necessarily make me small... because in so many ways, I already was.

And what Chase couldn't handle—what I refused to let go of once it took root in my soul and started to grow—wasn't a reclaiming of anything I had lost because of him. It wasn't about winning myself back. It was about discovering something I didn't even know I had.

It was strength.

It was the sense of self I had to develop just to keep loving him, to keep fighting for a relationship that should have fallen apart a hundred times over. A self I didn't know before, because I'd never had the opportunity to meet her, to test her, to see just how extraordinary and stubborn and resilient Victoria Anne Foster was capable of being.

I had to become someone who could stand her ground, who could demand answers, who could hold up the weight of a marriage and a man who couldn't hold himself. I had to become someone who could survive heartbreak after heartbreak and still get up in the morning.

And maybe I became that woman for him at first, but somewhere along the way, I realized I was becoming her for me.

So, yes. I may have attached myself to Chase Martin in an unconscious, feeble attempt to fill the void inside myself that needed more... that needed a purpose, something to make me feel less ordinary, and also so I could have a person to love.

And, yes, that naive fifteen-year-old girl was so far in over her head when she thought she could save the lonely, broken foster boy from his life of pain and tragedy.

But I did love him. Truly. Madly. Deeply.

I'll always love him in some way.

I don't regret loving him. We had some really wonderful times together.

Also, without all the decisions I made in the past, without the pain, the suffering, the heartache... I never would have met myself.

And I'm really, really glad that I met her.

She's a little bruised, but she's sharp. She's the girl who won't sit quietly when someone dismisses her. The woman who can survive a marriage cracking down the middle. The one who can look at herself in the mirror and recognize both the mistakes and the grit it took to keep walking forward.

She's feisty, and fun, and apparently goes down on grieving men in copy rooms.

Who knew?

And here's the thing—old me, the girl who lived to orbit around Chase, would never have done that. She would've been too worried about what it meant, what other people would think, what *he* would think.

She would've swallowed down her own curiosity (instead of his cum—*ba-dum-tss*), her own hunger, and let someone else's comfort or judgment dictate her choices.

But this version of me? The one who's met herself in the fire of everything I thought would destroy me?

She doesn't wait for permission. She doesn't apologize for wanting, for trying, for getting it wrong sometimes.

That's what the copy room was. Not just the hottest moment of my life—and God, it was—but a moment where I felt like *me*.

Not Chase's girl. Not the dutiful daughter. Not the peacemaker friend. Just me, flesh and bone and nerve endings, giving and taking in equal measure.

Well, until he ruined it.

One careless line, one reminder that even with all his intelligence, Leo Euler has a way of turning vulnerability into a weapon.

And just like that, the high of it—the connection, the electricity, the power I felt—slipped through my fingers.

But I took it back. Because no one, not even a grieving man who deserves a pass because he's hurting, is ever going to make me feel small or undeserving again.

Not even for a second. Not even as a joke.

And I made damn sure he knew that when I spit his own release back in his face and walked out. (I'm fully aware the swallowing joke just fell flat. Leave it.)

I laugh to myself at the memory.

I did that. I fucking did that. *flips hair*

And then... I think about what Skye and I walked in on. Stephanie, leaning into Leo. His arms wrapped around her. Her lips trembling, voice low. Skye's jaw clenched so tight she nearly cracked a tooth.

Was Leo comforting a woman who had lost her father? Maybe. Probably. But the picture was messy—faces too close together, sadness that looked more like longing.

Grief rearranges people. It remaps the borders between right and wrong, between comfort and something more reckless. It makes hands roam and words clumsy and touch feel like the only honest thing left.

Skye refuses to see nuance right now. That's fine. She's furious and she can be furious for a while. I don't blame her for how protective she is—that's Skye.

She loves hard and loud and she sees complications as a threat. She wants clear answers and tidy justice and Leo did something that night that made her want to punch a hole through the world.

I don't know what happened behind those closed doors.

I only know what I felt when I had him quiet and soft and broken against me a few hours later in that copy room—needed, in the most bone-deep way. I felt useful.

That's not noble. It's not holy. It's human.

And when he used his smart mouth like a scalpel, when he turned our moment into selfishness, it stung. Hard.

But here's the thing—I don't need him to be flawless to want him.

Wanting someone and sanctifying them are separate things. I can want him and still stand up for myself. I can take the good and set boundaries on the bad.

That's growth talking, loud and unfiltered.

And while part of me still wants to storm into his house and read him the riot act line by line, another part—the one that's quieter and less indulgent—knows he needs space.

So do I.

He needs to be with his family. He needs to spend the holiday break, this next week, with Linda, Stephanie, their family, and whatever grief looks like when it wakes you up at 3 a.m. and won't let you sleep again.

He needs to grieve without me making it about us. He needs to grieve without me taking it as evidence that he's choosing someone else. He needs to be their son and brother first, and whatever he and I are second.

Because no matter what history lies between the two of them, the reality is that Leo and Stephanie shared George as a father, and Linda is still their mother.

They will *always* be family.

I promised Skye I'd be okay here by myself. More than that—I promised myself I'd use this time to be honest about who I am and what I need.

Part of being honest looks like writing things I can't say out loud without devolving into an argument or crying or both.

So I grab a notebook. A pen that writes well and won't smear. Skye's bookstore candle because everything feels more official with a little dramatic light. And I sit at the kitchen table and write to Chase.

It's not ugly. It's not a rant. Just, a closing. A gentle but firm ending of a chapter.

I write like I'm explaining something to someone I once loved and still respect enough to want them to walk away with their dignity intact.

> Dear Chase,
>
> I've tried a dozen times to figure out how to put words to the ending we never managed to give each other.
>
> You were my first love. And for a long time, I thought you'd be my only. We grew up together in all the hardest ways, filling holes in each other that we never admitted out loud. I thought if I was steady enough, patient enough, strong enough,

I could be everything you needed. Maybe I even thought saving you would prove I was worth saving, too.

But the truth is, we broke ourselves even more while trying to hold each other together.

I don't regret us. Not one bit. I don't regret the nights we laughed until it hurt or the quiet mornings when it felt like maybe we'd finally figured it out. I will carry those memories with me always. They're stitched into my heart, forever.

But I can't carry them and keep carrying you, too.

You've been weighed down with so much pain since you were a boy. Pain you never asked for and didn't deserve. The parents who should have protected you left scars that never healed, and then they were taken from you. You and Trent were left to figure out survival in a world that wasn't kind to either of you.

That wound has lived in you all these years, telling you that you weren't enough, making you angry at yourself and everyone close enough to love you. And for too long, I stood as the primary target and outlet for that anger and pain, letting it chip away at me while I told myself it was my job to absorb it.

You used to come back to me because I was

your home. I used to cling to you because being yours made me feel like I mattered. But I've learned that home isn't supposed to hurt like that. It isn't supposed to cost you your peace. And I finally know I can be whole without being your safe place to land.

So this is me letting go. Not because I stopped loving you, but because love shouldn't feel like drowning. Not because you don't deserve love, but because you deserve to find it without the weight of my expectations, and I deserve to live without the weight of your projections.

I hope you get help, Chase. Real help. The kind that can sit with the broken parts of you that you keep trying to bury under anger and bravado. Therapy. Counseling. Something that lets you name the pain instead of deflecting and allowing it to ricochet onto the people who love you most. You don't have to keep living in survival mode. You don't have to keep proving or posturing. You can heal. I believe that. I always have.

I hope you love your brother well. I hope you build something that lasts. I hope you give yourself the chance to stop running and finally rest in yourself. Because you are worthy of both love and healing.

This isn't hate. This isn't even goodbye with bitterness in it. It's just the last page of our story. And I'm choosing to close it with gratitude for what we had, and with hope, for both of us, that we'll be better for letting go.

Take care of yourself, Chase. Please.

All my love, Tori

TWENTY-EIGHT

TORI

IT'S BEEN ten days since I last saw him.

Ten days of silence that, oddly enough, felt necessary. The university shutting down over the holiday was its own kind of mercy. We both needed the space, the time to let the sting fade and the heat settle before either of us said something we couldn't take back. He needed ten days to grieve such a tragic loss with his family.

But now that the days have stretched long and slow, I realize how much I've missed him. I didn't expect that. I thought the distance would make it easier to draw a clean line of friendship in my heart, but instead, every quiet morning has reminded me of his smart mouth, every empty evening of how easily his presence filled a room.

I hate admitting it, even to myself, but he's wound his way into the rhythm of my days, and without him, everything feels a little off-beat.

Tomorrow, campus opens once again. Tomorrow we go back to work, back to schedules and fluorescent lights and the constant shuffle of papers and people.

I've been telling myself I'm ready for that, but the truth is, I don't want our first words to happen under buzzing ceiling lights with the copier groaning in the background. I don't want to face him for the first time in an office where anyone could walk past and watch.

So when the knock comes at my apartment door, I know. My heart knows before my brain can catch up.

I open it, and there he is.

Leo Euler. Jeans, a dark sweater, hair rumpled like his hands couldn't leave it alone on the way over.

And his eyes—God, his eyes stop me. Not older, not exactly, but weighted in a way they weren't before.

Grief does that. It sharpens, etches lines you don't see until the light catches them. It puts years in your gaze you haven't actually lived, and his carry all of it.

"Hi," he says, voice low, raw from too many days unused.

"Hi."

For a moment, neither of us moves. The silence stretches, thick with everything we didn't say over break, everything we couldn't. It doesn't feel like absence anymore—it feels like the edge of something about to break open.

"Can I come in?" he asks.

I should hesitate. Instead, I open the door the rest of the way, a silent welcome.

Leo steps inside, careful, like he's not sure he belongs here. He stands near the door, hands shoved in his pockets, eyes flicking around the room like he needs a moment to find his footing.

I cross my arms, not defensive—just grounding myself. "You're here."

"Yeah." He lets out a short laugh, more breath than sound. "Didn't exactly plan it. Just... couldn't wait until tomorrow."

His words hang there, fragile, and I realize he means it. He couldn't wait.

I nod toward the couch. "Sit."

He does, leaning forward, elbows braced on his knees, head

bowed like he's carrying something he hasn't decided how to set down. I sink into the other side of the couch, my legs tucked under me, and wait.

When he finally lifts his gaze, it nearly undoes me. His eyes are raw, rimmed red like he hasn't slept, but steady, searching.

"I need to say I'm sorry," he starts. "For Stephanie. For the way that looked, for how it must've felt walking in on that. It wasn't—" His jaw tightens.

"It was messy," he admits, voice low but steady. "I was a wreck that night, and she was grieving too, and we leaned on each other in a way that didn't look good from the outside. I should've stopped it before it even looked like something it wasn't. Because it wasn't, Tori."

His eyes are pleading, earnest. "I swear I was not about to kiss her. I didn't want her. Not then, not now, not ever again. Whatever we were, that ended a long time ago. We're over. Truly over."

I nod. "I know," I whisper.

"But I should've known how it looked," he continues. "I should've thought about how it would feel for you to walk in on that. But I wasn't in my right mind. And that's not an excuse, but it's the truth. And I hate that I wasn't thinking straight, because the last thing I would ever do is hurt you like that. Not on purpose. Not in any way that makes you question what you mean to me."

I swallow hard, keeping my voice even.

"You both just lost your father. You were comforting her. I can understand that."

Looking down at my lap, I say, "It doesn't mean it didn't sting."

He nods, slowly. "I know. And then the copy room—"

His eyes close for a second, like replaying it makes him flinch. "I was cruel. You went there to offer me comfort, and I... God... I just had to fuck everything up. You didn't deserve that. You don't deserve half the sharp edges I throw around when I get uncomfortable."

"You mean when you feel vulnerable?" I say.

He nods. He knows.

His honesty pulls at me, and I hate how much I want to soften for him, how much I want to close the distance. But I don't move.

"You're right. I didn't deserve it."

Silence settles again, but it isn't empty. It's heavy with everything neither of us can undo.

Then he says, quietly, "I miss you."

The words hit me in the chest.

Simple. Unadorned.

"I miss you too," I admit, my voice softer than I intended.

"But missing you doesn't erase the fact that I'm still married. That every time we cross that line, I wrestle with guilt that I can't just switch off."

I sit up a little straighter. I need him to know that what I'm about to say... I mean it. And I need him to respect this boundary, even when I, myself, don't want to.

"My marriage is over, I know that in my bones, but until it's final—until the ink is dry—it feels wrong to keep... doing this. Not the physical part."

His shoulders lift with a breath, then drop. He doesn't argue, doesn't push. Just nods once, like he understands.

"Then we don't. Not until the ink is dry."

The relief that floods me is almost dizzying. Not because I don't want him, but because I need him to be my friend right now. Not my lover. And he gets that. Truly, he does.

Then he smirks, tilting his head. "Still allowed to flirt, though, right?"

I roll my eyes, laughing out my response.

"Of course you'd ask that."

He leans back, casual, though the gleam in his eyes is anything but.

"You know, if we were elements, you'd be oxygen."

I arch a brow, unimpressed.

"Because every time you're near, I forget how to breathe."

I stare at him flatly. "Wrong subject."

He throws up his hands, dramatic as ever. "There are only so many math innuendos, Tote!"

I turn slowly, deadpan.

"So the limit does exist? Thank God."

His grin spreads, smug and boyish all at once. "Technically, it's approaching infinity—but I'm a patient man. Also—did you just *Mean Girls* me?"

And just like that, everything is back to normal.

I laugh. I can't help it.

"Oh my gosh, that's my favorite movie."

"Classic," he declares, like the argument's settled. "We should totally watch it."

And we do.

Somehow, without either of us saying it out loud, we shift. I end up tucked against his side, his arm looped around me like it's the most natural thing in the world.

He keeps tossing out one-liners, and I keep pretending I'm not amused, but he knows.

He always knows.

When he leans down, voice low and ridiculous, and says, "Are you going to start telling people I'm almost too gay to function?" I lose it completely. My laugh shakes against his chest, warm and unguarded.

For a moment, everything else fades—the grief, the divorce, the loneliness.

I'm happy. And for the first time in ten days, the hole in my chest—the GBF-shaped one—is filled to the brim.

Eventually, the credits roll and the late-afternoon light slants across the living room floor. Neither of us wants to move, but reality waits on the other side of the door.

Work tomorrow. People. Responsibility.

Leo exhales, reluctant. "I should go."

I untangle myself from his side, then walk him to the door, every step a small tug in my chest. He pauses there, looking down at me, eyes soft in a way that makes me want to undo every boundary I just set.

Instead, he leans forward, pressing a kiss to my forehead—gentle, grounding, nothing more.

"I'll see you tomorrow," he says.

It's simple, but it feels like a promise.

When the door clicks shut behind him, the apartment is quiet again, but not empty.

Not anymore.

TWENTY-NINE

TORI

THE OFFICE IS BLISSFULLY quiet for a late morning. The heater rattles to life, pushing warmth into the corners, and the faint smell of burnt coffee drifts down the hall from the faculty lounge.

I'm halfway through an email to a panicked student begging to swap into a calculus section that's already three seats past capacity when a voice I haven't heard in months cuts through the air.

"Hey, Tori."

My fingers still on the keyboard. For a split second, I think I've imagined it. But when I look up, there he is.

Chase.

Standing just inside the doorway like he belongs here, but not quite. His hands shoved into the pockets of his jacket, his shoulders set, his eyes—calm.

Not cold, not furious, not the sharp edge I braced myself for the last time he showed up. Just... calm.

"Hello," I say, my voice even. Not defensive. A little wary, but not brittle.

I promised myself I wouldn't let him shake me anymore.

"How are you?" he asks.

I blink. Not the script I expected.

No accusations. No demands.

Just words that sound simple, ordinary, almost too plain to come from his mouth.

My guard goes up anyway. He's never led with "how are you" in his life.

"I'm... fine, thank you. Can I help you with something?"

He shifts on his feet, glances at the empty chair across from my desk. Nervous. *Nervous?*

I can't remember the last time I saw Chase look anything but sure of himself, cocky, or angry.

This is new. Or maybe it's an act.

Maybe he's calculating how long it will take Leo to step out of his office and haul him out by the collar if he raises his voice.

Too bad Leo is across campus teaching a class right now.

However, Chase doesn't know that.

"I was wondering if we could talk?" he asks.

I study him. Wait a few seconds to see if his face betrays the performance.

But there's nothing. No twitch of impatience, no simmering frustration under the surface.

Just sincerity. Or something that looks an awful lot like it.

"Give me just a minute," I say, my voice steady. "Then I can take my lunch break. We can go somewhere to talk, okay?"

Relief flickers across his face, softening his jaw. "That sounds great. Um... do you want me to wait outside, or...?"

I glance toward the chair in front of my desk, the one students use when they need me to sort out their schedules. Neutral ground.

"You can sit there. I'll just be a minute."

He nods and walks the few steps forward, dropping into the chair before letting his eyes roam the office like he needs something to focus on. He doesn't stare at me, which I appreciate. The silence stretches, but not in the old way—the tense, buzzing way that used to make me fill it with nervous chatter. This silence just exists, and I let it.

I finish my email, close the laptop, and slip into my coat. It's early for lunch, barely past eleven, but I don't care. I grab my purse and gesture toward the door. "Does pizza work for you?"

His mouth curves into the faintest smile. "Sounds good."

OUTSIDE, February air slaps against my cheeks, sharp and wet with the promise of snow. The quad is full of students hustling between classes, collars pulled up, scarves covering their mouths.

Chase walks beside me but not close enough to brush my arm, and for that, I'm grateful. We pass the student center, the library, and then step into the warmth of Nico's.

Garlic and dough and melted cheese wrap around us like a blanket. It's cozy, crowded, every table buzzing with students and professors trying to steal warmth from both food and each other.

We place our orders at the kiosk. Chase pays. I don't argue, just murmur thanks, and lead us to a two-person table tucked against the side wall near the back. It's the kind of spot where I can see the whole room, mainly, the entrance.

Leo's class doesn't let out until 11:20, so I didn't bother scanning the room when we entered.

But if he walks through that front door, I want to know it.

Chase sits across from me, his elbows on the table, eyes searching mine for a beat too long.

Then he says, "You look good."

I huff out a soft laugh, not unkind.

"Thanks. You look... tired."

Because he does. Dark circles under his eyes. Shoulders drawn tight.

He's always carried a certain recklessness about him, but today it looks heavier, like it's wearing him down.

He runs a hand through his sandy hair, chuckling quietly.

"Yeah, well. These last few months have been kinda rough."

I nod. I don't offer more. I'm not here to make this easy for him.

Silence again. I let it sit.

He clears his throat.

"I've been going to therapy."

"I heard," I say simply. He doesn't ask how.

I don't tell him about the disgusting phone call I received from my father the same day he called to cuss me out.

My nod is enough. I'm done carrying his words for him.

"I'm... I'm sorry, Tori," he says.

A blank stare from me. "For what?"

"Everything," he says. His voice cracks.

"All of it."

I shake my head, half laugh, half disbelief.

How many times have I wanted to hear those words? And how hollow do they sound now, echoing back after all this time?

"I'm serious, okay?" He leans forward, urgency creeping into his tone.

"I'm sorry. I've been an asshole. I've been selfish. I haven't touched a drop of alcohol since October—"

"Bullshit," I snap.

"I'm serious." His hands flatten on the table.

"That's when I started therapy. Real therapy. Not that 'pray harder, read your Bible more' crap at church. An actual therapist who knows what they're talking about."

That makes me look up. That catches my attention.

I don't bring up the fact that I spent years begging him to go. Literal *years* trying to explain how badly he needed professional help.

He rushes on. "I knew that if I just said it, you wouldn't believe me. And you'd never come home. I had to show you I was serious. And I am serious. About this. About us."

A waiter delivers our food to the table.

"Enjoy."

Then he's gone, and Chase doesn't even glance at the pizza. He keeps his eyes locked on me, like if he blinks I'll vanish.

"I've been going every week since the beginning of October," he says. "And I haven't touched alcohol—I swear I haven't. Not even when you had those fucking divorce papers served."

His hand curls into a fist on the table.

I brace myself for the eruption, the old familiar shouting match. But it doesn't come.

He inhales sharply, unclenches, and exhales.

Different. Almost unrecognizable.

"I shouldn't have yelled at you," he says.

"No, you shouldn't have."

"But you shouldn't have served me divorce papers without talking to me first."

I scoff. "I tried, Chase."

"When?" His voice lifts, but only slightly. Enough to sting, not enough to draw eyes from the tables around us.

"I've been trying to talk to you for years. You never listened. So I left. And I told you—first in the letter I left when I moved out, and then again to your face when you showed up here—that I was done."

His mouth presses tight, and then he exhales.

"I'm listening now."

I tilt my head, studying him.

"Are you, though?"

He swallows, and for a long moment he doesn't speak.

Then, softer, "Look, Tori."

His hand reaches across the table, covering mine.

Warm. Familiar. Heavy.

I don't pull away, but I don't lace my fingers with his either. I let it sit, let the weight of it press into my skin without pressing back.

"I'm sorry," he says again, voice earnest.

"I'm so fucking sorry. And I love you. I've always loved you. I haven't stopped therapy, and I won't. I'll keep going. We can go together, if you want. We can figure this out. If you'd just come home, we can fix this. Fix *us*. We can make it better this time."

I stare at our joined hands.

And I feel... nothing.

No spark. No ache. No pull toward the boy I once swore was my forever.

He's saying all the things I begged him for, year after year, but every word spoken is too little, too late. The emptiness between us is louder than his voice.

"If you'd just come home," he pleads. "We can fix this. Together."

My lips part, the words leaving before I can second-guess them.

"I'll go back with you."

Shock flickers across his face. He wasn't expecting that.

Relief floods in after, softening him in a way I haven't seen in years. His smile is small, genuine, unguarded.

Gratitude. Victory, maybe, but not smugness. Just thankfulness.

"You... you will?" he asks.

I nod once.

His smile spreads, full and bright. He looks like a man who just won back the world.

Chase doesn't notice that I'm quiet for the rest of lunch. Doesn't notice how I chew my pizza in silence, how my eyes drift to the window instead of him.

He fills the space with stories of Moraine, work, friends, all the pieces of his life I've been absent for.

He doesn't ask about mine. Not once.

In his mind, this is already settled. We're already back where we belong.

By the time we finish eating, he's talking about a second honeymoon.

Maybe tropical. Maybe Europe. Maybe both.

He's already spinning the future, building castles out of words, and I let him. I smile in the right places, let him talk until he's full of himself again.

When it's time to leave, I stand, slipping my arms back into my coat.

"You head home," I tell him. "I've got to grab a few things, but I'll meet you at the house around dinnertime."

His grin is soft, boyish. "Okay. See you tonight."

He leans in, places a soft kiss on my cheek, then turns and leaves.

And just like that, he's gone.

Out the door, into the cold, convinced he's won me back.

THIRTY

LEO

I GIVE my Calc II section a pop quiz this morning because I enjoy watching panic bloom, then immediately work through the answers with them so they can actually leave campus before conspiring to murder me.

They shuffle out early, grateful, and I text Dex to see where he is and what he's up to.

> Dexter, 10:45 a.m.: Free until 12:30 — lunch?

It's 10:45 and yes, I could eat.

> Leo, 10:45 a.m.: Nico's?

> Dexter, 10:45 a.m.: Bet.

We arrive just before eleven, order, and Dex heads to the back while I duck into the bathroom—three minutes alone, wash my hands, shake off the rest of the chill from the walk over.

I look at myself in the mirror and tell the face looking back that he's a sexy motherfucker, because obviously.

Then I step out and walk straight into my own trouble.

Dex is standing at the take-out counter when I come back, his head tilted, eyes fixed on something in the corner across from us. He doesn't even try to hide the way his jaw tightens when he sees me.

"Bro, is that who I think it is?" he asks, nodding toward the wall where a couple sits crowded in on themselves like they own whatever private bubble they have contrived in the chaos of the place.

My line of sight follows.

For a beat I don't register the rest of the world: the chatter, the clatter of dishes, the Nico's worker calling out names for take-out orders.

All I see is Tori — and the man across from her.

Chase.

The last person in the world I want, or expect, to see sitting with her.

He looks... calm. Not the loud, angry, impossible-to-ignore version of himself. Calm enough that for a second I think maybe I'm misreading a hallucination.

Tori is listening to him. Not flinching. Not rolling her eyes. Her expression is soft and contained.

Tori can handle herself. She doesn't need rescuing. She's not some fragile woman who will be easily manipulated by Chase's charm.

I tell myself all of that in the span of a second.

Then, he reaches across the tiny table and takes her hand.

The stupid normalcy of that gesture—just a hand, a casual squeeze—hits me like a punch. It isn't the grab of a jealous ex. It isn't the claim made by someone used to getting what he wants through sheer force of will.

It's the softer proof of the thing I cannot un-see:

She *lets him* touch her. She *lets him* hold her.

For an instant I am ridiculous with fury and the kind of childish ownership that's ugly and hot and stupid all at once.

My chest tightens. The air feels wrong. I can taste bile.

Dex sees it. Sees Chase's hand holding hers. Sees the rage boiling within me.

"Leo?" he asks.

I should get a grip.

I should step back. I should walk away.

Instead, something in me—a possession that has nothing to do with logic and everything to do with the stupid human animal part of me—pushes forward.

"No," I think. "No way. Not today."

I take a step.

Dex squeezes my shoulder—an attempt to stop me—but the motion is meant to buy time. Meant to say, *maybe think about whether you want to be that guy.*

I shrug his hand off like it's an afterthought. My strides carry me toward their table before my brain catches up.

She is not *his* to touch, I think. Not *his* to hold. Not *his* to love.

Then, as if a current snaps something into place, the thought that makes the rest of it honest and terrible slides under everything else:

She is *mine*.

Not in any legal sense. Not in some ownership logic that would make me ashamed.

In the blunt, aching way of needing someone so much it rearranges your insides: that small, private corner of me that stops at the name Victoria Foster and feels like home. She has woven herself so quietly into my days that I didn't notice until the absence of her is a room too large to stand in.

Only I can touch her. Hold her. Love her.

And I do. I fucking love her.

By the time I'm within one table of reaching them, literally five steps away from ripping his hand off of hers and telling him to back the fuck off, I hear Chase say something that makes my entire world tilt like a bad ride.

"If you'd just come home, we can fix this. Together."

But what freezes me in place is her answer.

It's immediate. No hesitation.

"I'll go back with you."

The sound of those five words hollow everything out inside me. The syllables sit between them like a promise, maybe a surrender, and the joy on his face spreads like sunlight across a wet street.

She smiles at him in the way that makes him soft and victorious and sure.

The truth hits me like a freight train—she means it.

She chose him.

Him.

I exhale. My legs move—not toward them, but away—because I cannot stand there and watch that tableau any longer.

I came here to grab food and head back to my best friend's office for an hour of uninterrupted bro time, but instead I find myself in the exact same position I was in just a few years ago.

In love with a woman who has chosen someone else.

She deserves happily ever after. And clearly, I am not it.

I slip back through the crowd toward Dexter. People brush past—a shoulder here, a backpack thud there—and the ordinary overcrowding of the restaurant gives me anonymity.

If she glances up from across the room she doesn't catch me. She doesn't see my face go blank. She doesn't see the way my fingers curl until the knuckles go white.

Dex is waiting, our lunch in hand, eyebrows lifted.

"You okay, man?" he asks again, with the genuine concern of someone who knows you well enough to read the train wreck before it happens.

I don't meet his eyes. I can't. I rub a hand over my face because if I look at him he'll know I am undone and I... I just can't right now.

I let out a breath that sounds like a laugh and say the only thing I can at this very moment.

"Just get me the fuck out of here."

THIRTY-ONE

TORI

I CALL Jake the second I leave Grand River, my Telluride engine humming against the cold as I merge onto I-70 east. Roughly four and a half hours lie between me and Moraine.

That's four and a half hours to brace myself for the conversation waiting for me when I get there.

He answers on the first ring.

"Hi, Tori. I'm assuming you have news."

I skip the pleasantries.

"Chase came to the office today. Calm. He just wanted to talk. I don't know if he'll stay this calm, but I'm not dragging it out anymore. I'm on my way to Moraine. This ends today."

"I'll have my co-counsel meet you at the house," Jake says evenly. "Call me when you're about an hour out so he has time to pull the paperwork together and drive over."

"Okay." My knuckles whiten on the steering wheel. "Thank you."

The line clicks off and leaves me with nothing but the road and the ache in my chest. The drive blurs—winter-bare trees that look more like bones than branches, snow crusted in the ditches.

I try music, then silence. Neither helps. Every mile closer, the weight in my chest gets heavier, but my resolve is steady.

Mountains crest and fall into foothills. I cut north, trading highway speed for narrower roads that twist along creeks and through shuttered towns. Snow dusts the shoulders, bare branches bow over the pavement, and every curve brings me nearer to the jagged outlines of the Rockies.

By the time I'm about a half hour out, I call Jake again.

"I'm on track," I tell him, my voice steadier than I feel.

He confirms the co-counsel will meet me there in an hour, and I end the call and drive the last stretch in a quieter, bleaker kind of focus.

The canyon leading into Moraine is narrow. Granite walls climb high on either side; the frozen river runs like a ribbon beside the road. The climb feels endless until the valley opens and the town spreads beneath the snow-capped peaks.

Finally, I'm driving down our street. The house comes into view, small under the mountain sky.

Chase steps outside—he must have been watching for my SUV from the window—and he stands, waiting on the porch. His smile is wide, almost boyish, and it cuts something deep inside me.

The drive has been long, but not long enough. Hours of winding canyons and snow-laced peaks, of trying to steady myself with coffee and silence, and still nothing could prepare me for the way Chase is waiting.

Chase steps off the porch when I pull into the driveway, shoulders squared against the cold.

For a heartbeat it feels like I've stepped backward in time, like nothing has broken between us.

Before I turn off the vehicle I send a quick text to Skye, realizing only now that in my hyper focus to make things happen I completely forgot to tell my roommate I wouldn't be home after work.

Tori, 5:02 p.m.: I'll be home late. Don't wait up.

I don't check to see if she responds, instead switching my phone to *do not disturb* before dropping it into my handbag.

Chase walks to my door and opens it, his voice warm, hopeful.

"Dinner's ready. We'll get your bags later."

There are no bags.

He doesn't even check.

I step out, letting him fall in beside me, but my chest is already tightening, bracing for the weight of what's coming.

When we step onto the porch I pause, my hand gripping the rail. I can't go inside.

It feels... wrong. Like a lie.

"Let's sit a minute," I say softly, lowering myself onto the top step. The wood feels frigid through my jeans—it's insanely cold right now, but we both have on jackets. We'll live.

I pat the spot beside me. He sits, close enough that our shoulders touch.

I take his hands in mine, look at them—at us. The way we've always fit, the way it once felt like home.

"Chase," I say, softly. "I need you to hear what I'm about to say."

He smiles faintly, still believing.

"Of course, baby."

He leans in to kiss me, but I turn away, eyes fixed on our fingers knotted together.

"What's wrong?" he asks. "You're here now. Everything's going to be fine, we can work on things—"

I lay three fingers gently over his mouth.

"No. Not this time. I need you to listen. Not to argue, not to twist my words, not only to hear what you want. Just listen. Can you do that?"

He studies me, something nervous flickering in his eyes, then nods.

I lower my hand and take a breath that cuts sharp in the cold. "I love you. I always will. But when I left... that wasn't an ultimatum. That was the end."

The hope drains from his face. His grip on my hands tightens, then falters.

"But you said—"

"I'm speaking," I murmur, my voice breaking. "You're listening."

His jaw tightens, but he stays quiet.

"I'm proud of you for going to therapy," I continue, voice trembling but steady enough.

"And you should keep going. But not for me. Not for us. For you. Because if you're only doing it to win me back, then nothing will change. You need to heal for yourself. Because you are worth fighting for, Chase. You are worth loving. Even if it's not me who does it anymore."

He swallows, and the quiet after that feels like a held breath.

"So this is it," he says finally, voice small. "This is really done?"

"It is," I answer. "It's not one fight or one problem. It's every time I picked myself up after you broke me and then smiled so you wouldn't feel worse. It's every time I swallowed my anger because your shame made you louder. It's the years of being the one who fixed, smoothed, and absorbed your darkness because you couldn't sit with what hurt you."

He looks as if he might argue, but words fail him; they stack behind his eyes like bricks.

"I didn't mean to make you feel like that," he whispers. "I didn't know how to be different."

"Then learn," I say, sharper than I want, then softer. "Learn for you, not because I asked. I won't be the reason you stop spiraling. I'm not your safety net."

His hands are shaking, not from the cold. I can feel the tremor run through him.

"I'm trying. I swear I am. Every week—there are things I say out loud that I never said to anyone. It's brutal."

"I know you're trying," I admit, and it hurts to say it because trying shouldn't be the only thing that keeps people together. "But trying is different from changing. Trying can be performative if it's shaped around getting me back. Change is slow, ugly work. And it has to be for you. No one else."

Tears slide down his face, silent at first, and then steady. "If I'm worth loving, and if you still love me... why are you ending this?"

"Because I've broken too many times for you." My own tears spill over. I've held them back too long. "And I can't do it anymore. As long as I stay, we'll keep breaking each other until there's nothing left."

He clutches at my hands like a lifeline.

"I don't want to lose you, Tor. I was scared—scared of failing, scared of being small. My parents—" He stops, the words too heavy for the thin winter air. "They did this to me. I don't want to be that man. I don't want to hurt you."

"My staying won't make you stop hurting me," I say. "Your childhood didn't make you a bad man, Chase. It made you wounded. But I won't let you keep using me as the place to bleed out. I loved you and I thought love could hold everything. I was wrong."

He closes his eyes, and the sound he makes is half sob, half apology.

"Tell me what to do. Tell me anything that could fix this. I'll do it."

My throat tightens. I want to give him a list—therapy sessions, reading lists, support groups, calls to Trent, consistent check-ins with a sponsor. I want to give him a plan that guarantees success.

But there's no guarantee. There's only time and work and a willingness he must find inside himself.

"Start with you," I say finally. "Keep going to therapy. Do the homework. Go when it's hard, not just when it's convenient. Talk to your brother and let him see you try. And stop drinking—really stop. Not for me. Not for your brother. For yourself. Then show up for the small things. People don't need grand gestures. They need daily proof that you can be a different man."

He nods, furious and desperate and heartbreakingly sincere. "I will. I swear I will."

"Then do it for that reason," I plead, still crying. "Not so you can come back to me. Do it so you can live with yourself without hating the man you see in the mirror."

He looks at me like that broken boy I fell in love with so many years ago, and he whispers, "I love you."

"I love you," I whisper back. "And that's why I can't stay."

His forehead presses against mine, his tears thick in his voice. "I ruined us."

"It wasn't only you," I breathe.

"But it was mostly me."

My throat tightens. "Maybe. Yeah."

He pulls back just enough to cup my face, his hands warm against my frozen skin, his thumbs wiping at tears that won't stop. His eyes are red, wet, so full of regret that I almost can't bear it.

"I'm sorry, Tor."

I choke on a sob, because this hurts. It hurts like my soul has cracked in two, my heart is breaking all over again. "I know."

Then he leans forward and presses his lips to mine. Gentle. Careful. A soft goodbye.

When he pulls back, he doesn't let go, just rests his forehead on mine again. And for a long time we sit like that.

Crying together. Mourning seventeen years of shared history —a complicated life and a turbulent love we built together, all of it crumbling into memory while the mountains watch in silence.

The sound of tires crunching over snow breaks the moment. A black Mercedes pulls up the drive and the attorney climbs out, briefcase in hand, and even without words Chase understands.

Inside, the house is the same—same furniture, same scent. But it feels foreign now, like walking through a photograph.

The papers are laid out on the coffee table, white sheets that weigh more than stone. The space next to his name waits for his signature, then mine.

Chase goes first. His hand shakes as the pen scrapes across the page. Then it's my turn. My fingers tremble, but I sign anyway.

And just like that, seventeen years are reduced to ink on paper.

He clears his throat, voice rough. "I'll call the realtor Monday. Start the process with the house."

"Please route everything through Jake," I say, my voice flat. "You already have his information."

He nods. There's nothing left to say.

The attorney leaves first, and I'm not far behind.

At the door, I pause. The air is sharp, my tears drying cold on my cheeks.

"Chase?"

He turns, weary and hollow.

"Thank you," I whisper.

He dips his head in acknowledgment, then disappears back into our—his—bedroom.

I walk to the SUV, each step heavy.

When I drive away, the house grows small in my rearview.

I wish this day could be over already, but I have one more stop to make before I leave this snowy mountain town.

BY THE TIME I pull into my parents' driveway, the stars are already out, sharp against the black sky. The porch light glows over snow still crusted in patches along the walk, and my headlights sweep across the yard before I cut the engine.

The house looks the same as it always has—warm light in the

windows, neat curtains drawn, the faint shadow of movement inside—but I feel like an intruder stepping onto this porch.

I knock, and a few seconds later my father opens the door. He doesn't notice the redness in my eyes, doesn't notice the exhaustion pulling at me.

His face softens in what passes for a welcome. "Tori. You want to come in?"

"Yes," I say quietly.

He steps aside, and I brush past him into the familiar foyer.

"We're just finishing up dinner," he adds, tone matter-of-fact. "You're welcome to join us."

I nod. "Thank you."

He leads me into the dining room.

My mother is there, sitting at the formal table set with candles and china. Her eyes widen when she sees me, surprised but happy.

Then, instantly, they narrow with concern when she catches what my father didn't—the swollen evidence of tears, the heaviness in my face.

She rises, crosses the room, and folds me into her arms without hesitation.

"Sweetheart," she whispers, holding me a second too long. When she lets go, her voice steadies into something brighter. "Sit, sit. I'll get you a plate."

She moves toward the kitchen, already pulling a fresh plate and silverware from the sideboard, while I sink into one of the side chairs.

My father sits back down at the head of the table as if nothing has shifted, knife in hand, cutting into his roast.

"So," he says, without looking up. "You're home now? Done with that nonsense in Grand River?"

The words land like a stone, but I don't answer right away. I wait until my mother returns, sets the plate in front of me, her hand brushing mine in quiet reassurance.

"Thank you," I murmur to her.

Then I lift my eyes to him, calm and steady.

"Grand River is my home, Daddy. I only came by to let you know that Chase and I signed the papers today. Our marriage has ended and the house will be on the market next week."

The scrape of his knife against porcelain is sharp enough to make my teeth ache.

He finally looks up, his face hard.

"You're divorcing your husband."

The disdain in his voice is sharp. "Ten years of marriage, and you just throw it away. All the prayers, all the work we put into that marriage—wasted. You're a selfish girl, Tori. You never learned how to endure. Marriage is hard, but you don't just—"

"I'm sorry, you must be confused." My fork touches down against the plate with a quiet click. My voice is calm, deliberate. "I didn't come here to have a conversation or to obtain your approval for my life choices. I'm here, as a courtesy, to inform you about an adult life decision my now ex-husband and I have made. Whether or not you agree with that decision is not my concern."

Then I pick up my fork again and start to eat, slow and unhurried, as if the world isn't cracking in two between us.

My mother watches me, torn between pride and fear, but she doesn't speak.

My father's face flushes red. He chews like the food is an offense, rage thickening in his jaw.

Finally, he slams his palm against the table. The silverware rattles.

"Get out. Get out of my house."

"Richard," my mom pleads, voice sharp with warning.

I set my fork down again, slower this time. Blot my mouth with the napkin in my lap, fold it neatly, and push back from the table.

I lean over and press a kiss to Mom's cheek.

"Thanks for dinner, Mom."

Before I can take another step, his voice whips across the room. "I said leave!"

"Richard!" she cries, sharp and desperate.

I look at her, then back at him, my voice calm but final.

"Don't act surprised, Mom. He's always been a dick."

And then I walk out, coat still unbuttoned, February air biting hard against my skin as the door shuts behind me.

Back in my SUV, I sit for a moment with the engine off, silence pressing in heavy.

Two goodbyes in one night—one to the man I married, one to the father who never really knew how to love me without conditions.

My chest aches with the weight of both.

Finally, I start the car, headlights cutting through the cold, and I drive away from the house that is definitely no longer my home.

THIRTY-TWO

LEO

THE HANGOVER WAKES me right before the doorbell does.

It sits behind my eyes like a hot coin—press, throb, press. When the chime goes off, it punches through that coin like a gong, pain ricocheting around my brain.

I peel one eye open and immediately regret it, tasting last night on my tongue—whiskey, toothpaste, and... why do my nostrils burn? Did I throw up and shoot whiskey out my nose?

The doorbell rings again.

"It's Saturday," I croak to no one. "Cease and desist."

I grope around for my phone, don't find it, shove off the blanket that's acting as my warm, fluffy hiding place, and swing my legs out of bed. Boxers, that's it. No T-shirt, no socks. My mouth is dry as a desert and the floor is so cold my arches rise in protest.

The bell goes again. Long press this time.

"All right," I mutter, staggering down the hall. My head does the thing where it pulses in time with my footfalls, like there's a subwoofer buried under my hairline.

I smear the back of my hand over my mouth—drool, fantastic —and catch sight of myself in the hall mirror. Bedhead like I've been electrocuted. Eyes the color of bad coffee.

I squint at my reflection and, out of long habit, deadpan, "Still a sexy motherfucker," and then open the door.

Stephanie.

"What the fuck," I say, not even bothering with hello, "are you doing at my house at this *ungodly* hour on a Saturday?"

I'm standing in the opening to my house, hand resting on the knob and forearm on the frame, so when she attempts to step in from the cold and I don't budge, Stephanie stops and stomps her foot like a petulant child.

"Leo," she huffs. She's bracing against more than the weather, hands shoved into the pockets of a long coat, cheeks pink from the air. "I need to talk to you."

"Not right now, you don't."

I start to shut the door. She plants a palm against it and leans in.

"Leo, please."

Great. Now I'm a half-naked asshole wrestling with his ex-wife on his own stoop at six in the morning. The neighbors are probably peeking through their blinds, judging the prick who won't let that poor woman inside from the cold.

Who am I kidding? Nobody's watching this. They are all asleep. Like normal people, this early on a Saturday.

I pinch the bridge of my nose, which does nothing helpful for the coin behind my eyes, and inhale air so cold it scrapes.

"Look," I say, exasperated. I just need this woman to leave, right now, so I can go back to sleep. "I promise, we'll talk. We can talk about whatever the fuck you want to talk about. Just not at six in the morning, on a Saturday, when I'm hungover and my head has a pulse and I'm in a terrible mood and I don't even have any fucking clothes on, okay?"

Her gaze slides down my bare chest, lingers a fraction too long at the waistband of my boxers, then zips back up.

"Right. You're right." She takes a small step back. "I'm sorry. I should have called."

"Yeah," I snap. "You should have. And not until after nine. Because, Saturday."

"I'll go," she says, voice small, apologetic. "I'll... I'll go."

"That's probably for the best."

She turns, starts down the steps, and that's when a Kia Telluride I know all too well jerks to a stop at my curb like God heard my prayer for more sleep and laughed.

Because of course Victoria Foster would show up at my house at 6 a.m. when my ex-wife is leaving and I'm standing at my open door practically naked.

The driver side door flies open. Tori barrels out. And damn, she's hot. Not like, good looking hot—which she is, because she always looks amazing—but like, fucking angry hot.

Stephanie startles like she's been shot at.

"Are you fucking kidding me?!" Tori yells, and the sound of it hits my porch, my chest, my stupid, hungover brain.

If the neighbors weren't awake before, they probably are now.

Stephanie freezes, looks from Tori to me and back. "I was just leaving," she says, and hustles toward her car like she's outrunning a storm.

Tori rounds the front of her SUV, hands waving, eyes burning with fury. She points at me like I'm a dead man.

"Your ex-wife, Leo? You couldn't even stick your dick in some random Tinder twat to get yourself off? You had to go and sleep with *her*?!"

She punctuates that statement by jabbing a finger toward the street where Stephanie is fumbling with her keys.

"Wait," Stephanie asks. "Who are you?"

"That is none of your damn business, Champagne Problems," Tori snaps. "Now go the fuck home."

I laugh. I can't help it. She's so sexy when she's angry. And— *ouch, fuck,* my head.

"You think this is funny?" she shrieks. "She's married, Leo. MARRIED."

I shrug because I'm stupid, and also because why does she care?

Which reminds me.

"I thought you went back to Moraine?" I toss out. "Back to your *husband*."

At first, Tori looks like I slapped her. Then the rage returns.

"I did," she fires back. "To get *divorced*, you dumb idiot."

All the air goes out of my lungs. I swear it's like someone just kicked me in the chest and I cannot breathe.

Wait. What?

I stand there in my doorway like a frozen gargoyle, mouth half open, nothing useful coming out.

Her expression morphs from fury to exhaustion. "I'm too fucking tired for this," she mutters, turns, and climbs back into the SUV.

The next thing I know her door slams shut and she's speeding away before my knees remember how to bend.

"Tori. Wait!" I call, and then I'm running down the steps, forgetting that I'm not wearing shoes. The porch is rimmed in frost and my entire driveway is a sheet of ice posing as concrete.

It's ten degrees, maybe twenty if the sun is lying. My soles hit the porch steps and pain shoots up my calves from the cold. I make it to the sidewalk, flailing for balance, and by the time I hit the curb, her taillights are a pair of rubies shrinking into the gray morning.

Fucking dammit.

I pivot, sprinting back toward the house to grab keys, phone, anything. I must have pulled the door shut behind me when I launched myself down the steps.

My hand meets the keypad and... nothing. No little lights. No cheerful beep. I press again. Dead.

No. No no no no no. The battery. The one that's been chirping for days. The one I kept telling myself I'd change "tonight" and then got distracted and said "tomorrow" and then got distracted again and said "later."

Guess what time it is, Leo? It's later.

I am now the living, breathing definition of *fuck around and find out*.

I punch the center button to reset it, get exactly zero response, and stand there, half naked, half hungover, entirely freezing, realizing I am locked out of my own house with no keys, no phone, no dignity, and no way to fix this situation without being the asshole who woke up his neighbors at 6 a.m. on a fucking Saturday.

I head back down the steps, trying the windows because I am nothing if not a man who prefers the obvious humiliation to the creative one. Every ground-floor latch is tight.

My alarm system is fancy, which means every sensible point of entry is sealed like it expects a raccoon army at dawn. I could break a pane, sure, but the second I do, the siren will go off, automatically signaling the police while Lois follows up with a call to 911 and the HOA. Then the HOA will send a sternly worded email about "seasonally appropriate attire on common-view porches," and I will become the next viral Nextdoor post: *Boxer-Clad Burglar Actually Just Hungover Homeowner.*

My feet go from freezing to pain to that alarming numbness where you can't tell if you still have toes. I hop back onto the porch, huffing steam like a dragon who regrets everything.

Options spool through my head and all of them are bad.

The only unsecured window in the entire house is the little one that opens into the weird bonus loft—a dormer tucked away over the side yard. It's not really a second story; it's a glorified treehouse someone slapped onto a cottage style house to make the blueprints more interesting.

The front dormers are ornamental—pure Potemkin village. But the side dormer? The loft? Real window. Real latch. And unless I'm wrong, I've never once told my alarm to care about it.

I glance at the pergola that frames the back porch. Snow crusts the top slats, weighty and white. There's a bump-out of roof not too far from it.

If I can climb the pergola, use something to clear the snow, belly onto the roof, and shimmy across, I might be able to reach the dormer ledge. Would that be insane? Yes. Would it be a better option than freezing my testicles off on the porch while composing a note to Tori with icicles? Also yes.

"Brilliant," I tell myself. "Let's do the dumb thing."

I pad gingerly around to the back, tiptoe-hobble-curse, and size up the climb. The pergola is solid cedar, anchored into brick, crossbeams spaced like a ladder if ladders were designed by a sadist.

The snow makes it slick, the cold makes it brittle, and I make it worse by being a tired, hungover idiot without shoes... or pants.

There's a broom leaning in the corner by the grill, bristles stiff with old ash. I grab it, knock off the crust, and test a foothold on the first crossbeam. It holds. I reach for the next beam with my hands, palms stinging instantly, and do the thing rock climbers do where they pretend they're not dumbasses with a death wish.

One rung. Two. My toes are screaming. I hug the post and rest my forehead against the cold wood.

"You're fine," I tell my entire lower body, which has decided to revolt. "We're fine."

I get another rung, plant my foot, shift my weight—and my arch slips. My right foot slides off the slick beam, my left knee slams into the post, and my full body slams forward into the ladder of wood with exactly one unfortunately positioned crossbar to break the momentum.

My entire universe reduces to a single, blinding point: I have just introduced the left side of my scrotum to a frozen piece of cedar at velocity.

Every man has a language for this pain. Mine is incoherent. Sound rips out of me—the noise you make when you've discovered an entirely new color of agony—and I cling to the beam with my chest and biceps and will my soul not to leave my body.

I see God for a second, or at least I see a cartoon of Him holding a sign that says, "Buddy."

I breathe through my teeth. I want to vomit. I want to ascend into a higher plane and leave my balls behind. "Initiate subspace," I whisper to my junk, and wait for the waves to recede from killing to maiming.

Cold helps. So does swearing. I do both. When the pain eases from white-hot to a deep, punishing throb, I re-set my feet and move like a contrite sinner: slow, careful, with the full knowledge that one wrong move and I'm back in communion with the cedar crossbar of doom.

At the top of the pergola, the broom earns its keep. I extend it, push snow off the small lip of roof that runs from the porch over toward the dormer. Sheets of powder slough off like blankets. Once there's a bare strip, I belly flop onto it. The roof is rough under my chest, the shingles grabbing skin.

My ribs complain, my stomach does not understand why it is being exfoliated, and my testicle is still not speaking to me. That's fair.

I keep the broom in one hand like a ridiculous tightrope pole and shimmy along the strip of roof, inching toward the little ledge in front of the dormer. Below me, the yard looks mean and far. Above me, the sky is bright and unforgiving.

I try not to think about falling. I try to think about Tori's face. She was furious and exhausted and still, somehow, the center of the only world I want to live in.

She said she went back to get divorced. I should have said something, anything, other than just standing there, speechless. I should have run down the steps, immediately, bare feet and boxer clad and begged for a do-over.

Instead I'm out here auditioning for America's Dumbest Home Intrusions. *Is that a show? We should make that a show.*

The ledge is a narrow lip—eight inches, maybe ten—the accumulated snow and ice making everything stupid, cold, and slippery as fuck. I knock off what I can with the broom, slide onto it, press my chest to the line of the dormer, and wedge my toes onto the shingle edges, calves trembling.

The window is right there. Salvation, quartz-cold and smug.

"Please be unlocked," I breathe, and curl my fingers under the bottom sash.

It doesn't budge.

I lift harder. Nothing. My breath fogs the glass and drifts back into my face. I drop my forehead against the pane and whisper a string of obscenities that could curdle milk.

I have two choices: negotiate my way back across the roof and down the murder pergola with a bruised ball, or break the window and crawl through.

The first is *maybe* safer, but also maybe break-my-neck-ier, and humiliating. The second is dangerous in a might-slice-something-open kind of way, and still, humiliating.

I look down again. My feet skitter slightly on the shingles. My stomach drops. Decision made.

I test the corner of the pane with my knuckles—tap, tap. Solid.

I think about all the movies where someone blasts through a window with a jacket wrapped around their fist, then remember that I have exactly one garment on my person and it is currently covering the two parts of my body that are not meant for public display. Also, if I take it off, I'm not just the idiot breaking into his own house—I'm the idiot breaking into his own house bare-ass naked in twenty-degree weather.

"Okay," I tell myself. "We're doing this."

I hook my thumb in the waistband of my boxers and pause.

There is a version of this story where I maintain a sliver of dignity. This is not that version.

Using my other hand to maintain my balance on the window, I peel the boxers down to my knees, then to my ankles, step out with one foot, and keep the other foot half-caught because the last thing I need is to drop my underwear off this roof and into the frozen yard like I'm stripping for a very specific OnlyFans.

I lift said foot up into some weird yoga pose—please God don't let me fall—and remove the boxers. I then wrap the fabric around my fist—once, twice—tighten it over the knuckles, and cock my arm.

"Leopold?" a voice calls pleasantly from below.

I freeze, half crouched, bare butt presented to the morning like an offering. I turn my head enough to see the side yard and, standing on her back porch in a robe, slippers, and one of those knit hats with a pom-pom the size of a softball, is Lois Schneider.

"Yes, Mrs. Schneider," I say, because I was raised with manners even when I'm committing misdemeanor self-entry in the nude.

"I told you, dear, you can call me Lois."

"I know, Mrs. Schneider."

She peers up, shading her eyes with a liver-spotted hand. "Do you need help? Should I call someone?"

"No, ma'am. I'm fine."

"Okay..." she says, unconvinced.

There is a pause long enough for me to hear three sparrows debate my life choices.

Then, "Leopold, why are you naked?"

"Not now, Mrs. Schneider!"

"You don't need to be embarrassed, you know," she says, matter-of-factly. "I was married to my Harold for sixty-three years. Your testicles are nothing I haven't seen before."

I close my eyes, then inhale what dignity I have left and exhale every stupid decision that led to this very moment.

"And I do know how cold it is outside. Why, this one time, my Harold, his testes—"

"Lois?"

"Yes, dear."

"Can we please stop talking about testicles? I'm trying to focus."

"Oh yes, of course. Of course. Be careful now, you hear?"

"Working on it," I mutter, and draw my arm back.

The first hit doesn't break it—just a crack, a sharp star in the corner. The second shatters the pane with a sound that feels like a slap across my entire nervous system.

Glass gives, a triangle falls inward, and a spray of glittering shards skitters across the loft floor. Cold air knifes out and through me, and a few splinters bite the skin of my wrist where the cotton slips.

I shake out the boxers, wrap them again tighter, and knock away the remaining jagged teeth, clearing a gap large enough for a dumb man—this one, specifically—to crawl through.

I brush the bottom sash, swipe shards off the sill with the edge of my forearm, and get one knee onto the frame.

"Almost there," I tell no one. The roof squeaks under my other foot. I plant my palms, tuck my head, and wriggle through.

For a second I'm a cartoon of a man birthing himself into his own loft: bare ass in the wind, shoulders scraping old carpet, boxers wrapped around my wrist like I just captured this flag.

Then I'm inside. I sprawl on the frigid floor, cheek against dusty carpet, lungs grabbing at the air like I ran a mile.

The pain in my left testicle thrums. Glass crunches under my palm when I push up. A small ribbon of blood slides across the back of my hand where a shard caught me.

I get to my knees and take inventory: skin scraped, hand nicked, pride annihilated, nut offended but intact.

The loft is empty. Nothing but dust, cobwebs, and now, glass hiding up here. I shuffle to the little half door, unlatch it, and climb down the short set of steps into the hallway.

The alarm panel at the end blinks a cheerful green like this morning never happened. I punch the bypass code for the broken dormer zone, just in case something decides to trip, and shuffle straight to the thermostat. Heat on full blast. My skin prickles as life returns to my feet in hot needles.

In the bathroom, I run warm water over my hands, wash the cut, dab at it with a towel, and catch sight of myself in the mirror once again.

New additions: a smear of blood on my wrist, an impressive scrape on my shoulder, hair that looks even more out of control.

I turn sideways, wince, and check the damage. The left side of my scrotum is already showing the faintest, traitorous bloom of purple.

"Buddy," I tell it, because we've been through a lot. "I'm sorry."

I shower, not to clean the night off so much as to stand with my head under heat and let the stupidity wash off my skin and out of my muscles.

The water scalds at first, then settles, steam fogging the glass. My body loosens. My brain does not. It keeps replaying the last forty five minutes of morning like a loop I can't stop: Stephanie on the porch. Tori in the street.

"I did. To get divorced, you dumb idiot."

I lean my forehead against the tile and breathe.

The truth is simple and humiliating: I didn't trust her. I made assumptions based on a snippet of a conversation I overheard, drank myself into oblivion, and then, when she showed up at my house and said the one thing I've been dying to hear for months, I pulled a Leo and fucked it all up.

I didn't say "I'm proud of you" or "Are you okay" or "Do you need anything."

I'd already made assumptions, let her believe a lie because I was angry, and was too far into my trip to Fuckupsville to reroute my internal GPS and fix the situation.

Maybe if I'd been clothed and caffeinated, I would have done better. But I wasn't.

So I stood there. Slack-jawed. A frozen, buffering buffoon.

I towel off, pull on sweats and a hoodie, and limp—God, I'm limping—into the kitchen.

Coffee. Water. Ibuprofen. I line them up like communion and take all three. The clock on the stove says 6:48.

These forty-eight minutes have been the longest three days of my life.

My phone is on the counter where I abandoned it last night. Ok, fine—yesterday afternoon. I pick it up and stare at the black screen, as if the thing will tell me how to fix any of this. When it wakes, there's a text from Dexter from after we fled Nico's:

> Dex, 11:32 a.m.: you need me?

There's also a text from Tori, time-stamped last night, that I didn't see:

> Tori, 11:31 p.m.: Sorry I had to leave early today. Had some stuff to handle. I'll be by first thing tomorrow morning.

Would you look at that. She called ahead.

If I had paid attention to my phone instead of blocking out the world to drown my sorrows in whiskey, well, it's safe to assume Lois wouldn't have seen my asshole this morning.

I type and erase three different drafts of apologies. The first is too defensive, the second too pathetic, the third too... I don't know.

I hate all of them. I set the phone down and stare at the cooling coffee until the skin on top shimmers. My head throbs once in solidarity.

The doorbell rings again.

"No," I yell at the door. "Absolutely not. Go away."

It rings again.

I shuffle to the door more carefully this time, crack it open, and there—because apparently the universe likes to revel in my humiliation—is Lois.

This time on *my* porch, a grocery bag in her hands, a knit scarf thrown over her robe like she's decided apparel is a buffet and you can add whatever you want to an outfit. Mixed genres allowed.

"I brought you a towel," she says, blithe. "And muffins."

I blink. "Muffins?"

"Blueberry. Your favorite."

We have never, not once, discussed my preferences in muffins. "Thank you, Lois."

"And a towel," she says again, pressing the bag into my hands.

I peek inside. Towel, muffins, and—for reasons beyond me—a travel-size bottle of aloe.

"Figured you might need that," she says, eyes perfectly innocent.

I close my eyes and accept that I now live in a daytime comedy written by a benevolent assassin.

"You are a saint."

"You looked distressed," she says, as if that covers the spectacle of my ass and nuts to our entire street.

"Also, there's a piece of glass sticking out of your hair."

She reaches up, plucks it, and drops it into my palm like a fairy godmother handing over a crystal.

"Thank you," I say again, because the alternatives are to laugh or cry and I don't have the energy for either.

"Is your girlfriend mad at you?" she asks, completely unbothered.

"She's not my girlfriend," I say, and wince because that's a technicality my heart resents.

"And yes. Maybe. I don't know. She was mad at me before she told me she divorced her husband and then left before I could say anything worthwhile."

"Hmm," says Lois, which is a full treatise coming from her. "Women don't get loud unless the quiet has been ignored too long."

I stare at her. "Did you just... quote Socrates at me?"

"Eat a muffin, sweetheart," she says, patting my cheek twice before leaving my porch and toddling back across the snow to her house, robe and scarf both fluttering like a flag.

I do as I'm told and eat a muffin. It's still warm and it's perfect and I hate that my eyes sting because Lois Schneider, that strange and inappropriate old woman, just surprised me with so much kindness after my morning from hell.

I drain the coffee, as much water as my stomach will hold, and then I text Dexter because that seems like a safe first move.

> Leo, 7:06 a.m.: locked myself out. keypads dead. broke my own dormer. frostbitten toes… and pride. also maybe a testicle. neighbor saw my naked ass. please prepare to never speak of this again.

> Dexter, 7:07 a.m.: on my way

> Leo, 7:07 a.m.: do not come here

> Dexter, 7:07 a.m.: coming with bagels

> Leo, 7:08 a.m.: i swear to god you cannot read

I set the phone down, then pick it back up. I scroll to Tori's name and stare at it until I mutter *fuck it* and just do it. Then I type, because if nothing else, the morning has taught me that silence will not save me.

> Leo, 7:10 a.m.: I'm sorry for this morning. Not for what you did—please keep yelling at me when I'm an idiot—but for what I didn't do. I let you believe something because I was angry. Then you told me something huge and I ignored it. I'm proud of you. Are you okay? Do you need anything?

I stare at the phone, waiting for bubbles that don't appear. I don't deserve a response. I send another, because if I'm going to be honest, I might as well be honest all the way down.

> Leo, 7:11 a.m.: Stephanie showed up uninvited at 6 a.m. I didn't invite her in. I didn't sleep with her. I will never choose that again. I know saying it doesn't earn your trust back, but I didn't want you to spend the day picturing the worst.

I put the phone down and pace, then regret pacing because my left thigh decides to repossess all the pain from its testicular neighbor. I stop, lean on the counter, and let the hangover and the grief rehearse their grim duet.

George would hate this. He would have stood in my kitchen, filled the coffee mugs, and waited me out.

"What do you actually want, son?" he'd have asked, and I would have tried to make a joke, and he would have let it die. He was like that—gentle in a way that made you tell the truth.

What do I want? I want to stop getting in my own way. I want to stop making the easiest words the first ones. I want to keep choosing the person who keeps choosing me, even when I'm unbearable. I want to knock and then wait until invited.

I want to hold space without filling it with noise. I want a life where I don't have to write sentences like *I love her* in my head without ever actually saying them out loud.

I want Tori on my couch, stealing my throw blanket and telling me my taste in movies is both impeccable and embarrassing.

I want to be the man who hears "I went to get divorced, you dumb idiot" and replies with, "I'm sorry you had to do that. I'm so goddamn proud of you. What do you need?"

Another text arrives—not from her, but from Skye.

> Skye, 7:19 a.m.: if you hurt her again i will end you

I type three drafts, land on:

Leo, 7:20 a.m.: Understood.

When Dex shows up twenty minutes later he doesn't knock, because—oh, look—he has a key.

He steps in, eyes take one sweep of my pathetic form—hoodie, limp, bandaged hand, dark circles under my eyes like a raccoon—and sets a paper bag on the counter.

"Bagels, juice, and an apology doughnut," he says. "And I brought a pack of AAAs for your keypad."

"You're a good man," I say, voice thick with relief that I pretend is about carbohydrates.

"You look like you wrestled a yeti," he observes, taking in the general aura of a man who has recently courted gravity.

His gaze drops. "And you're walking like someone angry kicked you in the gonads."

"Pergola," I confirm, grim.

He winces, then, because he's a good friend, doesn't joke. "You want to tell me why you were roof-crawling at dawn in February?"

"Locked myself out. Dead keypad, remember?" I take a sip of juice and make a face.

"Lois saw my entire ass."

"Lois sees all," he intones, then nods at the phone. "You text the Mrs?"

"Tori?" I swallow. He nods.

"You mean the *Ms*. Turns out assuming really does make an ass out of me. And, to answer your question, yes."

"Yeah," he says, sympathy aimed at my stupidity lacing his tone. "I just found out this morning."

Dexter unscrews the battery compartment on the keypad like he owns the place. "You going to text her again?"

"After a bagel? Yes."

He grins. "Good man."

I take a bagel from the bag, chew, breathe, and brace for whatever comes next.

Tori's name sits at the top of my messages. I don't know what she'll say. I don't know if she'll come over or tell me to give her space or send a single period that means *heard*. I don't know if I've done too much damage with my shitty words, terrible timing, and stupid porch pantomime.

But for once, I'm willing to sit in not knowing. To wait like a man who understands the difference between wanting and deserving, between love and possession, between noise and care.

My phone buzzes.

For the first time all morning, the coin behind my eyes cools, just a fraction, like maybe, just maybe, the worst thing I've done today won't be the only thing that defines it.

> Tori, 7:25 a.m.: Your neighbor saw your naked ass?

I yell at Dexter, "You fucking told Alis?!"

THIRTY-THREE

TORI

LIKE ANY NORMAL human being with an eight-to-five, I am not a fan of Mondays. But today... this one feels different.

The ink is dry. Papers are filed. There's no more almost, no more waiting.

Yes, the judge still has to give his official stamp of approval, but Jake has already assured me there won't be any hiccups.

For all intents and purposes, I am walking into work this morning without the invisible weight of someone else's name pressed against mine.

Although I've been going by Victoria Foster for the last seven months, I've still carried another name for so long that it feels foreign to imagine myself without it.

Still, officially severing that tie is freeing. Terrifying and liberating at the same time. (*Nobody ruin this moment for me by saying it isn't officially official until I change my name at the Social Security Administration office. I'm not an idiot.*)

The weekend blurred past me. A lot of texting with Leo, some of it serious, some absolutely ridiculous and fun.

He told me all about Lois, how she caught him naked and trying to break into his own house, and I laughed until I cried. I think she might be my new favorite person, and that's saying something since I haven't even met her yet.

Somewhere in between the laughter and the late-night honesty, I fully embraced how much lighter I feel with him. How much easier everything seems when he's the one on the other side of the conversation.

However, texting is one thing. Standing in front of him again is another.

The hum of the copy machine greets me as I step inside the small room mid-morning, balancing a ream of paper against my hip. The smell of toner clings to the air.

I slip into the rhythm of loading trays and pressing buttons, my body working on autopilot while my brain tries to convince me that this is just a normal day. Just a normal Monday.

The door opens behind me.

I don't have to turn to know who it is. The air changes— charged, aware, like my skin is suddenly more awake than the rest of me.

When I glance over my shoulder, there he is, leaning against the filing cabinet like he owns the place, his crooked grin doing terrible things to my heartbeat.

And in his hand, folded carefully, is a flower.

At first I think it's just scrap paper. Then he steps closer, and I see it properly.

A flower folded from the page of a math book. The petals uneven, a little messy at the edges, but still beautiful. Entirely him.

He holds it out. "For you."

"You made this?" The words come out breathy, my voice softer than I mean for it to be.

He shrugs, but there's a glimmer of pride in his eyes. "Yeah. I thought it was better than showing up with grocery store roses. And…"

His voice dips lower, gentler.

"You look really pretty today."

The words hit me harder than they should. Not because they're cute or clever, but because they're simple. Honest. No pun to hide behind, nothing fancy to soften the edges. Just the truth.

"Thank you," I whisper, pressing the flower lightly against my chest.

He clears his throat. "I wanted to say I'm sorry again. For being an idiot. For assuming the worst. For being loud when I should have been listening. For every stupid thing I said. And, again, for making you spit in my face. Which, also again, I deserved."

A laugh breaks free before I can stop it.

"You really did."

His grin widens, boyish and sheepish all at once. Then he pulls something else from his pocket.

A folded piece of paper, neat and precise, like he took his time with it. He presses it into my hand.

On it, written in his careful handwriting, are two words: *Formal Request.*

I arch a brow. "For what? A restraining order?"

His mouth twitches. "To step down from my current post as your GBF."

My mouth drops open in mock horror. "But Leo, why? Why ever would you leave me?"

"I'm afraid it must be done," he explains solemnly. "It is for the greater good."

Then his voice gentles, hopeful, eyes locked on mine.

"However, the position has not dissolved. It is simply... evolving."

"Evolving?" I inquire, eyebrow raised.

"Yes," he confirms, completely serious. "Rather than the one post of GBF, I've been told of promotions—elevating both your status and mine. The G simply transfers to you, making me your BF, and then you become my GF."

It's so ridiculous, so corny, and so utterly him that I snort. "Leo Euler—"

"Actually," he interrupts, puffing up like a peacocked dork, "it's Leopold Christopher Euler the Third."

That makes my eyes sparkle despite myself. "Okay, Leopold Christopher Euler *the Third*, did you just ask me to be your girlfriend like we're in middle school?"

"Yes," he says simply, no hesitation. "Yes, I did."

I press the paper flower harder against my chest, smiling despite the lump forming in my throat.

"Yes. I would love to be your girlfriend."

The relief that floods his face is so raw and genuine it almost undoes me.

He steps closer, closing the space between us. His hand comes up, brushing a strand of hair behind my ear, then lingers. His palm curves against my jaw, fingers sliding behind my neck, warm and steady.

"Can I kiss you?" he asks, voice low.

I nod, my heart tripping over itself.

"Yes. But only a small one. No making out at work."

His grin tilts. "I'll behave."

He leans down, brushing his lips softly against mine. Once. Twice. Sweet, steady, and dizzying all at once.

When he goes in for a third, I slip a finger between us, stopping him with a laugh.

"Don't you have class, Professor Euler?"

His eyes crinkle. "Shit, you're right."

He presses one quick kiss to the tip of my nose before pulling back, reluctant but grinning, and then he's striding out the door like he just won something.

I stand there for a long moment, the paper flower still clutched to my chest, lips tingling, my whole body humming with the aftershock of something that feels both brand new and long overdue.

When I finally make it back to my desk, there's a folded note waiting for me. My name written neatly on the outside in his handwriting.

I already know what it is before I even open it—he's too smug not to have planned something like this.

Inside, the words make me laugh out loud.

> *Dear Girlfriend,*
> *Please come to my house for dinner tonight. Seven o'clock. Wear something comfortable. But feel free to wear something lacy and uncomfortable underneath if you so choose. I will not object.*
> *Lovingly,*
> *Boyfriend*

I shake my head, grinning like an idiot at the sheer nerve of him. He left that copy room and went straight to class, meaning he wrote this note and left it on my desk before ever stepping foot into that copy room.

He was so sure of himself, writing this before even asking me. So perfectly, ridiculously Leo.

I pull out my phone and respond to his note.

Tori, 10:52 a.m.: Dear BF, I would love to come for dinner tonight. Will Lois be joining us?
Warmly, GF

His reply comes almost instantly.

Leo, 10:52 a.m.: No.

I laugh and type back.

Tori, 10:52 a.m.: But why not? She's my favorite!

Leo, 10:53 a.m.: She's seen me naked once. She will not see me naked twice.

My core clenches at the thought of the two of us, together, finally.

Before I get too lost in my thoughts, I take his note and refold it, tucking it into my planner alongside the handwritten incident report from a few months back. Proof of how far we've come— then and now.

Mondays are supposed to drag, supposed to weigh heavy with dread and preemptive exhaustion for the week ahead.

But this one? This one feels like the start of everything wonderful.

Leo

The knock comes right at seven.

I'm already standing in the entryway when it lands—because of course I am. I've checked the mirror three times, re-set the plates twice, and reheated the food once even though it didn't need it.

For a man who usually wings it, I've suddenly become incredibly meticulous. Every detail feels like it matters tonight, like I need to get this right.

I open the door and forget how to breathe.

She's there. Cheeks pink from the cold, hair falling in soft waves over her shoulders, peacoat hanging open like she's already halfway in.

Tori is wearing a wrap shirt tied at her waist, dark jeans that look like they were sewn specifically to test my self-control, and boots with a modest heel that somehow make her legs look a mile long.

But it's her smile that destroys me. That familiar, radiant smile —the one that never fails to level me.

"Hi," she says, voice warm, easy, as if we didn't spend all

weekend in that uncertain in-between space, texting through the wreckage of Saturday.

"Hi," I say back, and my voice cracks like a thirteen-year-old boy whose hormones haven't figured themselves out yet.

I open the door wider, letting her step inside, and that's when I notice the bag in her hand.

Small. Zipped. Unmistakably overnight size.

My grin comes without permission. I lean back against the door as I close it, arms folded for exactly one second before I can't resist.

"I see you brought an overnight bag. How very presumptuous."

Her eyes flash, just enough heat to make my chest thrum, and she swats me in the chest.

"Shut up."

I don't. Not really. I pluck the bag from her hand like it weighs nothing, set it aside, and slide my other arm around her waist. I pull her against me, and when her body lines up with mine it's like puzzle pieces finding their way home.

I kiss her—*my girlfriend*. My lips against hers, quick, deliberate, claiming. Not too long, not too deep, just enough to taste her. Enough to remind myself she's real, and she's here, and she. chose. me.

When I pull back, she sighs—a soft, involuntary sound that shoots straight through me. Makes me want to abandon every plan I had, skip dinner, skip everything, and get lost in her until neither of us remembers our own names.

But I cooked, and I set the whole damn scene, and I can't throw it away after all that effort.

"Come on," I murmur, lacing my fingers through hers and tugging her gently toward the kitchen.

The smell of roasted garlic and butter lingers in the air, mingling with the faint sweetness of the wine already poured.

Plates are set on the island, candles flickering low, shadows stretching warm and intimate across the counters.

I pull her stool out like a gentleman—which, frankly, is hilarious, because five minutes from now I'll be plotting how to undo those jeans with my teeth.

She glances toward the dining table, one brow lifting. "We aren't sitting there?"

"Nope." I drop into the stool beside hers with a satisfied sigh. "I like it better here. Feels more normal."

"Normal…" she repeats, skeptical, but smiling.

"Yeah. You know. Less formal, less stiff." I roll my shoulders, then swivel my chair sideways, demonstrating.

"If we eat at the island, it just feels like us. Side by side, talking. I can turn my chair like this—" I do it, the motion casual but deliberate. "Slide a knee between your legs—" I slide my knee, just a nudge against her thigh. "Maybe sneak a peek under your skirt, and… you know. Normal."

Her laugh bursts out, bright and sharp, filling every corner of the room.

"But I'm wearing jeans."

"Hey." I lift my hands in mock surrender, grinning. "It's not my fault you failed to read the subliminal assignment, Tote."

She keeps laughing, shaking her head, and that sound—it does things to me. Untangles every knot I've carried since Saturday, every trace of doubt.

Just like that, everything is easy again.

Dinner doesn't last long. Not because the food is bad (I nailed it, thank you very much), but because every other bite is interrupted by something else.

Her hand brushing mine. My lips brushing her cheek. A joke murmured against my mouth before it turns into another kiss.

I keep my arm draped across the back of her stool, fingers toying with the ends of her hair, grazing her shoulder, slipping against her skin. She leans into me every time like gravity insists on it.

Wine vanishes. Plates empty. And the rest of the world dissolves.

One kiss becomes two, then three, then something hungrier. She shifts, turning sideways, legs bracketing mine, and I rise without thinking, slotting myself between her knees.

Her arms loop around my neck, body pressed flush to mine like she was made for this.

My hands grip her hips, then slide lower, over the curve of her ass, and I lift. She gasps but clings tighter, legs wrapping around my waist as I carry her down the hall.

Tori's laugh breaks between kisses, her breath warm against my mouth, her body alive and pliant in my arms.

I trail my mouth down her jaw, along the line of her throat, tasting her skin. She tilts her head back in offering, and I groan into the hollow of her collarbone, already half mad with hunger.

That silky, tempting wrap shirt slips, neckline gaping. I tug at the edge with my teeth, growling against her chest, "Open it. Lose it."

Her hands obey, untying one side, then the other, until the whole thing comes undone. It falls open, then slides off her shoulders, landing somewhere behind us.

I keep walking, and my eyes catch what she's wearing beneath. Black lace, sheer, a balconette bra that leaves nothing to the imagination. And then I see the flash of silver.

"When. The fuck. Did you get them pierced?" My voice comes out guttural, torn straight from my chest.

I don't give her time to answer before my mouth is on her, tugging one of the bars with my teeth. She arches, moans, her whole body tightening against me.

"The day after the funeral," she breathes.

I freeze mid-step, releasing her nipple, staring at her. Confusion is written all over my face.

"But, you were pissed at me."

The look she gives me would undo a lesser man. Pity, amusement, a challenge in her eyes.

Tori pouts, taps my cheek twice like I'm a misbehaving child, and says:

"It's so cute that you think I got these for you. These were a Christmas present to myself, sweetie."

Naturally, I spank her ass. Sharp. Quick. And then I bite her other nipple, tugging at the piercing with my teeth until she cries out.

"More," she moans, hands gripping my hair, yanking me closer.

By the time I reach the bedroom, she's half undressed, wrapped around me, kissing me like she never intends to stop.

But I don't drop her onto the bed. Not tonight.

Tonight isn't about being careless or reckless. Tonight isn't about games. Tonight is about reverence. Worship.

About showing her, without a single shadow of doubt, that I love her. That I am *in love* with her. That whatever came before, whatever hurt or brokenness we dragged behind us, the old has gone and the new has come.

I lower her onto the bed slowly, gently, my body still pressed hard against hers. My hands brace on either side of her head, our mouths working furiously, until I finally pull back just enough to see her.

Her jeans. Her boots. They have to go.

I kneel, tugging off one boot, then the other, setting them aside. She watches me with heavy eyes, panting, gaze burning hot enough to sear.

"These jeans look painted on, Tote," I murmur, smirking up at her. "When I unzip them, will they obey, or will your ass fight me for them?"

She laughs, breathless. "They stretch. So they should behave."

"Should," I tease, leaning in to pop the button. I drag the

zipper down slowly, deliberately, and the sight that greets me nearly buckles my knees. Matching black lace panties, sheer like the bra, taunting me.

The jeans slide off easily, thank God, and now she's laid out before me in lace and nothing else.

"You're staring," she says, softly.

"I'm aware."

I don't stop staring, but I do peel my own clothes away—shirt, jeans, boxers—until I'm stripped bare.

My cock heavy in my hand, I stroke once, slowly, letting her see exactly what she does to me.

"We didn't have this conversation beforehand," I say, voice low, steady, "but I need to know right now if I'm allowed to take you bare."

Her eyes go wide. "I'm not on birth control."

"That wasn't the question, Victoria."

Her gaze flicks from my cock to my face, back again. "No. Not bare. I trust you, but I'm not ready for that."

I nod. Relief washes through me. She doesn't feel like she has to give me something she isn't ready for. She knows she can say no.

"Good girl."

Her thighs twitch and then clench at the words, and I file that away for later. *Praise kink, activated.*

"Now," I murmur, tracing my fingertips from her ankle, up her calf, to her knee. I push her leg wide, anchor my knee against hers so she can't close it.

My other hand grips her opposite thigh, spreading her fully.

Her breath stutters. Her gaze flickers between my face and my cock, anticipation written across every line of her body.

I lick my lips; she moans.

Dessert.

"Listen carefully," I tell her, voice rough, deliberate. "And do not interrupt."

She nods, wide-eyed. "Okay."

"I'm going to kiss every inch of your bare skin before this night is over. I will eat your pussy until you come on my face. You will suck my cock exactly how I tell you, and you'll swallow every drop. And I will fuck you—at least twice—before morning. I will bite your piercings. I will spank your ass. I will pull your hair. But I will not hurt you. I will not leave a mark. Do you understand?"

Tori nods. She squirms beneath me, panting, barely holding back sound.

"Is there anything in that list you don't want?"

She shakes her head fast. "No."

"Do you want control, or do you want me to worship you while you do as you're told?"

Her breath shudders. "I'll do as I'm told."

The smile that spreads across my face is dark, certain, hungry.

"Perfect. Now take off that bra while I remove these panties with my teeth."

THIRTY-FOUR

TORI

HE SAYS it low and certain—*Now take off that bra while I remove these panties with my teeth*—and I have never been more free to let go, completely, and obey.

I reach behind my back, the clasp giving under my fingers like it's been waiting. The sound is tiny, but it echoes in my ears like a door unlocking.

My bra loosens, straps sliding off my shoulders, fabric falling away. Air finds new skin, raising goosebumps across my chest, but before the chill can settle, the heat of his gaze replaces it.

My nipples tighten, bare and sensitive, and I know he sees it. I know he feels the way my body reacts to him without hesitation, without permission.

His breath brushes my stomach a beat before his mouth does, warm against my skin, and the first kiss there lands like a promise kept.

My thoughts scatter. His lips, his tongue trail a path down my body. A path that's new, untraveled. A pioneer exploring uncharted territory, but he's in no rush.

Every press of his mouth is deliberate, reverent, as if he's mapping me for the first and last time. He knows this land belongs to him, but he's savoring the claim.

He is careful and greedy at once, reverent and sure. Every place his mouth touches becomes the most important place on my body —until the next kiss argues with the last one, each one convincing me it matters more.

I expect him to reach my panties, to bite the edge and drag them down my legs like in so many of my favorite novels.

I brace for it, waiting.

But, no. Of course he doesn't follow the script.

Leo continues kissing, licking, sucking over the top of my panties.

And I feel it. All of it.

Every vibration through the lace, every drag of his tongue amplified by the thin barrier, every wet slip sharper because of the friction. The fabric clings, already soaked, turning every move into a tease.

Good God, this man.

He buries his face into my pussy, licking, sucking, kissing, using the lace of my panties as added friction against my most sensitive parts.

He finds my clit, sucks it into his mouth—fabric and all—and then bites, and I swear I'm about to explode. My hips jerk, my back arches, a helpless sound tears from my throat.

"Play with your piercings," he growls, surfacing for a second before burying himself in me again.

I do as I'm told. My hands fly to my breasts, tugging at the silver bars.

Each pull shoots sparks down my body, lightning bolts that converge on my clit where his mouth is working me through the fabric.

It's too much. It's not enough. I don't know how my body can survive both sensations at once, but I don't want it to stop.

Leo hasn't even pressed a finger inside me yet and I'm close, so close.

My fingers flick and twist at my nipples, my eyes locked on his as his own gaze follows the motion, hunger burning in him. He watches the way my hips jolt every time I tug, watches the way I can't keep still under him.

Then he bites down on the crotch of my underwear, tugs back, and—*snap.*

The wet, elastic fabric snaps against my clit at the exact moment I pull on my piercings, and the double jolt detonates inside me. I scream, the sound ripped from somewhere primal.

Holy. Fucking. Shit.

Every nerve ending in my body lights up at once. My muscles seize and release, a violent quake I can't control. I'm shaking, trembling, vibrating apart. My core pulses so hard I think I might break.

Back arched, body taut, I'm not even flat on the bed again before Leo slides two fingers into me, thrusting deep as his mouth latches onto my breast. His tongue circles my piercing, his teeth tug, and the overload is unbearable.

"Leo," I gasp, every syllable shattered.

"Tell me," he says, curling his fingers inside me, grinding his palm against my clit. His voice is gravel, wrecked with want.

I ride his hand shamelessly, hips grinding down, chasing every ounce of sensation. I'm still coming, still gasping, and it feels endless.

"More," I whisper—no, beg. It doesn't sound like me. It sounds like someone stripped bare, someone who has never wanted more in her life.

His laugh is low and wrecked, undone by my plea. He kisses me, tongue tangling with mine, and then I'm spiraling again, another climax ripping through me on his fingers.

I arch. I tremble. My hands clutch his hair like an anchor, because if I let go, I'll float away.

He slows our kiss, easing me down, and slides his hand from between my legs. His eyes never leave mine as he lifts those two fingers and slides them into his mouth. His lids flutter, his tongue curling, and he groans—lost in the taste of me.

I watch, spellbound, as he savors every drop.

When his fingers leave his mouth, his smirk is ravenous. He's had a taste, but it isn't enough.

I know it. He knows it.

"My cock is jealous, Victoria," he rasps, dragging his hand down my stomach until he hooks the string of my panties.

Even wrecked and trembling, I find my voice. "We can't have that."

"No," he agrees, pulling the panties down my legs and over each foot, tossing them aside. He reaches for the drawer, pulls a condom, and rolls it on with practiced ease.

"We can't have that."

"I thought you said you were going to take those off with your teeth?" I nod toward the discarded scrap of lace. My grin is weak, but it's there.

Leo doesn't answer.

Instead, he prowls up my body, slow and deliberate, kissing every inch of exposed skin on his way.

My stomach. My ribs. Each breast, where he pauses to suck, lick, and tug, nipping at my piercings until I gasp.

Only then does he grip my thigh, pinning it high against my chest, and slams into me in one long, relentless thrust.

"Give me your hands," he orders.

I give them. Both arms stretching above my head, fingers intertwining with his as he holds me down, utterly his.

He moves. Slowly. Deliberately. Possessively.

I rock my hips to meet him, every thrust dragging fire through me. My eyes flutter shut, but I force them open, needing to see him —this man above me, chest heaving, jaw tight, gaze locked on mine like he's drowning in me.

With my leg pinned high, my hips tilt at the perfect angle, his pelvis grinding my clit each time he rolls into me.

And he *rolls*. Not mere thrusts. Not just in, then out. Leo grinds, dips, drags, like he's embedding himself deeper with each stroke. Like he wants to fuse us together.

"Tori," he whispers, breaking me open with just my name.

"Leo," I whisper back, our eyes locked.

His grip on my fingers tightens. I squeeze back, needing the anchor.

"Do you love me?" His voice cracks with need, raw and certain all at once.

I smile through the heat and the ache.

"Is pi irrational?"

His laugh bursts free, breaking his rhythm, and then he kisses me hard, mouth bruising mine. When he pulls back, his whole face is alight.

I didn't just answer his question. I answered it in his language.

"I fucking love you, woman."

"I love you too, fuckboy."

And then it's chaos. His thrusts snap sharper, faster, harder. His grip on my thigh unrelenting. His hold on my hands like iron.

"Leo..." I pant, strung tight, seconds away from shattering.

"I know, baby." His forehead presses to mine, his breath ragged.

And then his mouth is on my breast again, sucking my nipple deep, teeth clamping on my piercing—

—and I shatter.

My core squeezes around his cock, pulling him deeper, refusing to let go. My free leg locks around his, binding us closer. My nails dig crescents into his skin, desperate to anchor myself as the orgasm rips through me, raw and unrelenting.

And the craziest part? The pleasure is so overwhelming, so brutal, so beyond words that instead of screaming, instead of crying out—

I bite my tongue.
You read that right.
I bite down. As hard as I can.
Straight. Through. My. Fucking. Tongue.

HE'S STILL inside me when it happens.

The last pulse of my orgasm is still fluttering around him, my body stretched and trembling beneath his, when I cough. Just a little—just enough to clear my throat.

But it's not air that comes out.

It's blood.

A hot, wet spray splashes over his chest, bright red against his skin. Droplets scatter across his collarbone, his throat, even his cheek.

For a second, I don't even register it. My brain is still humming from release, still melted around the feel of him inside me, heavy and perfect.

Leo freezes. Entirely. Every muscle in him goes tight. His eyes go wide, staring down at me like he's just witnessed a homicide.

"Tori!" His voice breaks. "What the hell—are you—oh my God, are you okay? Do you need a doctor? Do I call an ambulance?"

I try to answer, but the words slur around my swollen tongue.

"Bithh my tonghhehh."

Which, of course, sprays even more blood across his chest.

He flinches but doesn't move away, gripping my face, trying to peer into my mouth while I'm choking on laughter.

"Baby, you have to stop giggling. Tori, I'm serious—are you choking? Are you bleeding out? Tell me if you're dying right now!"

"Not—dyin'thhh," I manage, but the garbled mess only shoots another mist across his jaw.

Leo bolts off the bed, scanning the room like a man possessed.

"Fuck, fuck, towel—where the hell—"

He flings open the closet. Nothing. Yanks a drawer. Socks.

"Goddammit!" He snatches the nearest pillow, tears the case off in one hard pull, and shoves the cotton into my hands.

"Here. Press it. Press it hard."

I sit up and do as I'm told, pressing the pillowcase to my mouth. Blood blooms instantly, soaking it dark.

My head starts bopping back and forth before I even realize it —*Whip it!* now playing on repeat in my brain like a bad jukebox.

Maybe I really am losing too much blood.

"What's happening? Are you having a seizure?!" Leo's back on the bed in an instant, hovering close, eyes wild.

I shake my head, laughing into the pillowcase, still jamming to the music in my head.

"*Whip it!*" I try to say, but it comes out muffled, garbled, and bloody. His expression goes from panic to sheer horror.

I decide the explanation isn't worth his anxiety, so I stop my dance and shrug.

Leo watches me for a beat longer, eyeing me like I might start convulsing at any second.

When he's convinced I am not, in fact, seizing, he mutters, "Fucking hell, woman..." and steadies his breath.

Then, a few moments later: "Let me see. Maybe it's slowed down a bit."

He peels the fabric back just enough to check the damage.

I tilt my head back, open wide, but the blood starts to drain down my throat. The second he leans in, I start to choke, cough, and then—*splat.*

A spray of blood shoots forward, covering his face and chest in crimson freckles.

He freezes, blinking at me through the mess.

And I laugh. Oh God, I laugh so hard I can't breathe, clutching the pillowcase back over my mouth, shaking with it.

"Stop. Laughing!" he yells, swiping at his face, which only smears the blood worse.

"You're turning my bedroom into a Quentin Tarantino set!"

I can't stop. Physically, absolutely cannot stop laughing.

"Unfuckingbelievable," he mutters.

The knock on the front door interrupts him.

"Leopold?" Lois's voice filters through. "I've been hearing very loud noises. At first they sounded... enthusiastic, but now they sound angry? Or... afraid? Are you all right in there?"

Leo's head whips toward the sound, naked, bloody, and panicked.

"Jesus Christ," he mutters, blood dripping down his collarbone. "Does she sit by my front door and eavesdrop?"

"Lois! We're fine!" he yells back, frantic.

A pause. Then: "Leopold, you sound upset. I'm coming in."

"What? No—Lois, do NOT come in here!"

His voice cracks in a way I've never heard before.

"I already told you, dear," she says calmly, keys jingling. "I've seen everything before. Nothing will surprise me."

The master bedroom only has a sliding barn door for 'privacy,' so he doesn't even attempt to shut it.

Knowing resistance is futile, Leo lets out a string of curses. He grabs a pillow and slams it over his junk, then tosses another at me. I clutch it to my chest, still completely naked, blood-smeared, and shaking with laughter.

The doorknob turns. The door swings open. Light, childlike footsteps pad down the hall.

And in walks the most adorable four-foot-ten (on a good day), blue-eyed old woman—dressed in a bathrobe, fluffy bunny slippers, and a neon orange hunting balaclava—*with a shotgun cocked against her shoulder.*

I swear on my life, you cannot make this shit up.

Lois pauses just long enough to take in the scene: blood splattered literally everywhere, Leo clutching a pillow to his groin, me holding one across my chest, and a bloody pillowcase stuffed between my teeth.

She blinks. Lowers the gun. Then nods.

"Blood play? Kinky."

Leo thumps his head against the wall and groans. I'm laughing so hard I'm crying, still biting down on the fabric.

Lois is completely unfazed. Not one bit.

"I'm glad no one is trying to murder you, Leopold." She peels off the balaclava, her wispy white curls sticking up every which way with static.

"But listen here, kids," she continues, tone serious. "You have to be careful with these kinks, or things can get out of hand quickly."

She clucks her tongue, entirely unbothered. "As you experienced tonight."

Then she looks at me, her gaze softening. "Let me get you some ice, dear."

Before she can fully step out of the room, Leo blurts, "Lois, how the hell did you even get in here when that door was locked?"

She smiles at him, all innocence, as if she isn't holding a shotgun in a bathrobe.

"My key, of course. You gave me a spare in case you ever got locked out."

Leo stares at her. Horrified. And I collapse onto my side, laughing so hard I nearly roll off the bed.

Lois, still unfazed, shuffles toward the kitchen. "You two take a shower and clean that blood off your naked bodies while I make you some tea."

So, we do. Because what other option is there?

THIRTY-FIVE
TORI

I WAKE to sunlight spilling across a bed that doesn't belong to me and yet feels, somehow, like the safest place I've ever been. The sheets smell like detergent and Leo, faintly crisp and warm, and the pillow beside me is still dented from his head. For a long time I just lie there, staring at the ceiling, letting my own breath rise and fall.

I used to start every morning with a weight in my chest. A running tally of how I'd bend myself that day—what tone to take, what edges to soften, how much of myself I could risk showing without breaking something fragile.

That's gone now.

The absence is almost startling.

My body is my own. My choices are mine.

I am mine.

That's what so many people couldn't—wouldn't—understand: leaving wasn't about choosing someone else. It wasn't even about ending a marriage.

It was about stepping into myself. Finding the woman I'd buried under years of silence and compromise and shame.

She's here now. Awake. Breathing. Whole.

And because I know I'm whole, I can choose love without fear of losing myself again. I can choose Leo—not because I need him to fill the empty spaces (those belong to me now) but because life is so much brighter, so much richer, with him in it.

I roll toward the nightstand and find the note propped against the lamp.

This man and his notes.

> *GF,*
> *Ran to the store. Don't panic. Needed sherbet. Figured your tongue probably isn't ready for bacon and eggs, and I refuse to be the man who serves you a breakfast that hurts. Back soon. Don't move. Or at least, don't put any clothes on.*
> *I love you.*
> *BF*
> *P.S. I emailed Dr. Johnson and told him both of us would not be in the office today due to a late-night medical scare involving my neighbor. That is not, technically, a lie.*

I snort, pressing the paper to my lips. Sherbet for breakfast, of course. And the P.S.? Only Leo would turn last night's fiasco into an excuse to miss work.

I slide back beneath the sheets, tucking the note beside me like a talisman. The quiet hums in my chest, steady and certain.

For the first time in forever, I know that I could be fine on my own. But I don't want to be.

I want this. Him. Us.

The front door clicks. I hear Leo humming—Sinatra, maybe—and a second later, there he is: hair wind-tossed, grocery bag dangling from his hand. He takes one look at me sprawled across his bed, bare skin tangled in his sheets, and his grin curves slow and wicked.

"Hot damn, woman," he says, voice warm with mischief, "take a look at that ass. The square root of negative one isn't the only thing that's unreal."

I burst out laughing, tossing a pillow at him. He dodges, still grinning like a fool.

"Breakfast of champions, coming right up," he says, lifting the bag. "Raspberry sherbet. Don't say I don't spoil you."

"Sherbet for breakfast?" I tease, propping myself up on an elbow. "What kind of man are you?"

Leo kicks off his shoes and plops onto the bed next to me, back against the headboard. I adjust my pillows and join him, dragging the comforter along with me.

"The kind who knows better than to give his girlfriend scrambled eggs when her tongue looks like it went twelve rounds with Mike Tyson."

I roll my eyes, but my chest warms anyway.

"You're ridiculous."

"And yet," he says, leaning down to brush a soft kiss against my lips, "you're still here."

The kiss lingers in me even after he pulls back—light, certain, grounding.

Last night was just the first night of many, but it felt like a glimpse into something bigger. Not a promise of perfection, but of possibility—of dinners that turn into laughter, of stolen kisses in kitchens, of late nights that spill over into mornings.

And this life, this future, includes so much more than just the two of us. It'll be Skye with her unfiltered honesty, Alis with her quick wit and tender heart, Sunny pulling us into plans we never see coming, Dexter posturing himself as the refined one while secretly enjoying the madness. A whole family of people who remind us that love and joy are multifaceted, and beautiful, and complicated, and real.

Life with Leo will always lean toward the unexpected, a little messy, a little absurd—but as long as we are true to ourselves and surrounded by the people we love, it will never, ever be dull.

And if things ever get too quiet?

Well...Lois has a key.

EPILOGUE ONE
SKYE

STERLING LAW GROUP. Fancy.

The receptionist leads us down a hallway lined with polished wood and brass nameplates, like every door is guarding a secret club. The air feels heavy with formality, the kind that makes people sit straighter in their chairs and whisper instead of talk. My combat boots thump against the carpet, my jean skirt brushing against my thighs, leather jacket creaking as I fold my arms.

Do I look out of place here? Hell yes. Do I care? Not even a little.

Beside me, Tori is all steel. Her shoulders are squared, chin high, lips pressed together like she's holding the world between her teeth. I know that look—it's the one she wears when she's fighting her nerves with sheer willpower. She's been through hell and back, and this... this is her line in the sand.

I feel a rush of pride so strong it almost steals my breath. She's walking into this office to take her life back, and if anyone tries to push her down again, I'll fuck them up.

We stop at a door. The receptionist knocks lightly and opens it.

"Ms. Foster, Ms. Kennedy—Mr. Sterling will see you now."
What was I saying about a secret club? Because the way she just
said that definitely sounded like we were being escorted into a
private VIP room at a sex club.

Inside, the man himself stands with his back to us, phone
pressed to his ear, gaze fixed on a bookshelf stuffed with leather-
bound volumes. His posture is as rigid as his tone, voice clipped
and precise. Even without seeing his face, I can tell he's the kind of
man who never leaves a paper out of place.

Yes, sir.

The call ends. Which reminds me—shit. I forgot to turn my
phone on silent before walking in here.

I hear him walk across the room and introduce himself to Tori.
"Ms. Foster?"

Tori shakes his hand, steady, calm. "Yes. Thank you for
meeting with me."

In my periphery I see her gesture toward me, her voice softer
now. "This is my best friend, Skye Kennedy."

I'm too busy digging in my bag, setting my phone to Do Not
Disturb so I don't get ambushed by memes or notifications, to
notice him right away. My fingers fumble, I drop the damn thing
into the abyss of receipts and gum wrappers, and when I finally
look up, there's a hand waiting for me.

"Sorry," I reach out automatically, polite reflex. "Hi, I'm—"
Oh. My. Fucking. God.
"—Skye."

It's *him*. It's fucking *Asshole Suit Guy*.

And yes, before you say anything further, THAT Asshole Suit
Guy. The same Asshole Suit Guy who's ordered black coffee some-
time between 7:23 and 7:25 every morning since the day I started
working at my beloved little coffee shop without once cracking a
smile. The same Asshole Suit Guy who has ignored every joke,
every question, every compliment I lobbed his way. The same
Asshole Suit Guy who, the *one time* he dared to break his own

routine, showed up at 7:35, and then burned himself with his own damn coffee, then decided to unleash the fires of hell all over me like I—yes, me, the very demure, very mindful, very cutesy Skye Kennedy—was the root of his problems.

Like what the actual fuck have I ever done to him?! NOTHING. That's what!

My stomach drops, my pulse spikes, and I nearly yank my hand back—but too late, the handshake is already locked.

Fucking. Asshole. Suit Guy.

And now? He's standing here, smooth as ever, introducing himself as Jacob Sterling, attorney at law. Tori's attorney, if this meeting goes well and he's the right fit for what she needs.

I swear, if God, the universe, whatever has a sense of humor, it's a twisted one.

His eyes catch mine, and I know he recognizes me, too. There's a flicker—jaw tight, eyes sharp—but then he smooths it all away, his expression the picture of professionalism.

"Ms. Kennedy," he says evenly. Like we're strangers. Like he didn't once accuse me of having Kool-Aid colored hair and no life plan.

I paste on a smile sharp enough to cut glass. "It's a pleasure."

Inside, I am screaming.

But outside? I straighten my spine, plant my feet, and remember why I'm here.

Not for him. Not for this overpriced, leather-soaked office.

For Tori. For my best friend who just walked through that door braver than I've ever seen her.

I'll sit here in front of Asshole Suit Guy and swallow down every sarcastic comment clawing its way up my throat if it means she walks out of this office stronger than she came in.

Because if Tori can face down the end of her marriage, I can face a stuck up asshole with a vendetta against morning pleasantries.

But, just for good measure, I did my fingernail into his palm before letting go of his handshake.

That's for making fun of my hair, prick.

EPILOGUE TWO
TORI

THIS ENTIRE DAY has been magical. A perfect Colorado day in late April.

The wedding ended hours ago, but the glow of it lingers. The sky above the Rockies is a deep stretch of indigo, scattered with stars so sharp they look close enough to touch. Strings of twinkle lights crisscross over the open lawn behind the lodge, each one flickering like a piece of captured starlight. Laughter ripples from the tables, the clink of glasses blending with the swell of music from the speakers set up near the dance floor.

Dexter and Alis's reception looks exactly like the kind of dream you don't want to wake from.

And here I am, in the middle of it, swaying in Leo's arms.

His palm rests firm against the small of my back, guiding me easily among the couples. My hand presses against his shoulder, my head tucked into the familiar steadiness of his chest. The music is slow, low, wrapping around us like a ribbon.

"Look at you, Tote," he murmurs, his voice vibrating through me. "Acting like you actually like slow dances."

I smile against his shirt. "I like them when I'm wiped out from a full day of wedding festivities, a little bit tipsy, and the dance is more like you rocking me to sleep for a standing nappy nap."

He huffs out a laugh, the kind that never fails to loosen something tight inside me. "If you fall asleep while we're dancing…"

"You'll what? Think it's adorable and carry me like a princess somewhere quiet to rest?" I tease, tilting my face up toward him.

His eyes catch the glow of the lights above us, dark and warm, steady as they meet mine. "Yeah. Probably."

My smile is instant, undeniable—I love this man. "You're the best."

"The total package? The summation of everything you could ever want or need in a life partner?" he asks, and I laugh softly, snuggling back in.

"Something like that, yeah."

He dips his head, pressing a quick kiss to my temple before pulling me closer. "You didn't actually believe your nickname came from a dog, did you?"

"Wait, wha—"

"Shh. We're dancing. And I almost had you rocked to sleep." I let myself sink into him, into this night, into the rare and precious peace of being exactly where I want to be.

All around us, joy swirls: Skye laughing so loud her whole body shakes; Belanger cousins darting between tables; Dexter twirling Alis across the dance floor like he's waited his whole life for this moment. It's the kind of night that makes you believe in forever.

I'm just about to tell Leo that when a voice cuts through the music.

"Tori!"

I glance over his shoulder. Sunny darts across the lawn, her dress hitched up in one hand, curls bouncing with each hurried step. She's barefoot, her shoes dangling from the other hand. She looks half amused, half concerned.

"Sorry!" she says, skidding to a stop beside us. "I wouldn't interrupt, but your phone hasn't stopped going off."

She thrusts it toward me, the screen glowing with three back-to-back missed calls from the same number.

"They left a message," Sunny explains quickly, her words tumbling out. "I figured if someone's that persistent, it's probably important."

A pinch of unease coils low in my stomach.

"Thank you," I say, forcing my voice even.

Sunny nods once, her usual brightness dimmed by curiosity she doesn't voice, and then she disappears back into the crowd.

Leo studies my face. "Want to take it inside?"

"Yes," I nod, my throat tight.

We step off the dance floor together. The music fades as we cross the lawn and push through the wide doors into the lodge. The quiet inside is immediate, the thick wood beams and glass soaking up the sounds of celebration. Twinkle lights from outside filter faintly through the windows, casting fractured patterns across the floor.

I lift the phone to my ear and press play.

"Hello, Mrs. Victoria Martin. This is Grant Medical Center. We have you listed as Chase Martin's emergency contact. Mr. Martin has been admitted following a serious accident. He is unconscious but stable. Please give us a call at this number and head to the hospital as soon as possible."

The words echo inside me, dull at first, then sharper with every repeat in my head. My knees weaken. Leo's hand finds my elbow instantly, steadying me.

The second voicemail begins without warning.

"Hello again, Mrs. Martin. This is Grant Medical Center, calling again. If you could please return our call as soon as possible and please head this way immediately. Mr. Martin's blood alcohol concentration was more than twice the legal limit. He was not the only vehicle involved in the accident and police are present—"

A sob wrenches free before I can stop it. My hand clamps over my mouth, but the sound breaks anyway. My chest caves; my lungs burn; my vision swims.

Not the only vehicle involved.

The phrase carves itself into me, merciless.

I lift my eyes to Leo. Terror floods me, spilling over as tears streak hot down my cheeks. His gaze holds mine, steady, unwavering, even as I fall apart.

Without hesitation, he slides his hand up my arm, over my trembling fingers still clutching the phone. His palm is warm, firm. Gently, he eases the device from my grip and ends the message before it can go further.

Then he pulls me into his chest, wrapping me tight in his arms. I break against him, the sob tearing out louder this time, muffled by the fabric of his suit. He doesn't flinch. He just holds me, solid and sure, while the world tilts on its axis.

His voice rumbles low against my hair, calm and deliberate. "Here's what's going to happen. You can step into the bathroom if you need a minute, or sit right here. I'll grab your clutch and let Dexter and Alis know we have to leave. If I see Skye, I'll ask her to collect the rest of your things from upstairs. If not, I'll text her in a bit. I'm going to come right back here for you, and then we'll go straight to the hospital, together. I am driving. You don't need to think about anything except breathing. We'll be there as soon as possible. We'll make sure he's alright."

He eases back just enough to cup my face in his hands, tilting it so I can't look anywhere but at him. His thumbs brush away tears even as more spill over.

"Did you get all that?" he asks softly.

I nod, though the motion feels fragile, breakable.

"Good." He presses his lips to my forehead, lingering there for one quiet beat. Then he lets go.

"I'll be right back."

The loss of his embrace leaves me unsteady. I sink into the

nearest chair, my hands gripping the edge of the seat as if it might keep me from unraveling.

The reception hums faintly beyond the walls, muffled and distant. Out there, life goes on: laughter, music, joy. In here, everything feels fractured, like the air itself is too heavy to breathe.

I bury my face in my hands, but there's no shutting it out. The words replay mercilessly: *serious accident... unconscious but stable... over twice the legal limit... not the only vehicle involved.*

Images slam into me—Chase behind the wheel, his jaw set in reckless defiance; headlights screaming across the dark road; the sickening crunch of impact.

My stomach twists so violently I think I might be sick.

I'm devastated. That he was drinking. That he drove. That he's lying in a hospital bed, unconscious and broken.

Despite everything—despite all the nights I cried alone beside him, despite the verbal abuse and the neglect—I will always love him, and my heart aches at the thought of him like this. I never wanted any of this for him.

And I'm terrified. Terrified of what he's done, of who else he might have hurt. Whoever was out there on that road tonight didn't ask to be tethered to his spiral, to become collateral damage in his wreckage.

Tears burn tracks down my cheeks, my chest clenching tight with grief and guilt and fury and fear all tangled together.

Skye's voice echoes in my mind. *He'll have to hit rock bottom before any lasting changes take effect.* She was always so sure he'd have to completely fall apart if there was any hope of him being pieced back together.

Maybe she's right. Maybe this is what it will take for him to heal.

I just never thought rock bottom would look like this.

ACKNOWLEDGMENTS

I didn't include an acknowledgments page in my first book because I was terrified I'd forget someone. True story. Here's my attempt at remembering all the people who helped make this book happen.

Ashley: *I used up all my best words in this book, so I'll borrow some from George Clooney: "Whatever alchemy it is that brought us together, I couldn't be more [thankful] to [have you in my life as my PA and friend]." Thank you for late night and early morning texts, hours-long phone calls fleshing out specific scenes, helping me to verbally process things that were or were not working. More than all that, this book contains so much of your wisdom. Thank you.*

Hubs: *Thank you for your honesty and encouragement. I know this genre isn't your cup of tea, but it still means everything that you read my books and tell me you think I'm a great author. I hope you enjoyed the random inside jokes I dropped into the story as "I love you" nuggets.*

Krista: *I love you, bestie. You know these characters as well as I do, and I'm thankful to build the series with you through endless conversations. I'm so glad you slid into my DMs to tell me how much you loved my first book—even more glad we somehow ended up living down the street from each other. But I STG if you give this book a two-chilis spice rating I will punch you in the vag—it says the word "cock" ELEVEN times. That's <u>at least</u> three chilis.*

Carol: *You're such a blessing in my life. I'm glad we met in that hotel lobby and started chatting about books. Thank you for checking behind my writing and telling me when something sounded cool in my brain but didn't actually work on the page. I appreciate you so much.*

Shannon: *Thank you for talking with me about the heavy things so I could make sure to honor those journeys well. And thank you for still calling me Brittany, even when we're at events and everyone else calls me BJ. I don't know why my brain misfires when you call me anything else, but it does. lol. I love you so much.*

Sarah: *Thanks for convincing your husband to let me put your faces on the cover. I know it took forever to finish this book, but I hope now that you've read it you can see the emotional toll it took to create. I'm so proud of this story, and I hope you're both proud to represent the characters in it.*

Alina: *You say I would have finished this on time without your help, but we both know that's a lie.*

Kate: *Thank you for always pushing me to be better, steering me in the right direction, helping me think strategically, and reminding me this is a long game. You're my friend, but you're also my mentor in so many ways. Can I be you when I grow taller?*

Julia: *Thank you for checking in every few hours during that final stretch and providing all the best reactions to the scenes I sent. You're so good for my ego, but maybe kind of terrible for my sense of humility. "What's that? You don't like my books? Well, Julia says I'm a rockstar and I'm amazing, so... you are INCORRECT." I love you so so so much.*

Jessica: *Soul mate—I love you more than my own life. Thank you for always believing in me, and for being the yin to my yang.*

Jibbly Handlers (Katie, Kira, Nickie, Ashley again): *I wouldn't be able to write without the four of you running this company alongside me. I know I sound like a broken record, but it's true—I never could have imagined being blessed with a team who works so well together, whom I trust implicitly, and who fully embrace the mission and vision of our brand. And that's what it is— ours. WE are Jibbly. (Yes, I'm crying again.)*

Emotional Support Bitches: *Thank you for living up to our group name.*

Family: *I'm lumping you all together here because to list you* *one-by-one would be another book entirely. Thank you for your encouragement, support, and grace when I had to bury myself in my writing corner for days without speaking to anyone. It means the world that you're all so proud of me.*

Chandler: *(Op! Guess I did single one of you out.) Happy birthday, baby sister.*

Shauna & Becca: *Thank you for prioritizing my mental and emotional well-being over a deadline—stopping the initial book tour halfway through and restarting it a whole year later. I'll never forget sitting at my dining room table, crying on the phone, saying, "I can't do this right now," and hearing you say immediately, "You and your family are more important than a book. Whenever you're ready, we're here."*

Everyone I didn't mention by name: *It's not that I've forgotten you; I simply find mindself wandering off the path of acknowledging those who worked with me on this book, specifically, and into a babbling mess of "OMG I love you so much!" Thank you, each and every one of you, for your love and support.*

ABOUT THE AUTHOR

B.J. Hill wants to live in a world where it doesn't matter if you're a square peg or a round hole; where 'round' is a perfectly-acceptable goal for getting 'in shape'; and where unfiltered and messy life is not only welcomed, but celebrated. Her books explore the depths of human connection, the bittersweet taste of life, the redemptive power of love, and the belief that true strength is often found in vulnerability. They offer a space where passion meets purpose, where characters break and mend, and where readers can find solace in the shared experience of resilience and hope. She is the sunshine to her grumpy-ish college sweetheart, mom to the three coolest offspring in the world, and devoted subject to her canine and feline royal majesties. When she's not writing stories about her imaginary friends, you can find her reading, using her outside voice at inopportune moments, or being generally awkward (I mean, awesome. Totally awesome).

For all things BJ scan the QR code below!

B.J. is also the innovative founder and CEO of Jibbly, a company that embraces the vibrancy and authenticity of storytelling. Through Jibbly, she aims to extend that connection, crafting a community where stories uplift, challenge, and transform. Find Jibbly at an author signing event near you or online here: